LEGENDS ALL

Ike then put an arm around the blond-haired kid. "And this here's my brother Billy."

Wyatt couldn't see any resemblance between the brothers, but then who was to say how many wives a father of Ike would have had at one time.

"Billy tells me he seen you the other day," said Ike. "Tells me you're ridin' for Wells Fargo."

"You best watch how you ride," Billy said. "A body could sneak up on you, Earp."

There was a mean glint in his eyes, but mostly the kid looked like he was trying to keep up with the older hardcases with him. Wyatt wasn't sure if he was as bad as Ike.

"And then there's Ringo over here," Ike continued. "I especially want you to meet him. Maybe you've heard tell of him. I say he's probably killed twenty men. Maybe more."

"That right?" said Wyatt. "Tell me, Ringo, that twenty men, is that counting Mexicans you ambushed?"

Ike's smile froze.

The expression on Ringo's face didn't change at all, but he changed the way he stood, almost imperceptibly. Moving slowly, he turned his right side slightly away from Wyatt, the side that wore the revolver. If he were to pull the gun now, Wyatt wouldn't have a good look at the pistol until it had cleared its holster.

THE STORY OF WYATT EARP

LEGENDS:
THE STORY OF WYATT EARP

DAVID EVERITT

PaperJacks LTD.

TORONTO   NEW YORK

AN ORIGINAL

PaperJacks

LEGENDS: THE STORY OF WYATT EARP

PaperJacks LTD.

330 STEELCASE RD. E., MARKHAM, ONT. L3R 2M1
210 FIFTH AVE., NEW YORK, N.Y. 10010

First edition published July 1988

This is a work of fiction in its entirety. Any resemblance to actual people, places or events is purely coincidental.

ISBN 0-7701-0935-7

FOREWORD

THE LEGEND OF WYATT EARP is perhaps the most famous and most controversial story of the Old West. The number of versions of this tale has been matched only by the number of disagreements over what the story really was.

Some say Wyatt Earp was the greatest frontier lawman. Others claim he was nothing more than a vicious gangster. To some he was the man who brought law and order to such wild and woolly boom towns as Tombstone and Dodge City, while to others he was one of those towns' premier shady characters, a man who used his gun and his badge to back up his criminal activities. No one disputes that the Gunfight at the O.K. Corral was the great climax to Earp's career, but the question remains: Was this incident a classic Western showdown in which the Earp brothers vanquished the Clanton-McLowery Gang, or was it an act of cold-blooded murder?

These two schools of thought are a natural outgrowth of the controversy that surrounded Earp while he was alive.

He was a man with fiercely loyal friends and equally bitter enemies — there was rarely any middle ground. Those chroniclers of Earp's life who spoke to the man's friends came away with a glowing picture of a fearless, upstanding peace officer; those writers who relied on the memories of Earp's detractors created a completely different picture of this legendary figure.

Although the number of books and films about his life have assured Earp's place among the West's most prominent legends, he was a latecomer to mythic status compared with other frontier figures. Buffalo Bill and Wild Bill Hickok, for example, were immortalized in dime novels while they were still young men. The first major book on Wyatt Earp, on the other hand, was not published until 1927, when Earp was 79, just two years before his death.

Walter Noble Burns's *Tombstone, An Iliad of the Southwest* was, as the title suggests, a romantic and colorful account of the events surrounding Tombstone's Gunfight at the O.K. Corral and was the first step toward the creation of a Wyatt Earp legend. A much more important book, though, was Stuart N. Lake's *Wyatt Earp, Frontier Marshal*. Published two years after Earp's death in 1931, this fanciful biography shaped the way America perceived Wyatt Earp. Lake's Earp was the six-gun hero who tamed Dodge City, held off an outlaw army in Wichita and, with the help of his brothers and the formidable Doc Holliday, wiped out the Clanton-McLowery Gang of Tombstone. A definitive model of Western manhood, he was courageous, wise, righteous and unassuming — all of which would have been pretty hard to swallow if Lake hadn't been such an entertaining writer.

Over the years, Lake's romanticized vision of Wyatt Earp extended its influence through movies and television shows. *Frontier Marshal* was adapted to the movie screen three times and was the uncredited inspiration for many other films, while Lake himself served as a consultant for the popular Wyatt Earp TV series of the 1950s. Through films and television the Earp legend reached millions of people around the world in the person of such stars as Randolph Scott, Burt Lancaster, James Garner and Hugh O'Brien. The most respected of the Earp films is 1946's *My Darling Clementine*, starring Henry Fonda as Earp and directed by western master John Ford.

By the late 1950s, some writers were fed up with the Lake embellishments on Earp's life and began to swing the pendulum in the opposite direction as they set out to debunk the glorified myth. Earp was no longer a virtuous hero. He was a sneak and a killer. He had a criminal record as a young man, and he went on from there to become a boom town liar and bully who was not above pimping and stage robbery — or much of anything else either. Conversely, the Clantons and McLowerys were no longer an outlaw gang, they were a cowboy faction. Not only that, the Earp debunkers claimed, most of the Clantons and McLowerys were not even armed at the time of the O.K. Corral fight.

As is usually the case when writers set out to deflate an overblown myth, the Earp critics went too far. Such books as *The Earp Brothers of Tombstone* and *Wyatt Earp: The Untold Story* were obviously the results of a great deal of research, but, as some more recent writers like Alford Turner and Glenn Boyer have pointed out, the research was incomplete and one-sided. A writer wouldn't have to go far to find people who were ready to bad-mouth Wyatt Earp, but on the other hand, there were also documents and first-hand accounts that bore out some of the pro-Earp claims. The real Wyatt Earp lies somewhere between the Lake myth and the debunking diatribes, and probably closer to the good than the bad.

To one extent or another, every famous Western hero or villain is a shadow figure. Documentation along the frontier was sketchy at best and illuminated only part of any given Western personality. The most diligent researcher is likely to find gaps in the story he is trying to unearth. To bring the shadow figure into the light, a certain amount of conjecture is necessary. Wyatt Earp's life is no exception.

We have seen Earp portrayed as a white knight of the frontier and as a cold-blooded villain. This book places him somewhere between the two extremes in a story that is part fact, part fiction — the story of Wyatt Earp as it might have been.

LAMAR, MISSOURI

1

Five Earps stood side by side at the open grave. Their black-suited figures etched harshly against the pale spring sky, they watched in silence as mounds of earth were heaved onto the oakwood coffin nestled six feet below.

The blond hair, the long thin nose and the close deep-set eyes were the unmistakable Earp stamp on father Nicholas and all four sons. Somewhere between the older solidity of Virgil and the lean quick youth of Morgan, was twenty-two-year-old Wyatt, long and taut in figure, his arresting face bisected by penetrating eyes shaded under a sharply chiseled brow.

The words of the Barnetts were distant at first and encroached slowly on Wyatt's consciousness:

"Willa was a good woman," Mrs. Barnett concluded, and old Ned Barnett chimed in that the whole town thought the same.

Wyatt's gazed swiveled slowly toward the couple. His light eyes glazed as they stared somewhere between Barnett and his wife.

A good woman. Sudden heat speared across Wyatt's temples and his jaw set hard. Willa had been just sixteen when the typhus had taken her. She never had the chance to become a woman. She was only a girl when they were wed, and the nine months they had together could hardly be long enough to be called a marriage. Just barely a running start, Wyatt thought. Running start. The words repeated and echoed senselessly in his head.

Eyes fixed on the slowly rising level of dirt in the grave, Wyatt took little notice of the movement around him as the funeral party began to disperse. A big hand clamped on his arm. Wyatt turned away from the gravedigger's work to see Virgil by his side. Wyatt's older brother considered saying something but instead just tightened his hold on the arm. Looking past his oldest brother James, limping away from the graveside, Wyatt saw the fat barber from town coming toward him, an empty condolence on his tongue, just waiting to get within Wyatt's hearing. Wyatt had passed the man nearly every night when he made his rounds, but for the life of him he couldn't remember his name. And he had no stomach for the fat man's sympathy. Jerking his arm free of Virgil's grasp, Wyatt smacked his broad-rimmed hat across his thigh, planted it on his head, and marched toward his buckboard tied by the stand of cotton-woods.

Wyatt swung onto the seat of the wagon in one long step. Gathering the reins, he wheeled around away from the trees, and pointed the buckboard toward town. Once the trees were cleared, he braked. For the first time it occurred to him he had no idea where he was headed. He looked back at Willa's grave in the middle of the small hillside cemetery. On opposite sides of the grave the Earp women and the Earp men stood in ragged lines, all heads turned toward Wyatt. Past the downhill slope to the right were the outlines of orderly little farms stretching along the choppy ground to the horizon. Facing ahead, Wyatt stared at the rutted road sweeping south to the small tight network of streets and frame buildings that was the town of Lamar. Wyatt's mind latched onto a fast decision. He gigged the wagon forward.

Hunt's Cafe and Saloon wasn't the only bar in Lamar — Redfield's stood just across the street — but Hunt's was the only one that would serve a man during the day. Wyatt left the buckboard in front and strode to Hunt's open front door. He paid no attention to the Barnetts who turned onto the street and watched him in stunned curiosity.

Afternoon light slanted through the windows onto the saloon's chipped plank floor near the entrance and shone off the corner of the bar's buffed brass rail. It then gave up the fight quickly and left the rear of the saloon to its own murky privacy. In the shadows of a rear corner, Ben Hunt hunched over a broom and worked on a week's worth of dust and scraps; at the bar were three noisy customers.

Hooting over their latest joke, the cowboys at the bar gave Wyatt the briefest of glances as the tall young man in the black suit stepped up to the rail ten feet away. Wyatt studied the cowboys. Their mud-spattered chaps were still strapped on and their shirts were stained with old sweat. They had obviously just slipped away from the cattle trail to toss back a few before continuing northward with the herd. They had themselves another laugh. The sound stung Wyatt's ears. They laughed too loud.

The shortest of the three cowboys noticed Wyatt's stare. The cowboy's smile froze in place while his eyes riveted on the tall man in black. The man's ruddy, pug-nosed face irritated Wyatt deeply. Wyatt turned away from the face only when Hunt ambled over to ask what he'd have.

"Bourbon," Wyatt said.

When Hunt came back with the bottle and glass, Wyatt took the whiskey from him to pour his own. Looking back at the other end of the bar, he saw that the short man was saying something in a low voice to his two friends who smiled and looked at Wyatt. Wyatt's fingertips whitened as he gripped the glass.

The short man drawled, "These here sodbusters think it's some kind of big deal to see anyone bother to come to their town." The big, thick cowboy to his right laughed. "This one here can't take his eyes off'n us," the short man added.

"Aw, leave him be, Rollie," the big cowboy answered. "Most like this here's the shitkicker's big day for high livin'."

All three cowboys thought this was funny. Wyatt downed his glassful. His jaw tightened with the bite of the bourbon, and he reached slowly into his jacket pocket to take out a badge. He pinned the circle of scuffed silver to his lapel. The constable badge on, he faced the cowboys squarely. The words came out hard and even:

"You Texas scum."

He watched the cowboy faces stiffen. In reflex, the short one called Rollie let his hand dangle toward his belt, but came up empty; the guns for all three cowboys had been checked behind the bar.

"You son-of-a-bitch cowboys," Wyatt went on, "you bring your stinking herds up through here and run right across homesteader land. Land that doesn't belong to you."

Many a time Wyatt had watched Texas cowboys drive their herds past Lamar toward northern markets; sometimes they let cattle veer across farmland, trampling corners of wheat fields. The Texas herds also brought splenic fever to infect local stock. It had gotten under Wyatt's skin from time to time, but never so much as it did now. Never so much as to make him tremble with rage.

Virgil Earp balled his fists into his pockets as he watched Wyatt drive the buckboard away from the cemetery.

"He's headed for town," said Morgan.

Virgil moved his stocky six-foot frame around to face his father. Nicholas watched Wyatt disappear down the road, the lines in his face set grimly. James stood to one side, staring at the ground in front of him; he shifted the weight off the lame leg, the one that had caught the bad-luck Rebel slug outside Vicksburg. On the other side of the grave, the Earp women grouped into a tighter knot.

Nicholas, clasping his hands behind him, considered the top branches of the stand of cottonwoods as if intent upon counting the leaves. "Virgil," he said flatly.

"Yes, father?"

"You best keep an eye on Wyatt. He's hurting bad."

Not bothering with a reply, Virgil went over to the horse standing just beyond the graveyard and saddled up.

"Morgan," Nicholas said, "you help your brother James take the women home."

Young Morgan hid his grimace from his father and followed James. Nineteen years was too old to be traipsing about with the womenfolk as far as Morgan was concerned. Especially when there was something else to be done. He looked at Virgil riding off without him and cursed under his breath.

Slowing his pace with each step, Morgan managed to fall several yards behind James and the women as they neared the wagon under the cottonwoods. He looked over his shoulder to see his father paying off the gravedigger and turned ahead to see James helping his mother onto the wagon. With all eyes turned away, Morgan slipped behind a bole and, keeping the tree between him and the wagon, bolted for Ransum's livery alongside the road. At the corner of the stable he shielded himself from view, checked to see if he was clear, and ran after Virgil.

Riding into town at an easy lope, Virgil spotted the buckboard outside of Hunt's and hitched his horse along-side it. Through the window of the saloon he could see Wyatt, with his back to him, his broad shoulders held tensely, facing the three cowboys. For a moment no one moved. The shortest of the cowboys stepped forward, as if he was going for Wyatt, then stopped. Virgil went to the door to see the short cowboy let out a quick, gruff laugh and turn to the big man next to him.

"Would ya look at this one, Will. Give a sodbuster a badge and he thinks he's the top of the heap."

"The dung heap," Will added, and the three of them whooped in appreciation.

The rest of his body held motionless, Wyatt pushed his glass away from him with the side of his hand. He took a step forward.

Hunt reached across the bar to grab him.

"Take it easy, Wyatt," he said.

Will, the big cowboy, grinned. "You heard him, Wyatt," he mimicked in a nasal tone. "Take it easy."

Virgil stood silently on the threshold, still unnoticed by the men at the bar. He dared not move, feeling as if one step might set off a hair-trigger explosion. Even with Wyatt's back to him, Virgil could imagine the red rushing across his brother's pale cheeks and the glint flickering in his eye. Concentrating so much on the scene before him, Virgil never noticed Morgan slipping toward him along the boardwalk.

Wyatt shook off the bartender's hold. With his eyes set on Rollie, he said, "What is it with you Texas rebs? Why do you got to crap up our land? Is that your way of trying to get even for gettin' your ass whupped in the war?"

The cowboys stopped laughing. There was just a moment's hesitation, then Rollie lunged forward.

Expecting the charge, Wyatt whipped around as soon as Rollie barrelled into him and used the cowboy's momentum to swing him crashing into the bar. With Rollie stunned for the moment, Wyatt squared himself and pounded a right to the side of Rollie's face. The pain lancing across his fist after impact made little impression on Wyatt; he reared back again for another shot. The two other cowboys pounced on him before he could connect a second time, but not before Virgil set himself in motion.

Virgil took hold of one cowboy and yanked him away from Wyatt with a single powerful tug. He then stepped between Will and his brother and tried strong-arming the big cowboy to the side. Will moved off a couple of steps but no more. During the brief respite, Virgil shouted at Wyatt to hold off. Oblivious, Wyatt rammed a fist into Rollie's gut; before Virgil could say another word, the big cowboy was on him.

While Wyatt took on Rollie and Virgil grappled with Will, the third cowboy got up the nerve to rush back and help his friends. Letting loose a howl, Morgan angled at him at a dead run, sprang off his feet and tackled him to the floor.

Virgil grabbed his man by the arm and worked it around the cowboy's back to try to restrain him. The big cowboy resisted the pressure and threw a blind punch that caught Virgil in the chest and made him let up on the hold. Seeing the next one coming, Virgil jabbed the cowboy hard in the face. Off to the side, Morgan's man kicked his way free and stumbled toward the bar. A flash of light reflecting off glass on the bar's counter caught Morgan's eye and he bounded to his feet, grabbed the half-empty bottle, and cracked it across the back of his cowboy's head.

Wyatt continued to batter away at Rollie. The cowboy's legs finally buckled and he sank halfway to the floor. Taking him by the back of the shirt, Wyatt heaved him toward the middle of the room; Rollie was pitched onto an old chair, which collapsed underneath him. A dull, wicked shine in his blue eyes, Wyatt strode over to the groaning body and picked up a broken-off chair leg.

Hunt circled around the end of the bar and shouted at Wyatt to let him be.

Wyatt pulled Rollie up to his feet with one hand and, after a brief considering look, whacked the chair leg across the side of the cowboy's head. He did it once more, releasing his grip on the man upon impact and letting Rollie spill away, stagger and drop. The cowboy's head thudded against the edge of the table on his way down.

Wyatt dropped the chair leg and lifted the cowboy by the shirtfront. Rollie hung limply in his grip. Wyatt was suddenly aware of the others around him, aware that the other fighting had stopped. Big Will sat in woozy submission against the bar; the third cowboy struggled to his knees alongside Morgan and stayed there.

Wyatt stared at the man in his hands.

Hunt said, "Christ, Wyatt. I don't think he's breathing."

Studying the cowboy vacantly, Wyatt seemed not to hear. He let go of Rollie. The cowboy slumped in a heap on the floor.

Wyatt took an involuntary step back, away from the body. He looked at Virgil and Morgan, making a concentrated effort to clear his mind.

"Come on," he said, stepping toward his older brother.

Virgil moved to the window to see if anyone was looking in from the street. The fierce excited glow now gone from his face, Morgan gawked at Rollie lying still on the floor.

Wyatt pushed Morgan along. "Come on, move," he ordered. Morgan fell into step and the three Earp brothers left the saloon.

2

The wheels of the buckboard spun dirt out of the road as Wyatt drove it hard around the corner. Morgan held tight to the seat alongside Wyatt and, up ahead, Virgil paced the wagon on horseback.

Wyatt knew the roan in harness well. He could pull and slacken the reins and flick the whip with unthinking instinct and still manage to coax the animal into top controlled speed at every turn. His hands working themselves, Wyatt soaked in the passing sights: the seedman's, the dry goods shop, the blacksmith. All were sights riddled with a past; times with Willa, times of patrolling, catching vagrants, jailing drunks. Wyatt tried imagining these places as part of a future, or even a present. He could see nothing.

On the edge of town the buckboard sailed over the far side of a bump and pounded back down on the packed earth. Careening onto a road to the left, they wound through pasture land and crossed the beaten-bare trail where Texas cattle sometimes traveled. Farther on, they rattled past the big oak standing in the meadow where

Wyatt used to noon. Another memory. From time to time, sitting in the oak's cool shade, Wyatt had watched the cowboys herd north. Many cowboys had passed him by while he just sat and lazed. One less cowboy starting today, Wyatt thought calmly.

The two-story frame house commanded the front section of the Earp property. Corn fields stretched to the left and the refinished barn was back to the right. Braking the buckboard to a fast stop by the front porch, Wyatt walked into the house a step ahead of Morgan and Virgil. He left his two brothers at the foot of the stairs and climbed up to his room on the second floor. There was no doubt in his mind what had to be done.

He gathered up a change of clothes and the remainder of last month's constable pay. Below him, from the big room downstairs, he could hear voices murmuring; the sharp, precise voice of his father stood apart from the others. Rolling up his things in a blanket, he left his room for the last time.

Without a word, Wyatt stepped past his father, mother and brothers to take down the warbags from the hook beside the fireplace. Nicholas stepped close.

"Are you sure the man was dead?" Nicholas asked.

Wyatt wrapped some biscuits in a handkerchief and stuffed them inside a warbag pouch. "I don't intend to stay and find out."

"What're you running for, Wyatt? You have a job in this town. A law job."

"That's not enough to keep me here. And when people hear about the cowboy, I probably won't even have that. The son of a justice of the peace, with a barroom killing to his name. That'll look fine, won't it?"

"Stay, Wyatt. Whatever happens, we can stick it through together."

The last of his provisions packed, Wyatt hefted the bags across his shoulder.

His mother said, "We know how to take care of our

own. We always have.'' She sat by the fireplace, an arm around little Warren, the youngest of the Earp boys. Her warm voice pierced Wyatt's will for a moment, but he braced himself to stand by his decision.

"This is no time to rush to a decision,'' Nicholas said. "You've just been through a lot of misery. Stay here and sort it all out.''

Wyatt tried not to listen. He half-expected his father to bring up his old plans for Wyatt to study the law and make something of himself in Lamar. With a murder in his past, he could never study the law.

"I don't have Willa anymore,'' was all Wyatt could say. Deep inside he knew that even if the bar fight had never happened, he would still be sorely tempted to take off. During the war, he had rankled at the sight of James and Virgil going off to fight for the Union while he had been obliged to stay behind and tend to the fields; and two years ago he had watched restlessly once more as Virgil headed west for Kansas. Now was his time to go.

Nicholas finally gave in when Virgil pointed out that a posse might already be on its way for Wyatt. Nicholas bowed his head in thought, the stern authority gone for the moment. "Well,'' he said, "I guess I'm not about to let a jury tell me whether a son of mine did right or wrong.''

He gave Wyatt some money and told him to take the new bay mare. "She'll take you a good distance,'' he said, "further than any other horse in Lamar.'' At the doorway, Wyatt looked past his father at the rest of the family. His mother ran a hand up her sleeve and held tight just below the elbow, her eyes holding fast to him. Something wrenched inside Wyatt. He picked up the Henry repeater propped against the wall and hurried out the door.

Saddling the mare, he took off out of the barn at a trot, veering toward the westbound trail on the far side of the thicket-hedged meadow facing the house. Fluttering up from his stomach was the feeling pinned to his last look at his mother and the lancing sound of father's voice. His face cooled as the passing breeze chilled the tears zig-zagging down his cheeks, and with a jolting realization the thought came to him that Willa's funeral had been only an hour ago. His stomach sickened. He tried summoning up the image of Willa's face, but it obstinately stayed hidden, while memories of his family continued to bite into him. After a time, the memories faded from his mind and all that remained was the trail ahead of him in stark dreadful clarity.

Lulled by the rhythm of the mare's gait, Wyatt rode slouch-shouldered out of the thicket and heeled the horse into a strong lope. The meadow passed quickly beneath him. At the trail skirting the other side, he pressed on, looking over his shoulder toward town to see that no one was pursuing him.

Bringing himself up straight, he took in the view that was wide and far in front of him. Around eighteen miles ahead would be the Kansas line. He had imagined himself riding this way so many times.

The Earps had first moved westward from Illinois to Iowa, and then down to Lamar. Wyatt always thought he was fated to continue the Earp move west. Even though he had let himself be held behind when Virgil had gone off to Kansas to hire on with a stage line, Wyatt had always believed he would be taking this road one day. But he never thought he'd ride this trail on the mend, feeling like a limping sick dog inside. This feeling wouldn't go away in a hurry — he knew that. But maybe, in Kansas, or the Indian Nations, there'd be things to make a man forget, something a man could tear a big godawful chunk out of.

The mare snorted sharply when Wyatt's boot heels snapped fiercely back into her ribs. She bucked slightly, then powered forward and stretched into a long, mad gallop.

3

The prairie camp at end-of-track was a crooked line of tents and shacks, just two rifle shots away from the upper reaches of Big Cabin Creek. The Missouri, Kansas and Texas Railroad had crossed south into Indian Territory in June and had dragged its hangers-on fifteen miles into the Cherokee Nation. With dusk settling in, the first railroad workers came into camp; they tramped through the muddy road and splashed through pockets of rain water to make their choices of jerry-built saloons, gambling halls and cathouses. Prowling with them were the camp regulars: an occasional Indian or white and, more common, Negroes enjoying the pleasures they could only glimpse a few years earlier while enslaved to their Creek and Cherokee masters.

Wyatt Earp rode to camp from the southwest and tied his horse to a shaft of wood hammered into the ground behind a long tent. His white shirt pulled at his broad shoulders and stuck with sweat to the small of his back as he bent over to beat the flecks of mud off his denims.

Though he was otherwise clean-shaven, a moustache now sprawled across his upper lip and straggled over the top of his mouth. Pulling his hat down low on his brow, he walked the narrow passage between tent and shack to the camp road.

It had taken Wyatt three months to wend his way through eastern Kansas to the Indian Nations border. From Fort Scott to Chanute and Baxter Springs, he had let his money drift away while applying himself to nothing in particular. Feeling his way, as he put it to himself, he crossed paths with buffalo hunters, trappers and drifters; he kept his distance from towns, and kept his ears open. Talk of the Nations in roadhouses and buffalo camps at night stirred him to his innards, as did talk of great opportunity for a man who knew his horseflesh and could do something about it.

At the end-of-track road, Wyatt kept to the edge of traffic to let the men who were milling around the street pass. Through gaps in the growing crowd he could see tents yellowed by lamplight. Inside them agitated silhouettes of customers angled across the canvases. On the other side of the street, a White Cherokee badman strutted past a gambling hall and a wide berth opened through the crowd before him as he advanced. Passing an alley, Wyatt sidestepped out of the way of a hard-running Indian. Not too far behind came the shout of "Thief!" and a breathless old Negro in hot pursuit. Laughter rose from the passers-by as the two darted across the camp. Wyatt continued on his way.

He went into a gambling hall made up of a frayed tent fronted by a wooden-slat facade. The man he was looking for sat at a rear table dealing blackjack. The black-Irish Ed Kennedy flicked an extra card to the man on his right and asked if he was standing pat. Wyatt leaned over his shoulder.

"It's all set," Wyatt said softly.

Kennedy gave him a glance in answer and finished the

play on the table. Half-turning from the game, he then asked, "Shawn is in?"

"He'll have the wagon ready."

Kennedy told his players to keep their seats as he got up to talk to another dealer at the bar. When he got his replacement at the table, he was ready to leave.

Riding off to the southwest, they soon left the cluster of camp lights behind and tracked their way across the grassy flats by the three-quarter moon. The closing darkness sent a pleasing shiver across the back of Wyatt's shoulders. Anticipation of the night's work made his blood rush even though he had done this twice before. The first two times hardly counted — just piddling around, that's all. Tonight was a step up, a step worthy of him.

Keys Well was a small Creek settlement just three miles from end-of-track. William Keys, the top Indian there, had himself a fair string of horses and was selling some work animals to the Missouri, Kansas and Texas. Wyatt had noticed, when riding past yesterday, that Keys also had a pair of well-bred duns, damn good racers if Wyatt didn't miss his bet. He figured they could easily bring a good 150 apiece. Still a few miles ahead of the railroad and the drifters that went along with it, Keys hadn't learned yet to be too suspicious and left things pretty open. At least, that's the way it had been that first time Wyatt had eased out the Indian's young roan.

Only a few lights could be seen from the semicircle of huts in the valley of Keys Well. Wyatt and Kennedy dismounted some fifty feet short of the corral; leaving the horses with Kennedy, Wyatt slipped on ahead. Out of the shadows on the far side of the corral came a man. Wyatt lowered himself silently to the ground. The man made a pass across his side of the corral, watched the horses for a moment, then moved on back toward the huts.

Reaching the corral, Wyatt squatted on the outside and stayed in place to let the horses get accustomed to his smell. The two duns capered a few steps nearby, then gradually settled. Satisfied that his presence was accepted, Wyatt ducked between rungs of the fence and, murmuring softly, moved toward the pair. He brought out one of his ropes. The near dun shied a bit but Wyatt kept up his sweet talk and the horse held his place, his head cocked to get a better look at the man through the darkness. Wyatt slipped the loop smoothly over the fine head. The animal snorted and sent a ripple of quiet disturbance through the rest of the stock. It died away as quickly as it had started after Wyatt stroked his dun into silence. With one in tow, the second dun came easier. A quick look back at the village, then Wyatt was opening the gate, leading his pair through, and closing the corral behind him.

Wyatt and Kennedy walked their horses until they were well out of earshot of the settlement. Wyatt's breath relaxed as they trotted off across the inky flat, but the fine prickling across his neck remained. In the moonlight he could now and then make out the sheen of the duns' coats and the rippling of the long muscles. He almost begrudged giving them up. Sleek, fast horses like these had always been part of his idea of good living, and handling them had been his gift since he was small. But, hell, the money he'd get for them in Kansas would put him on his way. Some day he'd have plenty of horses like these.

At the bend of Big Cabin Creek, a patch of hackberry trees sheltered the east bank. Among the deep shadows beneath the branches was the deeper pitch-black shadow of a wagon hitched to a team of two. The outline of the thin man in the driver's seat stood out when Wyatt and Kennedy drew near. John Shawn stopped worrying the reins long enough to half-rise from the seat.

"You're late," Shawn said. "I was thinkin' you might not come."

Wyatt gave him a glance as he and Kennedy dismounted and brought the duns over to Shawn's team. The moonlight cast dim splotches of shadow across Shawn's pockmarked cheeks and picked up the worry in his pale eyes.

Wyatt started to unhitch the team, annoyed that Shawn hadn't done the job already, and swung the duns around to take the team's place in harness.

"I was here on time," Shawn chattered on. "I had to wait. I was here an hour, a good hour I'd say. For all I knew you wouldn't make it. For all I knew you could've called the whole thing off. I might've been just settin' here, not knowin' —"

Wyatt reached Shawn in two steps, grabbed the man's arm, and brought him back down on the seat in a hurry. "We got business here, Shawn. Are you going to hold up your end?"

Not trying to break free of the hold, Shawn mumbled that he would.

"All you have to do," said Wyatt, "is drive these horses up to Techopa Gully. Just ten miles. You got that?"

"Yeah . . ."

"We should be able to throw anyone off your trail by then. We'll meet at the gully and then it's just a few miles more and we'll be in Kansas. If you're with us, then just get a grip on yourself and get it done."

Shawn turned sullenly away, not bothering to reply. Wyatt went back to the horses and helped Kennedy finish up the switch. With the duns in harness, he checked Shawn once more. The driver sat hunched over, staring at the ground.

"You ready?" Wyatt said, his voice cold.

"Yeah. Yeah, I'm all right. Just got a bit jittery, waitin' and all."

Wyatt stepped away from the team. "Then get the hell going."

Shawn urged the duns forward, reined away from the hackberries, and headed for the open flat. Pleased to see that Shawn wasn't pressing the prize horses too hard, Wyatt saddled up and gathered the lead-rope on one of Shawn's animals to move on. He and Kennedy angled to the left of the wagon's route.

Kennedy jerked his head toward Shawn's path. "I've seen better men before — better and then some."

"I'm not asking him to do much," Wyatt said. "I think I put enough backbone in him to get the job done."

"Well, it's your play," said Kennedy. "You call it."

Their decoy ride didn't turn up any signs of trailers and by midnight they came upon Techopa Gully. After a final searching look at their back-trail, they picked their way down the slope and waited on the floor of the gully. Once Shawn showed up, they could cover the last few miles to the Kansas line within the hour.

Kennedy wondered out loud once more about Shawn making it and Wyatt snapped at him to keep it to himself. They listened.

Roaming across the plain, the wind swept through the tall grass and rustled softly in steady whispering waves. The scuttling of a jackrabbit cut through the regular swish of air from the flat, but nothing else reached Wyatt's ears. He sat his horse and waited. With growing irritation, he expected Kennedy to say something more about Shawn. Kennedy kept his silence and the two men strained to hear any sign of distant hoofbeats.

As long minutes passed, Wyatt got around to wondering if Shawn had the gumption to try selling the horses on his own. A wiser voice told him to settle down; the little runt didn't have that kind of nerve. Still, Wyatt spent the next few minutes imagining what he'd do to Shawn if he actually did try his own play. It passed the time.

He heard something to the east and dismounted to peer over the edge of the gully; he tried to distinguish figures through the blackness. The dim rattle might have been hoofs beating across the plain, but it thinned and then faded away before Wyatt could be sure.

"You see anything?" asked Kennedy.

"Can't see a damn thing." Wyatt slid back to his horse. "Could've sworn someone was coming."

Before Wyatt could answer, the clip-clop of hoofs

reached the draw. In another moment the dim outline of the wagon pulled into view along the top of the slope. Shawn's pinched voice called Wyatt's name.

Letting his breath go, Wyatt led his horses up the incline. Kennedy was quick to follow. The two men tied both their mounts and Shawn's original team to the rear of the wagon.

"You see anyone?" said Wyatt.

"No one," answered Shawn. "Just like you said, Wyatt, it was an easy ride. Smooth as could be."

Kennedy said, "You sure took your goddamned time."

"That's all right," put in Wyatt as he moved ahead to inspect the duns in harness. "At least he didn't work the animals hard." He ran a hand across the chest of one of the horses and felt him breathing easy.

"No one said I had to beat hell to get here," Shawn went on as if Wyatt hadn't already put the question to rest. "I was just supposed to ease 'em over here. Ain't that right, Wyatt?"

The darkness hid Wyatt's sharp glance from Shawn. Wyatt climbed into the back of the wagon with Kennedy, and told Shawn to get started. "Take her to the right of that ridge and then just follow your nose north."

As the wagon surged forward, the ridge rose bleakly against the moonlit sky just past the mouth of the gully. Beyond that, into the night, Wyatt imagined the station house on the other side of the Kansas line where he had spent a night just a couple of months ago, a scared young man on his way into Indian Territory. This time, he'd be coming with something to show for his trouble.

Shawn didn't care much for the silence. "If you told me before tonight that it would be this damned easy, I'd never've believed you."

"I *did* tell you it'd be this easy," returned Wyatt.

Shawn turned his head in reflection for a moment. "That you did," he laughed. "And I'll be damned if I *didn't* believe you."

Wyatt and Kennedy exchanged a look and shook their heads. His back to them, Shawn paid them no mind. "Well, I guess I learned my lesson," he mused. "And the little woman'll be glad I did at that. I'll be gettin' her some fine things now. And there'll be more to come, I can see that. You got to do that sort of thing for a woman, the way I see it."

Shawn had more to say about the little woman and what he'd get her, but Wyatt, looking off into the night, didn't hear him. He was looking at shadows at the base of the ridge.

Out of place shadows that moved.

The shadows, four of them, came out from behind the steep slope and soon became silhouettes of horses and riders. Thin black lines extending up from the knees of the horsemen had to be rifles. In another moment they were close by, close enough for Wyatt to see the Indian faces beneath the flat-brimmed hats. Shawn stopped talking.

The little man reined the team in hard. Wyatt swiveled on his heels to check their back-track. Up from the floor of the gully came two more horsemen, both armed. One of them was William Keys.

While his stomach churned, Wyatt's mind raced back over the last few minutes and a realization sprang out at him. The rattle of hoofs just before Shawn had reached the gully. They had come from the east. Shawn had ridden in from the south. The sound had belonged to the Creeks circling around to cut them off at the ridge. Wyatt fought down the panic.

"Let me go!" Shawn leaned forward on his seat. "Please! I just wanted a fresh team to take me to Kansas! They made me do it! I swear to you, by God! They made me —"

Wyatt spun him around and yanked him halfway into the rear of the wagon. "Shut up!" he hissed. "Shut the hell up or I'll kill you!"

4

The United States Deputy Marshal took custody of the three rustlers at Fort Gibson. Using his shotgun to point the way, he took Wyatt, Kennedy and Shawn from William Keys's posse and marched them to his wagon.

A cage on wheels, the wagon was ten feet by five across with rusting iron bars connecting the floor to its slat roof. Chips of paint on the hinged back door were all that was left of the circus emblem applied by the previous owner. Wyatt balked before stepping up. A prod from twin muzzles of the deputy marshal's shotgun got him up and inside.

The old circus wagon rumbled east on the Osage Road just north of the Arkansas River. Wyatt sat across from Kennedy. In the far corner, Shawn slumped, whimpering. A stench rose from the wagon floorboards, fumes from animal urine soaked deep in the wood. Swallowing hard to keep from throwing up at the smell, Wyatt desperately concentrated on the leaden river rolling by until the churning inside him subsided. Opposite him, Kennedy lowered his head and ran his fingers fitfully through his black curly hair.

Wyatt grabbed one of the bars to hold himself steady and edged over to the deputy marshal working the team.

"Where do you take us from here?" Wyatt asked.

The burly deputy marshal showed no sign of hearing the question. Wyatt was about to ask again when the answer finally came: "I guess you ain't heard, have ye?"

Wyatt waited for the rest of it. The deputy marshal cracked the whip over the animals' backs and tended to his chaw of tobacco as if he had forgotten Wyatt was hanging onto the bars behind him. He then spoke up suddenly. "The federal court," he said with a quick glance over his shoulder at his prisoner, "it just moved to Fort Smith. The whole ball of wax. Presides for the whole Territory, it does."

"We're going to Arkansas?"

"That's a fact." A low laugh rumbled in the marshal's throat. "I was you, boy, I'd hope the judge don't step in shit on his way to court, come your turn." The marshal tilted his head back and laughed long and loud.

Wyatt slouched back down on the wagon bed. Kennedy was staring at the roof when he spoke. His voice was thin. "They just built the gallows at Fort Smith," he said. "Hear they're hangin' for rustlin'."

Shawn's whimpering stopped. Not daring to look at either of the other two men, Wyatt fixed his gaze on a knothole in the floorboards; the swirl of grain in the wood stood out in vivid lines that his eyes followed over and over again in maddening circles.

For the first time in weeks, Wyatt thought of Willa. He groped for an explanation for the last few days that he thought would satisfy her, but the image of her was frittered away when a low, halting whine came from Shawn's corner. Wyatt wanted to shut the weasel's trap but said nothing.

They reached Fort Smith the following evening. The

ferry took the wagon across the Arkansas to the sharply banked shore at Belle Point where the Arkansas met the mouth of the Poteau. Fort Smith town crowded the bank on the left, while the cleared ground of the military-post reservation sprawled above the junction of the rivers straight ahead. After climbing up the shore, the wagon reached the level military grounds and the fort itself came into view.

The Army had left a couple of months before, but the encircling brick wall of Fort Smith still looked like it could stand up to an attack. Sullenly, Wyatt realized that it now served to keep men in. The wagon clattered through the gateway and moved along the rectangular line of road that connected the buildings inside. Rounding the corner of a two-story building, the wagon headed toward the new gallows constructed in front of the post magazine. Kennedy sidled up to Wyatt to take a look. The platform stood seven feet above the ground; a rope dangled from the crossbeam of hewn oak; two men fastened the rope to a weighted sack which was positioned above the trap door. Alongside the scaffold, a second gallows was under construction.

The deputy marshal called back cheerfully, "Finally gonna use one of them damn things tomorrow. Say they'll shoot 'em through like greased pigs down a chute." He grunted in admiration.

The wagon veered to one side and the scaffold was cut off from Wyatt's view for the moment. He heard a creak and a sickening whoosh as the trapdoor was sprung and the sack dropped.

The marshal braked next to another wagon along the thin strip of ground between the scaffold and the brick building that used to be the soldiers' quarters. He let the prisoners out, the shotgun cradled in his arm. Outside the wagon, Wyatt got a good look at the weighted sack swinging lazily below the platform. The fear that had been a tenacious, steady thing since boarding the deputy mar-

shal's wagon at Fort Gibson now clawed its way through
his gut like a hungry animal.

A shove from the marshal sent him toward the brick
building. On their way to the door, the three prisoners
passed two men walking, toward the wagon beside the marshal's. One of them planted his eyes on Wyatt. A big,
bearded man in a broadcloth suit worn thin at the elbows.
The gray eyes staring from under bushy black eyebrows infuriated Wyatt. He would be damned if he'd show any fear
before this gawking bastard. With a long stride, he led his
two accomplices inside.

The cocky front faded in a hurry when the deputy marshal took the prisoners down a flight of steps. In the base-
ment, the barracks kitchen had been converted into jail
cells. A narrow passage, pitch-black except for the swaying
light of the kerosene lamp held by the jailor, ran along a
series of barred doors. From somewhere came a groan that
reverberated the length of the passage. The fourth door
down was opened and the deputy marshal signaled them
inside. The setting sun outside left most of the cell in
darkness. Wyatt's feet were rooted in place at first, but,
knowing he'd receive another shove from the marshal, he
got himself going.

The threesome inside, the door slammed shut and the
metal bolt clanged into place. Shawn, pressed against the
door, arched his head toward the opening above. "You
could give us a break," he pleaded. "Let us go. We're just
three young fellers who made a mistake. One mistake.
We'd never do it again. We . . . ."

The footfalls of the deputy marshal and the jailor
resonated down the hall in response.

Shawn looked at Wyatt and side-stepped along the wall.
He posted himself as far as possible from the tall young
man. Wyatt returned Shawn's look but didn't bother with
him. He was too close to begging himself.

He stood in the center of the cell, giving his eyes time to
adjust to the darkness. The deep, thick voice startled him.

"Got any tobacco?"

Wyatt spun toward the corner to his right. Sitting in the shadows was a big man; Wyatt couldn't make out any details. The deep voice asked its question again. "Got tobacco?"

"No, I don't," Wyatt answered.

The man came to his feet in a smooth unhurried motion and took a step closer, picking up some of the fading light filtering through the barred window. He was a half-breed, built wide and strong with a scar running jaggedly down from his temple. The broad shoulders made the man seem big when seated, but on his feet he was a half-foot shorter than Wyatt. Still, the thick muscles looked like they could move with crippling speed. He leveled a stare at Kennedy and Shawn while his hands braided a length of horse hair.

"How about you?" the half-breed said. "Any tobacco?"

Shawn blurted "No" and Kennedy shook his head. The half-breed grunted, returned to his corner, and continued braiding.

The window faced the gallows on the other side of the yard. Wyatt stood and watched the scaffold crew adjust the bolt below the trap door and set up the weighted sack for another trial run. He was still watching when the sun disappeared altogether and the crew fired up a lantern to allow them to make the final preparations.

Kennedy shuffled over to Wyatt's side, glanced out the window, and turned away. He crouched by the wall. "What'll we do, Wyatt?"

Wyatt shrugged helplessly. Only one decision had come to him that entire day: he would never be afraid of anything again if he ever got out of this. If he ever got out.

5

The deputy marshal and the jailor came for the half-breed in the morning. The big-shouldered man got up out of his corner without being ordered and stood by the door while the jailor put on the leg irons.

"Bring the tobacco?" the half-breed asked.

"Didn't think of it," the jailor answered.

The half-breed seemed to muse about this awhile. When the shackles were tightened, he blandly said, "Damn you to hell, Travis. You said you'd get me some."

Travis shrugged and turned him toward the door. The half-breed, flanked by his two keepers, dragged his manacled feet down the passageway.

Going to the window, Wyatt and Kennedy saw the shackled man led out of the building. A crowd of about twenty people from Fort Smith was waiting for him at the foot of the scaffold. With difficulty, the prisoner side-stepped up the stairs, the leg irons rattling sharply with each step. Once on the platform, the half-breed was placed on top of the trapdoor, and the shackles were removed. A clerk of the federal court announced to the crowd that the sentenced, known only as Sixkiller, had been convicted by Judge Story's court of killing a man for his team and wagon. The minister then read a psalm, and the hangman checked the noose.

Wyatt kept his eyes riveted on Sixkiller's face, waiting for some sign of fear, any emotion at all, as the final rituals were carried out. He was still waiting for some visible reaction from the killer when the black hood was fitted over his scarred head. A moment later, the lever was pulled, the trap door opened, and Sixkiller dropped. His legs churned in a brief flurry. From the jail cell window across the yard, Wyatt could hear the man's neck snap.

The three men in the cell sat in silence for another hour. The door then opened, and the Deputy Marshal announced that court was in session. Shotgun in hand, he guided them down the passageway.

"Judge Story holds session in the Rogers Building in town," said the marshal. "Be sure to take in the morning air, fellas — it's a nice day for a walk."

Stepping out of the soldiers' quarters, Wyatt squinted against the sunshine. He adjusted to the light in time to see Sixkiller cut down and stretched out in a coffin beneath the platform. Another look at the gallows and his mind was made up. Walking close to Kennedy, he whispered, "We're going to make a break. I'll start it off."

With only one path leading out, the fort was no place to begin. They passed through the gate to the surrounding field. After a claustrophobic night in the cell, the open grounds made Wyatt's heart quicken, but escape here was no more practical than inside the fort. On this flat piece, they would be sitting ducks for the marshal's shotgun. Wyatt consciously measured his steps to keep himself in the marshal's orderly procession.

Bordering Fort Smith town was wide Garrison Avenue. Heads turned to watch the prisoners walk along the street and cross over to the northeast side. The deputy marshal then told them to turn left onto a side street. Wyatt figured the courthouse couldn't be much farther. A farmer walked out of a boot shop just up ahead. Looking the three prisoners over closely, he stepped off the boardwalk and passed just in front of the rustlers. When the farmer was within lunging distance, Wyatt grabbed him.

Pivoting on his heels, Wyatt yanked him off balance and heaved him back at the deputy marshal. Wyatt didn't wait to see what happened. He put his head down and raced for the alley to his right.

Dashing down the passage, he heard shouts from behind but no gunshots. The farmer must have barrelled squarely into the marshal and knocked him over. Glancing over his shoulder, Wyatt saw Kennedy run down the opposite alleyway. Someone on the street shouted that he caught one of them. That would be Shawn.

Wyatt turned left at the end of the alley and scrambled across a string of backyards. A boy taking out slop from a restaurant stopped and stared, but he was too surprised to do anything more than watch Wyatt reach the next block. Sticking to the back lots, Wyatt scaled fences from one yard to the next and ran for the next side street. He passed a livery corral and turned to see the deputy marshal charging down the parallel street on the other side of the pen. Wyatt pressed harder to reach the cover of the rear of the stable up ahead, but the marshal caught sight of him before he made it. A blast from the marshal's shotgun pelted the ground a foot behind him. He dove as the second barrel boomed and he sailed the last couple of yards to the protection of the stable corner.

Rolling and springing back to his feet, Wyatt made for the next road. At the edge of the street he halted, seeing a wagon moving away from him, some fifteen feet to the right. From the left, he heard hoofbeats. They sounded like they could be coming from the marshal's direction.

The street was quiet; no one was looking Wyatt's way. He ran for the wagon.

Running low to keep himself below the driver's view, he reached the back of the wagon, grabbed the top of the rear flap, and, with a quick double-step, vaulted inside. Among the grain sacks, he pulled the wagon's canvas over himself.

Though his body was now still, his heart raced on. He tried taking long slow breaths to settle himself but it made little difference to the pounding against his rib cage.

He took stock of what lay ahead. When he started for the wagon, he had noticed the street ended just two blocks farther on; from there the buildings began to thin out. He figured he would be clear of Fort Smith in another ten minutes, then he could slip out and take off on foot. Maybe head back toward Kansas, maybe try another part of the Nations. He counted seconds to keep time.

Squeezed into a narrow space between sacks, his limbs began to ache and then go numb. He started to shift his weight to uncramp a leg and then froze when a voice called out.

"Hold up there!" It was the marshal. He called out again and the wagon eased to a stop. Wyatt heard the clip-clop of hoofs walking past him, toward the driver.

"An escaped prisoner just came by here," the deputy marshal said. "You see him?"

The driver answered, "What'd he look like?"

Wyatt slowly lifted the canvas up an inch to get a look. He could only see the marshal from the shoulders down, but that was enough to see the Winchester in its saddle boot and the shotgun in the lawman's hands.

"Tall feller," the marshal told the driver. "Light hair. You'd notice him if you saw him."

"No, can't say that I have, marshal. Didn't see no one runnin' from nobody."

"Sure?"

"I'm sure all right."

"Damn!" The deputy marshal turned in his saddle. Wyatt backed off from the crack between canvas and wagon. "Where the hell did he go?" the marshal said.

Reining around quickly, the marshal swung back toward Wyatt, who pressed his face against the floor of the wagon. Hoof-beats came toward him, then stopped close by. Breath caught, Wyatt held himself motionless. The horse didn't move. He tried to remember what he had seen of the side of the street opposite the marshal's position. A place to scramble for, some sort of cover: a water trough, an alley, an untended horse, anything. He carefully flexed the muscle in his right knee. If he didn't move soon, the leg might be too cramped to support his weight. He heard the marshal's saddle-leather creak. Then silence.

Suddenly, the wagon lurched forward and rolled on down the road.

Over the rumbling of the wagon, Wyatt tried to hear if a horse was following. He counted the four horses in the team. Nothing more. The deputy marshal must have tried another direction. Wyatt pictured the street ahead in his mind, imagining the progress of the wagon.

He sectioned off the passing minutes into one street block, then two. The wagon now started to bump across ruts in the road, a road not tended too often. The road past the edge of town.

He pushed his torso up off the wagon floor and, shuffling his feet underneath him, braced himself for the jump. He edged toward the side of the wagon.

"No sense in jumping now, son."

Wyatt stopped. It was the driver's voice.

"Might as well just come up here with me," the man went on.

Unsurely, Wyatt pushed the canvas aside and faced the head of the wagon. The driver looked at him over his shoulder. It was the bearded man from the night before, the one outside the jail. The man spat out a stream of brown tobacco juice, which arced neatly over the side.

"Come on up," he said. "I could use a body to shoot the poop with."

Turkey Creek Jack Johnson had been lending a hand with a grain contract with the Federal District Court. When he had finished his business in the soldiers' quarters, one of the incoming prisoners had caught his eye. The tall one, walking nearly a full head above the other two prisoners; he had a way about him. Turkey Creek had seen outlaws herded into Fort Smith before, and it was usually a look of terror or rock-hard nonchalance that he saw in their faces. Here he saw a fierceness despite the fear, a smarter look than was common. He was not surprised the next morning to see the young man out of the corner of his eye, running to the mouth of the alley, looking for his best route away from the law.

The sound of the young man climbing into the back of his wagon started him thinking. His mind had been set by the time the deputy marshal called out.

Creeping up toward the front of the wagon, the young man now looked at him with quick, calculating eyes, like a stray cat eyeing a handful of food from a stranger. The young man took a seat beside him and looked straight ahead. Turkey Creek could sense the wiry muscles flexing underneath the fugitive's shirt-sleeves, poised for the next unexpected move.

Turkey Creek introduced himself. The young man nodded, but kept looking straight ahead.

"You got a name too, don't you?"

"Earp. Wyatt Earp."

"Glad to meet you, son. You did a pretty fair job of sneakin' into my wagon. But not so good that I didn't notice."

Wyatt's face snapped toward Turkey Creek. "You knew I was back there the whole time?"

"Sure did. If I didn't hear you I would've smelled the jail stink on you."

Confusion gave way to a hint of suspicion in Wyatt's

sharp blue eyes. "If you knew I was escaping from jail in your wagon, how come you didn't tell the marshal? You don't know me from shit."

"Just a whim." Turkey Creek snapped. "I got a good look at you last night and it started me thinkin'."

"What does that mean?"

"Well, it got me thinkin' that you didn't look like you should be goin' to jail. You looked like you were a cut above hanging." Turkey Creek's mouth curled into a half-smile. "Maybe not a big cut, but enough of one."

"You thought all that when you spotted me last night?"

"Partly, not all. I like to think I can size a man up just lookin' at him. If a feller's got something to him, I want to know about it right off. It can save a lot of trouble later on, wouldn't you say?"

Wyatt shrugged.

"Like I said," Turkey Creek continued, "I figured just part of it last night. The rest come to me after I heard you climb on back there. Hell, I figured you could use a second chance, is all. So I told the marshal I hadn't seen you. No skin off my ass. Who knows? You might be able to do me the same sometime."

Wyatt nodded slowly as he watched the road before him. "I guess I should thank you," he said.

"I guess you should," said Turkey Creek.

Wyatt glanced at the man, looked back at the road, considered it, and then finally said thanks as if he decided just then that he could spare it.

Turkey Creek let him ride in silence for a few moments. He then asked, "What'd you do? Kill somebody?"

"No," Wyatt blurted. Putting on a casual air, he added, "We just took some horses."

"You mean you stole them."

Wyatt grudgingly admitted he was right. Turkey Creek shook his head. "You sure don't look like you should be a penny ante horse thief."

"What *do* I look like?"

Turkey Creek turned to study the young man who still couldn't settle on facing him square. "I may have just saved your life, Wyatt. You think that gives me a right to give you some advice?"

Wyatt gave it a thought. "I guess it does."

"You're damn right it does." With a snap of his wrists, he slapped the reins across the horses' flanks. "You just come out west, Wyatt?"

"Three or four months ago."

"Not surprised." Turkey Creek narrowed his eyes. "You probably figured that everything's wide-open out here and you could just come out west like some fire-eater and take whatever you damn please. But that's not all of it. I think you know that now. You've seen the gallows at Fort Smith. From the wrong side."

"I saw them, all right."

"Well then, you should know it's not a bad idea to keep on the right side of the law. Now the law ain't something I'm religious about, mind you. I just know you got to respect it, like you would a man who's bigger'n you."

Wyatt put on a sarcastic face. "Is that your great advice?"

"Not at all." Turkey Creek moved the team up a hillside path. "I figure you to be a young man who wants to get somewheres. Probably that's what you figured you were doin' when you stole them horses. But outright stealin' won't get you nowhere for very long, not unless you're dead set on dyin' young and stupid. Someone with your looks and your way — and maybe some brains, too — you should be able to find smarter ways of gettin' along."

Wyatt was now looking straight at him. Turkey Creek let the young man wait a moment before going on.

"I ain't talkin' about being a pilgrim," he said. "I'm just talkin' about being smart."

His piece said, Turkey Creek put his mind back on the

hillside switchback. They rode on without talking for some time.

Out of the corner of his eye, Wyatt took in the burnished face and the leathery creases that stretched upward from Turkey Creek's black beard. The man still hadn't said where he was headed or how far Wyatt could tag along. For now, Wyatt felt no urge to find out. He was surprised to find he was willing to leave choices of where and how far to Turkey Creek. Absently, he watched the crest of the rocky hill come closer as the wagon made its climb.

Kansas and Indian Territory had been on his mind before he got out of Fort Smith; now he couldn't think of what he would do in those places. He wondered how smart Turkey Creek himself had been at getting along out west.

Feeling obliged to break the silence after a while, Wyatt made trifling talk about the team. After some easy horse talk, he got around to asking where Turkey Creek had been. Turkey Creek told him about freighting along the border, hunting buffalo, and scouting now and then for the Army at Fort Dodge. Wyatt listened closely to the stories at first, but soon his mind was wandering; when Turkey Creek finished his say, Wyatt let the conversation break off.

By late afternoon they reached the river and ferried across to Van Buren. Skirting the town, they headed north and traveled another couple of miles to a station house. Here Turkey Creek stopped the wagon.

"I'm headin' northeast for Mountainburg," said Turkey Creek. "You'd best take off on your own from here."

Wyatt thanked him, stuck out his hand, and shook on it. The tall young man swung out of the wagon. He didn't move off at first, and, for his part, Turkey Creek kept his wagon in place.

"What are your plans?" asked the bearded freighter.

Wyatt sunk his hands in his pockets as he took a step

back toward the wagon. "I guess hunting buffalo gives a man his share of staying to himself."

"His share, and then some. Could still be some money to be made by it too, from what I hear."

Wyatt nodded, turned away and started for the station house.

"Could use some money now, couldn't you?" called Turkey Creek.

Facing the bearded man, Wyatt saw him take a roll of money from his pocket and toss it over.

"Take it, boy. I don't think they left you a whole lot back at Fort Smith."

Wyatt leafed through the bills. "Seventy-five dollars," he said, his voice hushed. "How'll I be able to pay you back?"

Turkey Creek grimaced as if picking up a bad smell. "Now don't make me out to be stupid, Wyatt. Only reason I'm lendin' it to you is I got a hunch I'll be runnin' into you again. A strong hunch." He made a broad gesture to the right. "Over that hill there's a ranch, belongs to a man named Anson. He'll sell you a good horse."

Without waiting for a reply, he gigged the team and moved on ahead. Over his shoulder, Turkey Creek called, "After I unload this, I'm on my way to Newton, over to Kansas."

Standing alone in the road, Wyatt watched the wagon roll away as night creeped across the valley. The wagon descended down the pitch, nearly disappearing, then curled to the left, and, in the last oblique rays of soft light, vanished up a wooded mountain road. Wyatt listened to the spin of wooden wheels, the wagon a faraway creaking phantom in the darkness.

KANSAS

6

Most of Newton's saloons, dance halls and bordellos could
be found in the section of town called Hyde Park. Springing to life once the Atchison, Topeka and Santa Fe built a
terminal in Newton, the area was kept in business
throughout the shipping season by Texas cattlemen and
cowhands. The business brought in by the Texas trade was
a lively one. Some said that by August of the first season
four men had been killed in that part of town; others said
that was mostly brag.

The clerk at the Pioneer Store told Wyatt that Hyde
Park was where he could find Turkey Creek Johnson.

In the glare of midday, as the roughs and gamblers slept
off the night before, the streets of Hyde Park looked
orderly enough. Aside from a few farmers coming in for
supplies and freighters bringing in goods, Main Street was
almost empty. The buildings may have looked a bit more
sturdy than those Wyatt had seen at end-of-track down in
the Nations, but not by much. They still seemed like they
were ready to be uprooted, false fronts and all, and

transported to the next favored shipping point. The longhorn trade had already shifted from Abilene and Ellsworth, and there was talk stirring up that Wichita, twenty-five miles south of Newton and that much closer to Texas, might be the next cattle town to boom. But Wyatt had heard different. He had met a kid in a buffalo camp along the Cimarron by the name of Bill Masterson who was putting his money on the new town building just west of Fort Dodge. He was a game, amiable fellow and he had Wyatt just about convinced. Masterson was on his way to grade for the railroad outside of Fort Dodge; Wyatt might have even gone along with him if he hadn't had personal business to tend to first.

Hunting buffalo on the plains turned out to be lucky for Wyatt. With money made as a teamster outside Coffeyville, he had been able to buy a Sharps and wagon, and hire a man to help drive and skin. He killed as much as fifty at one stand and had his share of other respectable kills besides. More important, he and his man had found a deserted shack along Medicine Lodge River while the great blizzard in January was setting in. Other hunters had been ruined by the brutal weather, but Wyatt had been able to wait out the storm in fair comfort.

A good part of Wyatt's earnings was now worn around his waist. The brace of Colts had walnut handles and the gun belt was tooled along each holster. The added heft on each hip made Wyatt's walk more measured and, he felt, more confident. To go along with the firearms was a new brown suit whose trousers didn't reach quite as far down as they should have. On his way down Main Street, Wyatt stepped up onto the boardwalk to try to keep the suit clear of the rising dust in the road churned up by passing horses and wagons.

Wyatt saw Turkey Creek walk out of a saloon called the Side Track on the other side of the street. With Turkey Creek was a lean, dark man wearing a black gun belt under his duster. They both looked down the street and, by the time Wyatt reached them, were talking quietly.

"Hi, Turkey Creek," said Wyatt. "I guess you were right about seeing me again."

Turkey Creek said nothing. He glanced at Wyatt, then checked the street over his shoulder. It hadn't occurred to Wyatt until now that the bearded man might have forgotten all about him within a couple of hours of leaving him outside Van Buren.

Anxious to set things right, Wyatt said, "I've got that money I owe you."

"I could use some help, Wyatt."

Wyatt followed the man's look down the block. "What is it?"

Turkey Creek motioned for Wyatt to follow. As Turkey Creek and his friend started walking down the boardwalk, Wyatt fell into step alongside them.

"Been a killin' here," said Turkey Creek. "A bad one. A fella name of Fitzpatrick, he murdered the justice of the peace last night. He's been up and drinkin' since, and word is he intends to kill any lawman on sight."

"What do you want me to do?" Wyatt tried to keep the eagerness out of his voice.

"Well, I'm a lawman these days and this fella Fitzpatrick is in a gambling hall down the road. I need a couple back-up men to take care of any of his friends. You and Johnny Green here are those men."

Wyatt looked across at Johnny Green. The man nodded curtly and turned his gaze back to the street. Wyatt's thumbs curled tightly around his gun belt buckle in anticipation.

"I'm goin' down the street," Turkey Creek said. "You cover me from the sidewalk on the other side. Johnny'll take care of this end."

Turkey Creek stepped off the boardwalk and started walking down the road. Moving quickly but calmly, Wyatt

went to the opposite sidewalk. He glanced at Johnny
Green and Turkey Creek to his right, and stayed abreast as
they walked deliberately along the block.

A cowboy coming out of a saloon stopped in Wyatt's
path, saw the three men walking in time with each other,
and shuffled quickly out of Wyatt's way. Something in
Wyatt, galvanized by the moment, propelled him forward
at a steady, purposeful gait, his eyes and ears at razor-
sharp attention. The lingering feeling of fear didn't matter.

Up ahead, out of a gambling hall called the Gold
Rooms, lurched a thick-muscled man. He shouldered past
townsmen and walked heavily out into the street. Noticing
Turkey Creek coming toward him, the man wiped the cuff
of his new frock coat slowly across his wide mouth; his
eyelids drooped drunkenly but underneath there was still a
look of business to Fitzpatrick's gleaming eyes. He called
out: "Heya marshal! Keep on comin', that's it! Come on!
You lookin' for a fast cut to hell, I'll show it to ya!"

Turkey Creek didn't reply. He kept walking toward Fitzpatrick. A Mexican, walking on the boardwalk toward
Wyatt, studied Turkey Creek and came to a stop just three
steps in front of the young man with the two new Colts.

Fitzpatrick's laugh sounded more like a series of grunts.
He fell silent and watched Turkey Creek advance. When
the two men were about forty feet apart he yelled, "All
right, marshal! All right, don't talk, you bastard! You can
buy it just like this!"

As Fitzpatrick drew his gun, Wyatt saw the Mexican pull
a Navy Colt from his pocket. Sweeping his right Colt out
of its holster, Wyatt rushed forward and clubbed the Mexican across the top of the head. The moment the man hit
the boardwalk, Fitzpatrick let loose.

The outlaw triggered fast. Three times his Smith and
Wesson roared. Turkey Creek, not breaking step, pulled
his revolver as the three slugs sailed past. Fitzpatrick fired
twice more. Wyatt watched in amazement as Turkey Creek
took another deliberate step forward, as if oblivious to the

outlaw's fire. He then halted and, while Fitzpatrick reached for a second gun, raised his .44 slightly higher than waist level. Fitzpatrick now cleared leather, but Turkey Creek's Colt bucked once and the slug crashed through Fitzpatrick's rib cage. The outlaw wrenched. He gaped stupidly as a red patch spread across his chest, then, shuddering, he dropped to his knees. He struggled back up to his feet, took a single faltering step, and pitched forward into the dirt.

A groan from the Mexican on the boardwalk brought Wyatt up short. He took his gaze from the road to check the clubbed man at his feet. The Mexican was stirring but wasn't going to make trouble for now. Wyatt turned back toward the street and watched Turkey Creek inspect the motionless body; he studied the bearded plainsman as if seeing him for the first time.

Johnny Green joined the marshal and the two men headed back the way they had come. Wyatt followed suit. Just now he noticed the tremor in his limbs and realized he still hadn't holstered his gun. Self-consciously, he slipped it back into place.

When the young man drew near, Turkey Creek put a hand on Wyatt's back and gave him a twist of a smile. "Come on, Wyatt," he said. "The drinks are on you."

7

Wyatt brought the bottle and glasses from the bar to the corner table by the Side Track's front window. While pouring the whiskey, he gave Turkey Creek a sharp glance.

"You didn't tell me you were a lawman."

The marshal of Newton reached for his glass. "If you wanted to know you should've asked." He downed the whiskey with a single toss. "Only a sometime-thing with me. Just happened to be a need for a man with experience when I got here. Fact is, there's no government yet in Newton. Just some shopkeepers give me the badge and tell me to go to it."

Turkey Creek took the bottle to start the next round. To Johnny Green he said, "This here's the young fella from Indian Territory I was tellin' you about."

Raising his glass, Johnny Green kept his hard look on Wyatt. Wyatt, not knowing what to make of it, busied himself with knocking back his glassful.

Turkey Creek kept talking to Green as if he had gotten a response. "Looks like I'm a good judge of men after all. I help this fella slip by the law and here he is to pay my money back." Lowering his head, he looked at Wyatt from underneath his bushy brow. "You *are* goin' to give me that money you were braggin' on, aren't you?"

Smiling, Wyatt took a roll of bills from his jacket pocket and handed it over.

"A man who pays his debts," said Newton's marshal. "That's a good sign, ain't it, Johnny?" Green answered with a nod. "And how about the way he took out that backshooter? That was fast movin', son."

Wyatt acknowledged the compliment by gesturing with his glass and emptying it. The whiskey was burning off the rough edges now. Tipping back his chair, he looked over the advertisements for beer and whiskey tacked on the wall behind Turkey Creek and Green. As the drinking slowed him down a notch, his eyes rested on the Anheuser-Busch ad and its picture of a filled-out woman in a flowing dress, holding a beer stein high, a drooping sleeve exposing the soft ivory skin of her shoulder.

Johnny Green's voice, as if rusty from lack of use, sounded unnaturally deep and harsh. "Might be some use for a quick-thinkin' man around Newton."

Turkey Creek nodded. "That's something to think about. You ever done any law work, Wyatt?"

The gunshot roared just a second after Wyatt thought he heard something thump behind him. The slug blasted a hole through the wall, a foot to the right of Turkey Creek's head. Almost as one, the three men spilled out of their chairs and flattened to the floor. Turkey Creek and Johnny Green had their guns out as they hit the packed earth. Turkey Creek spun away from the table. "Check the window, Johnny!"

As Johnny Green went for the window, Wyatt reached for his Colt. All he grabbed was air.

He looked down and saw the empty holster. He scanned the floor. No gun. He was going for his second gun on his left hip when he saw the smoking hole in the skirt of his jacket, on the right side. His stomach sinking, he twisted around to get a good look at his gun lying on the floor behind him, smoke curling from the muzzle. It had slipped out of the holster and hit the floor; his own gun had discharged and nearly shot both him and Turkey Creek.

He came to his knees with the retrieved gun in his palm. Frozen in place at opposite ends of the table, Green and Turkey Creek stared at him. Slowly they got back on their feet. Turkey Creek was pale around the eyes. He ran a finger around the bullet hole in the wall, then faced Wyatt, his thick eyebrows one black, furious line. Withered by the man's look, Wyatt dropped his eyes and stood with shoulders slouched.

"Wyatt," Turkey Creek growled, "I think there's just a few things you got to learn. Right now."

They stopped on a flat crowded between flint hills a mile outside of town. Turkey Creek let Wyatt ride the distance without talk. He could see that the young man's embarrassment would teach him more than any strong words. They dismounted, left their horses ground-hitched, and, with Turkey Creek leading, walked toward a ledge of rock, three feet high, rooted in the side of a hill. Going to the far side of the slab, Turkey Creek picked up the tin cans he had left for himself the last time. He set five cans in a line along the top of the ledge.

"When you grew up," he said, "did you learn to shoot with a rifle?"

Wyatt tried looking nonchalant. "Mostly."

Slowly, Turkey Creek led the way from the ledge. "I figured you most likely didn't use a hand-gun much. And I *know* you never learned how to wear one." He stopped and put out a hand. "Give me one of your guns."

Wyatt took out the gun from his right holster.

"Not the one you dropped," Turkey Creek said. "The other one."

A trace of flush spread across Wyatt's cheekbones. He holstered the gun, pulled the left one and handed it over.

Turkey Creek hefted it in his hand. "The first thing you got to learn is never load bullets in all six chambers." With a quick, deft motion he ejected one of the cartridges. "Leave one chamber empty. Always. That's the chamber you rest the hammer on." Rotating the cylinder, he positioned the empty chamber. "That way you only got five loads, but the gun won't go off on its own."

He gave the gun back and started walking again. While Wyatt stared obstinately straight ahead, Turkey Creek took a good look at the young man. Wyatt rode his humiliation hard. His features drawn tight and severe, he was not about to let on that any of this information was new to him. With his brow bunched low, his mouth hidden under his thick moustache, and his nostrils flared, Wyatt put up a damned stony front. Turkey Creek had seen the same kind of look on Johnny Green. It was a look, figured Turkey Creek, that could come in handy. It might even make a fighting man back off, if Wyatt could harness it.

"That's how you load the gun," continued Turkey Creek. "Now all you got to do is learn how to shoot the damn thing."

They came to a stop about ten yards from the ledge and Turkey Creek held Wyatt's gaze. "Well, what will it be, Wyatt? You want teachin' or not?"

Wyatt's eyes shifted slightly before he got the words out. "Yes," he said quietly, "I do."

Turkey Creek hid his smile with a hand that scratched his beard. "Could be you got a body to teach you," he said. Reaching into his jacket pocket, he groped along the inner lining, found the hole in the cloth, and poked through to get ahold of his tobacco chaw. He pulled it out, then gestured toward the guns on Wyatt's hips. "Most important thing I know about fightin' with a gun is taking just enough time to make your first shot count for

something." He bit off a chunk of tobacco and tucked i
into the corner of his mouth. "You can squeeze off te
shots in two seconds and it won't do you a damned bit o
good if that first one don't hit the target. A lot of dea
men knew how to shoot fast. That feller Fitzpatrick back
in town was triggerin' mighty quick."

He moved a hand out in front of him. "I knew I wasn'
close enough to make sure of my aim; I took a couple extr
steps and set myself before I fired. That time I waited a
much as, oh, a few seconds. Other times, you have to take
just a part of a second before firing. Each fight is different." Turkey Creek turned slowly toward the ledge.
"You just take it one step at a time. Now don't get me
wrong. It don't *hurt* to be fast."

His body now facing the ledge, he swept his hand up
snapped his Colt clear and thumbed back the hammer. The
first can leaped back and four more shots boomed in a
controlled, rapid cluster. All the cans danced off the ledge.

Turkey Creek flicked open the cylinder gate and started
to reload as he headed for the slab of rock. He heard
Wyatt's steps following and could feel the young man's
eyes on him. At the ledge, Turkey Creek reset the cans; this
time Wyatt helped out.

"You been in many fights, Turkey Creek?"

"Enough," answered the bearded man. "But we'll talk
about you." He replaced the last can and leaned against
the side of the rock. "Last time I saw you, you were talkin'
about taking to the buffalo range, maybe to sort things
out. You figure what to do with yourself out there?"

The long days on the buffalo range had given Wyatt
enough hard work to clear his mind, and the lonesome few
hours before bedding down at night had been time enough
to turn things over slowly. Looking out across the dark
prairie, he didn't miss people and didn't give them much
thought. The peace of mind that sneaked up on him seemed
like a stranger at first, a feeling forgotten since those lazy

nights when he and Morgan used to camp out during hunting jaunts in the Missouri hills. Each day eased into the next and the hides piled up, but then the air frosted and the snow swept down from the north. While looking for wood along Medicine Lodge River to build a shelter, Wyatt's skinner, Bob Capson, had stumbled upon the deserted shack. Inside, they'd been able to protect themselves and their property while snowbound for nearly a month.

On the range, Capson's silence had been welcome, but inside a ten-foot square cabin the quiet wore a man down. It hadn't been long before restlessness had started nibbling at Wyatt. The memories soon followed.

Those damnable days during the war. Working the corn fields. A deadly, colorless life. While his two older brothers had fought the war, Wyatt was the one held back, leashed to the farm. He was the one who'd finish studying the law, said father. With Virgil gone, there had been no one to stand between Wyatt and Nicholas, and the arguments heated up to taint the monotony of work with an ill feeling that cut deeper every day.

In the close air of the Medicine Lodge cabin, Wyatt had bristled at thoughts of those days. One thing he'd been sure of was that he wouldn't be coddled and haltered again. He would step long and bold. The problem still was how to do it and do it smart.

Leaning now on the ledge outside Newton, he thought back about the cowboys stepping out of his way as he had walked side by side with Turkey Creek that afternoon in Hyde Park. Ideas he had had on the buffalo range started to fall into place. He said, "I want to be a town man. There's money to be made in these boom towns and I sure wouldn't mind taking my piece of it."

Turkey Creek nodded. "And letting everybody know it too," he put in.

Wyatt said nothing. No point in denying what they both knew was true. They started walking back across the flat.

Wyatt asked, "You think I'm talking too big?"

"Either that or too small." He gave Wyatt a considering look. "No offense, Wyatt, but you put me in mind of a young feller with a red-hot poker up his ass. You got something to prove to somebody?"

"Maybe to myself, is all."

"Well," Turkey Creek mused, "if you want to be a big noise, Newton's as good a place to start as any. It's not as big as some cow towns, but there's enough here to keep you in poker and whores for a time. Of course, it'd help if someone was to show you the ropes."

Wyatt smiled. "Might that be you?"

"Aw hell," Turkey Creek laughed. "Why not? Maybe you'll remember me when you're top man on the boom town run." He laughed again. "Go ahead, the cans are set up. Why don't you try your hand."

Thinking he might have gotten an answer to the letter he wrote in Coffeyville, Wyatt asked Turkey Creek where he could find the postmaster. He left the room at Bentley's Hotel that Turkey Creek had found for him, and walked across the street to the hardware store.

In the back of the shop, Jake Hurst sat behind a cluttered counter totalling up his receipts with a stub of a pencil and a scrap of paper. Wyatt spoke twice before the little man tore himself away from his figures.

"I'm looking for a letter," Wyatt repeated. "Addressed to Earp."

"Vill you be Earp?" Hurst asked in a thick German accent.

"That's me."

"Ah!" Hurst jumped from his stool and whisked the floppy hat off his balding head. The little German reached inside and pulled a folded, dog-eared envelope from a small packet of letters lodged underneath the inside headband. "Two veeks I have been holding this." Wyatt took the letter, checked the Missouri postmark and thanked the man.

Outside, Wyatt sat on a hitching rail and tore open the envelope; his father's handwriting was a grand scrawl that took up each of the two pages with just a few lines.

Dear Wyatt,

Your letter did your mother's heart good after not knowing for so long what had become of you in your travels. Just as your letter brought good cheer to our home, we have, for you, news that is good as well. The man with whom you fought before leaving us was confined to a bed for several days, but did not, after all, expire. As he has since left Lamar, no charges against you are, or will, be made.

We look forward to your return home.

Always,
Father

Wyatt read the letter three times. He then let the hand holding the message drop to his side. He faced the twilit street and watched the cowboys in their new finery swagger toward Hyde Park. From down the road came distant cowpuncher howling. Staying put, Wyatt waited for a sense of relief at the news he had just read. None came.

It had taken months to accept the death of the cowboy and find his way to live with that hard fact. But by now, if he thought of it at all, he simply considered the killing to be his reason for coming west. The cowboy's new lease on life meant nothing.

Wyatt read the Missouri letter once more. He then crumpled it in the palm of his hand, dropped it to the ground, and crossed the street to Bentley's to join Turkey Creek and Johnny Green for dinner.

8

Two years in Newton were enough to put Wyatt on the move again. Two years spent in saloons and gambling halls, practicing his gunplay, playing faro and poker, backing up Turkey Creek as deputy.

The first week in town, Turkey Creek had let Wyatt waste an evening losing at five card stud before he took him aside for some pointers. What passed for cardsharping in Lamar couldn't stand up long to the competition at cow town gaming tables. When not tending to marshal business or dealing faro, Turkey Creek took Wyatt into the back room at the Side Track and taught him all he could.

Wyatt's long fingers took naturally to handling cards and before long he could execute flourishes with ease. Applying ointment to his hands kept the fingers smooth and sensitive, able to feel each card as it flicked by. When need be, he could also turn a slippery move, but not too often. "Us gamblers are respectable professionals out here," Turkey Creek would say, "just as long as we look that way. Nothing wrong with a slick move to win here and there, but do it too often and you'll get tagged. Won't be too many comers for a gamin' man like that.''

One night, after two hours of faro at the Side Track — washed down with a quart of rye — Turkey Creek and Johnny Green showed Wyatt the Brazos Dance Hall down the block. On the dance floor, Turkey Creek collared one of the painted ladies for Wyatt. She gave him a dance and, after a signal from Turkey Creek, led the staggering young man to one of the rooms in back. The first time he had bed a woman since Willa's death, Wyatt was thankful for his boozy haze, but spent the next morning fighting off both hangover and clinging regret. The next time he found it easier.

Every fair-weather day, with or without hangover, Wyatt shot cans off the ledge and then each night disassembled his Colts to clean them until he knew each piece and its place by touch. In time, satisfied that the young man's eye was sharp and sure enough on the firing range, Turkey Creek decided it was time to put on some speed. He dismantled one of Wyatt's Colts and showed him how to ''file the dog'' so that he could fire by just pulling back the hammer and letting it go. The shots quickened, and his aim caught up with his speed soon enough.

Turkey Creek went along with him to the rock ledge one clear, cool day in March, just two months before Wyatt traveled on. After a few rounds of fire he was willing to admit that Wyatt was a dead shot. ''Still can't hold your liquor worth a damn,'' he added to keep him honest. The smile that Wyatt thought would come with these words wasn't there.

Walking with Wyatt to the ledge to replace the targets, Turkey Creek was quiet for a while, then asked if Wyatt was afraid of the first time he'd have to go up against a gun. Wyatt answered that he thought he could take care of himself all right.

''Personally,'' Turkey Creek said, worrying his beard, ''I always figured the best way to win a fight is not to get into one in the first place. You can make a man walk away real quiet if you got the reputation to make him think twice. The way you buffalo a man with your gun barrel might be enough to get you by without firing a shot.''

The cans set for another round, Wyatt turned away from the ledge with a laugh. "You're not afraid I can't use these guns, are you, Turkey Creek? After all this practice!''

Turkey Creek frowned as he stepped alongside him. "You can defend yourself well enough. If what you're aimin' for is to be top dog in town, you should do all right. If that's all you want.''

Wyatt studied his friend. The creases in the face seemed deeper and in the bright sun he detected for the first time scattered white hairs in the beard. Suddenly Turkey Creek looked old to Wyatt. "What're you getting at?'' he asked.

"Hell, what you want me to tell ya?'' Turkey Creek let out a long breath. "I been driftin' a good twenty years myself. Probably more if I troubled to count.''

"Would you take them back, all those years?''

"I ain't sayin' that.''

They walked on without speaking. Not sure what Turkey Creek was leading to, Wyatt put in, "You talk about me using these guns — you didn't seem to be shy about killing a man first day I came to Newton.''

"It's guns you just want to talk about, ain't it?'' Turkey Creek shook his head. "All right, Wyatt, it's up to you what you do with what I been teachin'. But about me gun-nin' Fitzpatrick that day, when you know a man wants you dead, you better not hesitate, not one second. That much you should remember. And you better make sure he don't get the chance to come after you. He just might come up from behind.''

Nearing the horses, Turkey Creek stopped and faced him. "Another thing. When need be, you can make gun-men back off without even thinkin' about touchin' one of your Colts.'' He swung away, pulled the double-barrelled shotgun from its saddle boot. "A whole pack of badmen can get awful peaceful in a hurry when they're facin' down these two barrels. Chances are that one of them could shoot a lone man with a shotgun, but just the idea of what one of these suckers can do to a man is a tough argument."

Turkey Creek thumbed back both hammers, looked over his right shoulder to spot a young cottonwood, and suddenly wheeled about. He triggered both barrels at once. The loads thundered, the echo bounced across the valley, and the top half of the tree snapped off in a flurry of splintered wood. Wyatt stared at the blasted dwarf of a trunk left standing while shavings and chips, exploded from the middle section, fluttered down behind it in a fast-falling cloud.

9

The sign by the Douglas Avenue Bridge read:

EVERYTHING GOES IN WICHITA. LEAVE YOUR
REVOLVERS AT POLICE HEADQUARTERS,
AND GET A CHECK. CARRYING CONCEALED
WEAPONS STRICTLY FORBIDDEN.

Not paying the last part too much mind, Wyatt shelled out
the toll and crossed over to the wide spread of buildings on
the east side of the Arkansas.

On his way past the Douglas Avenue House, he slowed
his packhorse and mare to a halting walk to get a good
long look at the three stories looming above. It was the biggest hotel he'd ever seen. He dawdled long enough to bottle
up some of the late afternoon traffic and, with a freighter
steaming and cursing to his rear, left the huge frame
building behind. Farther on, he rode by a hotel that, as far
as he was concerned, put the Douglas Avenue House to
shame. The Occidental was not only three stories high, but

solid brick and sure to last. By counting windows, Wyatt figured there to be at least fifty rooms inside. Calculating the price that must go with the rooms, he moved onward.

The sign above F.L. Plumlee's stables promised "Scientific Horseshoeing"; Wyatt wasn't too sure what that was, but he decided to leave his horses there and let the man prove it. He took a room at the Southern Hotel, changed into his new black broadcloth suit, and stepped out to get a taste of Wichita nightlife.

His first stop was the barbershop. Seventy-five cents for a haircut and fifty more for a shave may have been a bit dear, especially for a place with a dirt floor, but the new town had Wyatt riding high. Trimmed and spruced, with his moustache waxed and his face smelling of rose water, he forgot about his empty belly and, as night set in, strolled back toward Douglas Avenue for a better look at the center of the city. He detoured briefly to buy a new cigar for the occasion and walked the last two blocks to the summer night clamor and stir of the intersection of Douglas and Main.

Coal oil streetlamps illuminated the prairie darkness that encroached on the middle of town. Their red brick fronts rearing up against the night sky, the massive New York Store and Eagle Building faced each other across Douglas Avenue. Below, along the road, a stream of cowboys and gamblers passed through the intersection, some stepping with, some against, the music of a ten-piece band. As he walked into the center of the intersection, Wyatt could see where the music came from. Blue-uniformed band members played the "Red River Waltz" on a second-story platform built outside of Keno Corner. In the quick gaps between notes, the hoot of a satisfied sporting man would sometimes escape from inside the second-floor establishment. Wyatt headed for the stairs.

Inside Keno Corner he found a crowded bar and a string of gaming tables; along with keno, there were roulette, faro, chuck-a-luck and poker, each table busy with cowhands risking wages just collected at the end of their drive from Texas. By the roulette wheel, Wyatt recognized Hurricane Bill, a dealer the season before at the Gold Rooms in Newton. Other faces jogged his memory, faces of Newton men who had preceded Wyatt to this new terminus of the Atchison, Topeka and Santa Fe, the lifeline of the Kansas cattle trade.

A half-hour later, with fifty dollars to the good, Wyatt returned to the street and wandered on. From behind a real estate office came the roar of a gun and a booming Dutchman's voice: "Dere she goes again! Kick like mool!" Walking down an alley, Wyatt came to a tent marked "Professor Gessley, Armless Wonder." The professor, a nattily dressed man whose empty sleeves dangled limply at his sides, sat on a chair in the middle of a clutch of spectators; he was loading a pistol with his bare feet. Triggering the gun with his toes, the armless man fired again and, with three shots, hit a pair of bottles on a table twenty feet away. He nodded to the applause and cried again, "Kick like mool!" He got a couple of laughs from the crowd. Wyatt paid his admission and watched the next round up close. For his money, he also got to listen to a hand organ and take a look at a jar containing a preserved pig with one head and two bodies. The shooting exhibition done, Professor Gessley then wrote notes for the crowd with both his right and left feet. An uneasy feeling soon told Wyatt that he may have seen more than he should have.

Coming out of a cafe on Water Street around ten o'clock, he noticed that activity was increasing across the Arkansas on the west bank. Earlier that day, when he had ridden into town, he hadn't given a second glance to the ramshackle buildings he'd passed on his way to the west end entrance of the toll bridge, but now he could see that the night was their time to come to life. Brightly lit and churning out music, the buildings welcomed high-rollers from the east side for the night's final stand. The long day's ride was beginning to take its toll on Wyatt, but he would have to have a look at the other side of the river before the night was done.

Of the dance halls and cathouses on the west side, the biggest attraction seemed to be Rowdy Joe Lowe's place. Wyatt stood by the open doorway and looked in to see the girls finish up a number; as far as Wyatt could tell, if the girls wore any less they'd be practically buck naked. The song over, the men then moved in to pick their partners and kick up to the next tune. There were dandies, Texas cowpunchers, Mexicans and respectable businessmen. If any were picky about the company they kept they were too stinking drunk to remember. Men passed Wyatt on their way in, but Wyatt couldn't convince himself to follow.

He walked to the far side of Rowdy Joe's, passed some shacks used by the girls, and came to a new, two-story frame house. He leaned against a corner and lighted his cigar. He watched the lights across the river, making spidery streaks across the rippled black water; the tinkling of a piano came from inside the house at his side and a block away pistol shots cracked as cowboys started to hurrah the town.

Wyatt pictured the places he had seen tonight. No two ways about it, he had found his way to his first crackerjack boom town. Hell, he had been walking all evening, and he'd be damned if he'd passed the same place twice. There was some satisfaction in thinking about Wichita and all there was to it. But not enough to stop his feeling lonesome. Tilting back his head, he blew out a tall, slow column of smoke. He started thinking about Morgan and Virgil and the good times they'd had in Lamar.

A woman shrieked and then others joined in. Wyatt heard something smash inside the house. A deep voice bellowed and the room inside sounded like it was getting rearranged in a hurry. Wyatt turned the corner to see a squat woman in a red dress scurry out the front door. Spotting Wyatt, she swooped upon him.

"Please, mister. Help me. Please."

"What is it?"

"A crazy-drunk cowboy's going wild inside." Her hands fluttered in front of her rouged face. "He's tearing up the place, molesting my girls. No one can stop him. Please mister, my bouncer's just up and left." She pulled on his coat sleeve. "I need help or he'll wreck the whole place."

The same deep voice roared again and another crash followed. Wyatt let himself be pulled to the door, then stopped. The madam's fleshy, painted face turned to him pleadingly. Wyatt set his broad shoulders straight, pulled a waxed tip of moustache, and, pushing back his jacket skirt on each side, revealed the walnut-handled Colts. He said, "I'll see what I can do, ma'am."

A man pulling on his pants rushed out as Wyatt stepped in. Before him, standing tall in the middle of the parlor, was the big crazy cowboy. He had a squirming whore hefted under his left arm and was lunging for another with his right. A laugh rumbling up from his chest, he turned his mad pig eyes on Wyatt for just a second before grabbing the girl and jerking her toward him with a quick, powerful roll of his huge shoulders.

Around the cowboy were shattered furniture and girls cringing back along the walls. By the foot of the stairs stood two more drunken cowhands. "Go on, Dolph!" one of them shouted. "Give 'em hell!" The two of them cackled.

A red-headed girl ran over to one of the whores held by Dolph and tried tugging her away, but a growl and a lunge from the big man changed her mind. She dashed to the side of the door. Her round chestnut eyes looked at Wyatt in desperation. When Dolph lumbered for the door with the two girls in tow, Wyatt took a step forward.

With a couple of beers under his belt, the words came out easily, as if he were still working by Turkey Creek's side. "That's enough, cowboy," Wyatt said. "Put the girls down and get the hell out."

Coming to a stop, Dolph considered Wyatt with a dim glower. One of the other cowboys yelled at him to go at it. His gaze wandering around a bit as he made up his mind, Dolph dropped the girls to the floor and made an effort to concentrate on the tall, slim man in black.

"I don't see no one," he slurred, "what's goin' to make me go?"

The two cowboys by the stairs let loose shrill rebel yells while the freed girls scrambled to the side. Not about to waste his time, Wyatt pulled his right Colt and swung down hard on the top of Dolph's head. The big cowboy's head snapped to the side. The wide head then straightened slowly and the pig eyes fixed on Wyatt. The parlor was suddenly quiet. Wyatt's sharp blue eyes stared in disbelief, cold panic fingering up his back.

Dolph shook his head like a dog. He said, "Don't do that."

An instant passed before Wyatt got himself to move. He swung the Colt again and slammed the barrel across the side of the cowboy's head. Dolph staggered a step, stared emptily as if he were lost. Grunting deeply, the big cowboy then drew himself up. He blinked at Wyatt who felt as if his knees might buckle. He had given the big man his worst. Short of shooting him, which he wasn't altogether sure would do the trick either, he couldn't think of what else he could do.

Shifting his weight carefully, Dolph reared back for a punch. Wyatt brought his gun up once more. Dolph leaned back and, as he raised his fist, teetered on unsteady legs. He corrected himself by balancing forward, then, with eyelids flickering, wobbled once more. His body finally going slack, he stared off blindly and flopped back to the floor with a tremendous thud.

The breath slipped out of Wyatt in a long, relieved sigh.

Remembering himself, he noticed the red-head to his side, watching him closely, her warm gaze sympathetic. As he holstered the gun, he saw the two other cowboys marching drunkenly toward him. Their gun belts were in plain sight.

The taller one placed himself right in front of Wyatt. "Hold on, dandy," he drawled. "This fight ain't over yet. There's me and Cal still."

"Dolph wasn't heeled," Cal put in. "You wouldn't be so damn tough against another feller with a gun." He slapped his holster for emphasis.

Some kinds of drunk made a man quick to fight; others just made him mean but sluggish as molasses. These two weren't jumping to anything, and Wyatt, with his blood already up, wasn't going to wait for a change of mind. He whipped his gun back out and buffaloed the tall cowboy standing next to him. The cowboy dropped. Cal gawked, then worked up enough steam to take a defiant step forward. His pronunciation clouded by a drunken slur, he blurted, "You wouldn't try that ag'in a man who's filled his hand." While the cowboy groped for his gun, Wyatt cracked the Colt's barrel across his head and dropped him next to his friend.

Standing above the three inert bodies, Wyatt could see, out of the corner of his eye, the red-head smiling at him.

"I'll get these fellas out of your way," he told the madam, grabbing Dolph and pulling him toward the door. He huffed and strained at the big man's weight, and dragged him out to the road. Stepping back inside, he took ahold of Cal, but stopped when the madam put a hand on his shoulder.

"That's all right," she said and smiled. "The girls can get rid of these two. You've done your share."

Still out of breath from dragging Dolph, Wyatt didn't need any more persuading. Stiffly, he tipped his hat to the madam and said, "Glad I could help out, ma'am. Good night."

The madam caught his arm on his way out. "Not so

fast, fella." Wyatt gave her a quizzical look. "Nobody's going to tell you that Nadine doesn't remember a favor. You did such a good job for us, I think there ought to be something coming to you, don't you?"

"Well . . ."

"Verna," Nadine said, signaling to the pretty red-head. "Show this gentleman what the upstairs is like."

A coy smile dimpling her cheeks, Verna came over, took Wyatt's arm, and led him toward the stairs. Wyatt walked mechanically alongside her, the idea just starting to dawn on him.

"Like I told you before," said Nadine, "our bouncer just skipped town. Me and the girls could use a young man like you around here. Maybe we can work something out, something more permanent."

A full-bodied, dark haired girl took Wyatt's other arm and climbed the stairs with him. From his right side, Verna said, "How do you find Wichita, mister?"

Wyatt couldn't keep the shit-eating grin from spreading across his face.

10

Marshal Mike Meagher knew Virgil from Abilene. His lean, weathered face wrinkled with some unspoken, welcome memory as he connected the older Earp with the young man seated before him.

"If you think you've seen some sort of swift here in Wichita," Meagher said, "you should've gotten a bellyful of Abilene that first season. Yeah, Virgil was there. Him haulin' freight, me workin' for the railroad." He stared out the window at the New York Store. "Some times they were."

"Virgil's told me some."

That said, Meagher pulled in the long look in his eye and was all business again. "You come by for a reason?" he snapped, as if it had been Wyatt jawing about old times, wasting the marshal's afternoon.

Wyatt started in with the little speech he had made up for himself. He lied about hunting for a surveyor party in the Indian Nations, and after a while drifted back to the truth with the story of his good season on the buffalo range. "Then," he continued, "thanks to my days as a lawman in Missouri, I was hired by Marshal Jack Johnson of Newton."

"Jack Johnson? That be Turkey Creek Johnson, wouldn't it?"

"Yes, that's him all right."

"If your days in Missouri were all that good why'd you come out here?"

Wyatt hoped the flush of anger didn't show. "The way Virgil talked about life in Kansas — hell, I just had to give it a go. If you want, Marshal, you can write Johnson at Newton for a reference. I think you'll find that while I was there, I served . . . ."

Meagher waved him to a stop. "All right, Earp. That'll be enough. I don't have the damned time to write Newton or the Nations or any such. I need another special policeman, starting today."

Wyatt bristled at the marshal cutting him off, but kept his mouth shut.

"Virgil was a good man and for now I'll count on you having some of the same."

Wyatt forced out his thanks.

"They tell me since you came to Wichita you've shown folks on the west side of the river that you know how to take care of yourself. With the cowmen comin' in every week we can use another officer to help them have a good time over there without there being any bad trouble. You can show me what you can do."

From his desk drawer Meagher took out a badge and tossed it over. "Stop by here at six."

"Thank you, Marshal. I won't disappoint you."

Meagher leaned back in his chair and wrapped a thumb about his watch fob. "I sure as hell hope not."

Wyatt got up to leave but didn't reach the door before Meagher's voice stopped him. "There's one little thing I got to tell you right from the start, Wyatt." The marshal leveled a beady stare, then looked carelessly out the window. "There's a passel of sportin' fellas like yourself who are aiming for a lawman's job so they can keep their guns on in the city limits and line their pockets every which way." He turned back to Wyatt. "Now I hope you ain't going to do anything stupid."

"Like what?"

"Like what I ain't goin' to tell you because I don't want to be givin' you any ideas." Meagher let the room go quiet and, smiling coldly, looked at Wyatt. "If you got anything on the side," Meagher went on, "just make damn sure it ain't common knowledge. I've got to run for re-election down the road a bit and I don't want to drag a lot of dirt with me when I'm campaigning. You get me?"

"I get you, Marshal. I'll do my best."

Warming up to Meagher was not on Wyatt's mind when he left the man's office in the Eagle Building, but the marshal turned out to be easier to work for than he first thought. As long as Wyatt kept the high-rollers in reasonable check on the west side and brought in his share of arrests, Meagher let him go his own way.

For two dollars a day, Wyatt patrolled the west side at nights and sometimes lent a hand along the string of saloons and gambling halls on Douglas and Main. The important citizens of Wichita demanded some kind of order in the city, but not too much. Cattlemen brought their trade to Wichita for two reasons: the railroad and the recreation. Many days could pass between bringing a herd to cow camps outside of town and arranging a sale and transportation to beef markets. Cattlemen and their hired hands counted on living it up in that time; Wichita businessmen wanted to keep the customers happy. A gunfight might not be tolerated, but a little rough-housing was just business as usual.

Word of his fight with the cowboys at Nadine's cathouse let the roughs on the west side of the Arkansas know that Wyatt Earp could stand up to trouble, but some cowhands and gamblers, especially those soggy with Dutch courage, weren't so quick to be impressed. Taking Turkey Creek's words to heart, Wyatt set about to make things plain for anyone who still thought the new special policeman was fair game.

Early one evening, a gambler acquaintance from Newton by the name of Neal Brown told Wyatt that a young cowboy, half-crocked and armed, was making the rounds of the Douglas Avenue saloons. He had already shot out the music box at the Buckhorn Tavern and was surely lathering up for a fight. While the cowboy filled up at Schnitzler's saloon, Wyatt posted Brown and another gambler with shotguns at second-story windows on either side of the bar, and then stationed himself across the street.

The cowboy came out of Schnitzler's and, peering through the thin light of dusk, recognized Wyatt on the opposite boardwalk. He cursed out Wyatt, calling him a fighting pimp and stepped out into the road. Steeled by the insurance of shotguns trained on the cowboy from both sides, Wyatt walked toward him, speaking softly, telling the cowboy to put up his guns, soothing him the way he would quiet a skittish horse. Then, when he was within arm's length of the drunk, he pulled his Colt and beat the man to the ground right there in the center of busy midtown Wichita. By midnight, the story had gotten around.

Just to make sure the message was clear, Wyatt would practice his shooting once a week on the outskirts of town, near enough for people to take note. Pretty soon, just as Turkey Creek had said it would, facing down troublemakers became easy enough.

The nightlife kept Wyatt up and going until at least two or three in the morning, and sometimes straight through till first light. Sometimes, in the morning, he'd be roused from bed to help untangle the traffic of wagons loaded with wheat that occasionally clogged the route to the railroad. Mostly, though, he didn't see daylight until early afternoon.

As the law work became more routine, Wyatt had more

time to spare for the gaming tables. By the end of that first cattle trade season, he was spending many of his nights dealing faro at the Bon Ton Saloon to add to his policeman's wages; he was able to use his earnings to buy into the faro concession at the saloon soon after his second season began. With the money left over, he got himself a fast-running dun to race against other gamblers' stock.

The Wichita pace slackened in the autumn months when the Texas longhorn drives tapered off. Meagher now had less use for the added special policemen. Released from the force until spring, Wyatt decided to winter on his savings and whatever piecework came along. In between stints of poker and faro with travelers passing through, he would hire out as a guard for local cattlemen during ownership disputes, or as a bill collector to search out deadbeats, or sometimes as shotgun rider on the Cannon Ball Stage, the "jerkies" running from Wichita to Kingman and Pratt.

Once during the off-season, Wyatt was hired on again by Meagher to help keep an eye on a troublemaker named Bill Anderson who had been involved in a questionable shooting. The problem then solved itself when Anderson stepped into the crossfire at a gunfight at Rowdy Joe's and got both his eyes shot out. Wyatt was back free-lancing again.

At nights, whether on season or off, Wyatt would make periodic checks on Nadine's place to make sure rowdies were staying in line. Toward the end of his first Wichita season, as he became a fixture at her place, Wyatt was taken aside by Nadine for a talk about her fines. The more respectable element in town didn't think much of the wide-open ways of wicked Wichita, and thought even less of the big salaries they paid the lawmen who contained the violence caused by those ways. To appease the righteous, and at the same time raise money for the police without burdening the good citizens of the city, the Wichita council took the usual cow town route of imposing monthly "fines" on bordellos and gambling halls. These establishments weren't closed down because that would irritate the cattlemen, but the fines helped pay for the police and the court sessions needed to control sin. Nadine didn't relish parading through court each month and Wyatt agreed to add to his duties by passing the fines along to the city treasury.

He certainly didn't resent these extra duties; they only seemed right since the first room on the second floor had become a second home for him. That first night with Verna clung to his mind, and whenever he came back he would single out the redhead. A bit skinny maybe, but she was a supple, lusty young woman with a girlish, wide-eyed face that glistened every time Wyatt came through the door. Much of the time she was quiet, and that was all right with Wyatt too. A night with her left him lazy and satisfied for hours the next day; by nightfall he was impatient for her again.

Coming in from the crisp autumn night, the warm air of Nadine's place was a welcome, homey change. Wyatt snapped his frock coat collar back down, nodded to the customers waiting on the couch, and headed for the stairs. Nadine was scurrying down the steps. Darting a look over her shoulder, she told Wyatt he'd be better off coming back later. Maybe even tomorrow. He asked what was the problem; not till his words were out did the first suspicion hit him.

Nadine put a hand on his shoulder. "Nothing to fret about, Wyatt. Now's just not the time."

"What's wrong?" The stern lines in his face hardened. "She knows I'm due this time of night."

Nadine prattled on about how small a matter it was, but Wyatt hardly heard her. It had never occurred to him to think about the other men who came to see Verna. He had no illusions about what she was, but it was easier just to keep the thought of her screwing somebody else at arm's length. That let him think that she was somehow his. Until now she had kept herself free from midnight on and there hadn't been any competition for him to see. Nadine's nervous efforts to ease him away sent a patch of heat crawling up around the hairs on his neck. He stiff-armed Nadine, bouncing her off the wall, and bounded up the steps three at a time.

Not knowing exactly what he'd do to the man he'd find in the room, he rammed his shoulder into Verna's door and burst in. He swung toward the bed, then stopped short. His eyes raked across the room.

Verna was alone.

She was curled on the bed, half under the bedclothes, her face buried under one arm. When Wyatt's senses stopped galloping wild, he could hear her crying.

She turned her head slightly to check who it was, but said nothing. She pulled herself into a tight little ball. Going to her side, Wyatt touched her, and she sobbed convulsively. His insides freezing, Wyatt slumped onto the bed with her and, straining briefly against her resistance, pulled her arm away from her face.

A fat welt, faintly purple, spread from just above her left eye, across her temple, to the bottom of her cheekbone. The puffed eyelid made her left eye nothing more than a slit. Wyatt yanked her up to a sitting position and shouted at her to tell him what happened. She wailed horribly and said nothing no matter how many times he asked. Cringing, he finally drew her toward him and let her cry on his coat.

He held her a long time, his thoughts racing while minutes passed by. He squeezed her harder and waited. When she eased up, she raised her head, her sniffling interrupted sporadically by sobs, and, as Wyatt told her quietly to take her time, she got enough of a hold on herself to talk.

A cowboy had come by late that afternoon, she told him. He didn't seem too drunk, but she said that once he got her in the room he turned ugly. First there were insults, then pushing around, and it ended finally in a beating.

Wyatt took a few moments to sort out the words. "What'd he beat you for?"

"I don't know, Wyatt. He just went crazy. He took me one time, and when I told him it would cost him for another he just went wild . . . I don't know," she whispered hoarsely.

"Whose outfit he with? Where'd he head to?"

She wrapped her arms around him, her wretched, swollen face turned upward, her mouth held tight, quivering. She tightened her grip on him.

Wyatt labored to keep his voice level. "Where is he, Verna?"

She tucked her head against his chest. "He's gone, Wyatt. Please leave it be. His outfit pulled out. O'Brian's outfit — they're gone."

"I can still find them." He tried to look at her face but she kept it turned away.

"No," she cried, her voice breaking. "Stay, Wyatt. No reason to get him. I deserved it. Why shouldn't he do it. That's what I'm here for. As long as he's got the price, that's what I'm here for."

Wyatt stiffened, too twisted up inside to reply. Verna wailed on; her words were almost unintelligible among the gasps and tears: "No reason for him . . . not to haul off on me . . . why shouldn't he . . . how can I expect any . . . any better for Christ's sake . . . me leaving home for sin . . . what else can —"

"Don't say that," Wyatt finally snapped. He jerked her up and stared into her face. "Don't you say that around me, Verna. Nobody's goin' to put hands on you, you hear? They try and I'll tear their goddamn head off and kick it down the stairs. You understand? That's how things'll be. You hear?"

Her head rolled slowly up toward him; she shot a glance at him, couldn't meet his steely gaze, then stared across the room. Ducking her head back down, she quieted for a time. Then she started to laugh. Rolling thickly from her throat, the laugh pitched high and scaled back down to fade gradually away into a rhythmic moan.

Wyatt held her close until she fell silent and drifted to sleep. His broiling rage scattered before a cold feeling as Verna's shrill laughter seemed to reverberate in his mind and then finally pass away. The shrill laughter of a girl he had just given his word to.

11

Ike Clanton and Curly Bill Brocius came to Wichita with
Shanghai Pierce's outfit in the summer of '74. By the time
they reached the cow camp along the Arkansas, Ike's
stories had become more plan than talk.

Cal Roberts had told Ike about the pistol-whipping dandy
when they had crossed trails in a bar in San Antonio; that
put the notion into Ike's head. On the drive northward he
made big talk of it to Curly Bill. Brocius would wrinkle his
square face pensively as Ike told him what he figured he
would do if he came across the dandy at end-of-trail in
Wichita. Curly Bill would scrutinize the small, dark cowboy and then stretch his thick lips into a lopsided grin and
shake his head. "You surely are something, Ike. If your
talk is anything, I wouldn't mind bein' there to see you
make your play against this Earp."

To while away the little relaxing time they had by the
campfire, Ike and Curly Bill made a habit of this kind of
palaver. Before long Ike would talk about "what we'll do"
and Curly Bill wouldn't object to his inclusion. Ike took

comfort in that. He had heard about Curly Bill running
wild in the Panhandle a couple of years back, and Ike liked
the idea of a nervy border tough at his side should there be
need for action when they finally reached trail's end.

Their first night in Wichita got rolling after a bath,
shave and the purchase of new outfits to present themselves in. Strolling down Douglas Avenue, they talked
about where to make their first stop. Ike was for going to
the whores straight off but Curly Bill pressed for a few
toots at a saloon first. The discussion ended when Curly
Bill dragged Ike by the arm over to the Bismarck Saloon.
Smiling amiably, Ike relented and let himself be pulled
along. It was plain that not everybody was always ready
for the women as he was. And you couldn't help but see
why Brocius needed some limbering up; a face like his
might give a girl some cause for hesitation, which was
another reason Ike liked keeping company with the man. A
woman would take a look at the mashed-in nose on Curly
Bill's ruddy block of a face, and then grab an eyeful of
Ike's fine-featured face, and there would be no question
who'd she turn to for a high time. A man had to consider
that if he cared about being seen with the handsomest
woman he could find.

After the Bismarck came Schnitzler's Saloon, then the
Bon Ton, then Schattner and Short's, and, on their way past
Douglas and Main, a turn at Keno Corner. They danced at
the Variety Theater and if Ike had gotten his way they
would have picked out their whores right then and there,
but Curly Bill was for moving on. "We ain't found him
yet," he growled, and with a meaty paw grasped Ike by the
arm and led the way onward.

Fogged by the whiskey, Ike couldn't recall where Cal
had said he had run into the dandy, but he knew it had to
be in one of the bordellos. They crossed the river to the
west side, passed through Rowdy Joe's, and started checking from house to house.

Inside Nadine's place, Ike snagged a couple of girls

before Curly Bill could lead on to the next stop. The square-faced cowboy was finally ready for a distraction. He slipped an arm around the waist of a chubby little brunette and winked at Ike. Ike grinned, "You're flesh and blood after all, ain't ye, Curly Bill." They were moving their girls toward the stairs when Wyatt Earp walked in.

Wyatt glanced around the parlor, traded smiles with Nadine, and, satisfied that all was in order, headed back out the door. He then glimpsed the gun belts on the two cowboys taking their first steps up the stairs. He stopped at the threshold. Ike saw the tall man in the black suit and brocaded vest looking their way. He put out a hand to keep Curly Bill at the bottom of the staircase. Brocius grunted in question.

"Hey Curly Bill," Ike said. "What do we got here?"

Following his friend's gaze, Curly Bill faced the dandy standing by the door. Brocius's wide, thick mouth pursed and his eyes narrowed. Wyatt looked suspiciously from one cowhand to the other.

"That just might be him at that," said Curly Bill.

The low-built cowboy stepped back down to the parlor floor, leaving the girl behind. Ike considered the two men facing each other. This Earp doesn't look so tough, Ike thought, not like Curly Bill here. The dandy is tall and skinny. A scarecrow in a fine suit is all he is.

Ike moved down the steps toward his partner, feeling cocky, figuring on an easy play. Just the same, he was careful to post himself just slightly behind Curly Bill, not quite in the line of action.

"Hey dandy," Curly Bill called, louder than he had to. "Are you Earp?"

Wyatt answered, "That's me. Who might you be?"

Ike spoke up. "This here's Curly Bill Brocius. Maybe you heard tell of him, from down in the Panhandle." Ike waited for a reaction. Earp glanced at Curly Bill but betrayed no emotion. "I'm Ike Clanton," the cowboy added as an afterthought, as if he still might not deal himself in.

"We been through all the cathouses in Wichita lookin' for you," announced Curly Bill.

"Now you've found me. What of it?"

Curly Bill cocked his head toward his friend. "He's a cool one though, ain't he, Ike? Cool and pretty — like any other city whore."

Wyatt kept silent as the cowboys laughed hard at their joke. He eyed Curly Bill's hands inching along his gun belt.

"We heard," Curly Bill went on, "how you buffaloed a couple friends of our'n last season."

Straining to keep the smirk on his face, Ike tried sifting through the whiskey blur to keep a grip on himself. He watched Earp slowly shift his weight from his left foot to his right, the tall man's eyes stayed on Curly Bill the whole time. Ike now noticed something new about this dandy. He was skinny, sure, but his shoulders were wide and his arms seemed like they might be rawboned and strong. His drunken mind wandering, Ike imagined one of those arms snapping to, the long hand whisking a Colt out of its holster. Ike ignored the thought. He placed his hands on his gun belt to keep them from shaking.

"How about it, Earp?" Brocius sneered. "You think you can take us? Those damned fancy guns of your'n — you aim to throw down on us?"

The girls were backing off to the sides. Wyatt stood stock still.

"What's wrong, Earp? You afraid you gonna hurt your pretty hands?"

Wyatt waited to see if either cowboy would pull his gun. Neither did. He slowly ran a thumb along the bottom of his waxed moustache. He then stepped forward.

Ike's arm flinched reflexively. He quickly steadied himself, but the trembling still rattled through him. Wyatt kept walking toward them. He neared the cowboys in a few more strides, then angled slightly to one side, and moved on past them out through the back door.

Ike stared at the door that closed behind Wyatt, not absorbing what had happened at first. He jerked his head around toward Curly Bill, his eyebrows arched in puzzlement.

Curly Bill's smile creeped up one side of his face as he turned away from the dandy's exit. A snort of laughter burst from Ike.

"Look at that would ya," he cried. "Probably won't stop walkin' till he reaches Abilene! Eh, Curly Bill?"

They hollered and whooped and grabbed their girls back to their sides.

"Don't you worry about a thing," Ike said to Nadine, his sudden good luck making him giddy. "Your boy'll get his nerve back. Won't he, Curly Bill? Just as soon as we leave town!" The cowboys hooted and took their whores up to the second floor.

Nadine watched them climb the steps, the puffy flesh around her mouth pinched with worry. Disgrace, she figured, might make a young man like Wyatt skip town; another dependable protector might not be so easy to find.

The second floor room didn't leave much space for anything but the two cowboys, their women and the bed. Selecting which girl they fancied meant taking hold of whichever one was closest. Ike and Curly Bill started groping at dresses and soft flesh, but before they got too far along Ike announced that more celebration was in order and shouted out the door for Nadine to bring up a bottle.

They passed the whiskey around till it was gone — careful to pour some down the girls' dresses — and then held off just long enough to slur a verse of song before going at the whores again. They both dropped their drawers, Ike let out a rebel yell, and they pressed the two girls against the mattress, side by side. That's when the door smashed open.

Wyatt Earp pounced into the room, a double-barrelled 12-gauge American Arms shotgun in his hands. He cocked both barrels.

"Get up, you sons of bitches!"

The girl under Ike screeched. Ike had pissed all over her stomach.

Wyatt jerked the twin muzzles from one cowboy to the other. "Pull 'em up and move 'em out!"

Ike jumped back and slammed into Curly Bill. Grabbing wildly at his pants, Ike looked at the face of his friend for some reassurance, some sign of defiance. Curly Bill's block of a face was drained of blood. Wyatt jabbed the muzzles up close to that face.

"I said move, shitkicker!"

In a mad scramble of arms and legs and flapping trousers, Ike and Curly Bill plunged across the bed toward the open door. His ankles snagged by the dropped pants, Curly Bill flopped into Ike who then staggered out of control through the doorway. With Wyatt closing in on him, Curly Bill skittered in haltered steps to catch up to his partner, only to muscle past him so he could be the first to take the stairs. That left Ike as the one to get the swift boot in the ass from Wyatt. Ike bounced down the steps and knocked over Curly Bill while waves of laughter shrieked from Nadine and the girls.

Later that night, Wyatt strolled over to Douglas and Main. He stopped beneath the overhang of the New York Store and listened to the band across the way at Keno Corner. Taking a break from sprightly reels and pounding marches, Fehleisen's band slipped into a sweet round of "I Dream of Jeannie with the Light Brown Hair". The lilting tune fit Wyatt's mood. The fire that had driven him during the cathouse scuffle had burned itself out and he now relaxed and lighted a fresh cigar.

Smiling at the memory of the two stupid cowboys tugging up their pants at a dead run out Nadine's door, Wyatt idly noted the high-rollers and dudes passing by, the play of streetlamp light against darkened storefronts, the close summer air of the prairie — all things that he counted as the blessings of his new life. These boom towns were the place to be all right. Musing about the time he'd spend with Verna later on, Wyatt stayed put for now and stretched his smoke for all it was worth. He had no reason to hurry.

The last refrains of Stephen Foster's tune could be picked up in faint snatches on the west side of the bridge. Ike remembered a time in Sweetwater, teaching a pretty Mexican girl the words to the song. He tried concentrating on the memory, hoping it would shunt aside the experience of this night. But he couldn't forget the twin muzzles of the 12-gauge bearing down on him. He rode on with Curly Bill, traveling at a fast lope past the outlying dance halls on their way back to Shanghai Pierce's cow camp.

In deadly silence they had scrambled away from Nadine's place and hurried back to the east side of the river where they had stabled their horses. Along the way, they found a near-empty bar and they each knocked back a shot in the hope that whiskey would ease the terrible humiliation. It didn't work.

From there they went straight to the City Stables. Only a few words were said between getting their mounts and reaching camp. They made a solemn oath to keep this night a tight-cinched secret forever.

12

While helping the family move out of the Lamar home-
stead, Virgil got the news of Wyatt's whereabouts and sent
off a letter to Wichita to warn of a visit that coming fall.
At the close of the '75 season, he found his younger
brother in the midst of Mike Meagher's re-election campaign, stumping for his boss to keep up his own position in
town.

The '74 cattle season had not been the richest of times,
but Wyatt had not been discouraged. Competition from
local sheep and cattle raising on the other side of the
Missouri line had cut into the profits of the longhorn trade
from Texas, and less shipping on the Santa Fe line meant
fewer cowmen throwing their money around in Wichita
saloons and gambling halls. The Bon Ton Saloon had suffered like the others; but that only left an opening as far as
Wyatt was concerned. Over the following winter he had
been able to buy a bigger share of the Bon Ton's business
for a small price, and when the trade picked up again in the
spring of '75, he took in a handsome profit. He counted

himself as a prospering man even after parting with the money that went toward Verna's upkeep in her new home away from Nadine's place. Good money and a woman of his own — he couldn't complain.

Good fortune rested easy on the younger brother. Virgil noticed a ready grin now on the face that so often could turn sour, and a healthy glint in the deep-set blue eyes. Taking time off from pumping hands along Main Street, Wyatt showed his brother some of the sights around town. He showed him the rowdy west side, quiet now in the daytime, and told him the latest about Rowdy Joe Lowe. "That feud of his with Red Summers has been going on ever since I got here. Their fight last week was a long time coming," Wyatt said. "A knock-down-drag-out fight it was too. When Meagher broke it up, Rowdy got real sorry-looking and said to Red he wanted it all to end. 'Come here, I want to kiss and make up,' he said. Red went over to him and Rowdy Joe bit the end of his nose off. Even for Wichita that turned out to be too much. He's already packed up and on his way." Going back to the east bank, they passed the Variety Theater, and Wyatt went on to tell his brother about the small riot that had demolished the Variety stage just a couple of months before. The sporting men and the cowboys got upset when the owner, Jim Allen, closed the place at four in the morning. By the time it was all over, there was little more than kindling where the stage had been. "Some folks got into a tizzy about the roughhousing coming to the east side," said Wyatt, "but Jim Allen didn't blink. He just built himself a new stage and made sure not to close at four anymore. With his money he can afford to be easygoing."

For each saloon and dance hall they passed there seemed to be another story from Wyatt about all the high times and easy money to be had. It had been years since Virgil had seen him so talkative.

Despite all Wyatt's tales about freewheeling Wichita ways, Virgil couldn't help but notice something else afoot in the cow town. On Emporia Street they passed a sturdy, brick Methodist Church under construction. It was a far cry from the first Wichita church he'd heard of, the one built back in '69 of log slabs with nothing better than a dirt floor to kneel on. At the north end of Main, they saw laborers draining the road to clear the way for a graded street.

"We're becoming real citified here," Wyatt said proudly.

But Virgil knew there was something else here for a boom town gambler to take heed of. He had seen the same thing in Abilene. A bad season comes along and doubt starts to creep up on some people about how long the town can count on Texas cattle business and the cowboys' free-spending binges. Before long, something else more dependable and respectable is liable to take their place.

Virgil filled Wyatt in on the family's trek to a new home in California, and told him about his new wife, Allie, and their house outside Council Bluffs.

"Did Morgan really leave home?" Wyatt asked.

"Less than a year after you did," Virgil said. "Went drifting for fortune, following in your footsteps. He was somewhere in Montana the last I heard from him. Not that I hear too often. Like I said, in your footsteps."

Wyatt nodded amiably, not bothering to acknowledge the needling.

At the Eagle Building the two Earps got ahold of Meagher on his way to his office. Virgil and Meagher slapped each other's back and traded friendly insults for a bit before they decided to walk to the Bismarck Saloon to talk over old times. After three rounds of rye the old friends had exchanged news and rumors on just about everyone they knew from Abilene: Butcher Knife Ann had passed through Wichita but the cow town's wild times weren't wild enough for her. She moved on to the Nations. Johnny Redden had come to Wichita and stayed, while Billy Brooks, Doc Skurlock and Cheyenne Jack had gone to

Montana. After the trouble with his brother in Ellsworth, Ben Thompson had drifted to Dodge and George Peshaur met up with him there.

"Abilene," Virgil mused. "We sure were full of piss and vinegar back then, weren't we."

"You were there when Tom Smith met up with that damn shitkicker, weren't you?" asked Meagher.

"I left town just before that," Virgil said, "but I heard about it."

They each took another drink and let the conversation drop for the moment, remembering Marshal Tom Smith, who'd been blindsided with an axe by a crazed farmer. Took Smith's head off for no damn reason.

"Finish up," said Wyatt as he poured the last of the whiskey into his glass. He had heard enough of the past. "You still haven't seen the Bon Ton, Virge. I'll show you what my business interests look like there."

They gulped down their last drinks and, sporting a whiskey glow, the three men left the Bismarck behind. To make it to the Bon Ton, they had to pass through a crowd gathered in the street listening to Bill Tyler explain how he would set things right if he was elected marshal.

"Hold on," said Virgil, taking hold of his brother's arm. "Let's hear how he's goin' to whip Mike come next Tuesday."

"That's an idea," Meagher said straight-faced. "Tyler tells me I ain't got a chance."

"As long as he tells the truth about you, you don't."

"Tyler's nothin'," Wyatt said, his tongue thickened by whiskey. He dismissed the crowd with a wave of his hand and started to walk away, but Meagher and his brother seemed set to take in the show.

On a makeshift platform in front of the land office, the squat Tyler thrashed his arms up and down as he brayed on about Wichita being "a growing city, a town of the future." Supporters behind him heaved up their BILL

TYLER FOR MARSHAL signs and waved them about to excite cheers from the crowd. Some spectators clapped out of politeness.

Wyatt grumbled, "If I wanted hot air I'd go down to the bean parlor on Topeka Street."

"Don't be in such a hurry," Virgil said. "Mike here might have to find a new line of work soon. Leave him in peace for a moment." Meagher grinned along with him.

"Now Mike Meagher is a good man," conceded Tyler as he mopped his brow. "But that don't make him a good lawman. What we need is a strong reliable police force and we don't have that now. Ain't that so?" Not getting an answer from the crowd, he plowed on.

"What we got now is a corrupt force, a corrupt force that's more concerned about themselves than you. Corruption, my friends. That there's the byword of Meagher's force."

"Bullshit," Wyatt muttered. Meagher shrugged but kept silent.

"And believe me, friends," Tyler pressed on, trying to work up a lather, "this ain't no careless accusation. No sir. Not at all. You want a specific? You want names? How about Wyatt Earp, policeman for Meagher." In an exaggerated stage whisper he added, "Mr. Earp, I'll let you know, has got very strong ties to a certain house of ill repute on the west side of the river."

Meagher wasn't taking his eyes off of Tyler now, but Virgil sneaked a look at his brother, trying to catch his attention. Wyatt, eyes riveted on Tyler, showed no sign of noticing him.

"This house," Tyler bellowed, "has got to pay a fine, every month, just like every other business of its breed. And I've got it on damn good authority, my friends, that the madam of this establishment hasn't bothered once to come to court to pay these here fines ever since Earp got himself a job on Meagher's force." Tyler shook a fist. "Now where has this money gone? You can bet it hasn't gone to the city treasury where it belongs! Thanks to Earp and others like him working with Meagher! Thanks to them our city's funds have been depleted! How can our city grow, I ask you, with the likes of them bleeding our resources —"

"Lyin' pig!" Wyatt lurched forward but Virgil was on him quickly, holding his brother by the arm, trying to hold him still.

Wyatt shouted again, the crowd rumbled excitedly, and Meagher grabbed his other arm. Wyatt twisted madly to get out of the hold. With a simultaneous heave, Virgil and Meagher shoved him back a good ten feet. Before Wyatt could bolt forward again, they caught him, wrestled his arms behind him, and dragged him struggling toward the opposite boardwalk.

Virgil glanced back at the speaker's platform. For the first time that afternoon Tyler looked satisfied.

At the near corner, Virgil and Meagher pulled Wyatt out of view of the crowd, and pinned him to the side of the building. Seething, Wyatt finally stopped resisting, then suddenly tugged again. Virgil drove his shoulder into him and shouted in his ear: "Wyatt, no more!"

Locked into place, Wyatt started to let up. His breath pulled in and pressed out hoarsely.

"What in the goddamned hell," spat Meagher, "do you think you're doin'?"

"He can't get away with that! He's talkin' trash!"

"Leave it, Wyatt," Virgil warned.

Meagher and Virgil waited a few moments, then let him go. Wyatt hunched against the wall, his arms hanging, his eyes staring at the ground.

Meagher let himself cool off before speaking. "All right, Wyatt. What's all this? You got something to tell me about the west side?"

"He's lyin'." Wyatt's voice wavered with the last of his rage. "Nadine pays up every month. I take it for her."

"What's this about her not goin' to court?"

"I told you. I take it for her. I bring it to court as a favor." He glanced uneasily at Virgil. "She pays up. She just doesn't show up at court."

"That's no big deal," Virgil put in. "This fella Tyler's twisting things around, Mike."

Meagher's beady gaze never left Wyatt. Shaking his head, the marshal then took a breath, considered Virgil. He paced off a few steps and faced Wyatt again. "One more thing. You tell me you're playin' it square, but then you go haywire out there. What the hell's the matter with you?"

"Let me and him talk," Virgil said. "Just Wyatt and me — let us talk."

Unwilling to give it up so easily, Meagher stared at Virgil, then looked around as if searching for someone to appeal to. He said to his friend, "He's your brother, Virge. You talk sense to him. I sure as hell don't have the time." Jabbing a finger at Wyatt, he added, "I told you I ain't draggin' dirt with me! I told you that." He wheeled and stalked off.

Virgil leaned against the building alongside his brother and let the dust settle for a few moments. "You're in politics now," was what he finally said.

Wyatt gave him a questioning look.

"You say Tyler's lying," Virgil went on, "but you got to expect that."

Wyatt petulantly shrugged a shoulder. "I'm not in the mood, Virge."

"You're not in the mood!" Virgil snapped. "Well, that's too goddamned bad! Meagher's a friend of mine and you're doin' him no good! He doesn't have just Tyler to buck here. He's got Tyler and all the reformers that must be backing him. And you're bollixing up the whole show!"

Wyatt looked away and fell silent.

"Doesn't that mean anything to you?" Virgil demanded.

"There's something going on here, Virge. Tyler singled

me out in front of everybody. Everybody! What'd he do that for? You tell me."

"Wise up, Wyatt. He's running for marshal. He couldn't get a rise out of that crowd, you could see that. So he took a stab in the dark. He took a stab at you. And you served it right up for him!"

Wyatt didn't respond.

Pulling back a step, Virgil let his brother stew for a few moments. He figured Wyatt was seeing his point; it wasn't in Virgil to badger him anymore.

When enough time had passed for some calm to sneak in, Virgil told Wyatt to show him the Bon Ton. "Come on, we'll hoist a few. We'll get a new look on things."

In the dim light of the saloon, the two brothers eased up some, and the liquor soon started up some more talk about the family and Virgil's Iowa freighting contract and plans for wintering in the coming months.

Virgil knew he should say more to his younger brother about the election, steer him as best he could, but he still sensed Wyatt's anger, and realized his brother was waiting for an excuse to flare up once more. Virgil had to admit to himself that he was afraid of Wyatt's temper, had been ever since Wyatt was in his teens. It was easier to try to get around it somehow. He only wished he had more time than the next twelve hours before pulling out for Iowa, more time to settle Wyatt, as father would have wanted him to do.

The day after Virgil left Wichita, Wyatt was dealing faro at the Bon Ton Saloon when Neal Brown came in. Seeing Wyatt at the gaming table, he hurried over.

"Wyatt, you hear about Tyler's speech this morning?"

Wyatt completed the play before turning to Brown. "I'm not about to wake up early to listen to him."

"Seems like he heard your brother Virgil had been to town. Now he's talking about your brothers, about them coming to Wichita. He says you already brought in Virgil for a look-see and now you're gonna bring in Morgan."

Wyatt's jaw tightened. "What's he getting at?"

"He says you're bringing in your brothers and getting them on the police force. He says you're building up a gang to take care of —" Brown hesitated when he saw the look in Wyatt's eyes. He then decided he would have to finish it. "He says you're making a gang to take care of your dirty dealings. Dirty dealings is how he said it."

For the first time since buying into the Bon Ton, Wyatt left a gaming table without a dealer to replace him.

He found Tyler holding forth at Schattner and Short's bar, mixing business with pleasure in the company of a pack of drinkers and two dance hall girls. Without breaking stride, Wyatt stepped up to him, turned him around and hammered him in the stomach. Tyler doubled up. Smashing his fist into Tyler's face, Wyatt yelled, "Bad-mouthing my brothers, are ya! Time I shut you up, you bastard!" He rammed a knee into Tyler's chest and beat him to the floor before two men could pull him off.

Tyler was slumped against the bar, bleeding from the nose and mouth. The blood from his lip gushed down to his white silk shirt. "You fucking son of a bitch," Wyatt roared as he was dragged out through the door.

Within the hour, word of the incident had gotten around town. Meagher heard about it on his way out of Ketzler's barber shop. The marshal went to his office and closed himself inside, speaking to no one.

His choice was clear: either fire Wyatt or let him stand trial for assault — while Wyatt still represented Meagher's force. And all this at the height of the election campaign.

He stared out the window at the New York Store for nearly a half-hour before sending out a man to fetch Wyatt.

Verna hovered in the hotel room doorway, unsure whether to step in. She watched Wyatt fold his shirts and stack them into his carpetbags. His long fingers worked precisely despite his obvious agitation.

"They told me at Bitting's drygoods about your leaving," she said quietly.

"Well, they weren't kidding you," he answered curtly.

"Where'll you be goin'? Do you know?"

"I keep hearing about Dodge City. I figure I might as well see it too."

"Bibulous Babylon," she said.

"What?"

"Oh, you know what they say in the newspapers. Dodge City, the Bibulous Babylon of the Prairie."

"Yeah, that's what they say."

Out of the corner of his eye, Wyatt saw Verna's hand worrying her calico dress. He knew she had something to say but he couldn't take the time to coax it out of her. He had to keep busy with packing to fend off thoughts of his humiliating last talk with Meagher. For all his bustling, though, certain memories wouldn't disappear.

The look in Meagher's eyes had told it all, even before the marshal had gotten around to bringing up Virgil and what he had expected of his old friend's younger brother. Wyatt saw it wasn't anger in the man's hard stare. It was disgust. Meagher had hired Wyatt on faith, faith that the brother of a steady, true man like Virgil would measure up. And Wyatt had shattered that faith.

"I'm glad Virgil ain't here to see this," was what Meagher finally said.

Wyatt stood there, meek, pathetic; unable to say anything to defend himself. The rest of Meagher's words wafted by him, mostly unheard, until the marshal asked for Wyatt's badge.

On his way over to the office, Wyatt had figured he would at least volunteer the badge before being asked, at least hang on to that much pride. But his humiliation had driven that thought from his mind. When Meagher held out his hand, Wyatt was stung with the realization that the time for that gesture, small as it may have been, had already run out.

A shuffling step from the doorway now recaptured Wyatt's attention. Verna's pointed chin tilted up to face him directly. "I want you to know I'm beholden to you, Wyatt. For all your help."

"Don't worry about it."

"No, I've got to tell you, Wyatt." She took a half-step forward. "I was wasting away at Nadine's and if you hadn't moved me out I'd still be there. It was all my fault of course," she added, now starting to chatter, "if it weren't for my own wickedness I wouldn't've been there in the first place. But for all that you treated me like I was something fine and good anyway. There's not many that would have, and God knows I didn't give them no reason to." She stopped abruptly. Uncertain where her story was heading, she stopped talking altogether.

The strained silence stopped Wyatt in his tracks. He had given up months ago on telling her to quit cutting herself down. The only thing he could do now was let her run out her string. Though less frequent recently, these pathetic outbursts of hers still wore him down. At first they had made him impatient, infuriated. How could she talk like that about herself? But today it just made him feel tired. He had thought that taking her out of Nadine's might help her peace of mind, but little had changed. He stood by his half-full carpetbag, facing the look of desperation in her sad chestnut eyes.

She stepped toward him. Her look now was almost an accusation. She waited for him to speak first.

"You want to come with me," Wyatt finally said.

"You will take me, won't you? I can't stay here. You know that."

Wyatt felt big and awkward next to her small, sensual figure. He fingered the leather handle of the carpetbag.

"Wyatt, I've tried awful hard," she said softly. "I've worked at sewing and such to earn something and keep myself away from Nadine's, but you know I'd starve without the money you give me. I've got to stick with you."

She clasped her hands around his waist and pulled herself to him. Wyatt's senses prickled wildly with the press of her lithe body against him.

"With you I won't fail," she went on. "I'd be like a wife to you, Wyatt. I'll sew for you — not for strangers. And I'll cook and take care of you. You'll need me, Wyatt. You'll be a big man in Dodge City, I just know it. And you'll need a fine house, and you'll need a woman to look after it. I'll do that for you."

Her round eyes took on a warm sheen and penetrated Wyatt's gaze. All Wyatt could think of now was their tumbles in the sack, the feel of her flesh, the trusting looks, so much like the expression before him now. Taking her soft shoulders, he half-lifted her off her feet. He cleared his throat once, then found it very easy to say, "You can come along, if you want."

She smiled crookedly. His grip loosened, and she slipped down and flattened herself against him. She held on fiercely. "Thank you, Wyatt." She then buried her face in his silk shirtfront. "God knows I don't deserve it."

13

The idea of traveling all the way to Dodge City by rail excited Verna. She chattered about it off and on the whole morning while waiting for the 11:30 to arrive and get stoked up for the first leg up the Wichita spur line to Newton. The notion of leaving her home of the last four years didn't seem to trouble her at all. For his part, Wyatt couldn't leave Wichita fast enough.

The first few miles of the ride Verna sat in a tense hush, leaning slightly forward, her hands clasped in her lap. She had never traveled this fast before and wasn't quite sure if the train could stay on the tracks the whole way. Wyatt gave her a reassuring pat on the leg to put her at ease. He didn't let on that he had never taken a long train ride either. He draped his arm nonchalantly along the ridge of the window, but he gripped that ridge tight enough to make his fingertips white for the first few minutes that the locomotive hit top speed.

Pulling into the Newton depot later that day, the train was held up for an hour for refueling and some minor adjustments. The passengers were told they could step out to stretch their legs.

"Come, Wyatt," said Verna, "I never seen Newton. You can show me the sights."

"I'm staying," he said.

"Come on. It's awful hot in here."

True enough, the close Indian summer air in the car was stifling and the back of Wyatt's shirt was soaked with sweat, but he had no intention of leaving.

Looking out his window down Main Street, Wyatt forgot the ideas he had a short time ago about returning to Newton as a conquering hero. The buildings facing each other across Main Street looked shabby. He couldn't imagine why he had thought it was such a crackerjack place just a few years ago. Getting off the train now would seem like taking a step backward.

"You can stroll around if you want," he told Verna, "but I'll sit it out."

Verna flashed him a nasty look but said nothing. She stayed where she was and suffered with the heat.

Once headed west along the main line of the Atchison, Topeka and Santa Fe, Wyatt started to forget all about Newton. He was even able to put Wichita out of mind. The rhythmic rattle of the train was soothing, and once out on the prairie a sweet autumn smell breezed into the car. Flat lands gave way to flint hills and then leveled off again. Wyatt dozed off, slipping into a light, fitful sleep. His arm jerked reflexively a couple of times as he fended off something in his dream.

The sleep was unsatisfying, seeming to last only a short time, but when Wyatt awoke he checked his pocket watch to see that he had been out for nearly two hours. Off to his right the limestone bluffs of west Kansas rose massively from the plains floor. They were well on their way, Wyatt thought, his mind filled with nothing but thoughts of Dodge City and the chances waiting for him there.

They reached Dodge City that night. After passing the

cattle pens they continued along the Arkansas River to the depot at Railroad Avenue and Front Street. As they carried their luggage off the train, they faced the Dodge House, a large, bustling hotel with a lamplit porch and a billiard hall next to it. Coming and going through both buildings were fancy gamblers and cattle buyers in swallowtail coats. The hotel was obviously the place to be seen for the newcomer wanting to make a good impression. Wyatt led the way across the street, stopping just long enough to let a galloping horse pass and then shake off the coat of dust left in its wake.

They checked into a room on the second floor. During the last leg of the train ride, Wyatt had imagined stretching out on a soft hotel bed as soon as they hit town, but that urge quickly faded. The little he saw of Dodge City from the railroad depot looked real interesting and he was ready to make his first rounds right away. He heaved the carpetbags onto the bureau, checked himself in the mirror and then suddenly found himself facing Verna, glued to the spot, not sure what to say.

He hadn't thought of making his first stroll through the town with Verna at his side; he figured that would be something a man did on his own. He watched her now, opening the bags and unpacking, and he took stock of what bringing her with him would really mean.

Feeling bad about not showing her Newton, he asked if she was ready to take a look at their new town. Without glancing at him, she stacked shirts in a bureau drawer and said, "You go ahead. I'll set us up here." She reached into the carpetbags again, pulled out some more clothes but still didn't look his way.

Wyatt knew something was brewing, something that could lead to one of those scenes of hers that he didn't understand, but his impatience to get going didn't let him think about it too much. He might have been bothered more by the way Verna was acting if it wasn't for the fact that he preferred to be alone anyway. You can't hardly blame a man for that, he thought.

Outside of the Dodge House was Front Street, the widest road Wyatt had ever seen. Nearly one hundred yards across, it was more like two streets running side by side, divided by the Santa Fe railroad tracks. The depot was planted right in the middle and along the north side were two or three blocks packed with commercial establishments. On the south side were just a few businesses spaced well apart on prairie lots. Wyatt quickly judged the lay of the land here in Dodge City.

A fella could certainly have his share of high living on the north side of the tracks; Wyatt counted six saloons within two blocks, mixed in with the boot shops and general stores. But the places looked pretty orderly. Gazing across the tracks, though, Wyatt saw a couple of dance halls, subdued now in the first half of the night, but promising the wild and woolly times found in places like Wichita's west bank and Newton's Hyde Park. Wyatt noticed that the city jail was built right in the middle of Front Street, just south of the tracks. Saves the south side rowdies a long walk when it's time to check into the calaboose, Wyatt figured.

The time had come to christen the town; there was no question of that. The only question was where. As he walked along the north side, he passed the Occident Saloon, the Old House Saloon, the Alhambra Saloon. Wyatt stopped counting the possibilities when he reached the Lone Star. He stood stock still on the boardwalk. Heading toward him was a man about his height, but more broadly built, with slate blue eyes, thick, black hair and a drooping moustache. The last time Wyatt had seen him he was in ragged buckskin, worn thin at the elbows by a hard season on the buffalo range. Decked out as he was now in a tailored suit with bowler and silver-tipped cane, the man wasn't recognizable at first.

"Masterson," Wyatt said. "Billy Masterson."

An easy smile came to Masterson's face. "Wyatt. Well, good God damn." He thrust out his hand. "Where the hell you come from?"

"Wichita. Just got off the Santa Fe."

"Wichita you say. I heard one of the Earps was a lawman there, but I couldn't get a straight story about which one it was. Some cowboy drifted through last summer, had also been to Montana. You've got a brother Morgan there, don't you? Up to Butte? This cowboy couldn't keep it straight who was who. Said you two look so much alike it was anyone's guess."

"People always said we favored each other," answered Wyatt, thankful they had gotten off the topic of Wichita so easily.

He was glad to see Masterson. He had taken a liking to him the short time they had spent together in the buffalo camp at Salt Fork a few years back and had wondered if he might be crossing Masterson's path sooner or later along the cow town circuit.

"Goin' into the Lone Star Saloon?" asked Masterson. "I wouldn't do that if I was you. Actually, you wouldn't do that if you was me. My credit's run out there. Let me show you a good place." He led the way a bit farther along the boardwalk and guided Wyatt into a bar a few doors down.

The Long Branch Saloon was a bright, freshly painted place, with a polished brass chandelier hanging from the ceiling. Wyatt noticed two doorways in the back of the seating area.

"They have a separate room for private gambling," said Masterson, "and another for lying down when you can't do anything but."

The bartender asked, "What'll it be, Bat?"

"I'll take a beer. Good and cold. A beer for you, Wyatt?"

"That'll do." When the bartender ambled off, Wyatt turned questioningly to Bill Masterson. "Bat? Is that what they call you here?"

"On account of this cane here," Masterson said. "I've batted my share of rowdies with it."

"You get paid to do that?" asked Wyatt.

From his vest pocket, Bat pulled out a badge. "Under-sheriff for Ford County," he said. "There's an election coming soon enough and I might even try for the whole ball of wax. Sheriff Masterson — how do you like the sound of it?"

"I won't kick. You say you've batted your share — do you have many toughs here?"

"Some. Mostly just cowboys who don't know when to stop. Truth is, I don't have to bat 'em as much as I used to. Seems they're starting to get the idea, which is fine with me. Mostly the trouble's on the south side of the tracks. That's where — hell, I don't have to tell you, Wyatt. You've been on the circuit long enough. Here in Dodge we have our own name for it. The tracks are called the Dead Line. South of there it's wide open. Like I said, I'm sure you figured that for yourself."

A cowboy in fresh-bought clothes walked in. Bat turned leisurely to look him over, then motioned to the man. Without a protest, the cowboy unbuckled his gun belt and handed it over to the bartender before ordering his whiskey and taking it to a table in back.

Wyatt carefully watched Bat operate and could see that Masterson, despite his easygoing ways, was all business when it counted. A man didn't command that kind of respect without making some hardcases either back off or drop to the floor in a hurry.

"I see you're not carrying tonight," Bat said, indicating Wyatt's waist.

"I had a hunch I'd only have to take the guns off the first place I went to. I figured I should learn the ropes around here before strapping them on."

Bat said, "You'd be wanting to wear those guns again by and by, wouldn't you?"

Wyatt gave him a curious look. "I was thinking about it."

"You might be able real soon. Things'll slow down through the winter but a fella name of Hartman is about to leave and that'll leave an opening on the marshal's force. I'll introduce you to Charlie Bassett. He's the Town Marshal. I think you'll like it here in Dodge, Wyatt. From what I hear, it could be more to your liking than Wichita."

Bat sipped his beer and let the remark stand at that. Wyatt studied him, wondering how much Bat had really heard about Wichita. The idea occurred to him that Bat might've dropped the subject of Wichita so neatly when they first ran into each other tonight because he knew Wyatt wouldn't want to talk about it. A man could pick up news pretty fast along the cattle town circuit, if he made it his business to know. Wyatt had a feeling Bat liked to keep himself informed.

As for Bat coming forward so quickly to help him with a lawman's job, Wyatt was a bit surprised. Thinking back, though, to their first meeting in the buffalo camp, he remembered the respect that Bat — Billy at the time — had shown right away. Being a few years younger, he must have thought of Wyatt as a man of experience.

"I'd appreciate the introduction to this fella Bassett," Wyatt said.

Bat nodded affably and took another sip of beer, as if the deed were already as good as done.

Walking back to the Dodge House two hours later, Wyatt was riding high, excited by his prospects in Dodge City. Bat had shown him the night life on both sides of

Front Street, or the Plaza as people in Dodge called it, and had introduced Wyatt to Marshal Charlie Bassett, a stocky, friendly man who seemed to be impressed by Bat's recommendation of the new sport in town. Life could be easy here, Wyatt thought. He felt something that reminded him of his first few wide-eyed days in Wichita, long before things had gone bad. He was sure he had a live one by the tail and he was going to hang on for all it was worth.

It was a giddy feeling coursing through him, but it didn't last much longer. The feeling abandoned him when he stepped into his hotel. He was on his way to Verna. Crossing the lobby and climbing the stairs, he thought of her strange moods, especially the latest one that had overcome her as soon as they'd arrived. He tried to think of what he would say to her now. As he turned the doorknob to their room, he hoped that she was already asleep.

14

Verna didn't leave the hotel at all during their first week in Dodge. She would putter about the room, visit the lobby and go to the Dodge House restaurant with Wyatt, but that was as far afield as she would go. "I just don't feel settled yet," was all she would say when Wyatt mentioned it.

Sometimes Wyatt would ask her if she wanted to take a stroll with him. "Oh, I've been out today," she would say. "I was out while you been off tending to business." Wyatt didn't believe her. She seemed to spend most of her time sitting by the window, staring out at Front Street. She sat erect, worrying her fingers, and when Wyatt would say something she would jump, startled by the interruption.

Wyatt finally got her out on a Sunday afternoon. He wanted her to meet Charlie Bassett's wife, Helen. She was a cheerful woman and seemed pleased at Wyatt's request that she take Verna under her wing and introduce her to other women. Wyatt congratulated himself for doing such a good deed, but the fact was he wanted someone to take Verna off his hands. He hadn't even been good at turning

Willa's mood around when she was sad, and that had happened little enough. She was one of the most cheerful, even-tempered people he'd ever met. With Verna he was forever standing around, not knowing what to do.

Verna put on a new blue dress and hat and was as pretty as Wyatt had ever seen her. Walking out of the hotel arm-in-arm with her, seeing the autumn sun reflected on the fair, clear skin of her face, he had no trouble remembering how he'd been drawn to her so quickly in Nadine's place. They passed Bat lazing in a rocker beneath the overhang of Zimmerman's Hardware. "Wyatt, get a hold on yourself," Bat said. "You can't steal a woman that good-looking. Some man's liable to shoot you." It was enough to get a small smile out of her.

They met Charlie Bassett and his wife on the corner of Front Street and Bridge Avenue. After Wyatt made the introductions, Helen Bassett allowed only a short pause before taking charge of the conversation.

"Some friends will be coming by my house tomorrow," the plump woman said. "We'd sure like to see you come around, Verna. It'll just be two women I know. I'm sure they'd be happy to make your acquaintance."

"That sounds nice," Verna said softly.

"Once I get my chores done in the morning, I sometimes have them by."

"So they can eat all my food," Charlie said and smiled.

Helen disregarded him. "It's a nice house. We can walk by it, show you where we live."

Wyatt first saw the pint-sized cowboy on the street as the man turned around to look back at Verna. Figuring the drover was just admiring her, Wyatt thought little of it. He shot him a cold glance by way of warning and left it at that.

Helen was telling Verna and Wyatt about how civilized it was on the western edge of Dodge, past all the stores and saloons. "Don't think it's just drifters here," she said. "Some good families have houses over that way. Most times it's peaceful, except when the south side starts whoopin' and hollerin'."

The short cowboy stepped onto the boardwalk, a silly grin on his sunburnt face. Wyatt now saw that he was working on an early afternoon drunk. He also saw that it wasn't admiration in the man's expression. It was recognition. He knew Verna. Now getting a good look at him, Wyatt recalled seeing the drover in Wichita, outside of Nadine's place.

Verna looked away.

"Still as pretty," the cowboy said, his voice slurred. "You west bank gals."

Wyatt considered cuffing the cowboy once across the head, just hard enough to send him into the street. Glancing at Charlie and Helen, he then decided against it. A fight in the middle of town wouldn't be the best way to impress a new boss and his wife. Wyatt took Verna's arm and started walking away.

The cowboy's reedy voice followed them, taking on a defiant edge. "I never forget a redheaded gal," he said. When Wyatt turned, the cowboy was already walking away, moving quickly. Charlie casually put a hand on Wyatt's arm, gripping him tightly to tell him to let it be.

Helen picked up her talk where she had left off. "Maybe you'll be wanting to build your own house near ours," she said. "There are some good lots we can show you. You feel like scouting the possibilities, Verna?"

Verna was silent, and she stayed that way. Whenever there was need for an answer, she would smile weakly or just shrug, staring straight ahead the whole time, not daring to meet anyone's eyes. Wyatt wished he had knocked the cowboy down. For starters.

After a stroll past the Bassett house, Verna finally spoke up to tell Wyatt she was tired, that she should go back to the hotel. Helen nodded in understanding and said that she and Verna could spend time when Verna felt better.

They walked back to the Dodge House without saying a

word. Back in their room, Verna slumped down onto the bed, not bothering to take off her hat. Wyatt considered saying something about the busthead cowboy from Wichita, but thought better of it. Leaving her to sleep, he started for the door. "Bat said to meet him today about a job dealing faro," Wyatt said. "I'll be off to the Lady Gay."

"Don't go," Verna called out after him.

"It's business," he said. "I'll be back later."

"Wyatt —"

He turned to her, waited for her to go on. She gazed at the floor and said, "Ain't there some better business for you to tend to." She shrugged off the top of her dress. "You can tend to me."

The remark should have been light and fetching, but her voice was indifferent, lifeless. From somewhere she conjured up a smile and then she was off the bed and pressing herself against him. Her brown eyes still sad, she pulled him back to the bed.

He was slow to get excited, unable to forget that woeful look of hers from just a few moments before, and not sure why it haunted him. But Verna knew how to make him forget. For the rest of the afternoon and into part of the evening he stayed with her.

The next day she was smiling and said she was off to see Helen when Wyatt was on his way out to tend to business. For a time, living with her became easy. The doubts Wyatt had about his decision to bring her with him to a new town stopped closing in on him. She spent time during the day with Helen and acted more at home in town. Wyatt gradually began to feel like the burden was off him. He couldn't say for sure how she got along at nights when he was off around town, meeting the right people and making his way. She was usually asleep by the time he got back to the room at three or four in the morning.

Sometimes he would wake her up, getting into bed alongside her, hiking up her bed clothes, running his hand up along her leg. Other times he would just lie there on his back and listen to the noises outside the window. A voice or two would ring out loud, wheels would rasp in the dirt as a buckboard rolled out of town, a south side piano would tinkle its last quiet notes. They were friendly sounds. Sleep came easily to Wyatt.

15

The winter months were slow, but Wyatt was satisfied, knowing that the pace would surely pick up in the spring when the first Texas longhorn herds moved up the Western Trail toward the Dodge City depot. In the meantime, Deputy Marshal Earp was free to wear his guns in town and there was time enough on the side to make some money with cards.

He had Bat to thank for clearing the way, and in return he campaigned for Masterson at election time. Running for sheriff as a Republican, Bat found a lot of support among the many Northerners around Ford County, and he also did himself a lot of good with his affable ways and his understanding of the men who were drawn to a cattle town about to boom. When the votes were counted, Bat had the job.

Although he was with the town marshal's office, Wyatt worked most of the time with the new county sheriff. "The town's got to work close with county officials," he told Marshal Bassett. Wyatt figured that sounded more serious-minded than just saying, "Hell, Charlie, I like the fella's company."

Wyatt couldn't think of many people he had known who were as expert at their work and as able to enjoy themselves as Bat. When he was with Masterson, the job and the high living seemed to become the same thing. Once he was sitting with the county sheriff at the Long Branch, listening to a tall tale about Bat's stint as a scout in the Red River War. "Not much to tell really," Masterson said, before launching into a twenty-minute account of his exploits. After hearing about the third pitched battle that Bat the scout had survived unscathed, Wyatt asked, "How come you never showed me all your medals?" He kept his face straight.

"I couldn't be bothered with that," said Bat. "I was in it for the sport." From there he went on to the next bloody battle in which he distinguished himself. The more amused Wyatt got, the taller Bat made the tale. As Bat worked on his next story, a drunk soldier at a nearby table started a fight with a cowboy over a girl named Polly from the south side. Masterson got up, whacked the trooper across the head with his cane and came back to Wyatt's side to finish his story before hauling the soldier off to the calaboose. He didn't miss a stitch of the tale or a drop of his beer.

After the warm weather set in, the Texas herds turned the town around. With the thousands of cattle coming up the Western Trail there was a surge of business and wild times that bested anything Wyatt had seen at the height of the Wichita boom. Cowboys showed their appreciation of Dodge by hurrahing the town on a regular basis, and notorious toughs from all along the border rode into Dodge throughout the summer to take a shot at the Bibulous Babylon.

Some of these men Wyatt knew only by reputation: Ben Thompson, gone for the last nine months, was back in Dodge after a jaunt through Indian Territory; Shotgun Collins, the Wells Fargo express messenger, arrived from

Montana; Mysterious Dave Mather drifted in from Wyoming; Luke Short the gambler rode in from the Dakota line. Others, like Jack Bridges and Prairie Dog Morrow, Wyatt knew from the buffalo range. There was talk for a while that Clay Allison, the New Mexico shootist, would be moving in, but that turned out to be someone's whiskey talk that others passed along just to make things interesting.

From Wyatt's Wichita days came Rowdy Joe Lowe and his wife Rowdy Kate. Naturally enough, they built a dance hall on the south side, a place called the Green Front Saloon. Since getting kicked out of Wichita, Joe had run into some more trouble in Ellsworth.

"Bad luck, that's my problem," Rowdy Joe said. He seemed to be already halfway into a speech when he stopped Wyatt in front of the Lone Star. A peculiar way to say hello, Wyatt thought, after not seeing a man for two years. "Bad luck's been doggin' me every which way. First gettin' thrown outa Wichita. Hell, I gave back the bastard's nose. But no one cares. And then Ellsworth. More bad luck with that damn mule business."

"I heard you stole the mule," said Wyatt.

"Bad luck!" Rowdy Joe roared. "How'm I supposed to keep my business goin' with luck like that. And you know something else, Erb?"

"Earp," Wyatt corrected.

"You know something else?" Rowdy Joe continued. "How much you want to bet Rowdy Joe's luck runs out here in Dodge too? How much you want to bet?"

Before Wyatt could say whether or not he'd take up that bet, Rowdy Joe was ambling down the boardwalk, grumbling to himself. A shriek then cut through the air from the other side of the street, and Rowdy Joe crossed over to see what Rowdy Kate was up to.

As it turned out, Joe was right: he did run into more bad luck in Dodge. A month later, he was on his way to the next town after a fuss was made about his stabbing another man's horse in the neck for no particular reason.

In a way it was Rowdy Joe's leaving that led to Wyatt's becoming a deacon, although Bat had more to do with it than Joe did.

"Dodge is getting to be mighty persnickety," said Masterson the day after Rowdy Joe was run out. "Sending Lowe packing like that. Hell, he could've done a lot worse things than stabbing a horse and he didn't even get the chance to do 'em."

Wyatt gave him a sidelong look as they walked along the wooden planks that provided a makeshift bridge across mud-filled Front Street. He had a feeling Bat was kidding him, but he thought he'd play along. "Weren't you the one to tell Rowdy Joe to get out?"

"Sure, but I was just doing my job. Fact is, with reformers trying to bust up the south side and get rid of them that frequents it, folks have got to watch their step."

This was news to Wyatt. Last Tuesday night, he and Bat had had to haul in three cowboys riding their horses through Zimmerman's Hardware — through the side wall of Zimmerman's Hardware — and the next morning Judge Harrison let the drovers off when they promised to try to contain themselves from then on. Not exactly Wyatt's idea of clamping down real hard.

"Tell you the truth, Wyatt, I'd keep an eye on them reformers if I was you." Bat's advice stopped there for a moment as he stepped aside to avoid mud splashed by a passing freighter. He was the quickest man Wyatt had ever seen when it came to keeping his clothes clean. "Yeah, them reformers could really cut you down if you're not careful," Bat said.

"Now why would they do that if I was such a good friend of an upstanding fella like you?"

"Not something to fun about, Wyatt. I'm serious. If you figure to make your way around here you got to show what a respectable, forthright citizen you can be."

"Maybe I can become a parson," Wyatt said, his smirk hidden by his moustache.

"No, I don't think so," replied Bat. "Deacon is more like it, I think."

Not hearing anything worth responding to, Wyatt just kept walking. Bat kept after him.

"I mean it, Wyatt."

Wyatt laughed. "Whatever you say, Bat."

"I'm dead serious."

Wyatt stopped and searched his friend's face. If Bat was still kidding, he was really dragging it out — and was keeping up a damn good deadpan.

Bat said, "I didn't win a landslide victory as sheriff without knowing something about handling people, you know."

"Landslide? You won by three votes."

"And it would've been a sorry day for me if I didn't know how to rope in those three fellas."

Wyatt nodded his head slowly as he mulled this over. "Deacon, huh?"

"Let's you and me talk to Reverend Williams," said Bat. "We'll see what we can do."

Just to see what would happen, Wyatt decided to go along with Bat's suggestion.

By the next Sunday, Wyatt still wasn't sure if it was all a joke or not as he found himself standing in as the Union Church deacon at the morning service. His gambling friends were all there, attending church for the first time in years. Neal Brown, Cold Chuck Johnny, Luke Short, Hurricane Bill and a few of the others were all in the last two rows. As for Prairie Dog Morrow, Wyatt doubted he had ever been to church before. Reverend Williams' round, ruddy face beamed from behind the pulpit; he thought he had finally gotten through to the Dodge City sinners and brought them back to the fold, finally cut a swathe through the field of wickedness that was all around him. But the sinners were there only to get a look at Deacon Earp swaggering down the aisle during the sermon, the skirts of his coat drawn back to show the walnut handles of his Colts, the leather of his gun belt creaking as he strode through the church.

The joke might have been on him, Wyatt conceded, but now that it was really happening he found he didn't much care. It was a joke he could appreciate. He turned away from the reverend to hide the smile growing beneath his wax-tipped moustache. He made quite a sight, he knew that much.

His deaconship may have been good for a laugh inside the church, but outside it turned out to be a pure business deal. To Wyatt's surprise, the effect on the City Council was exactly what Bat had said it would be. Within a month the council promoted Wyatt to chief deputy marshal and awarded him another fifty dollars a month. Wyatt never doubted Bat after that.

Tobe Driskill's cow camp was pitched west of Dodge along the Arkansas River. While Driskill dickered over the selling price of the beeves, the first shift left for town to get their chance to spend their month's pay in a day's time. That left a handful of men to tend to the herd, a handful of men to do all the work while everyone else got to live high and easy. And that was just typical, according to Ike Clanton who was tired of working his butt off, while the rest of the cowhands got the whiskey, the cards and the whores.

To be exact, the only thing Ike was working on now was a bottle of bourbon. But then what was the harm in that, he told himself. If I have to sweat out another day — or maybe two if the first shift doesn't make it back in time — then I damn well deserve a good drink. Pretty smart on my part to slip this bottle out of Driskill's wagon last week; otherwise I would be dry as could be.

The two horses pounded past and sped toward the finishing line marked by the end of the chuck wagon. That show-off kid Hoyt was riding along the side of his sorrel, hanging on the way he had seen Comanche horsemen do along the Mexican border. And damned if the kid didn't beat the other man, who was riding straight-up like a white man should.

That called for another drink. Ike tilted the bottle and gulped three times, the fine bourbon going down as smooth as hot silk. The kid's winning made it two bets in a row that Ike took in. Fifteen more dollars for the lucky girl who would get her chance with him in town, he figured.

Squatting next to Ike, Phil Benton shook his head — he was the man betting against Ike. Turning toward Clanton, he said, "What do you say, Ike? Think you can spare a swig of that good whiskey for a beaten man?"

Ike looked at him sideways. "Phil, let me ask you a question. Now I've been totin' this bottle around for a whole week, keepin' it hidden so's nobody would swipe it and so old man Driskill wouldn't find it. And now I finally get my chance to enjoy it, and I'm supposed to give it to *you*? Doesn't that sound just a tad stupid to you?"

"I didn't ask for the whole damn bottle. I just want a drink. I'm dry. I've been dry for three months."

Ike relented. "All right, here you go. But just a gulp. And don't let Driskill know that I've been hidin' it."

If he wasn't so damn dry, Phil would've spat in that damn Clanton's face. But he knew, just as Ike knew, that Ike held all the cards. He took his gulp.

Hoyt flopped down beside Ike. "I won for ya good, didn't I, Ike? How about that?"

Ike passed the bottle to the big-eared kid, which was cheaper than cutting him in on the bet winnings. "George, did you really see Comanches ride like that?" Ike asked.

"Well," George Hoyt said, obviously stalling, "not really seen exactly. My brother, he told me about it. He rode with the Texas Rangers. He fought them Comanches plenty."

Ike smiled. The kid was dumb, but he was good for a laugh. Like the time Ike got the kid to try to buy a poke with that yellow-haired girl in San Antonio, when Ike knew full well that she belonged to the two-gun pimp sitting right there at the table with her. That sure started a hell of a fight.

"Hey George," Ike said, "I hear there's some Comanches that ride standin' up. Standin' right straight up on the saddle."

Hoyt looked at Ike for a while, then said, "No. They do not."

"Sure do. They can go full tilt, standin' there on the saddle and not even lose their balance."

"A feller can do that?"

Ike could see the kid was already halfway there. "Pure fact. They start doin' it when they're little. They grow up on it."

Hoyt scratched his head. "My brother never told me none of that."

"You know what, George? A horseman like you, you could probably do it the first time you try it."

Seeing where Ike was headed, Benton shook his head, got up and walked away. Hoyt didn't seem to notice he had left. The kid was too busy thinking.

Pretty soon there was no more thinking about it. A couple more drinks and Ike had Hoyt lined up against another rider for the next race. Hoyt climbed onto the horse, trying to find his footing on the saddle. One of the other cowboys wanted Ike to bet on Hoyt again, but he turned it down this time. "This one's just for fun," Ike said, smiling.

That was a decision Ike soon regretted. Hoyt was wobbly at first, and for a second there he looked like he might fall off altogether, but he straightened up, holding the reins from a standing position, and slipped past his opponent just before the finish line.

When Hoyt scrambled off the horse and came walking back, Ike shook his head and smiled. "You beat all, kid," he said. He let Hoyt have another drink.

"I just might come ridin' into Dodge tomorrow like that," said Hoyt. "What do you think of that, Ike?"

"I think you just might be loco enough to do it."

"We are going to have us a time when we get there."
Hoyt took another drink and let loose a rebel yell.

Talk of Dodge started souring Ike again. "By rights I
should be there now. I done my fair share on this drive,
and then some, damn it."

"Don't you worry, Ike. We'll tree this here Dodge City.
All them women — they best hide themselves when they
see us comin'."

"Yeah, we'll tree it all right," said Ike. "Just as long as
that damn Earp don't get in our way."

"Who's this Earp?"

"Some fightin' pimp from Wichita. I hear tell he's
workin' Dodge now. A blind-sidin' son of a bitch is what
he is. About time somebody took him down a notch."

"You gonna take him, Ike?" Hoyt looked at Ike wide-
eyed.

"I'm just sayin' someone oughta, is all. Someone
oughta. I'm not sayin' who exactly."

Hoyt scratched himself as he thought this over. "That
mean you got some kinda plan, Ike? About takin' Earp?"

"What's the matter with you, you dumb shit! I just said
someone oughta! That's all!"

Hoyt should have been insulted, but he just stared at
Ike, his brow furrowed in thought. Finally he decided,
"The hell with this damn Earp."

Curly Bill came over to Hoyt from the remuda. He
shoved the kid hard. Hoyt made a big noise as he hit the
ground in a sprawl.

"Get out!" Curly Bill Brocius said.

Hoyt didn't consider questioning Curly Bill. He got up
in a hurry and left, not even bothering to look back.

"What are you doin', Curly Bill?" said Ike. "What'd
the kid do?"

"What've you been talkin' to him about?" said Curly
Bill, his square face still red with anger.

"We was just talkin'. Just passin' time." Ike already
realized what he had done, even if he wouldn't own up.

"You was talkin' about that Earp. I heard ya."

"Sure. I was tellin' him what a blind-sider he is."

Curly Bill got close to Ike. "You tell him what Earp done to us in Wichita I'll break your neck."

"I didn't do that," Ike said quickly. "I don't want to tell nobody that. We swore about that. I'm not tellin'."

"You're not lyin' to me, Ike." It was not a question. It was a plain threat.

"Swear to God, Curly Bill. Swear to God. I ain't lyin'."

Curly Bill stared at Ike, then wiped the sweat running off his broken nose and stepped away.

"You got no call to worry," said Ike. "When we go to town, we'll just steer clear of Earp. It won't never come up. Easy, right?"

Curly Bill turned to Ike. He wasn't glowering anymore. His face didn't show anything at all.

"The hell we'll stay away from him," Curly Bill said.

16

Wyatt first saw Doc Holliday outside the Great Western Hotel.

He and Bat had just run Mike Roarke to earth along the Arkansas River and had brought him back to Dodge on charges of taking part in the Kinsley train robbery. The ride had been hard, part of it through a hailstorm out on the open prairie, and after stashing Roarke in the calaboose, Wyatt was planning on nothing but a beer at the Long Branch and a day or two of sleep. He had noticed the skinny man in the gray tailored suit stepping out of the Great Western, but hadn't given him much thought at first. Bat pointed him out and told Wyatt who the man was.

"Doc Holliday — the man-killer?" said Wyatt incredulously.

"That's the one. I just got the word about him."

Wyatt wasn't sure how Bat had found out. Since coming back to Dodge with Roarke in tow, he had been with Masterson almost the whole time, except for a few minutes at Ham Bell's livery. Wyatt had waited outside with the prisoner while Bat had gone into the stable to put up their mounts. But then a few minutes was a lot of time for Bat to find out anything he needed to know.

Looking at the man standing in front of the south-side hotel, Wyatt still found it hard to believe it was Holliday. The man had moved gingerly on his way out the hotel door and he looked as if a strong wind just might blow him over. Wyatt couldn't see much of the man's face from halfway across the plaza, only the pale tone of his skin.

Wyatt said, "Looks kind of feeble for a gunman."

"Might be," replied Bat, "but I heard he wasn't too feeble with his gun down to Texas. Heard he left there just a jump and a holler ahead of a lynch mob. I guess they take exception to murder in Texas, too." Bat turned and started walking away. "I think that Holliday can stand some checking up on."

Bat wasn't the only one who thought it was a good idea to keep tabs on Doc Holliday. Before Wyatt and Bat had finished their first beers at the Long Branch, Charlie Bassett came in and stepped over to their table. He wanted Wyatt to find out what the newcomer did and where he went the next few days.

"What's the fuss?" asked Wyatt. "It isn't as if Holliday is the first gun-thrower to come to town. Not by a long ways."

"That's not it," said Charlie. "We've had others who came here with a reputation, but there was usually somebody who could vouch for them. Hell, Bat here could say something in Ben Thompson's favor and sure enough he didn't give us any trouble. But this fella — nobody even seems to know him except by what they hear."

"Then maybe he's nothing to worry about." Wyatt knew it must have sounded like a lame remark, but the fact was he was just too tired now to think about following some skinny gambler around town.

Charlie shook his head. "I don't know what'll set him

off. And I don't know anyone else who does neither. If he settles in after a few days then you can leave him be."

After a bath and the time it took to put on some fresh clothes, Wyatt started off by going to the Great Western. Dick Paxton was sitting behind the desk, gazing idly across the empty lobby as he sucked his teeth. He obviously had nothing to do but talk.

"Holliday ain't been back yet," was his answer to Wyatt's first question. Looking disgustedly at the empty lobby, he added, "And don't expect I'd miss him in this crowd. Did see his woman, though."

"She staying with him?"

"Sure is. She come to Dodge with him. All the way from Texas, around Fort Griffin I think she said. Look here." He pushed the register toward Wyatt. "Look how they signed in: Mr. and Mrs. John Holliday. How do you like that? Him a family man. A feller like that!"

"Who's the wife?"

"The name's Kate. I hear she was a sportin' woman. Used to be on the line down to Texas."

"What has he been doing since he got here?"

"Not much that I can see. Of course, I don't got the time to keep track of every mother's son that checks in." Quickly Paxton scowled, to fend off an expected remark. "Not every day's as slow as this, you know," he pointed out. "Usually this here lobby's crawlin' with high-rollers and such. One thing about Holliday, though. Kind of funny."

Paxton reached for something under the desk. "He asked me if I'd put this up out front. Let me show you. He wanted me to hook it onto the overhang out there."

Paxton handed over the sign, the sort that announces a small business. The wood was slightly weathered and flakes of rust had collected on the two hooks at the top. Some of the black paint had faded inside the professionally chiseled letters, but it was still plain to read.

"Him a dentist," Paxton laughed. "Said he would like a

room to rent as an office in back. It's a joke, right Wyatt?''

Wyatt examined the sign. At the bottom it read: "Where Satisfaction Is Not Given, Money Will Be Refunded.'' Wyatt glanced up at Paxton. "You think it's a joke, Dick?'' he asked blandly.

"I knew a feller called Doc once. Doc Evans, over to Ellsworth. We called him Doc because he could fix a lame horse like nobody's business. What do you think, Wyatt? You think Doc Holliday fixes horses?''

"If he does, he might do some business here. I know I wouldn't ask him to pull my teeth.''

After nightfall, Wyatt made the rounds, checking the saloons to locate Holliday. One thing he had heard about the man was that he liked his whiskey — bourbon, rye or any kind he could find. Wyatt went through the north side saloons without any luck, then crossed the Dead Line to the Varieties Dance Hall. In the gambling room off the dance floor he saw Doc Holliday at a table, playing poker head-to-head with Bill Forrest, a discharged Army corporal from Fort Dodge.

Wyatt posted himself against the wall behind the ex-trooper so that he had a clear look at Holliday. He saw no reason to hide the fact that he was watching. He had a feeling the skinny gambler was used to this kind of treatment when he came into a new town.

One thing was for certain: Holliday was no stranger to cards. Sweeping up the cards at the end of a play, his thin, white hands worked nimbly, stacking and cutting the pasteboards with swift, deft motions and shuffling rapidly without taking his eyes off Forrest. The eyes seemed to bore into his opponent, and Wyatt had no doubt that the trooper was returning the look for all it was worth. This game was not being played for fun.

Looking past Forrest, Holliday saw Wyatt facing him. The features of Holliday's face were fine, but drawn and pallid. The blue eyes stared at Wyatt with an unhealthy glow, and beneath the man's moustache Wyatt could see the corner of the mouth curl up in a lopsided smile. Holliday almost looked as if he recognized Wyatt. The gambler then quickly executed a flourish, riffling the deck in an arc from one hand to the other.

"Play the goddamn game," Forrest growled.

Holliday looked squarely at him, but didn't bother to reply. He let Forrest cut the deck, then dealt the hands.

Discards for the hand were placed in the deadwood in the center of the table. When Forrest put one of his cards there he dragged his hand along one of the other cards, just long enough to sneak a look at it.

His hand didn't linger long on the card; some people might not have paid any attention to it, but to a trained gambler it was obvious — obvious and damned sloppy. But then, Bill Forrest wasn't known for his skill at cards. He wasn't known for his skill at much of anything.

Holliday sat perfectly still. He stared at the trooper, who shifted his weight in the chair and tried acting as if nothing had happened. Holliday then slowly placed his cards down on the table.

"You out?" Forrest said lightly.

"No, but you are," replied Doc in a Southern drawl.

Wyatt considered stepping in to nip this in the bud, but he couldn't see any gun on Holliday, and if Forrest tried anything Wyatt figured he could reach him before the trooper could do any damage. Besides, moving in on another man's game was meddling, no matter how you looked at it, even for a chief deputy marshal.

"Play your hand, Holliday," said Forrest.

"You tinkered with the deadwood. And you tinkered with it once before that."

"Play your hand."

Holliday leaned just slightly forward. "You tinker with the deadwood, you forfeit the hand," Holliday said quietly. "I told you before."

Taking his eyes off Forrest, Holliday reached for the pot

of money and brought it over to his winnings pile. He fingered through the money to see how much he had. Wyatt thought he was being careless.

"The game is over," Holliday announced.

"What did you say?" Forrest was inching his right shoulder away from his opponent. "Just what the hell did you say, you skinny bastard? Do you think you make the rules?"

"The rules are plain enough."

"I been playing here six months, Holliday. Everyone knows me here."

"I expect they do."

"They all know I gamble clean. You come around here, you make your own damn rules. What the hell sort of damn play is that —"

Already tensed, Wyatt was quick to notice the first movement of Forrest's right arm as the elbow bent and the hand curled toward the small of the back. He was already moving when Forrest grabbed the Remington out of his waistband. Wyatt lunged forward, reaching for Forrest's arm.

That's when Holliday pulled out the knife.

It had an eight-inch blade and had been hidden in a vest pocket that was specially tailored to conceal it. With surprising quickness, the frail Holliday jumped to the side of the table and lunged toward Forrest.

Holding himself back to avoid stepping between a gun and a knife, Wyatt watched as Forrest fired. His gun boomed with deafening force inside the small room and sent a bullet through the far wall. If Cold Chuck Johnny hadn't flattened to the floor he would have been hit. Holliday moved in to make sure there wasn't a second shot.

He cut Forrest just below the sternum and rammed the knife in to its hilt. Taking hold with both hands, he turned the knife and sliced open the stomach in a vicious, jagged line down to the left hip.

Forrest was hunched forward, a sickening wheeze coming out of his mouth, his body still held up by Holliday's grip on the knife hilt. Swiftly reversing his motion, Holliday then ripped the knife out. Forrest wobbled down to the floor on both knees, then slumped down to his side, his eyes cold and wide open, a bulge of intestines showing through the wound.

Like everyone else in the room, Wyatt was frozen in place. The killing seemed to happen too fast to comprehend. He found himself stepping closer to Holliday. "Give me the knife," he said, hearing his words as if they were spoken by someone else.

Holliday didn't seem to hear him. He drew the side of his blade slowly across the rim of the table to wipe the blood off, then mopped it clean with his handkerchief. Wyatt wondered why the handkerchief was stained with blood before Holliday used it on the knife.

The blade clean, Holliday handed it to Wyatt, hilt-first, and said, "I'm ready." He led the way out of the room.

17

Wyatt ran the brim of his hat through his fingers, working the hat around full circle before he forced himself to put it in his lap. Shifting in the wooden witness chair, he tried to make himself comfortable and failed whichever way he sat. Willing himself to stop, he then fought the impulse to mop his brow.

The air in the courtroom was hot, damp and motionless, the open windows letting in no breeze. For all the discomfort, though, the trial was still the best show in town that day, and the spectator section was almost filled. At least some of the townspeople had their jackets off, Wyatt thought. A justice of the peace's son, Wyatt never gave a second thought to dressing in suit, vest and tie for the occasion. His father would always put on his best suit to carry out any of his duties, regardless of whether it was a wedding or a dispute over a pile of fertilizer straddling the line between two properties. "Honor befitting the law," was how he had put it. In this damnable heat, Wyatt hadn't considered dressing any other way although now he would have gladly gone barechested if given the chance. Another act of will kept him from cursing his father under his breath.

Wyatt waited some more for the defense attorney to finish going through his notes. The county prosecutor objected to the delay, an objection Wyatt would have seconded if anyone had asked, and the two lawyers went at it again. Wyatt was beginning to think that maybe Bat was right about not bothering to testify.

"Let the miserable son of a bitch take his chances without you," Bat had said the night before at the Long Branch.

"I saw what happened," Wyatt said. "Why shouldn't I testify?"

"Because he's an ill-tempered, cold-blooded misfit and the little I've seen of him makes me think he should be locked up on general principle. That a good enough reason?"

"I'll say my piece," was all Wyatt answered.

Bat shook his head and left it at that.

Judge Harrison finally put a stop to the lawyers' jabbering, but the defense attorney then wasted some more time by consulting with his client.

Whenever lawyer Frank Lillis took on a client, he managed to stretch an open-and-shut case into hours of courthouse wrangling. He was one of the first lawyers to set up practice in Dodge, but to his great annoyance he found he spent most of his time tending to his business interests in Zimmerman's Hardware rather than going to court. To make up for that, he prolonged court appearances for all they were worth.

"Get on with it," the judge told Lillis.

"May I remind the court," said lawyer Lillis, "of my client's right to the full benefit of my legal advice."

"May I remind the attorney for the defense that if he doesn't get to it I'm going to have him taken out and bullwhipped."

Unflustered, Lillis straightened his lapels and walked away from his client, leaving Doc Holliday to stare at Wyatt on the witness chair. Holliday sat intently at the defense table, resting forward on his elbows. There was no sign of anxiety as he took in his own trial for murder; there was only keen interest.

"Mr. Earp, to continue, please describe the events of last night, following the exchange of words between my client and William Forrest," said Lillis.

"Well, the other fella, Forrest, he went for his gun and then Holliday took out the knife."

"Let me make sure this is absolutely clear to the jury. William Forrest brought out his pistol before my client armed himself?"

"Yes, that's right."

"Go on, Mr. Earp. Please."

"Then Holliday killed Forrest with the knife. He did it in self-defense."

Lillis waited for some elaboration. When none came, he scanned his notes, then looked at Wyatt in disappointment. This was too easy. Even Lillis could see there was no point in furthering the examination.

"You are absolutely certain of all this?" he said, for lack of anything else to ask.

"Yes," Wyatt answered.

Lillis grudgingly relinquished the floor to the prosecutor.

The county attorney tried to find discrepancies in Wyatt's testimony through a series of questions about minute details of the incident but Wyatt never stumbled in his account.

Throughout the cross-examination, Wyatt felt a steady gaze upon him. Whenever he glanced at Holliday, he saw him looking straight at him, as if studying him, always in the same position, never moving. Once he saw the killer dentist smile coldly at him, amused by God knows what.

To Wyatt's relief, once all the evidence was presented,

the jury deliberated for only half an hour before returning to the courtroom. Sitting in the back row of the spectator section, the back of his jacket already soaked through with sweat, he waited for the decision.

"Has the jury reached a verdict?" Judge Harrison asked.

"Sure have," said Prairie Dog Morrow, foreman of the jury.

"What is the verdict?"

"He done it fair and square. In self-defense."

"Not guilty?"

"That's it," said Prairie Dog.

"Well done," said the judge. "The charge against the defendant is hereby dismissed. I want to thank the jury for its dedication to civic duty." He turned to Holliday. "I also want to thank the defendant for his gentlemanly behavior during the trial. Your deportment, Mr. Holliday, could serve as a model for future defendants in this court-room. I can only hope that they follow your example in conducting themselves with dignity and not busting up the furniture. All right, everybody, you go on home."

Wyatt walked his best racing horse one more time across the lot behind the Dodge House. In the cool night air, the animal breathed easily, showing no signs of the limp that Wyatt thought he had noticed two days before. He brought the big bay mare to a stop, stroked her neck and spoke quietly. "No one's getting the best of you," he said.

Kneeling, Wyatt checked the front, left leg just to make sure. There was nothing he could see or feel. "You were just dogging it, weren't you?" he said. "You don't like working in this damn heat no more than anybody else does."

"Good evening, Marshal," The voice came from behind Wyatt. It was a quiet voice, but it intruded abruptly in the still night.

Wyatt turned around slowly, his hand covering the Colt on his right hip. The figure stood ten feet away in total blackness, then stepped forward into the yellow light thrown by the rear window of the hotel.

"Hello, Doc," Wyatt said.

Holliday took a moment to look at the bay. The pale light left his hollowed cheeks in darkness, making his face appear hatchet-shaped.

"I hear there's to be a race along the Arkansas tomorrow," Doc said matter of factly. "Some good money is already piling up on your side."

"I like to think that's the smart money," said Wyatt.

"You did a good job for me in court today." Doc didn't even pause before changing the subject.

Wyatt didn't bother to answer. He was looking at Doc, trying to imagine this soft-spoken man as the killer who gutted Bill Forrest just the day before.

"I just told the truth," Wyatt finally said.

"I know that. But my lawyer told me no one else came forward to tell the truth. You could have just let it slide and watched them run me out of town — or done it yourself."

"That probably wouldn't have happened," said Wyatt. "You picked the right man to kill. Forrest was a no-account runt. Nobody was too troubled when he died."

"I just wanted to thank you, that's all."

Wyatt shrugged as he adjusted the bridle on the bay. "Just doing my duty as a peace officer."

"Horse shit."

Wyatt turned to him.

"That's no big concern to you," said Doc.

Not about to answer that, Wyatt took hold of the bridle and led the horse away. He stopped when he heard the coughing.

Doc's wasted body was wrenched forward as the coughs started coming in rapid succession, loud and racking. He fumbled quickly inside his jacket pocket, pulled out a handkerchief and held it to his mouth.

The coughing subsided after a while. Turning away, Doc wiped his mouth and slipped the handkerchief back into his pocket. Wyatt thought he saw a dark spot on the handkerchief, like the blood stain he had noticed the night before at the Varieties.

"You all right?" Wyatt asked.

Doc was able to bring himself upright again. "It's all right," he said, forcing a thin smile. "Just consumption, that's all."

"How long have you had it?"

"Long enough. They tell me this dry air is helping me." Doc suddenly grimaced and grabbed his chest. His knees buckling, he looked like he was going to drop. Wyatt hurried over to take hold of his arm and keep him on his feet. The arm he grasped was nothing but bone and sinew.

Doc braced himself, his eyes closed, and waited for the pain to fade. Soon he was able to let up. Regaining his footing and his composure, he slipped his arm out of Wyatt's hand and walked unsteadily for a few steps. His face was ashen.

Wyatt let him walk off by himself. A neighbor in Lamar had had consumption and from what Wyatt had seen then he knew there wasn't much point in taking Holliday to a doctor.

He busied himself with the bay, glancing occasionally to see Doc standing to one side, looking off toward the northern edge of town, taking out a flask and drinking a few swallows.

Doc said, "I got an idea why you stood up for me in court today."

"What would that be?"

"I've got a feeling the two of us have got something in common."

Wyatt looked at Doc and the wasted man met his gaze.

"You can think what you want," said Wyatt. He took a currycomb from his pocket and worked on the horse's coat.

"Wyatt Earp," said Doc. "Always a good man with a horse."

Doc sounded like he was enjoying himself, as if this was

some kind of game. An uneasy feeling stirred in Wyatt's stomach.

"A marshal told me that," Doc went on. "You see, I had to ride up through Indian Territory to come to Dodge."

Wyatt stopped brushing the horse.

Doc said, "U.S. Marshal J.G. Owen was the man's name. He said he knew you, you and a couple of friends of yours. He knew you between Fort Gibson and Fort Smith. Then it seems he just lost track of you."

Wyatt looked straight at Doc, trying to show nothing.

"Don't worry, Wyatt. I'm on your side. I didn't get along with that son-of-a-bitch marshal either." Doc smiled, then touched the brim of his hat. "I'll be going now," he said. "Good night, Deacon. I'll be seeing you." He walked off.

"I'll be seeing you," said Wyatt.

18

Wyatt heard about the three cowboys early in the evening.

Bob Wright told him they were drinking hard at Hoover's and were making talk about treeing the town. "I just thought I better tell you fellas," said Wright. "They sounded like they meant business."

Wyatt turned the next play at the faro table. "Are they heeled?" he asked.

"Hoover got them to check their guns. At least for now."

"Doesn't sound like they can make much trouble like that," Wyatt said.

Bat agreed. "They'll probably be tame enough, Bob. But we'll check on them anyway. They just might take their guns with them when they leave Hoover's."

"You'll be checking?" Wright said hopefully. "They're just a couple doors down from my store, you know. My place could be the first one they light into."

"I'll take a stroll by there," Bat said. "Wyatt here, he's working, but we'll be checking in later on, the both of us."

Wright seemed satisfied and left the Lady Gay to take a look at his store before heading home.

Wyatt finished his stint at the faro table at nine. Not having heard anything from Bat, he assumed the cowboys at Hoover's didn't amount to anything. For his part, the biggest problem that night had been the arrival of Mysterious Dave Mather.

"He's on the prowl tonight," a drover at Wyatt's table had said, glancing furtively at Mather on the other side of the room. "I hear he's gonna kill himself a trooper tonight."

The talk was the same at the other tables and some gaming men were just edgy enough to get up and leave rather than wait for the fight. The others, though, couldn't be dragged from their seats. They weren't about to miss Mather's first murder in Dodge.

But Mysterious Dave wouldn't oblige tonight. He walked through the place, sat in for a few hands of stud poker, then was on his way without so much as an angry word.

"He ain't primed yet," the drover at Wyatt's table explained. What that meant the cowboy didn't bother to explain. The others at the table just looked at the drover in disgust, as if it were his fault Mather didn't shoot anybody.

The night was warm, but a breeze was picking up off the Arkansas to stir the air. Downwind of Ham Bell's livery, Wyatt didn't appreciate the breeze very much and started walking along Front Street to get clear of the dung smell.

Crossing the entrance to Ham Bell's place, he saw a drover leading a pair of horses out of the stable. He was a tall man, powerfully built, dressed in a vest, shirt and trousers that looked like they were fresh off the shelves of Wright and Beverly's. The creases where they had been folded were still sharp.

Something about the man caught Wyatt's attention immediately. The cowboy didn't wear a gun belt, but there was something about his stance, the way his free hand dangled, the cast of the deep-set eyes. Most gunmen Wyatt had known seemed to have light eyes — blue, gray or something in between — usually hard and piercing. This man's eyes were dark — black in this light — but they were hard as glass, unrelenting. Those eyes have watched men die, Wyatt thought, and not just once.

Something about the man reminded Wyatt of Turkey Creek's friend Johnny Green. There was that, and something else that Wyatt didn't like but couldn't put a finger on.

Wyatt stopped to take out a cigar and light up. As he took out the match from his vest pocket, he made a point of pulling back his jacket so that the man at the stable could see the chief deputy marshal badge. With the cigar fired up, Wyatt glanced over once more. The cowboy paid the stable boy, picked up a saddle from the ground, hefted it easily onto the back of a dun and half-turned to Wyatt. He watched the lawman closely, then pulled the cinch tight.

Wyatt crossed the Dead Line and started his patrol along the north side. He passed the Alamo, Long Branch and Hoover saloons and, seeing they were still fairly quiet, he checked Wright and Beverly's. Open late tonight, the store was catering to drovers fresh from the trail who got a late jump from the cow camps. Looking in, Wyatt saw Mr. Samuels and Mr. Isaacson fitting a vaquero with a new set of clothes. Mr. Samuels talked to the young Mexican in Spanish to get his tailoring requests, which he then relayed to Mr. Isaacson who was marking the sleeves with pins. The haberdashers talked to each other in their own strange language, not Spanish, not German. Bob Wright said it was a kind of Hebrew that Jews spoke in Europe.

Wyatt walked up Bridge Avenue and turned on Chestnut to check the *Dodge City Times* office and, doubling back, he looked in on the competition, the *Ford County Globe*. Both offices were empty and so was the street. Wyatt stopped to relight his cigar. He lazed for a few moments as he looked at the light of the three-quarter moon slanting against the houses along the north side, brightened here and there by the Plaza's lamps. He considered going back to the Dodge House to stretch out and rest his feet until the night life really picked up. That's when the first gunshot cracked.

A cowboy whoop followed, then another gunshot, coming from the Plaza. Tossing his cigar aside, Wyatt ran to the corner. Horse hoofs drummed along the dry, packed earth of Front Street, then pounded around a corner toward Chestnut. Wyatt saw three horsemen, silhouetted by the lights of the Plaza, their guns glistening in their hands, galloping in his direction.

Wyatt's Colt was drawn. He made no conscious decision about it. His hand just grabbed for it some time after he had started running. He braced himself at the side of the street as the cowboys raced toward him. In the moonlight he now saw Curly Bill's square, ugly face above the head of the lead horse. The cowboy swung his gun around. Just as the gun fired, Wyatt saw Ike Clanton's face behind Curly Bill.

Throwing himself to the ground, Wyatt heard the shot pelt the earth next to his head. Dirt flew into his eyes, blinding him. Without hesitation, he rolled across the ground, over and over, toward the near lot. Gunfire exploded in a rapid-fire barrage. The ground was peppered on all sides of him.

Wyatt rolled, then scrambled, then dove to the rear corner of Wright and Beverly's. His blood racing, he quickly wiped the dirt from his eyes and saw the three cowboys round the corner toward his side of the building. Wyatt snapped off two shots, hitting nothing, and saw the cowboys draw their spare guns. In the instant before they cut loose again, the third rider's horse reared. In the saddle of that horse was the big man from Ham Bell's livery.

As the three-gun volley started, Wyatt ran along Chestnut Street and flung himself behind a water trough.

The tattoo of bullets splintered the wood and a single shot whined as it ricocheted off a metal corner brace. Wyatt hugged the ground, then heard the gunfire stop, to be replaced by the beat of hoofs. He heard the horses draw close, to the left. The hairs on the back of his head bristled as he heard another horse close in on the other side. Two horses on the left and one on the right. They were going to flank him on both sides and cut him down in the crossfire. Thinking he was going to die, Wyatt quickly grabbed his second Colt and steeled himself to give them his worst before he went down.

The next barrage thundered, searing past Wyatt from both sides. The ground seemed to shake with the force of the hail of bullets. As the sound of the gunshots got closer and shifted toward Wyatt's side of the trough, he plunged to his left, landed on his shoulder and leveled both Colts at once.

Before he fired, he heard the stray shot, a gunblast that didn't fit in with the volley that had been bearing down on him. The shot came from the right, the subtle difference in its sound giving Wyatt the split-second impression that it was not aimed at the trough. With Ike Clanton in his sights, Wyatt saw the horse beneath the cowboy lurch and flop to its side. The stray shot Wyatt had heard now left Ike without a mount.

Out of the corner of his eye Wyatt saw the source of the shot. Doc Holliday stood to his right. His nickel-plated Colt was smoking from its first discharge, and was now spitting the flame of its second round. Wyatt didn't hesitate any longer. He fired at Ike Clanton. The shot went high as Clanton flattened himself behind his downed horse. Hoofs drummed as Curly Bill rode hard toward Ike's side. Wyatt lined up on Brocius, but gunfire from the other side pitted the ground next to his head and made him roll away. The big stranger was firing fast to cover for his friends, triggering so swiftly that he was able to drive Doc to cover as well.

In the few seconds that Wyatt and Doc had to lie low, Curly Bill managed to pull Ike onto the back of his horse and spurred away along Chestnut. Wyatt and Doc squeezed off a few more rounds, but the horses galloped out of range, heading west out of town.

Wyatt watched them over the barrel of his gun, holding still as the hoofbeats receded into the distance. Slowly, reluctantly, he let his gun-hand drop. The delayed reaction then set in. He could feel himself shaking, not just his hands, but his arms and his legs too. He stared at the horsemen racing toward the horizon, telling himself to do something, but knowing there was little to accomplish.

"With that kind of jump they'd be hard to catch." It was Doc's voice. Wyatt turned suddenly to find Holliday standing next to him. "Leastways," Doc continued, "you probably couldn't catch them before they reached the cow camp. With all their friends around your badge wouldn't mean very much. Not out there." Doc laughed dryly. "Hell of a thing for me to tell you not to kill some bastards."

Wyatt kept staring down Chestnut. The riders had now been swallowed up by the darkness outside Dodge. Doc was right. In the cow camp Wyatt would really be up against it. He hated the idea, but his best chance was to wait till they came back to town. If they were stupid enough to try it again.

He turned to see Doc placing a cigar in his mouth. The wasted man held out another one for Wyatt. "This might help," he said.

Wyatt gratefully took the cigar. After lighting up, he drew the smoke in several times and waited for some of the shaking to stop before he got around to saying what needed to be said.

"Thanks for saving me, Doc."

Doc took an extra few puffs, turning his cigar slowly above the match to make sure the tip was evenly lit. "No need to thank me," he said. "It was purely a matter of self-interest on my part."

"What does that mean?"

"Well, I might need you to testify for me again. People believe you, Wyatt. And now I figure you're liable to oblige. One favor deserves another. And who's to say I couldn't do you another turn also."

"You make it sound like a business proposition," said Wyatt.

"Business, that's your lookout, Wyatt. I'm just here to get along." Doc smiled, his pale eyes taking on a glint, as if sharing a good joke with Wyatt.

"Well, Wyatt," said Doc, "I haven't gotten drunk for several hours. You care to join me?"

Wyatt wasn't sure what sort of drinking company Doc would make, but nothing sounded better now than a bottle of whiskey. "Let's go," said Wyatt.

As they started walking toward Front Street, Doc asked, "Any special reason those boys were shooting at you before? Or was it just for the usual bonehead cowboy reasons."

"Two of them I knew," said Wyatt. "Name of Clanton and Curly Bill. I know them from Wichita." Wyatt didn't go any further than that.

Doc nodded. "And just how foolish did you make those jaspers look in Wichita?"

Wyatt shrugged.

"I guess that means you didn't know the third one," said Doc.

"I just saw him tonight for the first time. Just before they jumped me."

"Maybe you ought to know him, Wyatt."

"Why's that?"

"He's John Ringo. The Texas gunman."

Wyatt turned to him, looked at him intently.

"That's right," Doc said. "*The* Texas gunman."

Wyatt nodded. "Now I know."

19

Under the scorching July sun it turned out to be a relief to lie beneath the wagon, even if it meant wrestling with the cracked axle. The ground wasn't exactly cool under there, but at least it didn't burn a man's bare back and was just comfortable enough for Virgil to toy with the idea of snoozing for a bit in the wagon's shade. He might have actually done it if he didn't think Allie would be coming by to see how the job was going. He couldn't put off fixing the axle any longer.

They needed the wagon for a trip to Council Bluffs to stock up. Supplies were running low — not dangerously low, but there was no sense in letting them get depleted any more. On top of that, Allie was starting to complain about not having a new bolt of calico with which to finish her dress. Virgil couldn't blame her. She had let her dress-making slide for two weeks without saying anything. "I'll pick up the calico when I go into town for supplies," he kept saying. That, of course, meant fixing the wagon and Virgil was always finding other chores that had to be done first. And some of those chores he didn't do either.

"How does it look?" Allie asked.

Virgil turned to see his wife's feet at the rear of the wagon. She knelt down to take a look at him. "Can you shore it up?" she asked.

"A few slats should do it, at least for a while."

She smiled at him, then got up and walked off to tend to the chickens. He watched the back of her strong, lean frame as she crossed the yard.

They never talked about it, but Virgil had a feeling that she suspected what had been going through his mind these past couple of months. Any woman who would put up with his laziness lately would have to be understanding. Either that or not have a mind of her own, and Allie definitely had a mind of her own. The way she prodded him without nagging him told Virgil that she must have some idea.

The freighting business had been good for a while, but once he had it running smoothly, Virgil had tired of it and sold his interest in the line. Since then he had been farming, and now he was wondering if he had made a mistake. Mike Mullin had already asked if he wanted to buy back into the freighting line. At times the proposition sounded tempting. Even so, another notion was holding Virgil back.

Virgil lined up the axle, set it straight and drove the first nail through the slat to shore up the cracked section. The clip-clop of hoofs drifted toward him from somewhere behind his head. Since the sound came from the northwest, his first thought was that it was one of the Schafer boys coming around to ask for help putting up the roof on the barn. Virgil finished with the second and third nails before it occurred to him that the rider might be somebody else. He calculated quickly. His last letter had been posted well over a month ago, he figured, maybe as long as two months by now. That would surely be enough time.

"Do you see the rider?" Allie called.

Virgil crawled quickly out from underneath the wagon to take a look.

The rider was still some fifty yards off. Moving at a sluggish walk, he looked like he had been traveling a long way. Virgil walked toward him to cut down the distance. Normally, he would have called out to make the horseman identify himself before letting him come any closer, but he had too strong a feeling about this.

While the set of the rider's shoulders was familiar, the head was slouched forward tiredly, making it impossible to get a good look at the face. "Morgan?" Virgil called.

Morgan looked up and smiled weakly at his older brother.

"Allie, he's here!" Virgil called back over his shoulder.

When Morgan reached him, Virgil could see his brother's sickly, pale complexion. He also saw a patch of moisture oozing through the white shirt at Morgan's left shoulder, a pale yellow circle speckled with red.

"Good God, what happened to you?" Virgil said.

"I think it just opened up," said Morgan, his voice thin. "A couple of miles back or so."

Morgan was listing toward his wounded shoulder, almost sliding off the saddle. Virgil hurried to his brother's left side to hold him in place. "Keep the horse walking," Virgil said. Morgan gigged the horse forward and they headed for the house.

Drawing near, Allie took in the situation quickly and, not bothering with words, went inside. By the time Virgil had his brother off the horse and in the house, Allie had the bed ready and was tearing an old sheet into strips to make bandages.

Letting Morgan rest on the bed and dressing the wound with a poultice seemed to revive him some. While Allie prepared a hot broth, Virgil found out what had happened.

"Was it Sioux? Blackfeet?"

"No, it happened before I left Montana," said Morgan. "Just a few weeks ago. Just after I got your letter."

Virgil gave him a tired look. "Was it over a woman?"

"No. I had some trouble with Billy Brooks."

"I know him. From Abilene."

"Yeah, he said something about that. They say he had experience as a lawman, which I guess is why he thought he should've been appointed town marshal instead of me."

"He always had a bad temper, but you usually could get around it."

"That's not the way it was, Virge. You already decided I prodded him, but I didn't."

"All right," Virgil said. "You tell me what happened."

"Well, like I said, I got appointed marshal. I was a deputy marshal for a bit the year before, you know that. And the council in Butte was choosing between me and Brooks and they picked me. Brooks started saying he was going to throw down on me and then everybody'd know who was the better man. When I heard about that I let it be known that I was gunning for him on sight."

"Now wasn't that a smart idea," Virgil said. "If you'd just let him get over his drunk it probably would've been all over."

"How the hell do you know that?" demanded Morgan. "You weren't there. He was going to kill me, drunk or not drunk."

"That's what you say."

"Virgil," Allie called sharply across the room. "Let him be. We're trying to mend him. You can argue later."

Morgan cocked his head toward Allie. "The smart one in the family."

Virgil said, "All right, Morgan. Just tell me what happened."

"Not much more after that. I saw him coming out of a saloon and he must've seen me at the same time because he pulled his gun as soon as I did. I think our guns went off right together. That's when he got me in the shoulder, but I hit him too. In the leg it was. On the ground I was able to shoot again and I hit him even better. That's it. By the end of the day he was dead."

"Did that sour you on the marshal's job?"

"I think it soured the council," said Morgan. "I wasn't much good to them lying in a bed with a hole in my shoulder. After a while I looked at your letter again and it seemed like a good time to move on."

"Now don't you think it might not have been a bad idea to at least wait till you were healed before riding here? That's a hell of a ride, even without a hole in you."

Morgan looked off. "I thought it was pretty much mended."

"And on horseback! You could have brought a rig of some kind. At least take some of the wear off of you."

"Please the Lord, Virgil, let up on him," Allie called again. "You haven't seen your brother for three years at the least and here you are badgering him. I swear, you'll sicken him before he can mend, you surely will." She was shaking the ladle at him now. "What do you think we gave him our bed for? So that you could weaken him with all your hard questions? If you want to be helpful, then leave him be and fix the wagon so we can haul some supplies in for him."

She turned back to her broth and stirred it furiously.

Virgil stared at the floor, clasped and then reclasped his fingers, then got up. "I'll be back," he said to Morgan and walked out to work on the axle.

Morgan lay quietly for a while, looking out the window across the Iowa flatland, listening to Allie stir the broth and start the preparation of dinner. "I didn't much like mending up in Butte," he said.

Allie turned to him and stopped her chores to wipe her hands on her apron. Morgan was still looking out the window. "Were there any good friends you had up there?" she asked.

He looked at her briefly, then settled back to gaze up at the roof, saying nothing.

"You decided right coming down here," Allie said.

"You just rest and I'll have some broth for you in no time at all."

That evening's dinner was the best meal Morgan had eaten in a long time. The chicken, biscuits and greens were good, and the talk at the table was better. Morgan hadn't heard anything about their parents for several years.

"They were looking fit, the last I saw them," Virgil said. Under Allie's watchful eye, he decided not to mention anything about Morgan not writing to their father.

"And how about their ranch?" Morgan said.

"Good land in the San Bernadino valley. The last I heard, father had just sold a section of it and got himself a good price. He was also elected to the county court."

"Not surprised," said Morgan. "You can't keep him from finding some way of telling folks what to do and getting paid for his trouble."

Virgil smiled. "You might be right about that."

"And Wyatt — I heard he's a tough character around Dodge."

"That means you've heard about as much as I have," said Virgil.

"All that learning your father tried to give you boys," said Allie, "and hardly one of you will put pen to paper to write to each other."

"You can't fault me," said Virgil. "If I hadn't written Morgan he'd never be here."

"Right enough," answered Allie, "and if neither one of you tells me what was in that letter I'll die not knowing, I suspect. Well, Virgil, I know you've been building a notion. God knows how long you got to build it before you tell your wife. I'm not begrudging you, Morgan, but I think sooner or later I have to know as much as you do, even if I'm not a brother in this family."

"You can know everything for all I'm concerned," said Morgan. He turned to his brother.

Virgil pushed some food around his plate with his fork before getting started. "It's about that time Schafer's oldest boy came by here on his way back home," Virgil began. "We were talking for a while when you went to get him some water."

"I know that, Virgil. I got eyes to see around a corner with," she said. "What did you talk about?"

"Well, he was coming from Arizona — you know that. He had a lot to say about all the mining down there."

"I thought you said there was nothing but sun, death and Apaches down there, all of which was the same thing."

"There was, that's right. But people have been moving in there, and life is starting to get settled. At Prescott, well, they've got a real town there now. A man can get rich down in Arizona now without dying in a hurry."

"Were you serious about pulling up stakes and settling down there?" said Morgan.

"Well, like Allie says, it's been a notion."

"A notion," Allie added, "that he's been taking to while nothing gets done around here."

"I'm sorry, Allie. You're settled here," Virgil said. "I was unsettled when we first got here and nothing's changed since. I'm no farmer, but I just didn't have the heart to come right out and say it until there was something else for us. Something I was sure about. I wrote Morgan because I thought it might make more sense if we all went to a new territory together. We could make more of it that way."

Allie put a hand on Virgil's arm. "For mercy's sake, Virgil, don't tell me how right you are. I know you're right. I've got no roots here if you're moping around all day and night. Get something you can do. It sure isn't farming, I know that much."

Virgil just looked at her. He had been uneasy about telling her that he wanted to leave. Now that he saw that it was so easy, he wanted to laugh.

"In case you thought I rode down from Montana just to

pass the time, I'm interested in going too, Virgil," Morgan said. "You say Prescott's the place?"

"That's my thinking. Looking at you now, I'd say you won't be ready to travel for a few weeks. It would be best for me to ride ahead, set us up down there. By the time I get back, you'll be ready to go with Allie and me." He turned to his wife. "I think that's the best, Allie."

"Of course it is," she said. "I'll get Morgan back on his feet while you're gone. And once I do, Morgan, I'll have you fixing up the place. If we're to get a good price for this farm we're going to have our work cut out for us."

the drover was identifiable by the bright green bandana around his neck and the nickel-studded belt around his waist.

20

Wyatt found his man coming out of the Varieties dance hall with three other cowboys. Just as Neal Brown had said, the drover was identifiable by the bright green bandana around his neck and the nickel-studded belt around his waist.

The faces of all four men were slightly flushed, meaning that they probably had been to the dance hall's back rooms and had come directly from the whores to the street. Laughing at some joke, they turned on the boardwalk to head toward the Lady Gay. Wyatt pointed to his man before the cowboy could move away. "You," Wyatt said, "I want to talk to you."

The drover smiled nonchalantly, looking to his friends as he was about to reply, the street lamp showing the glint in his eye. Whatever he had planned on saying remained unspoken. Seeing no support from his companions, he kept his mouth shut and stepped over to the chief deputy marshal.

Wyatt took him aside and stared straight into the cowboy's eyes. "Your name's Rayburn."

"Yeah, that's me."

"I hear talk about you."

"What kind of talk?" asked Rayburn. "Me and my friends, we're just having ourselves a good time. That's all."

Wyatt didn't like the cowboy's smile. He couldn't think of any reason why Rayburn should be smiling. "Just having a good time?" Wyatt said, never moving his eyes.

"Sure, why not?"

"That's a peculiar way to go about it."

"What're you talkin' about, Earp?"

Wyatt said, "A fella out for a good time doesn't need any weapons."

One of the other drovers called from farther down the boardwalk. "Leave him alone, Earp."

Wyatt studied Rayburn another moment before glancing briefly at the other cowboy. In a sudden motion he grabbed Rayburn by the cowboy's right collar, spun him around and slammed him face-first into the false front of the Varieties. Before the cowboy could say a word, Wyatt pulled a knife out of the man's vest pocket. He then kicked him behind the knee to make Rayburn drop to the walk. In the next instant, Wyatt pulled a hideaway gun out of the cowboy's boot.

Wyatt had his back to the other drovers, but he was listening intently for any sound of movement. He heard nothing. They're beginning to get the message, he thought.

When Wyatt hauled him to his feet, Rayburn said, "You son of a bitch." Wyatt shoved him along the boardwalk.

Staggering forward, Rayburn got control of himself after a few steps and wheeled about. He charged at the lawman. Wyatt sidestepped at the last second, tripped Rayburn and then waited just long enough for the cowboy to jump back up so he could punch him in the face.

Dragging him by the collar, Wyatt pulled the cowboy out into the street. "No son-of-a-bitch cowboy goes around armed in this town," he said through clenched teeth.

"You bastard!" Rayburn growled. Somehow he still had some fight left in him. He threw a punch that missed, then tried throwing an arm around Wyatt's neck. Not planning on putting up with any more of this, Wyatt pulled his Colt. He whipped it across Rayburn's head, opening a gash across the cheek, and watched the cowboy topple into the mud of the street.

Rayburn was tame the rest of the way to the calaboose.

Wyatt's blood was up as long as he was putting the cowboy in place, but after the man was locked up he gave no more thought to it. This work was getting too routine; it almost didn't feel dangerous anymore.

Clanton and Curly Bill hadn't returned to Dodge since the night they had treed Wyatt. Neither had Ringo. Since that time, though, Wyatt hadn't turned his back on anyone he thought might have been armed. The drovers looked at him differently now and that was all to the good as far as Wyatt was concerned.

On his way from the city jail, he stopped outside the Alamo when he noticed Rayburn's friends shooting billiards in the saloon. He looked in long enough to let them know he still had them on his mind. Two of them glanced his way. There was some defiance in those faces, but they turned away quickly. The third cowboy didn't even bother to look. Wyatt nodded his head as he walked away. My job will become easy, he told himself, like it used to be. These shitkickers are starting to get the idea.

Crossing the Dead Line, Wyatt set out to complete his partrol before taking a stint at the Lady Gay. On the south side, he decided to post himself outside the Comique Theater. It was a new establishment, a place where some of the rowdies and toughs thought they should try some of their woolliest stunts. If there is any trouble tonight, Wyatt figured, I'll be close to it if I stay near the Comique.

As he leaned against the thin side wall, he could hear the audience roar with laughter inside. Wyatt remembered that it was Eddie Foy and Jim Thompson performing tonight, two troupers that Bat considered the funniest to pass through Dodge. He decided that while he was here he might as well stay long enough to see if Bat was right.

Coming along in the middle of a section of songs and jokes, Wyatt wasn't sure what Foy and Thompson were up to, or why the crowd was laughing so, but he was able to pick up the phrase "Kalamazoo in Michigan," the name of the routine that was supposed to be the best part of the show, at least according to Bat. While Wyatt tried to listen, a cowboy loped past on a sorrel, headed along Front Street in the direction of the cattle pens. Wyatt kept an eye on him as he rode on for another block, then stopped and turned his horse. Wyatt stiffened when the cowboy seemed to look in his direction; he instinctively let his right hand drop and gripped the gun belt just in front of the scabbard. The cowboy didn't move for several moments as he looked from one side to the other. He seemed to be lost.

Wyatt told himself to ease up. Not every drover is gunning for you, he thought. And this one doesn't even look smart enough to know how to get out of town.

More laughter came from inside the theater. Whatever's going on, Wyatt figured, it seems to be funny enough to a lot of people. He decided if he was going to take in the show he should do it right. Set aside an evening, maybe tomorrow, and take Verna. She could probably use a night on the town and Wyatt was sure he wouldn't mind giving himself some slack.

Hoofbeats made him turn toward the cattle pens again. The cowboy was coming back, no longer lost, riding back at a gallop with his revolver in his hand.

In the darkness Wyatt couldn't see the drover's face.

What he could see plain enough, though, was the gun aimed at him and the flame spitting out of the muzzle. He flattened to the ground, his Colt in hand, cold fury rattling through him. The shot punched through the wall above him, and the cowboy fired twice more to send two more bullets into the Comique. The sound of the show suddenly stopped. In its place were shouts and the commotion of a mad scramble for cover.

Wyatt fired quickly and missed. He lined up another shot, taking more time to aim at the middle of the drover's body. He had the cowboy in his sights, but his target galloped on past him and around the corner.

Wyatt sprang to his feet and ran to the corner, ready to pursue the cowboy on foot if necessary. To his surprise, the hoofbeats, after a brief stop, started up again, heading back in Wyatt's direction. Who the hell is this? thought Wyatt. The cowboy barrelled past, no more than a few feet away, and turned onto Bridge Avenue. Wyatt swung his gun around to follow the man as he went by and snapped off a shot. Fired too quickly, the shot went wide.

The cowboy charged away, down the road. Wyatt was sure he would make a getaway, but the drover suddenly reared his horse and started firing again. Wyatt saw another bullet go through the Comique Theater wall, no more than a foot away. The cowboy's horse was bucking, but still the man didn't stop triggering. He was crazy drunk and unwilling to stop for anything.

Wyatt dropped to one knee, leveled his Colt and steadied the gun with his other hand. A bullet whistled past him. He took another second to take aim, then fired twice. Both slugs crashed through the cowboy's rib cage. The cowboy twisted horribly in the saddle, his rebel howl suddenly pitching to a sickly, fractured shriek of pain and ending in a gurgle of blood.

He stayed on his horse, slumped forward, the animal's eyes wide with panic as it bucked, then skittered, then bucked again. Wyatt was able to get hold of the bridle and, after getting pulled for several feet, soothed the horse to a stop. Charlie Bassett and Neal Brown reached Wyatt's side as he took hold of the cowboy and started pulling him out of the saddle.

"Get Dr. McCarty," Wyatt said. "Go on. Get him."

He pulled the cowboy free of the stirrups and slid him off the horse and onto the ground. Propping up his head, Wyatt could now finally get a good look at the attacker. He had a young, wide-featured face, with big ears and straggly, greasy hair. Wyatt stared at the face in disbelief. He had never seen the cowboy before.

At the city jail, Dr. McCarty told Wyatt and Charlie to stretch the cowboy across the big wooden desk. The doctor then tore away the bloody shirt and went to work. For a moment, the cowboy seemed to regain consciousness, but only long enough to slip into a yammering delirium.

"Who the hell is he?" Wyatt asked Charlie.

"I saw him in town, this afternoon some time. That's all I know," said Charlie. "You sure you don't know him, Wyatt?"

"I'm sure," said Wyatt as he turned away.

"He's with Driskill's outfit." The voice came from the lockup in the rear. Wyatt turned to see it was Rayburn, his bandaged face up against the bars, his eyes suddenly widening. "Don't you come near me, Earp," Rayburn said quickly. "I know he's with Driskill, I told you that, but that's all of it. I don't know nothin' else."

Wyatt considered Rayburn before speaking. "Is Simpson in town?"

"Who?"

"Al Simpson," Wyatt snapped. "Ramrod for Driskill's outfit. Have you seen him?"

"The ramrod? Yeah, I think I saw him, over to . . . I can't remember. I can't think good with this beatin' you gave me. Don't ask me where he is because I don't know any more."

Wyatt went out to make the rounds and by the time he

got to the Long Branch he found Al Simpson drinking at the bar with Luke Short. Simpson was surprised when he saw the wounded cowboy stretched out on the desk. The drover was quiet now, the delirium gone. "He's not even supposed to be in town tonight," said Simpson. "He's supposed to be with the herd. He was on the town last week. Damn it all, what's he doing here?"

"Who is he?" Wyatt asked impatiently.

"Some jarhead from the Panhandle. Name of George Hoyt. I tell ya, he's supposed to be with the herd tonight."

Wyatt stared at the still body on the desk, deciding to ask the question at the back of his mind.

"Ike Clanton's with your outfit," he said. "Does this kid know Ike?"

"Clanton? I don't know. Maybe. I don't pay much mind to Clanton. We just cut him loose yesterday. Him and Curly Bill both. The two of them're more trouble than they're worth. I could tell you something about them, all right."

Wyatt stopped listening. After Simpson left, and after Charlie Basset went out to take his patrol, Wyatt stayed, sitting across from the wounded George Hoyt, who was still lying on top of the desk. For two hours, Wyatt and Dr. McCarty remained by Hoyt's side, neither saying a word.

Wyatt had to stay. There was still the off-chance that the cowboy might come to, that he might be able to talk. The idea of a stranger trying to kill him was much more unnerving than the gunfight itself.

Although he watched Hoyt slip away for two hours, Wyatt was surprised when Dr. McCarty finally pronounced the young man dead. The death still didn't seem real to Wyatt when he walked away from the jail along Front Street. The south side was strangely sluggish now. A band performed at the Varieties and someone was playing the piano at the Lady Gay, but the clamor and the shouts weren't there, as if the musicians played for no one but themselves. Wyatt had no doubt that word had gotten around about Hoyt. Even crazy-drunk Texans are liable to show respect for the dead, he thought.

Wyatt walked beyond the slanting light thrown by the dance halls and crossed the tracks, almost as inky black as the prairie stretching beyond the pens. Just to keep walking, he followed the Dead Line all the way to the Dodge House, then moved over to the north side boardwalk and started back in the opposite direction along the Plaza. All he could think of was the heavy weight of the cowboy in his arms as he pulled him from the saddle.

Doc was standing outside the Lone Star, by himself as usual, when Wyatt headed west along the north side. Feeling no particular reason to keep walking now, Wyatt stopped alongside Doc and accepted the flask when it was handed to him. Doc let Wyatt finish his second swig before speaking.

"Did the cowboy die?" he asked.

Wyatt simply nodded and Doc shrugged. "Two .45 slugs through the chest wouldn't give him a whole lot of time, would it?" Doc said.

Wyatt passed back the flask, met the consumptive's eyes for a moment and then looked out toward the street.

"Was that the first man you killed," Doc asked.

Wyatt said, "I left a man for dead in Missouri once, but he ended up getting up and about some time later. The cowboy tonight — he was the first one."

Doc nodded and grunted in acknowledgement. Then he took another swallow of whiskey. "Well, welcome aboard, Deacon."

Taking out a cigar and match, Wyatt lit up a smoke. The cigar was old and tasted foul, but Wyatt smoked nearly every inch of it. There was nothing else he would rather have done. When the cigar was reduced to a blackened stub, he tossed it into the dirt of Front Street and walked away from Doc without a word.

21

"That old skinflint Fowler, how could he kick about that? Him with that measly store. What damn difference does it make how much bacon and flour he's got in there?" Ike Clanton waited to get a reaction from the line rider at the door. The man just spat tobacco juice onto the ground, shifted his rifle from one arm to the other and wiped his mouth on his flannel shirt sleeve.

Ike went on: "You ever see the store he keeps, Hobie? Measly — measly and mean. How does he expect to keep a whole ranch runnin' on those supplies? You want to know how he does it, Hobie? By starvin' us. There's days out with the herd I'd like to die, I was so hungry. How's about it, Hobie? Just loosen this here rope. I ain't about to go nowhere, not with my daddy ridin' in. How's about it?"

He held out his wrists as far as the halter rope would allow. Hobie barely looked at him. "Give it up, Ike. Mr. Fowler says to keep 'em tight."

"Mr. Fowler says! You gonna listen to him? You gonna listen to him after what he done to me! Look at this,

Hobie." Ike pulled on the halter rope, tied to the stove at one end and knotted around his wrists at the other. "This could be you, Hobie! Tied like a goddamned animal because of that cheapskate Fowler. This could be you."

Hobie shook his head. "That ain't so, Ike."

"Why the hell not? I'm just one of the hands, just like you."

"I didn't steal no supplies from the store," Hobie said.

"Steal from the store!" Ike rolled his eyes. "I wouldn't call that no store. You should see what Shanghai Pierce had. And Tobe Driskill — the both of them. They had stores that could feed an army. But Fowler — you couldn't keep a cat alive in his place. So what if I took some bacon and just a little bit of flour so's I could get by. It was a measly store before I took them things and it was a measly store after. Fowler's a skinflint and that's that."

Hobie still didn't respond. Ike finally gave up and turned to look bitterly out the line-shack window at Toyah Creek.

Mentioning Shanghai Pierce and Tobe Driskill made Ike reflect very briefly that he would've been better off if he hadn't been fired by those two men. Pierce had told him to ride on during the spring roundup of '75 when he found someone to take Ike's place, a man who wouldn't try to do his work sitting under a cottonwood. "Just shows you how much Pierce knows," Ike had said at the time. "I can afford to laze some, seein' as how I do the work of two men once I'm a'saddle. He'll see." Driskill had kicked him out of camp outside Dodge last summer when he heard about Ike borrowing his bonded bourbon. Ike took a dim view of that also.

If it weren't for getting fired, Ike would have been doing all right. He wouldn't have had to hire on with Caleb Fowler who held onto every dollar like it was his firstborn. Twenty dollars a month was all Ike was making with Fowler, while he had made thirty-five, sometimes forty, with the bigger outfits. As far as Ike was concerned, for that money you could hardly blame a man for making do.

The bacon and the flour from Fowler's store had brought Ike only a few extra dollars when he sold them to the sutler at Fort Davis, but at least it was something, enough to keep a man in snakehead whiskey for a while.

One thing Ike had been able to count on through it all was a good friend who was ready to stand by him. Driskill had been willing to overlook the fight Curly Bill started with Jacklin the wrangler, the one that left Jacklin's leg cut wide open, but then Curly Bill told Driskill he would give him some of the same if the cattleman tried firing Clanton. For friendship Curly Bill lost his job alongside Ike. Curly Bill had backed him up then and he was backing him up now.

When Fowler had said he would hold Ike prisoner until he could pay for the stolen property, Ike had known he was really in for it. Of course he didn't have the money — how could he with the measly wages he was getting? Lucky for him that Curly Bill volunteered to ride to Arizona to find Ike's father and get him to bail out his son. Old Man would know what to do. That was certain.

"Rider comin' in with Mr. Fowler," said Hobie.

Ike hurried to the side for a look out the window. The halter rope brought him up short, keeping him from seeing the trail leading from the ranch house.

"Just one rider?" said Ike, still straining for a look.

"Just the one. He's got an extra horse with him. But it don't look like it's Curly Bill."

"What's he look like?"

"An old man," said Hobie. "Just an old man with a beard."

"That's my daddy," Ike blurted out. "That's him. He's come to get me outa here."

Ike heard the horses come to a stop at the side of the shack and then heard footsteps circling around to the door. Stepping aside, Hobie let Fowler walk into the shack.

"You see, Mr. Clanton," said Fowler, in his Eastern accent, turning to someone just outside the door. "Your son has been well taken care of. No harm has come to him while he has been in my custody."

Old Man Clanton stepped into Ike's view and peered into the shack.

It had been six years since Ike had seen his father. In that time his father had aged considerably. The beard, which had been speckled with gray for as long as Ike could remember, was now pure white, and the creases on the leathery face were now bordered by a dense patchwork of sun-burnished wrinkles. But as Old Man got older he also seemed to have gotten tougher. The added lines made him look even more formidable, while the lean body still looked as strong as ever and the eyes beneath the hooded lids just as uncompromising.

Old Man Clanton sized up his son from the doorway, as if looking for any obvious injury on a horse that had strayed from the herd.

"As I said," Fowler reassured him, "he is as fit as can be."

Old Man grunted. He walked over to Ike and looked straight into his eyes. After six years, that look would have to serve as a greeting. The Clantons didn't dawdle on such things.

"Mr. Fowler here says you stole from him," said Old Man. "Be that true?"

Ike started to answer.

"Don't lie to me, boy," the old man warned. "I've ridden too far to listen to lies."

Ike looked at the floor. Old Man sure hadn't changed, Ike thought. Always going hard, never interested in anyone else's way of looking at things. "Yeah, that's the truth, Pa," Ike admitted.

Old Man shook his head and walked away from his son. "All right, Mr. Fowler. The boy's fit and you've been robbed. Looks like you got some money comin' to you."

"Only what's mine by right," Fowler said. "I don't ask

158

for anything else. It's nothing but just consideration for my losses.''

Old Man lifted the warbags from his shoulder and dropped them onto the bed on the other side of the shack. Fowler looked sympathetically at the old man.

"It's not easy to keep them on the straight and narrow, is it, Mr. Clanton? I try to impart some sense of virtue to my employees, but guidance is not always welcome. I can appreciate your difficulty."

Old Man glanced at Fowler from beneath his shaggy white brow. Instead of answering, he unstrapped a warbag and emptied its contents onto the bed. "One hundred twenty dollars. Count it up and I'll be taking my boy," he said.

"Whatever you say, Mr. Clanton."

Ike had just about lost faith in his father. He hadn't said a word to Old Man since leaving the line-shack, and the old man hadn't offered anything in return. Right in front of Fowler I had to say I was a thief! was all Ike could think. He was certain that his father didn't care a hoot for him — until he saw Curly Bill riding toward them at lope from the other side of the valley. Seeing Curly Bill changed all of Ike's ideas because Brocius was riding toward them with the gunnysack in his hand, the gunnysack in which Fowler had put Old Man's 120 dollars.

Meeting up with them underneath a cottonwood, Curly Bill told his story. "I stayed up in them hills just like you said, Mr. Clanton. And sure enough, when you and Ike lit out that damn Fowler came ridin' my way." Curly Bill let out a laugh. "He was sure surprised some when he saw me. Listen here, Ike. He asked me if I was stayin' on at the ranch. A good one, huh? He said I was one of the hard-working boys, one of 'em that he liked. I think he stopped liking me in a hurry when I put my gun on him. You should've seen his face, Ike, when I told him I'd put a hole in him if he didn't stop yappin' and hand over the money.''

Ike was sorry he hadn't seen it — the old skinflint must have been a sight. But he was happy enough just to find out what Old Man had been up to. Making Ike eat crow back at the line-shack had been just a way of putting on a good show for Fowler, to set him up. Looking at his father now, Ike had to smile: Old Man never missed a lick, you had to say that about him.

"The idea of Fowler getting 120 dollars from Old Man," Ike said to Curly Bill. "It'll be a cold day in hell when the old man has to pay for what's already his.''

Old Man Clanton finished counting the money, then grunted in satisfaction. It was all there. "No offense about the countin', Curly Bill," he said. "A young feller like you can just lose a dollar or two from here to there.''

If Curly Bill was offended he didn't show it. "It's your right," he told Old Man.

Nothing more was said about it. Old Man reined around and led the way along the base of the ridge.

"You'd best stick close to home, Ike," Old Man said. "You've been driftin' long enough. Time has come for you to stay with the family.''

"I don't know, Pa. Driftin' gets in the blood after a while.''

"Then it's time to get it out of the blood, boy. Curly Bill here, he told me he's ready to plant himself in one place. Now it's time for you. Besides, what with the silver strike in Arizona these days, the family needs to pull together.

"There's silver there?" Ike said. "And us with all our land — we'll be sittin' pretty. A silver strike!''

"Don't you get so keen all of a sudden," Old Man said.

"But, Pa, silver — that's money for us.''

"It'll be that," Old Man said. "Money's gonna be spread all around the territory, with plenty for the likes of us. But there's also gonna be more folks. Hell, there's

more already. And that means more law too, breathin'
down your neck every which way you turn.''

"You make it sound like the silver's something bad,"
said Ike.

"Not bad. Just something for us Clantons to figure out.
Like always, it'll be what we make of it. Ain't nothin' gonna be handed to us. You know that. That's why you're
comin' home — to lend a hand. About time you done
something for the family instead of traipsin' about like a
poontang-crazy shitkicker.''

Curly Bill laughed at this. Turning in the saddle, he then
cut the laugh short. "Riders comin'," he said. "Three of
'em, looks like.''

Ike followed Curly Bill's gaze to their backtrail. He
couldn't see a damn thing except patches of short grass all
the way to the horizon. Then the clouds of dust appeared,
small and far away, but coming closer and moving quickly.

Old Man didn't even bother to look back. Instead, he
looked along the ridge to their right and studied the land
straight ahead. Ike and Curly Bill glanced at each other,
waiting for Old Man to say something.

"We'll ride up ahead a piece," he finally said. "Don't
you two look back until I say so.''

Curly Bill handed Ike a pistol as they rode. Slipping it
into his waistband, Ike gigged his horse up to his father's
side. He wanted to talk — that might help to settle his
jumpy nerves — but he could see Old Man wouldn't want
to hear it.

By a scalloped bend in the ridge, Old Man said it was
time to stop. They turned to face the three riders loping
toward them. Ike could see the faces plainly now. It was
Hobie and two other Fowler outriders, Ramirez and
Mallon. Ramirez and Mallon were holding rifles, while
Hobie kept his in the saddle boot. Ike remembered uneasily
how good a shot Ramirez was.

"Don't none of you jerk your guns till I say so," said
Old Man.

Ike looked at him in disbelief. "What the hell we supposed to do while they —"

"Shut up," said Curly Bill.

The outriders reined in about ten feet away. Ramirez held both reins and rifle barrel in one hand, ready to aim and fire and control the horse at the same time.

"Mr. Fowler's real angry, Ike," said Hobie. "He sent us to get that money back."

"Let him stay angry," Ike yelled, "because we ain't givin' him nothin'."

"It ain't because of the money, he says. Mr. Fowler says it just ain't right. We gotta take the money," said Hobie.

"We can't give it to you, boys," said Old Man. "We just can't."

Mallon smiled and shook his head. "It don't seem like you got much choice, you old coot." Mallon leveled the rifle. "We got two guns on you already."

"And we can make it three," said Hobie.

Ike stared wild-eyed at the two rifle muzzles and at the beady eyes of Ramirez. Glancing at Old Man and Curly Bill, he looked for some sign as to what they should do. The two of them sat their horses, unflinching. Hell, they didn't even look like they were sweating. Ike's own perspiration was pouring down his sides.

"Well," said Old Man, "if'n you think you got to take this here gunnysack, all I gotta say is this ain't your day, boys."

Hobie glanced at the other two outriders, then squinted at the old man, perplexed. "You're a crazy man," he said.

"I don't think so," said the old man.

That's when Ike saw a stream of blood suddenly jet from Ramirez's throat. The crack of distant rifle fire then followed. Ike stared open-mouthed as Ramirez toppled from the saddle and thudded to the ground. Another distant shot ran out, and Mallon clutched his shoulder, blood creeping through his fingertips. All at once, gunfire seemed to explode all around Ike.

Old Man and Curly Bill had their guns out just as Hobie grabbed for his pistol. In his hurry, Hobie triggered the gun just before he had it leveled and grazed his own horse behind the right shoulder blade. The animal reared. Old Man and Curly Bill shot at the same time and Hobie flew back out of the saddle with the impact of both slugs.

Mallon left his shoulder wound alone now and was reaching with his left hand across his body for the revolver on his right hip. He managed to work it out of the scabbard, but Curly Bill was ready. He fired three times. The first shot whizzed past, but then Mallon's body jerked twice with the entrance of the second and third. Curly Bill fired once more and Mallon slouched to one side, sliding off the saddle a bit at a time until the horse bucked and threw him to the ground.

Ike's gun was still in his waistband. As he settled his horse, he turned toward the ridge and saw two men stand up from behind the cover of rocks, rifles in their hands. They started moving down the slope.

"God damn it all!" Ike shouted. "God damn it, Pa. You knew they were there all the time and you didn't tell me! Why the hell didn't you tell me!"

"Had my reasons," Old Man said as he walked his horse over to the three bodies.

"The hell you did!" roared Ike.

Curly Bill drew up alongside Ike and spoke to him quietly as he reloaded his revolver. "Old Man thought you might tell these fellers here — you know, kind of by accident."

Ike was speechless for a moment. "He thought I'd tell 'em! What the hell!"

"Sometimes," Curly Bill said, "you talk faster'n you do anything else, Ike. It's true. We had to keep that in mind."

"God damn!" was all Ike could say to that. "God damn!"

"We got us a breather over here," called Old Man, his horse standing over Hobie. The outrider's fingers curled and his chest rose and fell ever so slightly. Old Man cocked his gun and blasted Hobie's face open. He then walked his horse back to Ike and Curly Bill.

A groan came from Mallon, who tried to turn onto his side but soon collapsed.

"Another one," said Old Man. He reined his horse toward Mallon, but before he could make another move, Curly Bill shouted, "I'll get 'im," and gigged his horse forward. He bolted over to Mallon and, firing on the run, blasted a hole through Mallon's skull, leaving a cavity where the outrider's nose had been.

Old Man nodded at Curly Bill's work. "Good boy," he said.

Curly Bill and Old Man now got off their mounts. Seeing what they were up to, Ike decided it was time to do his part. He helped them take the gun belts and boots off the bodies and volunteered to go through their pockets, finding an old watch on Ramirez and some wrapped matches, a small knife and two dollars on Hobie. By the time he finished his work, the two men from the ridge were drawing near, leading their horses by the reins.

The set of the eyes was almost the same in both men, as was the thin face, but the one on the right, the one with the moustache and goatee, was taller and more handsome.

"I want you boys to meet my son Ike," Old Man said. "Looks like he's comin' back to the family at Lewis Springs."

"Glad to meet you, Ike," said the handsome one.

"Ike," said Old Man, "this here's the McLowery boys. That's Tom and the tall one, that's Frank. They staked out a ranch a couple years back, right near our'n. Remember the Ortega place? That's theirs now. While you been away they been lending a hand. They're good boys."

22

Wyatt didn't consider himself a finicky man, but he did have his limits. Waking up in his house off Military Avenue, he swung out of bed to see his shirts in need of washing, piled on the floor in front of him. The next thing that caught his eye, after he pulled on his clothes and walked into the kitchen, was the mound of unwashed pots and dishes sitting in a basket by the door, exactly as it had for the last three days. It was a mystery to Wyatt how so little cooking could produce so many dirty pots and dishes.

The stubble on his face itched and irritated, but he was in no mood for shaving. He wasn't even sure if he could find his razor and soap in this mess. He buttoned up his white shirt, grabbed his hat and gun belt off the peg by the door and stepped outside onto the porch.

There he found Verna sitting in the rocker. She held the needle and thread to mend the pants that rested on her lap, but her hands were still. She occupied herself by gazing across the field toward the eastern edge of the Plaza.

"Damn it, Verna, what do you do here all day? Are you keeping a cattle pen here or a house?"

She looked at him sharply, then turned to her sewing, shifting the pants in her hands, checking the threaded needle; not really doing anything, just fussing. "Sorry, Wyatt," she said, not sounding very sorry. "I'm just feeling lazy these days."

"Lazy, is it? There's a cure for that, if that's what's ailing you. You can do some work."

A couple of years ago, Wyatt would have been reluctant to push this, thinking there were better things for a man to do than spend his time ordering a woman around the house. That might be fine for a haberdasher or a schoolteacher, but Wyatt didn't come to Dodge City to fret about a house or a garden or chores or any such thing. He wasn't sure now why these matters should bother him, but it just seemed that a marriage, even a common law one, entitled him to expect something.

"And sitting on the porch isn't going to get that work done either," he continued.

When she looked at him again, tears were welling at the corners of her brown eyes, but the voice wasn't sorrowful. "I'll be gettin' to it, Wyatt," she snapped. "Damn it all, I'll get to it." A sob in her throat then muffled the anger. "I can only do so much," she said weakly.

He looked past her, at the row of houses and the new court house beyond them. He had nothing to say. He had no stomach for butting heads with Verna today. Mindlessly, he adjusted the buckle of his gun belt from one hole to the next, then stepped off the porch. Once more he relented: "Don't worry yourself, Verna," he said. That was better than carrying this argument any further. He started down the road toward Railroad Avenue.

He shouldn't complain, he told himself. Verna didn't make life easy, but you couldn't call her a bad woman. Wyatt knew men who were badgered half to death by their wives. Jack Pulley was hounded day and night by his — at least that's what Wyatt had heard. The woman spent all her days in bed, saying how sick she always was, but when it came time to keeping Jack on the run with this chore and that, she had the energy of a cyclone. And that black eye Jack was walking around with these days — that woman could pack a punch when she had to, no matter how sick she said she was. Wyatt had no complaint like that. After three years of living with her in Dodge, he had to say Verna was harmless enough. Sometimes Wyatt thought of the few months he had had with Willa in Lamar and wondered why living with Verna couldn't be more like that. But that notion didn't occur to him very often. He had never really expected Verna to take Willa's place.

He reached the Plaza with the gun belt still draped over his shoulder, not seeing much point in buckling it on. Under the late summer's midday sun, Front Street was as slow and quiet as it was dusty and hot. The few people on the street went about their business in no hurry at all. The only reason for moving quickly today was to reach the shade of an overhang.

Bat Masterson had already found his slice of shade in front of the Long Branch, sitting on a chair tilted back against the front of the saloon.

"There you are, Wyatt," he said. "About time you came by to help me keep the peace. I've been at it the better part of the morning and I don't mind tellin' you my butt's had about as much peacekeeping as it can take."

Wyatt pulled over a chair and slung his gun belt over the back.

"Better not sit down," said Bat. "We got us a drunk bothering Bob Wright over at his store. We just might have to round him up any minute now."

Wyatt sat down alongside him. "Who's the drunk?" he said with little interest.

"Some drover. Seems he forgot to pull out when Pierce's outfit left last week."

"What about Charley Goodnight's crew? Prairie Dog was telling me they might be reaching the Arkansas next week."

"Might be. Or it might be next month," said Bat. "What I hear is Goodnight had some rustlers to hang before hitting the trail."

Wyatt nodded. He and Bat then watched dust swirl toward them from the wheels of a passing buckboard. As the silence lengthened, Wyatt guessed that Bat was keeping quiet only because he was working up to something. He glanced at his friend, who was waving away the dust with his bowler and waited for him to start in with him again. Sure enough, when Bat had the derby perched back on his head, he said, "The time's for leavin', Wyatt. If this place gets any slower I think you'll have to kick me just to make sure I'm awake."

Wyatt was in no mood to hear about moving on. He couldn't argue with Bat's saying the town was slow, but he still was in no mood.

"You know they're liable to cut you from the marshal's roll soon enough," Bat went on. "The way things're going, they won't need you to do nothing for something. As for me, I don't plan on sticking around to watch myself get beaten by Hinkle at the next election. You know how strong the farmers are getting in this county."

I should know, Wyatt thought. You told me about it only yesterday.

Bat took off his bowler to shake off the few specks of dust that had settled there in the last minute. "The time's for leavin'," he said once more.

Wyatt couldn't dispute anything Bat was saying, but the idea of pulling up stakes just made him feel tired.

When he had first rolled into Dodge, Wyatt hadn't any notions about staying forever. It had been just the next town on the circuit for him. Looking at things now, though, he didn't much care for packing up and starting all over again. There were still fast towns to go to; every year or so another one seemed to crop up. But Wyatt couldn't muster up the ambition that Bat had to move on to some-place else. He conceded that he might shake the feeling next month when the season came to a close. That was the most definite thought he could latch onto. Verna wasn't the only one who couldn't take hold of things these days, Wyatt thought.

"What do you say we earn our pay," Wyatt said. "The drunk's over at Wright and Beverly's you say?"

By the time they got to Bob Wright's store, the drunk drover was no longer a bother. In fact, he was now a customer, consulting with Mr. Isaacson in the back of the store about buying a new hat. His old hat wasn't any use to him now as he had pissed in it on a dare.

"There's no call for you comin' around now," said Wright. "You can see that for yourself."

"I don't know, Bob, it just doesn't seem right," said Bat. "Us comin' all the way over here to take care of this here fella, and you're tellin' us to leave. If we wanted to leave be, we could've stayed where we were. I say we still haul him off to the calaboose. What do you say, Wyatt?"

"Seems fair."

"But he's a customer," protested Bob Wright.

"We've decided, Bob," said Bat. "He goes to the calaboose."

"I'm just buyin' a damn hat," cried the cowboy, his tongue still thick from drink.

"I can see that," said Masterson, "and so can everybody else, but we can't just be lazin' around all day. We've got to arrest *somebody*."

"What about my hat?" whined the drover.

"You can buy the hat. Then you come with us." As a charitable afterthought, Bat added, "You can take the hat with you."

The cowboy mulled this over. He then nodded his head slowly. "Seems fair," he said.

Walking down Front Street with the drunken cowboy staggering in front of them, Wyatt and Bat headed for the calaboose.

"Two grown men to arrest one drunk," Bat said. "That's not your idea of living, is it, Wyatt?"

"No, it's not," Wyatt had to say.

"Just think it over some. Hell, the way things're going you'll have plenty of time to think about it."

Wyatt didn't say anything. He knew if he encouraged him, Bat would drag this out all afternoon.

As they were about to cross the Dead Line, Wyatt saw a solidly built man in a black suit talking to Charlie Bassett outside the city jail. Wyatt didn't give the man any thought at first glance, but then, as something registered in the back of his mind, he looked again. When the man turned to face him, Wyatt called out.

"Virgil!"

Virgil smiled broadly and stepped away from Bassett to meet Wyatt by the tracks.

"Damn it, Virgil, where the hell did you come from?"

"On my way back to the farm in Iowa," Virgil said. "Thought I might give you a surprise."

"You did that," said Wyatt. "Virge, this here's Bat Masterson."

"Good to meet you, Bat."

"Same here, Virgil."

Wyatt clapped his brother on the back. "Come along with us to the calaboose. We can show you around after that."

"Don't bother," Bat said, rolling his eyes at the cowboy beside him. "I think I can ride herd on this desperado the rest of the way by myself. You two can start making the rounds right now." He took hold of the cowboy, who was about to collapse in the road, and led him toward the jail. "Virgil, take your brother for a drink," he said over his shoulder. "He can use it. He's been on the job close to an hour now." After another step, he added, "After a couple of drinks he can tell you how I've taught him everything he knows."

"He's got a lively tongue," Virgil said, cocking his head toward Bat as the sheriff led the prisoner away.

"That's the truth," said Wyatt, "but he's a good enough man to back it up. What about you, Virge? You didn't just happen to show up in Dodge to surprise me." Suddenly Wyatt lost his smile. "It's not bad news, is it?"

"No, not at all. Just wanted to talk something over with you."

"Come on. You can tell me over at the Long Branch."

Wyatt led the way back across the tracks.

"You said you were on your way back to the farm," Wyatt said. "Seems that means you're coming from somewhere."

"That's what I wanted to talk about. I was in Arizona. Been there on and off for the last two years."

"What happened to the farm?"

"I've sold it," said Virgil. "Actually, Allie sold it while I was prospecting in Prescott."

Wyatt gave his brother a quizzical glance. The idea of Virgil setting off for the other side of the country to go prospecting didn't ring true. Solid Virgil would never become a fortune hunter.

"I guess you've heard about the gold and silver boom down to Arizona," Virgil said.

"I've heard talk."

"Allie and I will be heading there as soon as I get back to Iowa."

Then again, Wyatt thought, Virgil was the first of the brothers to leave home for the west after the war, to pass through Abilene and then on to Wyoming. Some of the wanderer's itch must still be there. Wyatt held the door to the Long Branch open for his older brother.

"Morgan's coming too," said Virgil as they settled down at a back table with their beers.

"Morg? It's been years since the three of us were together." Wyatt drank from the mug, staring off, an idea starting to take shape.

"You're already figuring, aren't you?" Virgil laughed.

"What's so funny?"

"The look you just had," Virgil said. "I'll be damned if you're not a step ahead of me."

"What does that mean?"

"I came here to talk to you about the three of us going to Arizona and here you are, looking like you're already figuring it yourself."

Wyatt smiled. He could hide his thinking from just about everybody, but Virgil had always been quick to size up Wyatt's mind. When they were kids, Virge always seemed to know when he was up to something before it even happened. When he was planning mischief or figuring some way to slip out of doing chores, Virgil could catch him just thinking about it.

"Well, if you really are figuring on it," Virgil said, "then figure some more. There's a lot of opportunity down that way."

Virgil told him about the boom that had taken hold of the Arizona Territory while he had been there. Ore discoveries were luring men from all over the west and drawing them in from the east too. Virgil had had some small luck finding gold, but he found there were other opportunities that were better suited to him.

By buying claims and then either leasing them or selling them, he made some money in a short period of time and also built up a reputation for himself with Prescott's respectable businessmen. It turned out they had some use for him. A string of stage robberies committed in the area created a need for another lawman and, hearing of Virgil's police work in Abilene, the businessmen convinced U.S. Marshal Crawley Dake to appoint Virgil a deputy. Between keeping order in the county and doing business, Virgil found himself becoming a prominent citizen, but he also learned that, as fast as Prescott was, it was a small-chance town compared to what was going on to the south-east, closer to the Mexican border.

"Tombstone," Virgil said. "Have you heard of it?"

"I heard it's something fast," said Wyatt.

"It might be — but not as fast as it will be. That's where Morgan and I are headed. And we won't be starting with nothing. I'll be bringing my U.S. deputy marshal commission with me. I figure if we get there soon enough, we can register our claims and start the ball rolling." He gave Wyatt a long look. "This isn't some circuit stop, Wyatt. Before too long we'll be planting roots there. Least that's what Morgan and I are thinking. The Earps can be something in that town, especially if we pull together."

The idea of starting up somewhere with Virgil and Morgan struck a chord in Wyatt. It made him think of the old times, of riding the wagon with his brothers during the trek from their home in Illinois to their new home in Missouri. For all the hard times and the Indian scares during that trip, Wyatt remembered it almost fondly. The three of them had taken charge of their own wagon. Just boys really, they had faced the border country together.

He tried to picture Morgan now, how different he must be from the kid brother he had left behind nearly ten years ago. Thinking of the three of them together again gave him a sense of being able to get the best of anything. Suddenly, all the indecision about Dodge faded from his mind.

"I don't aim to ride and pull out in a couple of years," said Virgil. "Like I said, Wyatt, we should be making a stand there."

"I don't mind," said Wyatt, finishing his beer. "I don't mind at all."

TOMBSTONE, ARIZONA

23

The train from Tucson took them as far as the stamp mill town of Contention. Not wanting to wait till the next day for the stage, Wyatt bought a spring wagon and team for himself and Verna, and set out along the road for the last nine miles. For the first leg of the journey he didn't give this decision a second thought, but soon after leaving the San Pedro River behind he began to have his doubts. He sensed that the horses were drying up fast in the fierce desert sun. They might make it all right, he judged, since this wasn't a long haul, but he wasn't able to put himself at ease. In unfamiliar terrain with a woman, he might have been better off letting the stage line supply the transportation. And this land was very unfamiliar.

Parched bedrock flats stretched for miles to the east, interrupted only by occasional scrub vegetation, by creosote, ocotillo and mesquite. Here and there were some yucca plants and bald outcroppings, as stark as the jagged mountain skyline on the far horizon. A patch of tall, golden grama grass along the road put Wyatt in mind of the prairie he and Verna had left behind, but otherwise the land was sun-blasted and forbidding. Apache land, Wyatt thought. Although he was happy to admit he had never come across Apaches, he had heard enough stories to know it was reasonable to be afraid in their stomping grounds. He glanced at Verna sitting beside him, watching the road intently, looking like a perfect target. Wyatt wished he were traveling with his brothers instead.

His mind eased somewhat when, a few miles short of Tombstone, he saw a ring of chaparral, a fringe of thicket that surrounded and shaded a waterhole. At least water won't be a worry, he thought. Veering off the road, he brought the wagon through a gap in the thicket that led to the water's edge. Wyatt braked, stepped down from the seat and was about to unhitch the team when an uneasy feeling brought him to a stop.

Verna noticed the look on his face. "What is it, Wyatt?"

He turned toward the waterhole, certain that someone was there. He saw nothing, but he didn't have to wait long. A short, thin man showed himself, stepping clear of the chaparral on the other side of the hole.

He wore dust-caked denim and had a gun belt strapped around his waist. Walking stoop-shouldered, he moved toward the wagon, a meaningless grin on his long, pointy face. His green slit eyes lingered on Verna, but kept shifting nervously back to Wyatt.

Wyatt glanced at Verna. She was scared, gathering herself together, trying not to look at the man. Wyatt couldn't blame her.

Feigning casualness, Wyatt walked to the other side of the wagon and busied himself with checking the lead horse's hoof. From this angle, out of the corner of his eye, he now could see the edge of a tent, pitched behind the thicket. Beyond that was a hollow, a likely place to picket horses, provided a man wanted to hide his presence from anyone passing along the road. Wyatt thought he heard something from the direction of the far side of the water-hole, something other than a horse. He kept his eye on the edge of the tent, but couldn't see anything.

The slit-eyed man touched the brim of his hat. "Howdy there," he said, "the name's Pete Spence. Anything I can do for you folks?" The friendly tone belied the weasel face.

"Just stopped to water the team," Wyatt said.

"Why, I can sure enough help y'all with that. Want me to lend a hand?"

Before Wyatt could answer, Verna cut in. "Let's move on, Wyatt. The horses'll hold up."

Spense laughed. "Well, miss, they might hold up but no need to press 'em. You're just shy of water as it is. Might as well march right on in."

"That's the way I see it," said Wyatt, keeping his tone neutral as he glanced at the partially hidden tent and took an inconspicuous step back.

"And it won't hardly cost you nothin'," said Spence.

Wyatt narrowed his eyes as he realized his suspicions were justified. "What cost would that be?" he said.

Spence smiled. "Won't cost you but five dollars."

Wyatt stopped moving. He leveled a hard stare at the man. "That's a tall price. Do you own this water?"

"Me? Hell, no. I'm just lookin' after it for a friend. You know, there's some folks think they can just waltz in here and swallow. No respect for a man's property, that's what it is. Me, I got my eye on a lumber camp, over to the Dragoons. I just hope to God I can get a body to look after that lumber camp the way I'm lookin' after this here water."

"Your friend is lucky," said Wyatt, "to have you to see to his business." He had now taken two more steps back, bringing him even with the wagon bed.

"Most folks get the water for just three dollars." Spence sounded almost apologetic. "But you're strangers, after all. If you stick around this country maybe we can make a better price later on. You fixin' on stayin' in Tombstone, mister?''

"Yeah, I am," Wyatt said, now seeing no point in putting this off any longer. "But I'm not fixing on paying five dollars. You haven't earned it. You haven't even earned three."

Wyatt heard the sound again. This time the other man showed. He was a half-breed, dressed like a Mexican, with a small face and black eyes. He carried a rifle.

Spence called out to him. "Charley, you want to help this feller get his water?" He turned back to Wyatt. "How about it, mister? Indian Charley here can help you real good. Me, I can help the lady if need be." His gaze drifted toward Verna again.

The half-breed came forward, getting closer to Spence. Wyatt glanced at the wagon bed and then at Verna, hoping she would know enough to get out of the way. His shotgun was a long reach, lying as it was in the wagon bed, but he thought he could grab it quickly enough and bring it around before the waterhole squatters could react. With luck, Wyatt wouldn't have to fire. He could disarm them, water the team and be on his way without any more trouble.

Although Indian Charley had his rifle ready, Wyatt could see him glance nervously from side to side. He lacks nerve, Wyatt figured. He then concentrated on Spence, the one with the gumption. But that gumption only went so far. As Wyatt looked into the man's face, he saw a hint of uncertainty pass through the eyes, then disappear.

Wyatt sensed that this was his moment.

Verna looked at Wyatt next to the shotgun. "Don't do it, Wyatt! Don't do it!"

Wyatt froze, his hand halfway toward the shotgun. Spence and Indian Charley flinched, but then held still. Now that his element of surprise was taken away, grabbing for the weapon would be nothing more than a suicide play. He studied Spence and Charley to see how long they'd hesitate.

Verna realized — too late — that she had left Wyatt wide open. Afraid of a gunfight, she had done the first thing that had come to mind to stop it. Thinking quickly now, she did the next thing that came to mind, the only action she could think of to save Wyatt and herself.

"He'll kill you!" she shouted at Spence and Indian Charley. "He's got a shotgun and he'll kill you dead! The both of you!"

When Verna had stopped Wyatt short, he already had placed his hand in the wagon bed. The squatter rats couldn't see that hand from where they stood. Wyatt now kept it there. For all they knew, he had the gun in hand and could fire both barrels at the first provocation. They had to realize that standing as close to each other as they were, forty-two loads of buckshot would tear both of them apart, even if they would be able to shoot Wyatt in the process. The glint of worry returned to Spence's eyes.

Wyatt decided the time had come to complete the bluff. "You can keep your damn water," he said, "and you can also keep yourself in one piece. How about it? We have a deal?"

Indian Charley's hand flexed nervously on the rifle barrel, then suddenly stopped, as if he thought the motion might trigger a fight. He looked at Spence.

The short, pointy-faced man was able to manage a smile now that Wyatt was giving him a way out. "Hell, it's a free country. Don't drink my damn water if you don't want to." The smile looked like it was stuck on his face, but his slit-eyes were penetrating and still full of hate.

Wyatt swung a long leg over the side of the wagon and then stepped on board, his gaze never leaving Spence.

"Move the team," he told Verna.

She snapped the reins, turned the wagon, and drove it back onto the road, heading south. Wyatt kept his hands below the side of the wagon, to keep the squatters thinking about the shotgun.

When the waterhole was out of view, Wyatt moved up

next to Verna and took the reins. Her hands were clammy cold. She was silent a while longer before saying, "Wyatt, were you really going to kill them?"

Wyatt shrugged, putting on a nonchalant front. "Not over water I wasn't." He gave her a smile and worked the team up the road.

Rumbling inside of him was an icy trepidation about this place. It had first come to him as they had set out across the hardpan south of Contention and had taken a firm hold after finding men here as hard and treacherous as the land. Wyatt stopped worrying about Apaches and thought more about other dangerous creatures. Pushing down the road, he felt the biting smell of alkali in his nostrils.

At Drew Station there was water for the horses that cost nothing, and from there Wyatt and Verna took on the last leg of the bedrock road to town. Rolling toward the northern outskirts of Tombstone, Wyatt saw a group of men afoot and two riders up ahead, across from a small cemetery. At first, he thought they were setting up a race, but coming closer he could see two of the men kneeling, each burying something in the dry dirt. He then realized that each of the men was burying a chicken up to its neck. After the bets were made, a pistol was fired and the two riders bolted forward. The chicken-pulling contest had begun.

The lead rider leaned over the side of the horse, half out of the saddle. Going full tilt, he grabbed at the chicken head and got hold of it, but then his fingers slipped and he raced on empty-handed. Coming on hard right behind, the second horseman made his grab, managed to take hold under the beak and snapped the head off cleanly.

When the horsemen rode in for the grab, Wyatt had turned to Verna to tell her to look away. He stopped when he saw the way she was watching the contest, transfixed, fascinated. She didn't blink when the chicken head was torn off. She then turned in the seat as they rode by to get a look at the bloody chicken stump.

Wyatt drove past the gamblers and miners settling their bets and rolled on by the outlying adobe houses toward the center of town.

The first man Wyatt recognized in Tombstone was walking along the boardwalk outside the Cosmopolitan Hotel. After checking into a room, Wyatt stepped out through the hotel door to catch sight of the oncoming figure. It was the briefest of glimpses, just long enough to tell Wyatt that the man had a stocky build and a bearded face and that he was heading right toward Wyatt. Wyatt's right hand instinctively went for his hip, even though he had left his guns in the room. The next thing he knew he was staggering away when the man's thick body plowed into him.

Wheeling on the man, Wyatt braced himself for a fight, then suddenly eased up when he saw the face clearly.

"The first man I run into in Tombstone," Wyatt smiled. "Rowdy Joe."

Rowdy Joe Lowe looked at him curiously, showing no sign of recognition. For his part, Wyatt was glad to see the woolly whoremaster. A familiar face made him feel a little better about this new town.

"Joe, you remember me," Wyatt said. "From Dodge — and from Wichita before that."

Rowdy Joe scratched his beard, then pulled absently on the crotch of his pants. "She just picks up and leaves," he said, waving his arm, as if already in the midst of a heated conversation. "Her takin' offense like that. I treat all my gals the same, don't I? When they're on the line at my joint, I treat 'em like what they are. If'n a whore don't want to be treated like one, she can go be a schoolteacher, all I care. She holds out on me and I hit her one. My luck, she takes offense. A goddamn queen she thinks she is. You know my luck. Before long I'll most likely have to pull up stakes and leave. A goddamn queen."

He was now already crossing the street, grumbling to himself, carrying on the conversation on his own, leaving

Wyatt in front of the hotel. Wyatt shook his head and started walking along Allen Street. "Good to see you, Joe," he said to himself.

The Oriental Saloon was another sight that put Wyatt in mind of Dodge and the other cattle towns. According to the clerk at the Cosmopolitan, Virgil was considering buying into the place and was likely to be found there. At first glance Wyatt could see the Oriental was worthy of the Front Street establishments he had just left behind.

Outside the saloon's batwing doors, Wyatt looked in to see a newly built place, not quite finished, but well on its way. It had a mahogany bar, clean tables and a large painting on the wall of a full-figured woman reclining in a filmy, flowing dress. A large mirror rested against the back wall, ready to be mounted above the bar. In just the two months he had been there, Virgil seemed to have found a good investment.

Still a couple hours short of nightfall, it was quiet in the saloon. Only one game of poker was in progress at a back table and only a few men stood at the bar. The chuck-a-luck and faro tables were empty. At a table nearby, a gambler in a brown suit and checkered vest sat toying with a deck of cards, waiting for his work to start rolling in with the end of the miners' shift. He looked at Wyatt standing by the door, sized him up, then turned back to his deck, apparently figuring the tall stranger was not enough of a pigeon.

Wyatt didn't see Virgil, but his eyes rested on a man at the bar, who was dressed in a black broadcloth suit and black hat, his back to the door, talking to a cowboy. The drover, facing Wyatt, was a tall man, with a moustache and goatee. Clearly worked up, he stared at the man in front of him, his hand near his gun belt. By the tense set of the black-suited man's shoulders, Wyatt could see that the bad feeling went both ways.

"His marker's good," said the cowboy. "You sayin' it ain't?"

"I'm just sayin' he should pay up and pay up now," the

other man said. The man's voice snapped Wyatt to attention. He pushed through the batwings and stepped inside, heading toward the argument.

"Big talk, tinhorn," said the cowboy. "You talk like you beat my brother on the square."

"Learn to play poker or don't play. Every time you damn cowboys lose you say you've been cheated. It's not my damn fault you fellas can't hold your own."

Nearing the bar, Wyatt could see the cowboy was about a breath away from making his play, but the other man pressed on.

"And you don't know any more'n your brother does. The two of you are the sorriest, dumbest card players I've ever seen."

Wyatt wasn't about to wait any longer. In one more long step he reached the man in the black suit, grabbed his arm and swung him around.

Under the brim of the black hat, Morgan's face seemed a little older, mature enough to sport a full moustache and weathered enough to show the beginnings of crow's feet around the eyes. To Wyatt, though, it was still somehow the face of a kid.

Wyatt stepped quickly between his brother and the cowboy, checking to see that there was no gun belt underneath Morgan's jacket. The sight of his older brother made Morgan's expression freeze.

Wyatt noticed the beginning of a motion that told him that the cowboy was about to throw down. Before the cowboy could go any further, Wyatt grabbed his right wrist. At first the cowboy was too startled by this sudden move to do anything about it, then he tried to jerk his hand free. Wyatt's vise-like grip didn't let the hand budge. Wyatt then pinned the other hand to the bar.

"Give it up," Wyatt warned.

The cowboy's eyes blazed. He pulled against Wyatt's hold, still getting nowhere, then struggled frantically like a chained animal.

Wyatt held onto the arms. He pulled the right one up

and was about to spin the cowboy around and slam him against the bar when the voice reached him from behind:

"Frank, what the hell you doin'?"

The cowboy stopped struggling and turned to look.

The man approaching them was black-haired, slightly balding, with a tuft of a beard on his chin. He wore a badge on his vest.

"Get away, John," the cowboy growled. "This don't concern you."

"The hell it doesn't," said the lawman. "I let you keep your gun on. Don't make me regret it."

Wyatt could still feel the tensed muscles in Frank's arms. After a few more moments, they started to ease up.

"You can let him go, mister," said the lawman named John. "He's tame now. I'll take care of him."

Satisfied that the fight was out of Frank, Wyatt released him. Frank pulled away. Rubbing his wrists, he then let the wrists alone, as if to show that Wyatt's grip hadn't bothered him at all. He glared at the Earp brothers.

Putting an arm in front of the cowboy and taking his shoulder, John tried steering him away. "Let's go, Frank," he said. Frank shrugged off the hold, turned toward the door and stormed out of the place. John gave Wyatt a curious look and was about to say something, but then decided to go after Frank instead.

Morgan glowered at the doorway that Frank had walked through, not seeming to be aware anymore that his brother was next to him. Wyatt considered his brother but said nothing at first.

"Hell, Morg," he finally said. "After not seeing me all these years, you can't even look at me?"

Morgan's face was still flushed with anger. Wyatt could see the effort his brother had to exert to smile.

"A hell of a way to meet," Morgan said. He let out a short dry laugh. Getting more of a hold on himself, he then turned to the bartender. "Give us a couple, will ya?"

Wyatt placed a hand on his brother's shoulder, searching his face, trying to get used to his kid brother all grown up, a man of twenty-seven. Or was it twenty-eight?

"It's damn good to see you, Morg," he said.

Virgil came into the saloon, walking quickly. He slowed his pace when he saw his two brothers alone at the bar. "Wyatt, you're here," he said, going directly to Morgan, not bothering with any more of a greeting. "I heard there was trouble between you and McLowery. What happened?"

"He was bellyachin' about the money his brother owes me," said Morgan, taking his glass of whiskey off the bar and handing the other to Wyatt. "He figured he could come in here and make me back out of calling in the marker."

Wyatt said, "Who is this McLowery fella?"

"A no-account rustler who calls himself a rancher," replied Morg. "He also thinks he's some kind of shootist."

Virgil shook his head hopelessly. "He's not the only one who thinks so, Morgan."

"From what I saw," Wyatt said, "it would've been pretty damn easy for him to be a shootist going up against someone who's unarmed. Morg, what the hell did you think you were going to do if he went for that Remington of his?"

Morgan turned to take another drink of whiskey, his eyes averted. "I could've taken it away from him," he said under his breath.

Wyatt stared at his kid bother, hoping for a better explanation than that. He then exchanged a look with Virge.

"One other thing," said Wyatt. "How come this McLowery walks around heeled and Morgan doesn't?"

"That's the sheriff's doing," said Virgil. "His name's John Behan. He got elected with the help of Frank McLowery and his friends, and now he's real partial to them. Other fellas might have to put up their guns, but the McLowerys and the Clantons and their bunch can slip by."

Clanton's name brought Wyatt up short. "Clanton? Would that be Ike Clanton?"

"That's one of them," said Virgil. "You know him?"

Wyatt said, "He used to ride with a fella name of Curly Bill. An ugly bastard."

"That'd be Curly Bill Brocius. And he's still riding with him." Virgil looked at Wyatt quizzically. "How well do you know these boys, Wyatt?"

Wyatt knocked back his whiskey. The idea of Clanton and Curly Bill close by made his stomach twist around. His earlier uneasiness now seemed to be brought to completion. The memory of their attack on him still returned from time to time, the memory of his mouth full of dirt, of being flat on the ground behind the trough on Chestnut Street, of the bullets splintering the wood inches above him. He could still feel the rage that had rattled through his body on that night.

Wyatt spoke quietly. "The last I heard, they were cowboying."

Morgan laughed. "Yeah, cowboying other men's cattle and calling them their own."

"That's part of it," said Virgil. "From the talk I've heard since coming here, they're up to plenty else too. And there's plenty of them. This strike has attracted all kinds of men from all over, and a lot of them have thrown in with Old Man Clanton. They do whatever he tells them."

"Does he tell them to squat by waterholes?" asked Wyatt.

"Whenever they can get away with it. Why do you ask that?"

"I met a couple of them on my way from Contention. If there's more like those two around then I'd say the marshal's got himself a big job."

"You're right about that," said Virgil. "Which is why I'm not just a U.S. deputy marshal. I'm also working with the city marshal. Fella named White. He just made me a deputy to help him out. Morgan too, sometimes."

Wyatt finished his whiskey and gave his older brother a long look. "U.S. marshaling for the county and city marshaling for the town — I thought you said you came here for business, Virgil."

"This is business, as far as I can see. Nobody can take care of their affairs with the Old Man's bunch running wild. Last week four men were killed and a bullion stage was held up. There's no business without running herd on these fellas."

Wyatt smiled. Sometimes Virgil talked just like his father, he thought. Nicholas would be proud to hear such talk.

"Something funny?" Virgil asked, irritated by the smile.

"No," said Wyatt. "You're absolutely right."

Virgil took Wyatt to the western edge of the Tombstone town site to show him the mining claims he was lining up. He showed him the claim already registered under the family name on the First North Extension of the Mountain Maid Mine and pointed out two others he had his sights on just a bit farther westward. Right now, Virgil explained, all that was needed to buy this property was the recording fee.

"That won't last for long, though," Virgil said. "Already some investors are coming in to buy some claims. They're coming from San Francisco. Some of them coming all the way from New York."

Virgil went on to tell him about Wells Fargo needing a shotgun messenger, something for Wyatt to think about. "These stage robberies're making it hard for respectable people here," he said. "The payrolls, the mine shipments, the mail — everything depends on the stage."

Wyatt pretended to be listening to all of this but his mind kept drifting, wandering to thoughts that he would rather not visit. The memory of getting treed in Dodge by Ike and Curly Bill had not quite left him yet. After a while, his thoughts then shifted to the friend of Ike and Curly Bill, the man who rode with them on that night. He remembered seeing John Ringo at Ham Bell's livery and recalled how much the man looked like a killer.

Flopping back and forth between the treeing and Ringo's cold, hard eyes, Wyatt's mind then returned to Morgan at the Oriental Saloon. He kept seeing his kid brother, unarmed, standing up to Frank McLowery, ready to take the cowboy on, despite the man's gun and his ability to use it.

24

Old Man's dying made Ike Clanton feel shaky all over.

As long as Old Man was alive, Ike could hold onto a certain respect among the others. Some of them might not like him — he knew for a fact that Floyd Stilwell was outright against him — but Old Man called the shots, and no one questioned his determination to see his sons as top hands. Since there were only three Clanton boys in all, that meant that Ike could count on some say-so.

Ike had to admit, though, that Old Man might not have liked him too much either, but then that just went to show how important it was to be a Clanton. Old Man liked his younger brother Billy more and, to Ike's dismay, even seemed at times to favor older brother Phin, that old busthead. Just the same, when Ike was in trouble in Texas with skinflint Fowler Old Man had come to help, and when Ike got into a fight with Pete over that strawberry roan from the Del Rio raid it was Old Man who stepped in and decided for Ike. That kind of thing made a body feel good.

But then the ornery old coot had to go get himself killed

by beaners. If there was some comfort to take in all of this, it was that Ike was supposed to have gone along on that raid and had been able to slip out of it with a lie about busting up his leg riding the roan. If it hadn't been for that, Ike might have been killed also.

Old Man had ended up taking Joe Hill, Jim Crane, Pony Deal and brother Phin. Pony Deal and Phin were the only ones who had gotten away, and they had brought the story back with them.

Old Man's plan had been to hijack a shipment of silver being smuggled into Mexico by Delgado and his bunch. The problem was that Delgado had set out for the border five days sooner than expected. Given a choice, Old Man would have taken the mule train by ambush in one of the canyons criss-crossing the border, but this time the caravan got ahead of him. Not to be cheated, though, he had set out with Hill, Crane, Deal and Phin because he had a hunch Delgado would stop at a cantina along the road to Santa Cruz.

"You had to give Old Man credit," said Pony Deal. "He didn't miss much." When they had ridden into sight of Aragon's cantina, they had seen Delgado's mules picketed in front, exactly where Old Man had said they would be.

In the moonless darkness, Old Man hadn't been able to see if the silver packs were stored outside. They had had to ride closer. Beside a hogback, Old Man had told Joe Hill to go forward with him on foot, Apache-style, to scout the roadhouse. They had returned around fifteen minutes later, Pony Deal said, with some bad news.

"Delgado, that mean-spirited son of a bitch," said Old Man. "He stashed it all inside. Seems he don't want it too far from his poontang, the old goat. That means we're gonna have to really work for it, boys."

As usual, the Old Man had had his plan pegged out in no time at all. He, Crane and Hill would sneak up to the back door, then Pony Deal would ride hard by the front to get the beaners' attention. When Delgado and the rest had their backs turned, the Old Man, Hill and Crane would come in blazing. Phin's job was to hold the rest of the horses and ride them in at a gallop right after the shooting started so the others could hop on and make a quick getaway.

Phin said he had seen the Old Man and the other two reach the back of the roadhouse as quiet as could be. "They didn't give themselves away. I'm sure them beaners couldn't hear them." That meant that Delgado must have been already waiting for him, because no sooner did Pony Deal start riding in than the shooting from the back began.

Pony and Phin never saw what happened to Crane. They figured he must have gotten it in the first few shots. They saw Joe Hill staggering out from behind the cantina and into the corral, already on his last legs. He tried to fire back, but muzzle flames striking out of the desert blackness cut him down.

Somehow, Old Man had shot his way inside the cantina, the only place for him to go, even if it didn't do him any good. From the hogback, Phin could see the gun flashes inside the lamplit roadhouse. The Mexicans had been waiting for him in there also. There had been a scream, then another, and some Mexican words shrieked by a woman. Only one man had come out the front of the cantina, and damn it all if it wasn't Old Man — what was left of him at least.

Pony Deal had seen that Old Man's left arm was drenched in blood, and at least two fingers were missing. A line of blood also ran down the middle of his creased face and through the white beard below. Pony Deal guessed that there might have been another bullet hole in the man's stomach.

Delgado and his men had run from the back of the cantina to the front. They all had fired at once. Spinning away with the force of one of the slugs, Old Man had snapped off a shot and nailed a Mexican venturing too far forward.

Another shot hit Old Man, plowing through him just above the hip, but still the tough old bastard hadn't fallen. Deal had no idea what had kept him on his feet because half his body must have been smashed with lead by that time.

The gunfire had stopped for a long, eerie moment as the Mexicans had stared in disbelief, perhaps hoping that a gust of wind might do the work that their guns had failed to do. Old Man had tried to bring his second gun up, but it was no use — he hadn't had enough of an arm left for the job. One of the Mexicans — it looked like Delgado himself — had raised his rifle to his shoulder and taken his own sweet time to aim. The shot had drilled right into the middle of the torso. Old Man's body had wrenched with the hit, froze for a moment, then seemed to teeter slightly like a knotty, gnarled old tree buffeted by a shifting night breeze. The body had finally overbalanced forward, still locked with arms bent outward, and crashed to the ground.

The way he told it, Pony Deal never had a chance to throw in once the shooting started. "From where I was, them beaners were out of range. If I charged in the only thing I'd do was get myself killed also." When Old Man went down, Pony Deal had turned his horse, galloped back to Phin, and, after gathering the other animals, the two of them had ridden hard across the flat toward the Arizona border.

Ike knew something would have to be done to keep the bunch together now that Old Man was gone. Everyone else knew it too, which was why they all gathered at the Clanton ranch house as soon as the news got around. Someone was going to have to take charge, and between Frank McLowery, Floyd Stilwell and Ringo, there would be plenty of locked horns in making that decision. Ike wasn't too sure where he would stand with any of them.

A Clanton's got to stand by and watch who takes over, Ike grumbled to himself, after all that us Clantons did to set up this territory. But he wasn't about to kid himself about taking the reins on his own. If Stilwell and a couple of the others had their way, Ike would be told to ride on. And there wasn't much hope for Billy either. He was well-liked enough, but still too young and too quiet to make his mark. As far as Clantons went, that left only Phin, and no one even gave him a thought. It was plain enough, Ike thought, my only chance to hold my own is with Curly Bill.

Ike leaned against the wall by the hearth, too jittery to sit down as he watched the others in the room. He took the bottle from Tom McLowery, swallowed some and passed it along. A bottle of whiskey was usually enough to loosen tongues and fire up some fun, but tonight the boys drank in silence.

Just the sight of all of them here struck Ike as strange. Both McLowery boys, Stilwell, Spence, Indian Charley, Ringo, Hank Swilling, Pony Deal. Two or three might stay over at the ranch at a time, whenever they were on the run or if they needed a place to meet before setting out on business. Otherwise, Charleston was usually the place where they would meet in large numbers.

Ike's sister Hettie came in with a plate of biscuits and set them on the table by the window. As she made a big deal of wiping her hands on her apron, she looked hopefully toward John Ringo sitting to the side of the door, his back to the adobe brick wall. But he didn't pay her any attention. The only one even to notice the biscuits she brought was Indian Charley who was over at the table before Hettie could set the plate down and had already wolfed down four or five by the time Hettie left the room.

Squirming in his chair, Phin couldn't tolerate any more silence. "Maybe we should ride down there and kind of bring Old Man's body back," he said. "Give him a decent buryin'."

Frank McLowery let out a quick, nasty laugh. "Fine time for you to be thinkin' of that. You could've taken him from the beaners when you were there."

Phin turned sheepish and fiddled with his rope belt the way he always did when he had nothing more to say.

"I ain't draggin' no stinkin' corpse up here, I can tell you that," Stilwell put in.

"Me neither," agreed Pete Spence.

"Well, I'll tell you all one thing we can do," said Frank. "We can all ride down there and make that Delgado bleed for what he done. I say we make things square for Old Man. He was good to me and my brother and I ain't about to let that Mex get away with this."

Ike didn't much like that idea. Who the hell knew where Delgado was now? And who was to say the old Mex bastard didn't have ambushers waiting for them along the way? He was about to say as much, but then he saw Stilwell staring at him, like he was daring Ike to say something he could cut down. Ike kept his mouth shut. He looked to Curly Bill.

"No, Frank," was what Curly Bill said. He didn't offer any more than that.

Frank looked at the others to show his impatience with Curly Bill's remark, as if he thought they were already on his side. "What the hell does that mean, Curly Bill?" he said. "Old Man was like a father to you, just like he was to me and Tom here. You fixin' to just sit around pickin' at yourself and let that Mex get away with it?"

"Frank's right," said Stilwell, his meaty face looking smug and defiant. "We got to do right by Old Man."

Ike looked from Frank to Stilwell, trying to gauge whether there was some agreement between them to gang up on Curly Bill.

Curly Bill just shook his head and said, "No." Nothing more.

Frank said, "What're you talkin' about? You got something against shootin' beaners all of a sudden?"

The way Frank was going, Ike half-expected him to now call Curly Bill a coward for not going along with his plan, but Frank wasn't dumb enough to call Brocius out before knowing exactly where things stood. Ike figured that just having Stilwell on his side wasn't good enough for Frank.

"I bet if'n you asked everybody here," said Stilwell, "most of 'em would be ready to get Delgado. Why not you, Curly Bill? I'd like to know that."

Curly Bill stared at Stilwell. If Stilwell knew the man he was dealing with he would know to start watching his step right now, Ike thought. "Old Man was good to me," said Curly Bill, "but he also taught me good. And I don't remember him tellin' me to ride off wild, not knowin' exactly where to go."

"Well, there's some who know a thing or two about trackin' a man." Stilwell glanced at Frank, looking for support. "You know damn well what I've done for Johnny Behan's posses, and he can tell you something about my trackin'. With Spence here, I can run down this Delgado and then the only thing the rest of you gotta do is waltz in and pull the trigger."

"You don't know shit about trackin' a man." Curly Bill's tone was matter of fact. "That's how come we ain't goin' after Delgado."

"Me not knowin' how to track. That's funny."

Curly Bill got up, rubbing the side of his face, and started pacing in the middle of the room. "For what we gotta do, we don't need no trackin'," he said. "There's this mule train ridin' out of Tucson tomorrow with bullion, headed for Sonora. We jump 'em just this side of Bisbee and then we'll be even for Old Man. That's what we gotta do."

"Is this here Delgado's mule train?" asked Spence.

"It's beaners," Curly Bill said simply. "That would be good enough for Old Man and it's good enough for me." He turned to Stilwell. "That's the plan, Floyd."

Stilwell met Curly Bill's stare for a moment, then tried to laugh it off. "I ain't heard nobody else say it's the plan." He laughed again.

Ike looked at Frank to see if he was ready to throw in

with Stilwell now, knowing there wasn't going to be any other time to do it, if Ike knew Curly Bill. Frank leaned back in his chair and folded his arms across his chest, waiting, saying nothing. If he had made a deal with Stilwell, all bets were off now. That damn fool Stilwell, Ike thought with some satisfaction. Ike even considered speaking up now, but he wanted to make absolutely sure first.

Curly Bill walked over to Stilwell, who was seated by the wall. "That's the plan," he repeated, giving him one more chance to see the light.

Stilwell glanced at Frank and, seeing his ally sitting tight, he jutted out his chin to show that he really wasn't bothered by Curly Bill standing over him. All of a sudden, he started to get up.

Just as Stilwell got off the seat, Curly Bill swung out a foot and knocked Stilwell's left leg out from under him. Stilwell dropped hard to the packed-earth floor. Curly Bill then kicked him in the chest, making a dull, wicked thud of boot against flesh.

As his wind came back, Stilwell started to groan. Curly Bill then turned to Spence. "That's the plan," he announced. "Right?"

Looking at Stilwell curled on the floor, Spence didn't answer at first.

"Why don't you ask what Ringo thinks?" said Curly Bill.

Spence looked nervously toward John Ringo. The Texas renegade returned the look with a twist of a smile, in no hurry to speak up. "Curly Bill's got it all figured," Ringo finally said. It was a deep voice and, seldom used, it got a lot of attention. "We both like the plan."

So that's what made Curly Bill such a cock-of-the-walk, Ike realized. He had Ringo in his hip pocket the whole time. Suddenly, Ike felt his tongue loosening. He stepped forward.

"What do you say, Spence? You fixin' on goin' against Ringo?"

Spence just shook his head no.

Curly Bill faced Frank McLowery. "The same for you, Frank?"

Frank met Curly Bill's look, then dropped his gaze to the floor. He didn't bother to answer.

Ike put on a big smile. "We need some whiskey here. What do you say?" Using the correct deferential tone, he added, "Curly Bill, what do you say?"

"Get Hettie in here with another bottle, Ike. And get her to bring in some food too. I'm hungry."

"Sure thing, Curly Bill." Ike ran to the next room and snapped at Hettie for being so slow.

Just below the rim of Sawtooth Canyon, the air in the hollow seemed to stagnate and get hotter all the time. Slumped against the rocky side, holding the reins and sweating like a pig, Ike brooded about people's lack of consideration.

Sure, let Ike hold the horses, he thought. Let the man's work be done by everybody else. Naturally, he didn't begrudge Ringo and Curly Bill the right to sit over there on the other side of the rim with their rifles ready. They were the aces, they had to be there. And even Frank McLowery — he was a dead shot. But Stilwell and Indian Charley! If there was some reason for them to be taking their places alongside Ringo, Ike would like to know what it was. One of them was a jackass and the other wasn't even a white man, for Christ's sake.

Stilwell, of course, was the first one to say Ike should hold the horses. But Ike had to admit: Stilwell wasn't the only problem. Curly Bill was to blame also because he sure went along with the idea quickly enough. And he was supposed to be Ike's friend. That's what really got under the skin. After standing by him for years, Curly Bill was letting Ike down now that he was top dog.

An idea that had been nagging Ike now began to gain momentum. He was beginning to wonder why Curly Bill had stuck with him as long as he had.

Ike had figured all along that friendship was all it was, but now he had his doubts. There could have been something else on Curly Bill's mind. Chances are he had known the Old Man by reputation all along, and when he came upon Ike during that cattle drive up to Wichita, maybe the Clanton name had started him thinking. Maybe he thought that riding with Ike would some day put him in good with the Old Man, give him a chance to move into the Old Man's outfit. There was a price to be paid for having such a big man for a father, Ike mused.

Of course, hanging around somebody for three years seemed like an awful long time if all Curly Bill wanted to do was meet that somebody's father. On the other hand, Ike was starting to see that Curly Bill was a shrewd operator, much shrewder than Ike had first thought. In any case, would a real friend leave him to hold the horses? Ike didn't think so.

Across the shrub-spotted plateau Ike could see the Mexican mule train approach the canyon. Going further to the west or east would have meant that the train would have had to wind through the mountains. The fastest way for the beaners, Curly Bill had told the boys, was through the Sawtooth, and that was exactly where the Mexicans were going. Yes sir, Ike thought, that Curly Bill is a lot smarter than I figured.

The seven Mexicans Ike saw disappeared from view behind a craggy, cruel-looking ridge at the mouth of the canyon. The clip-clop of hoofs resounded hollowly as the train rode deeper into the pass. Minutes later, the lonely sound was suddenly drowned out by the burst of rifle fire crashing across the canyon floor.

Even after the firing stopped, the gunshot echoes bounced

between the Sawtooth walls, rippling and diminishing in the thin air. Ike then heard a drumming of hoofs, a far off sound, then three more shots as the last escaping Mexican was taken down.

"Ike!" a voice rang out from the other side of the rim. "Ike, you get over here!"

Ike led the horses to the other side and saw Curly Bill, Ringo, Frank and Indian Charley reaching the canyon floor. Curly Bill called again. "Let Stilwell take 'em," he said, pointing to the horses. "Get down here."

Stilwell worked his way across the ridge to reach Ike's side. When he took the reins from Ike, his meaty face was creased into a smile. Ike glanced uneasily at him as he started down the slope.

Ike found Curly Bill standing over a gut-shot Mexican. "What do you want, Curly Bill?"

"Frank says he ain't sure of you."

Ike saw Frank following Ringo and Indian Charley deeper into the canyon, well out of earshot. "What the hell does he mean by that?"

"He says you got to do your share," said Curly Bill.

A screech split the air. Ike turned to see Indian Charley standing over one of the other Mexicans, nudging the man's leg wound with his boot. The wounded man screamed once more.

Curly Bill looked blankly at Charley before turning back to Ike. "Frank says you can't be trusted unless you pull your weight with the rest of us. This ain't me talkin' now, Ike, this is just what Frank says. His idea is that we gotta make sure of you."

Frank's against me too, Ike brooded. As disgruntled as he was, though, he didn't let it show to Curly Bill. "What do you what me to do?" he asked eagerly. He then jumped as a bullet blasted from Charley's rifle, ending the wounded Mexican's screaming.

"This here beaner's still breathin'," said Curly Bill. "You know what the Old Man would've said about that."

"Right you are," said Ike. He could see the Mexican's nostrils flare repeatedly from the intake of breath. He then turned in time to see Curly Bill toss him a rifle.

"It's your job," said Curly Bill. "Just to satisfy Frank."

Ike almost dropped the weapon, but managed to get a good hold on the barrel before it hit the ground. He had never held Curly Bill's Winchester .44-.40. The heft felt good in his hands, the long barrel and the rear sight speaking well for its long-range accuracy, an accuracy Ike had seen Curly Bill prove. Not that Ike had to worry about range now.

"Hell," Ike said, "is that all you want? I guess I can do that much."

He levered the Winchester and lined it up on the sweating Mexican's face.

25

Adjusting his spectacles, Fred Aikens, the transfer agent, checked the contents of the treasure box against his records. Wyatt figured this would be a procedure of no more than a few minutes, but Aikens was a careful man and was clearly going to take his time about it. Wyatt stood around on the boardwalk and waited as long as he could, but the heat and his impatience got the better of him, and he stepped back into the office.

Sitting at Aikens' desk, he loaded powder and buckshot into four more copper casings. He was sure he had enough ammunition already, but the task was a painless one and it passed the time easily. After filling the remaining loops of his cartridge belt, he broke open the new shotgun to load both barrels.

The Stevens ten gauge had a different feel to it, a shade lighter than what Wyatt was used to. Wells Fargo had given it to him because, as Aikens had pointed out, a shotgun messenger needed an easier-handling gun than the twelve gauge that Wyatt owned for street work. In the stagecoach boot, a messenger had to maneuver quickly when trouble came his way.

Leaning back in the chair and laying the Stevens across his legs, Wyatt looked out the window at Aikens. Perspiration making his nose slippery again, the transfer agent pushed his spectacles back up, then leafed back to the first page of his documents to check the treasure chest once more. Exasperated, Wyatt sighed. He knew there was no need to step out into the scorching sunshine right away, but, getting restless, he stood up and headed for the door anyway. His first run to Benson about to roll, he was itching to begin his work for Wells Fargo. The past two weeks he had been settling into Tombstone, doing little except tagging along on Virgil's mine speculation jaunts. He was ready to do some work.

Standing alongside Aikens, Wyatt appreciated seeing Virgil come his way, glad to have someone to talk to for however long Aikens would prolong the procedure.

"Did father tell you to see me off on my first run?" Wyatt said straight-faced.

Virgil grimaced. "Just thought I'd pass the time," he said.

Wyatt gave him an incredulous look.

"Allie wants you over to the house for dinner tomorrow," said Virgil, not sounding very hospitable.

"All right, I won't argue. I'll eat your food." He glanced at Virgil again to see him standing stiffly, his hands clasped behind his back, looking straight ahead. Neither said anything for a moment.

"I'll tell you, Virge," said Wyatt, "you're no better at passing the time than I am. You got something itching you. Spit it out."

Virgil didn't seem to mind the needling. "It's about Morgan," he said. "I wanted to get to you when he wasn't following you around."

"What about him?" said Wyatt.

"Well, he needs somebody to steer him. I think you're the one to do it."

"He can be a hothead, no doubt about it," said Wyatt.

"One of these days he's going to walk into something without thinking and he won't be able to walk out of it. He's a hothead, all right. Fact is, Wyatt, he's a little like you. Always was."

Wyatt nodded, but didn't say anything.

"I've tried to drive some sense into him," Virgil continued, "just like I used to do with you — for all the good it did anybody. But he won't listen to me."

"You think he'll listen to me?" said Wyatt.

"Could be. He's always taken after you. When you were kids, you'd jump on a horse at a run and the next thing you'd know Morgan would come right along behind you to try the same thing. He still looks at you the same way, Wyatt. You've got to know that."

"Something's got to be done, you're right about that, Virge." Since seeing Morg go up against Frank McLowery his first day in Tombstone, Wyatt had seen other signs — arguments when there was nothing to argue about, a fistfight with a miner. He didn't like what he was seeing, but he had to admit, he hadn't done anything about it.

Virgil said, "Father used to send me along to keep an eye on you. I think it's time you do the same for Morgan."

Wyatt considered his brother's words, letting an idea take shape. "Maybe there's something I can do," he said. Acknowledging the signal from Aikens, he then put the shotgun into the boot and took hold to climb aboard. "Let me think on it," he told Virgil.

Sitting next to the driver on the way north to Benson, Wyatt did think of Morgan, but he couldn't let his thinking get too far. He couldn't dispute what Virgil had said; if someone was going to help his younger brother stay away from trouble it would have to be him. Virgil never could bring Morg into line — probably because he was too much

older. That much Wyatt could settle on. But he didn't have
the luxury now of dwelling on exactly what it was he could
do for his kid brother. On his first stage run he wasn't
about to let his mind wander to things that weren't essen-
tial at the moment. The country was still new to him and he
made a point of committing to memory as much of the
land as he possibly could.

The stage was traveling across a flat plateau with little
growth to provide cover. Someone could not approach without Wyatt seeing him from a good distance across the flat.
Along other stretches of the route, though, there were
gullies and chains of hills, places where a man could hide.
At some places, Wyatt saw, a man could hide close enough
to jump the stage if he timed it right.

Passing the waterhole alongside the road between Tombstone and Contention, Wyatt noted that there was no
longer any tent pitched behind the thicket and there was no
sign of squatters. He hadn't seen the man called Spence
since that first day, and had only seen Indian Charley
once, riding along Fremont Street the week before. The
half-breed had passed Wyatt without even noticing him
and had moved on out of town. Just the same, neither man
had been out of Wyatt's mind for very long. The fact that
they weren't collecting tribute for water only meant that
they were up to something else.

The stage now passed redstone mesas and the foothills to
the mountains rising farther to the east. Eyeing the piercing, broken lines of the yellow and red formations against
the deep blue sky, Wyatt saw something pleasing in this
harsh land for the first time, a striking quality that had
been masked before by the severity of the region. As he
watched the ridge to the right, he then saw two riders, sitting their horses, skylined at the top of the ridge. They
seemed unconcerned that they were so clearly exposed, but
Wyatt believed there was nothing casual about them. He
thought they were watching the stage.

After a while, they came down off the crest and rode

across the slope, keeping pace with the coach. Wyatt braced himself. He thought they might try a charge across the thin stretch of flatland. He also thought he knew who they were. The distance was too great to identify them, but he had a hunch.

A furlong farther along the ridge, the riders turned their horses toward the stage. Wyatt pulled back a hammer on a shotgun barrel. They then turned again, this time away from the stage, and disappeared through a draw.

For the next few miles, Wyatt concentrated on the broken ground to the right. He expected to see the two men again, thinking they might try another approach, but no one showed. Then, as the road curved westward, Wyatt saw a rider, sitting his horse alongside a boulder, just fifty yards away, staring at the stage. Certain that this was one of the men from before, Wyatt was surprised, now that he had a better look at him, to discover that the rider was neither Spence nor Indian Charley. From what Wyatt could see, the horseman was a young man, dressed like a cowboy, about medium height, his hatless head topped with a mop of sun-bleached light brown, almost blond hair.

Wyatt quickly scanned the line of hills to either side of the young man to search for the second rider. The hills were low here, trimmed with cottonwood, almost shimmering in the heat. Wyatt saw a small black spot move quickly across a slope and then vanish behind a rock. A jackrabbit, he figured. Perhaps a jackrabbit scared by something, perhaps spooked by a man with a rifle tucked away in a cut, just near enough for a sure shot. If the man was there, though, Wyatt couldn't see him. He turned back to the boulder. The first rider was gone. Wyatt's eyes raked the area. Like the jackrabbit, the rider had vanished.

For the rest of the drive to Benson, Wyatt saw nothing more of the trailers.

That night Wyatt thought Morgan was murdered.

His idea for helping Morgan occurred to him on the way back from Benson. As soon as the stage returned to Tombstone he went to the Wells Fargo office to talk to Aikens about his scheme. Aikens didn't rule it out, but he wasn't a man to be hurried into anything.

"I will have to speak with Mr. Bruhl," Aikens said. "He is the route agent for this area, you know. He is the one who will have to make the decision."

Aikens returned to cleaning his pocket watch, the parts of which were spread across his desk, washed in the yellow light from the lamp at his elbow. Aikens had been a watchmaker back east in Philadelphia, Wyatt had heard, but that profession became nothing more than a sideline after Wells Fargo had taken him on. Some said he went through this intricate operation once a week just to show off his fancy eastern know-how. Aikens, on the other hand, maintained it was merely a necessary step to keep his watch running perfectly, which in turn ensured Wells Fargo's punctuality.

"He can handle himself," said Wyatt. "Morgan was a marshal up to Montana before coming here. I wouldn't recommend him if I didn't think he could do the job."

"I'm sure he can," said Aikens, turning back to the minute pieces of the watch on his desk.

Wyatt stayed put, standing in front of the transfer agent's desk. He wasn't through yet, and he figured his silence would let Aikens know.

Aikens busied himself for just a moment longer before Wyatt's silent presence took its toll. He slowly raised his eyes to look at Wyatt, his patience obviously strained. "All right, Wyatt. I will recommend him. I will tell Mr. Bruhl I want your brother in the company."

"You're a good man, Aikens," Wyatt said. "I'm sure Bruhl will listen to you."

Wyatt was feeling proud when he left the Wells Fargo office. Working as a messenger could help settle Morgan, give him something he had to account for. It would also take time away from Morgan's nights on the town. Judging from how badly Morg handled the high-rolling life, the less time spent at it the better. And one other thing Wyatt liked about this prospect: as a shotgun messenger, Morg was not about to be caught unarmed. No brother of Wyatt should have to go around without insurance, and ten-gauge insurance could sure be comforting.

Wyatt started looking for Morgan in the saloons along Allen Street. As the night brought in a wave of miners just off their shift, Allen Street bustled and howled, and the crowds in the bars made it harder for Wyatt to spot his brother. He passed through the Oriental, the Occidental, Hafford's and the Crystal Palace without any luck. Gunshots from the east end of the street then turned Wyatt around.

He ran down Allen Street and saw a crowd gathering outside the Bird Cage Theater. As he drew closer, the terrible thought flickered in the back of his mind, then suddenly rushed to the fore: the Bird Cage was one of Morg's favorite haunts. If Wyatt had gone there first, maybe the gunshots would never have been fired.

Wyatt pushed his way through the crowd.

Dashing through the red brick doorway, he peered through the smoky air to see Virgil and Marshal White by the stage at the other end of the building. Virgil held a miner by the back of the collar; in his other hand he held an old Dragoon revolver. Not a gun that Virgil would carry, it obviously had been taken from the miner. White was looking at something on the floor, something hidden from Wyatt's view by the front row of tables and chairs. Wyatt's stomach sickened. Keeping himself in check, he strode forward, the only thing going through his mind was that he would have to look at the body, like it or not.

Before Wyatt moved very far into the theater, another gunshot roared. White and Virgil hit the floor, pulling the captured miner down with them. As painted ladies near the stage screamed, White squeezed off a pistol shot that went

wide of the cowboy firing from the box seat on the opposite side of the theater. The marshal's shot, though, was
enough to make the cowboy run.

Jumping out of the box, the cowboy headed for the
doors. He plowed into a table, knocked it onto its side,
then scrambled back to his feet. As the man came abreast
of him, Wyatt vaulted over a chair to get at him. After a
few long strides, he dove, piled into him shoulder-first and
brought him down hard. Without a pause, Wyatt was then
up on his feet again to drag the drover by the foot toward
the stage. The cowboy yelped as he was pulled rapidly
across broken furniture, but Wyatt never heard his pro-
tests. He couldn't get to the stage fast enough. He had to
see the corpse at Marshal White's feet.

Wyatt sagged with relief at the sight of the little man in
the tattered frock coat stretching across the floor, ashen-
faced and glassy-eyed but still breathing. That breathing
wouldn't last much longer, Wyatt thought coldly — the
bullet in the little man's chest would soon cut it short. It
occurred to Wyatt how indecent his relief might be in the
company of imminent death, but there was no arguing
with it. What mattered was that the wounded man was not
Morgan.

Virgil told Wyatt what had happened, a story that Wyatt
only half-heard. Something to do with an argument about
the magician performing on stage. The little man on the
floor wanted to run the magician out of the theater, and
the miner with the Dragoon had objected. "Damned if I
know why the cowboy dealt himself in once the shooting
started," said Virgil. "Hell, we can't even figure out who
shot this fella here."

Wyatt didn't really care. All of a sudden he was disgusted with these fighters, all three of them, the little man
on the floor as much as the other two. In a short time they
had already brought him too much misery.

After helping bring the fighters to the jail, Wyatt started
his search for Morgan again, agitation now making his

step quicker. He stopped by Hafford's once more and the Crystal Palace also and then moved on to the Alhambra.

He didn't have to go any farther. There at the Alhambra bar was Morgan, smiling and drinking. This irritated Wyatt, as if his brother's good time mocked the fear that had flared up in him this night. Wyatt stepped toward Morg, working out what he would say to him. The words were then forgotten as the man standing next to his brother turned Wyatt's way.

"Bat!" exclaimed Wyatt.

"Been looking for you," said Bat Masterson, tipping his bowler to the back of his head. "For a minute there I thought this brother of yours was you."

Wyatt looked past Bat at Morgan. By the look of it, his brother and Masterson had been at it a good while, and the liquor had loosened them up some.

"Bat," said Wyatt, keeping a deadpan, "you come here and the first thing you do in Tombstone is spend money at some place I don't own."

"Just tryin' to even up the competition. Fact is," Bat said, "the first thing I saw was the name Alhambra up there. You coulda knocked me over. I just had to look it over, see if it was the same as the Alhambra in Dodge. Here I am, I travel hundreds of miles and it's all the same names."

"Yeah, it seems a lot of Dodge is coming this way," said Wyatt.

Morgan said, "I was about to take Bat over to see our saloon. Told him Luke Short might be dealing for us. One of your old pals from Dodge."

"And another thing," said Bat. "Was that Cold Chuck Johnny I saw down the street before? He was just about ugly enough."

"Yeah, he came in from Dodge too," Wyatt said.

"Wyatt, about this Oriental Saloon of yours. Any chance for another honest dealer to work there?"

"There's a chance."

"Mighty white of you, Wyatt," Bat said and smiled.

When the voice reached them from the side, Wyatt could see Bat's smile become strained and a cold look creep into his eyes. "Hello there, fellers," was all the voice said. Before he turned to look, Wyatt knew who it was.

Doc Holliday stepped up alongside Bat. There was a little more color than usual in his face. The consumptive glow was still in the eyes, perhaps more than ever, but he looked somewhat healthier.

Wyatt said, "Doc, I heard you were in New Mexico. Las Vegas somebody said."

At the mention of Doc's name, Morgan turned to Holliday, his face showing quick interest. Wyatt had mentioned Doc to his brother, and Morgan had heard a lot more from others. A twinge of unease flickered inside Wyatt as he saw the intrigued look on Morg's face.

"Las Vegas was passable," said Doc, "but I couldn't see staying put there."

Bat said, "Now don't tell us they objected to you killing that saloonkeeper there." He barely looked at Doc.

In Dodge, this sort of bad-natured ribbing from Bat was liable to get nothing from Doc but sullen silence, but now Holliday seemed unconcerned, his mouth twisting into a smile. "I declare, Bat," he said cheerfully, "you're so well-informed."

"Whatever you say, Doc," Bat said as tolerantly as possible.

Doc clapped him on the back. "I do believe this dry Arizona air agrees with me. What do you say, boys, which of you is buying?"

Knowing Doc well enough not to be surprised by his moods, Wyatt didn't let this one faze him, even if he had never seen the mood before. Perhaps it was the climate after all.

Not bothering to wait for Bat to take up Doc's suggestion, Wyatt called the bartender over to order the drinks.

As he turned toward the bar, toward the front window, something on the other side of the street made him stop.

On the opposite boardwalk he saw Verna, all dressed up, in a way he hadn't seen for a long time, walking along with two other people. One was a girl named Ginnie, a whore who worked at the Bird Cage Theater. At least she had been working there until a couple of days ago when she got into a fight with the owner, Billy Hutchinson. Wyatt had helped Marshal White break up the scuffle, which had taken place during showtime and built up a second attraction for the crowd at the theater. Wyatt didn't know if she was back on the line now, but she was certainly dressed for it, all painted up with a low-cut dress and cheap finery. Ginnie walked at Verna's left arm, while on Verna's right was Rowdy Joe Lowe, listening for a change, and laughing raucously at something Ginnie said. Verna smiled at him.

"Wyatt," the bartender said. "Wyatt, I asked you what'll you have . . . Wyatt?"

Wyatt took a moment to focus in on him. "Drinks. For all of us. Whiskey. Yeah, whiskey."

26

From the road, the Mexican's body looked like a black bulge halfway to the horizon along the bleached white ground. Wyatt wrestled with his thoughts for a few moments before telling the driver to bring the stage to a stop. As he was braking, the driver protested.

"We got to keep time," said Levi. "You know what Aikens says. We got to pull into Bisbee right on the dot or he'll have kittens."

"I'm taking a look," said Wyatt, swinging a leg over the side of the boot.

The passengers inside the Bisbee stage looked at Wyatt curiously. One of them, a dry goods storekeeper from Prescott named Helm, offered to go along. "If you catch any trouble," Helm told Wyatt, "I'll clean them out for you." He reached into his pocket for cartridges and started loading his old Henry.

"You just stay here," said Wyatt. "I don't see anything out there that's liable to jump up and bite me." He slipped off his duster, put it in the boot and set off across the flat.

The Mexican had been shot once, as far as Wyatt could tell. The entrance wound was just below the right shoulder blade. There may have been other wounds, but Wyatt saw no reason to turn the body over to see. The Mexican had obviously been dead for quite a while — the top skin of his face and hands was completely peeled from the sun and he already stank. Wyatt would just as soon leave him be.

More interesting to Wyatt were the tracks that led from the body in a southwesterly direction toward the brush-covered mountains. Wyatt couldn't see where the trail ended, but he guessed that the Mexican had dragged himself a long way before he had finally died. Black specks could be seen in the distance, above the mountains, weaving through the air: the dance of buzzards.

When he returned to the stage, Wyatt told Levi he was going to follow the dead Mexican's back-track. He might not have done so if he didn't have a spare horse tied to the rear of the stage. At the Bisbee end of the run, he had planned on riding back to Tombstone on his own, leaving his post on the return trip to another messenger so that he could be back at the Oriental in time to set up the gambling concession. He had brought the spare horse along for that purpose. He now reached up to pull the horse's saddle from the top of the coach.

"For cryin' out blue Jesus," said Levi. Remembering himself, he turned toward the mail order bride riding in the coach. "Excuse me, ma'am," he said, then turned back to Wyatt. "How the . . . how're we supposed to finish this here run on time with you traipsin' around the valley? Aikens'll take it out of my pay. He's a vengeful man, Wyatt, you know that."

"The stage'll keep," Wyatt said, heaving the saddle onto the horse's back.

"The driver's the one what gets trouble if'n the stage is late," said Levi. "You're killin' me, Wyatt."

"I'll talk to Aikens. I'll take care of it."

"You will?" Levi seemed appeased. "You best do that

little thing. I surely mean that." He was appeased but still fidgety.

By the time Wyatt tightened the cinch, Levi had found another worry. "You're crazy, Wyatt." He was now keeping his voice low so that the passengers wouldn't be able to hear him. "You find a dead man out here, you leave be. Especially a dead Mex. If one man gets himself killed, another man can get himself killed just as easy, and it could be you this time, Wyatt. Might be Apaches out there. Won't do for you to be alone if there is. And won't do us no good neither if'n you're not here. Think on that."

Wyatt took the shotgun and handed Levi the extra Winchester. "Won't be long," he said. "You can always make a run if you have to. I'll catch up."

When Wyatt rode off, Levi had run out of talk. He sat morosely and spat over the side, even though he wasn't chewing tobacco and his mouth was just about bone dry.

Levi was right: the gun that had killed the Mexican could have been fired by an Apache as easily as it could have been fired by anyone else. Even so, Wyatt was counting on it not having been an Indian attack. He didn't fool himself into thinking that he was enough of a desert scout to know Apache sign at a glance, but he did know from what Marshal White had told him that most of the bushwhacking near the border was between Americans and Mexicans. An instinct told him that that sort of business was facing him here.

Trailing back from the Mexican's body, Wyatt was able to move at a trot across the sparse flat and still see the markings clearly. Past the stretch of exposed ground was a broad swathe of tall grama grass where he had to slow to a walk to read the sign. At times he had to dismount for a better look, and twice he had to double back and change direction. It was odd that the dying Mexican had left the grass's protection from the sun and its cover from possible pursuers for the wide-open land beyond. Wyatt figured that the man, losing his grip in the final moments, had thought he might still reach some point of safety, either real or imagined. He would have died soon enough either way.

On the other side of the meadow, the land started to climb as the grass thinned and gave way to creosote and mesquite. The shoulder of a ridge rose sharply in the near distance, its sharp, jagged lines partially concealing the mouth of a canyon. Hovering above were the buzzards.

When Wyatt would tell Aikens about this place later, he would find out that it was known as Sawtooth Canyon. For now, though, he only knew it as a passage through the mountains, headed southwest toward Sonora, a hidden route that might have been used by smugglers.

Following the back-trail of the Mexican, Wyatt entered the canyon — almost small enough to be a ravine — at first to find an empty tail, but then farther on he reached the rest of the Mexican party he had been expecting to find.

He counted six of them, sprawled on both sides of the canyon floor like carelessly thrown dolls. He walked his horse close enough to one of the bodies to see that it was bloated and spoiling. Riding by another, he discovered something else. The Mexican was on his back with his head propped against a rock, apparently placed there by someone's peculiar whim once the work was done. Certainly no one in the Mexican's condition would have taken such an incongruous, leisurely pose by himself.

As far as Wyatt could see, the bullets through the leg and stomach would have been enough to get the job done, at least after a while. Most likely, the knife slashes were someone's afterthought. They were short, deep cuts along the length of each arm, slashed across at regular intervals. The twisted expression frozen on the dead man's face probably meant that the knife had been used while the Mexican had still been alive.

To make sure his suspicions about these killings were correct, Wyatt left his horse ground-hitched and climbed up the west slope. He wound his way up a zigzag trace, lined with talus at the base and bordered farther up by a badland jumble of ledges and rock outcroppings. Just about any spot along this broken incline would have provided cover for a sniper, but Wyatt didn't find the ambush nests until he neared the crest. Here were boot prints and spent shells at four different locations beneath the rim. Wyatt stopped to lean against a boulder before starting back down. Looking at the corpses from above, he saw them as being small and helpless, an impression that struck Wyatt as curious. The Mexicans were, after all, only smugglers, regardless of how they had been gunned down. He didn't move for a while as he let his thoughts settle.

He rode back to the stage at a lope. After unsaddling and tying the horse, he got back in the boot, ready for the last leg to Bisbee. Levi was shaking his head. "Dern, Wyatt," he said, "there weren't no reason for goin' out there. And you know it."

"Let's move," said Wyatt.

"Just some Mexes what got themselves shot up — ain't that right?"

"That's right, Levi." For no good reason, Wyatt broke open the shotgun to check the loads. "Let's drive on," he said.

"And we got a responsibility here, ain't we? Now don't tell me to put on some hurry. We're late and no hurryin' is goin' to change that. You can't leave me here on the road with a mess of passengers just awaitin'. You know I'm right, Wyatt."

Wyatt reached out, took the whip from Levi's hand and lashed it twice across the team. The stage lurched forward. Grabbing the whip back, Levi took control of the team and pulled on the reins, coaxing the animals until he had set a steady pace.

"Dern it, Wyatt," he said, putting the whip to the horses once himself.

Wyatt sat silently, scanning the land around him. His nostrils still seemed to bristle with the stink of the dead men in the canyon. The stench didn't leave him until they were just short of Bisbee.

27

Aikens seemed satisfied with Wyatt's explanation for the delay of the Bisbee stage. Wyatt said he had called for a halt because of movement in the hills up ahead that he had suspected might have been an ambush in the making. "Levi was all for moving on," Wyatt said, "but I told him to wait until I was sure it was all clear. Can't say for sure what it was. We got through, though." Wyatt figured this story would be more acceptable than the truth. Aikens wasn't likely to be in favor of scouting for a party of ambushed Mexicans in the middle of the Bisbee run.

Not only didn't Aikens blame Levi for the delay, but he shook Wyatt's hand and thanked him for his caution. "Commendable, Earp," he said. "I am sure the company is grateful." Wyatt had noticed that Aikens called him by his last name whenever he was speaking for the company. They weren't back on a first-name basis until Aikens saw Wyatt to the door of the office a few minutes later and wished him a good night.

At the Oriental, Wyatt met the man Virgil had thought

could hire on as a stud poker dealer. With Bat now dealing
from time to time, just one more man was needed and this
new man looked like he could be the one. Named Ab
Richardson, he had worked Deadwood, San Antonio and
Leadville, or at least said he had. Wyatt liked the look of
the trim, short man right from the start and was willing to
take him at his word as far as his experience was concerned.
He told Richardson to sit at the side table across from the
bar where he could get started on a trial run. Doc was
already at the table, along with a big miner and a drummer
from Sacramento. If Richardson could keep the peace at a
table where Doc sat, then Wyatt figured he would do.

Taking a turn around the place, Wyatt checked on the
other games. Monte, faro and chuck-a-luck tables were
already going strong and had been bringing in a lot of gold
and silver money for a couple of weeks now. After the arrival of the roulette wheel from Kansas City in another
week or two the Oriental would become even more profitable. And the trappings were keeping pace with the
money. The big mirror was up behind the bar, new trims
were in place along the walls, and a set of longhorns had
been mounted above the backbar mirror. The longhorns
were Bat's idea. He figured if there were longhorns in the
Long Branch, there should be longhorns in the Oriental as
well. For good luck, he said.

With Morgan riding messenger on the Benson stage, it
was Wyatt's job to stand lookout tonight. Feeling restless,
he didn't bother to climb into the watchman's pulpit and
sit with the twelve gauge. Instead he placed himself by the
back wall to get a full view of the place, from the gaming
room in the rear to the bar in front. Noticing a miner about
to get his back up at the faro table, he strolled over to
make his presence known. That was when he heard the
rush of new voices and laughter coming from the front of
the saloon.

One of the voices registered with Wyatt. Raucous and
with an abrasive drunken drawl, it triggered a sharp sensa-

tion of urgency down the back of his neck. He turned
toward the front to see Ike Clanton with a bunch of
cowboys swaggering toward the bar. Like the others, Ike
had his guns belted around the waist.

"I'm buyin'," Ike shouted as he and his friends lined up
at the mahogany counter. Wyatt could now see Curly Bill
standing on one side of Ike and Frank McLowery on the
other. At the end of the line of cowboys Wyatt saw the
sharply etched profile and powerful build of John Ringo.

Two of the crowd were unfamiliar to Wyatt. One of
them bore a resemblance to Frank McLowery. That would
make him brother Tom, Wyatt figured. The other was a
kid, around eighteen years old, with thick dirty blond hair.
Wyatt thought he could have been the blond-haired trailer
that he had seen briefly by the boulder on his first run to
Benson.

Wyatt moved toward the front of the saloon. If this
bunch was going to make trouble he wanted to be close at
hand. Considering the six to one odds in their favor, he
angled to the right and posted himself against the wall facing the bar, alongside Doc Holliday.

Busy losing, Doc didn't notice Wyatt at first, but when
he did, he then shifted his gaze toward the cowboys at the
bar to see Curly Bill ordering another round. He leaned
back in his chair and checked his hole card. "Heard about
the silver shipment hijacked in Sawtooth Canyon," he
drawled, his eyes still on the game. "The fellas who did it
would most likely have scads of money to blow on drinks
in Tombstone, wouldn't you say, Wyatt?"

Wyatt nodded in acknowledgement, his eyes planted on
the hard-drinking cowboys.

The first one to notice Wyatt in the new mirror was Ike.
For a couple of moments, their eyes fixed on each other in
the reflection, Wyatt staring intently while Ike showed no
reaction at first. Clanton, dulled by whiskey, just seemed
mildly interested, but then something lit behind his eyes,

and looking slyly to his friends on either side, he started to smile. He turned around.

"Now just look who's here," Ike said. "You see that, Curly Bill? Our good friend, Wyatt Earp."

The faces of the other five cowboys turned toward Wyatt. He took note of the smirk on the face of the blond-haired kid.

"This here son of a bitch's been doggin' us since Wichita," Curly Bill told the rest of his friends.

"He don't learn too good, do he, Curly Bill?" Ike smiled. "Especially after the deal we gave him in Dodge."

Out of the corner of his eye, Wyatt saw Doc casually take his arm off the table and shift it below, out of the cowboys' view. Wyatt also noted with some satisfaction that Ike and his friends didn't seem to be aware of the move.

"Evening, fellas," said Wyatt.

Ike put the bottle back on the bar and took a step forward, the others moving with him. "Been a while, ain't it, Wyatt?"

"Could've been longer."

Curly Bill smiled thinly. "Still the cocky bastard, ain't he."

Wyatt slowly brought his right hand over to his gun belt and took hold of it. Ab Richardson watched this, frozen in place. The drummer was already getting out of his seat and muttering about getting something to wet his whistle. The big miner looked like he was ready to follow but couldn't get himself in motion yet.

Having Doc at his side was something for Wyatt to consider in this standoff, but he knew it hardly made things even. He also knew, however, that he had no choice in the matter. If he let any bunch of men make him back off in his own place, he might as well pack up now and leave tomorrow morning because he would never to be able to keep order after that. But more important than that, he wasn't going to back off from Ike and Curly Bill, not this time, no matter how many friends they had with them. They had treed him once when they had had surprise on their side. But this was head-on. Wyatt was counting on a strong face-to-face bluff turning the cowboys around. No other possibility entered his mind.

"Hope you fellas plan on behaving yourselves here," he said. "This place belongs to me and my brothers."

A gruff laugh jumped out of Curly Bill. "You ain't learned yet, have ye, Earp?"

"What's that, Curly Bill?"

Ike quickly spoke up for his friend. "You Yankee sons of bitches ain't the cock-of-the walk around here like you was in Kansas. We're the ones who call the tune down here."

"May I remind you," Doc cut in mildly, "that I might be a son of a bitch, but I'm no Yankee son of a bitch. I come from Georgia."

Curly Bill laughed again. "Well, we won't hold that against Georgia," he said. The other cowboys thought this was funny. Curly Bill laughed with them, but Wyatt could see that behind the lopsided grin Brocius was noticing Doc's hand under the table. One piece of the bluff was taking hold to set Curly Bill off balance. It might very well work, but only if the others had their doubts also. Wyatt kept flicking a glance at Ringo. The Texas gunman stared back, unblinking, a faint smile on his lips.

"Damn," Ike said, "now where are my manners? A Clanton oughta know better than that. There's some here you don't know yet, Earp." Ike smiled at Wyatt, looking for a reaction. He got none. "Over there," Ike went on, "that there's my neighbor, Tom McLowery. He's a good boy, Earp. You'll like him. Tom's brother to Frank here. I think you met Frank, didn't you, Earp?"

"We met," Wyatt said, making a point of returning Frank's icy glare.

Ike then put an arm around the blond-haired kid. "And this here's my brother Billy."

Wyatt couldn't see any resemblance between the brothers, but then who was to say how many wives a father of Ike would have had at one time.

"Billy tells me he seen you the other day," said Ike. "Tells me you're ridin' for Wells Fargo."

"You best watch how you ride," Billy said. "A body could sneak up on you, Earp."

There was a mean glint in his eyes, but mostly the kid looked like he was trying to keep up with the older hard-cases with him. Wyatt wasn't sure if he was as bad as Ike.

"And then there's Ringo over here," Ike continued. "I especially want you to meet him. Maybe you've heard tell of him. I say he's probably killed twenty men. Maybe more."

"That right?" said Wyatt. "Tell me, Ringo, that twenty men, is that counting Mexicans you ambushed?"

Ike's smile froze.

The expression on Ringo's face didn't change at all, but he changed the way he stood, almost imperceptibly. Moving slowly, he turned his right side slightly away from Wyatt, the side that wore the revolver. If he were to pull the gun now, Wyatt wouldn't have a good look at the pistol until it had cleared its holster.

The other cowboys became grim. Frank inched a hand toward his gun, as did Billy Clanton. Seeing this and the way Ringo had positioned himself, Ike began to look worried. He glanced from his friends to Wyatt and Doc. He saw that he was standing right in the middle of any possible fire.

Wyatt was watching the cowboys so closely that he just now glanced at the table next to him to see that Doc was sitting alone. He had never even seen Richardson and the miner walk away.

"You got something to say," Curly Bill said quietly,

"you say it, Earp. You think we done something, just you say it and see what happens."

Darting glances right and left, Ike shuffled back a step.

Frank said, "You want to back up what you say, go ahead. A fancy gun belt like you got there — maybe you want to show us how you use it."

His pulse quickening, Wyatt felt the situation running out of his hands. He didn't know why he had said anything about the dead Mexicans. If he had just stood his ground, moved on along the same straight line, the cowboys would have either gotten jittery or tired, and then made some excuse for leaving. Someone would have said it was time for another bottle or time to get some whores, and that would have been that. But now Wyatt had pushed them, and he could see no way to get things back under control.

"Frank, you've got things wrong." It was Doc's drawl at Wyatt's side. "The name is Frank, isn't it?"

Frank McLowery glowered at him, in no mood for polite chatter.

Doc continued, unfazed. "Like I say, you got it wrong. It's not really the gun belt that matters, no matter how fancy it is. It's how much Wyatt's filed the dog on that Colt of his. If he's got a hair trigger then he can really go to work. The gun belt doesn't enter into it. And anyway, none of that really matters because I can shoot your damn eyes and nip one of your balls before Wyatt could even get started."

In the course of the last minute, Frank's expression had gone from killing rage, to irritation, to disorientation, the kind of disorientation that sets in when a sure thing becomes not so sure. Wyatt and Doc could be killed but Frank wasn't quite sure now whether he'd live to see it.

Doc had almost gotten the play back on track. Wyatt saw what had to be done now. There had to be a way to put the cowboys on the defensive — if the situation hadn't already gone too far.

"Don't let Holliday call it for you, Earp," said Tom

McLowery. "You're the one we've heard tell about. How fast can you pull that gun of yours?"

"Yeah, go ahead," chimed in Billy.

The problem, thought Wyatt, was who to single out, the way Doc had singled out Frank. Except for Ike, and now maybe Frank, they all seemed ready enough. Time was running out, and there was little left to do but fight.

Ike sensed the same thing and also saw how comfortable the odds were, whether he threw in or not. "How about it, Earp?" he said. "Here's your chance to show us something." Inspiration hitting him he added, "Maybe you want to take a crack at Ringo. Just you two, Earp. We won't interfere."

Curly Bill liked Ike's idea. "Sure," he smiled, "we won't do nothin'. I swear."

Wyatt figured his only chance depended on Doc taking out Ringo. With the Texas gunman out of the way, there might be some chance with the others. Either they would back down or someone else in the saloon might throw in with Wyatt. He set his sights on Curly Bill. The plug-ugly cowboy would be his first target.

The tapping on the plank floor then distracted him. It also got the attention of the cowboys.

They all turned toward the source of the sound at the front of the saloon. Virgil and Bat stood there, no guns in their hands, but their gun hands ready. Now that he had everyone's attention, Bat stopped tapping his cane against the floor. Right behind Virge and Bat was Ab Richardson, the man who had brought the reinforcements.

The cowboys still had the advantage of numbers, but with the entrance of Virgil and Bat, they found themselves flanked. This was not lost on Ike, whose eyes glazed and who tried to take another step back. He was stopped when Frank blocked his path. Wyatt could see the uncertainty in the eyes of Curly Bill, Tom and Billy. The tables were turned.

A nervous laugh broke the silence. It came from Ike.

"This is funny," he said. "Everyone standin' around not knowin' what to say."

He tried another laugh, then glanced around him as everyone else stood their ground without speaking. "Damn it all," he said, "the funnin's over. Time for a drink." He yelled quickly over his shoulder, "Bartender! Drinks over here! On me! Hell, why not."

When Ike stepped around Frank toward the bar, Billy took a step in the same direction, glanced back at Wyatt, then joined his brother. Tom was the next to go. Curly Bill then dropped his hand from his gun belt.

Ike brought back a bottle and two glasses. "Good thing we got that settled, eh Wyatt? Here you go. Why don't we drink on it."

Placing the glasses on the table, Ike poured two shots. Wyatt noticed that as scared as Ike might be, he could still pour drinks without a tremor. Wyatt took the glass offered him.

"Hell," said Doc, "I got this thing settled as much as anybody, but I don't get a damned drink." He brought his right hand up onto the table again and began shuffling the deck of cards.

"Right," Ike said and smiled. "Get you a glass the next round, Doc."

Wyatt watched Bat post himself at the front end of the bar to keep an eye on the cowboys returning for drinks. Virgil headed toward the back so he could box them in if he had to.

Ike said, "Hell, Wyatt, we got our differences. Guess we did right from the start, way back in Wichita. Sometimes things just happen that way, am I right?"

"You're the one talking," said Wyatt.

Ike didn't seem to mind the lack of encouragement. "What do you say we just settle things in a sportin' way. I'm a sportin' man and I hear you are too."

"What do you have in mind?" The gall of the man almost got a smile out of Wyatt.

"Well, how about this," said Ike. "I hear tell you got yourself one hell of a fine racin' horse. They say you claim that your horse can beat anything."

"I think it can."

"Well, I dabble in horses myself. Got one lined up right now I think can run like hellfire. Why don't we set up a race sometime and see which is best. See what I mean? The sportin' way."

Wyatt was amazed at how fast the man could come up with this way out for himself. He wanted to see how far he'd go with it. "I'm not doing anything tomorrow. Bring your horse around at one o'clock. To the east side of the Combination Mine."

Ike looked at him blankly for a moment, then said, "Okay, I'll do just that. But I'm warnin' you, you'll be going up against something fast." Ike raised his glass for a toast to seal the agreement. "Let's drink on it," he said.

Wyatt glanced at Ike's glass, then gulped down his own drink and put his glass on the table. "I already did," he said. He headed toward the faro table in the rear of the saloon.

Returning to the Cosmopolitan at three in the morning, Wyatt found his room already dark. He moved in quietly so that he wouldn't wake Verna and felt his way to the bureau where he started to undress. He put his shirt down on the bureau to find a pile of clothes already there. Damn cramped room, he thought. He was going to have to change that soon, get a house to live in, maybe one already built. The couple that shared the house with Virgil and Allie might be leaving, he heard. The husband wanted a more orderly town in which to do business than Tombstone. Wyatt and Verna would move in if he left; Wyatt only wished it could be tomorrow.

He sat on his side of the bed looking at the dim outline of the chest of drawers in the dark and thinking about the race with Ike tomorrow. His big gray was certainly a fast one, but it occurred to him now that he hadn't raced it for at least a week. Hell, he hadn't even looked in on it for a few days. Between Wells Fargo and the Oriental and making plans for running for sheriff, the horse hadn't come to mind. He was less sure now. He couldn't say what sort of shape the gray was in; he didn't know if Gonzalez at the O.K. Corral had been exercising the animal.

The possibility of losing to Ike was unthinkable. But then, he told himself, I'll be riding the gray, and if there's any kind of handling that could get an extra burst out of the horse, I'll be able to manage it.

He decided that it had just been tiredness that had been nibbling away at his confidence. "Ike'll be taken care of," he promised himself under his breath. He wondered if he had spoken loud enough to wake Verna. Stretching out, he rolled onto the bed and reached out to lay an arm across Verna. He touched nothing but sheets.

He swept his hand along her side of the bed. Getting up, he went to the bureau and took his watch out of his pants pocket to confirm that it was after three o'clock.

28

"You were just talking and drinking all that time? Who the hell were you with?"

"Just Ginnie and another girl over to Hafford's," Verna said. Still in bed, she sat with her head resting in her hand, trying not to look at the midday sunlight streaming in through the window.

"What're you staying out till four in the morning for?" demanded Wyatt. He had been asleep when she had finally come in and had only her word that she had returned at four. It might have been five or six for all he knew.

"You stay out all night," she snapped. "How the hell do I know what you're doin' all that time?"

"You know because I tell you what I'm doing. I'm working. How the hell do you think I make my money?"

"Wyatt, I ain't even woke up yet. Leave me be."

"Try sleeping at night. It makes it easier to wake up during the day."

She didn't say anything. Still holding her head, she stared at the crumpled sheets at the foot of the bed. Wyatt turned away from her and stared out the window, craning his neck to look toward Fremont Street.

"Damn," he said, "where's Morgan? He could've gone to the corral and been back again three times by now." He checked his watch. It was nearly one o'clock.

Moving away from the window, he paced along the side of the bed. "The whole time you were at Hafford's, huh? You didn't just happen to stroll over to Rowdy Joe's, did you? Is he pimping for Ginnie now?"

"You want to check on me, Wyatt?" she yelled. "Ask over to Hafford's. They'll tell you."

"Ask them! That's funny. Why the hell do I got to ask people about you? They come tell me all the time. About you hanging around with whores, not just Ginnie, plenty others too. What're you up to, Verna? You planning on going on the line again? What the hell is it?"

"What do you want me to do, Wyatt? You talk about plantin' roots here and about becomin' friendly with the right folks. I can't do that, Wyatt. I can't get close to that kind."

"Why not? Just talk to them. I introduce you to enough of them. All you got to do is be sociable. You might even like them."

"I can't do that!" she said. "Don't you know that? You bring me around to Mayor Clum and his wife and all she does is give me that look. I know what she's thinkin'."

"What look?" he asked, exasperated.

"That look. She can tell. She knows what I come from. She looks at me and says to herself, 'She's just a whore. All dressed up nice but still a whore. That's all she knows and that's all she's good for.' That's what his wife thinks. She don't know I come from a decent family, but she knows where I've been along the way."

"Why would she think that? She doesn't know you from Wichita."

"She don't have to," Verna said. "A woman just knows

that about another woman. That's all there is to it. And she's not the only one.''

Wyatt ran his fingers through his hair, paced off a few steps, tried to think of something to say. He came up with nothing.

"So I spend time with whores," she said. "At least they're girls I can talk to. They don't care. They can't kick about what I am.''

"What the hell did I take you out of Nadine's for?" Wyatt shouted.

She stared right at him. As he returned the look, Wyatt had the feeling that something was out of place, something was not there. It didn't take long to figure it out.

All the times he had pushed her along, tried to get her to take care of herself, and all the times he had argued with her, there had always been some point where she had started to cry. Lately, he would see it coming and would usually back off just for the sake of not going down that same tiresome road. Looking at her now, he sensed that she should have reached that point. He figured the time had come for a hint of breaking down, the eyes welling or maybe just the sullen downcast look that had become so familiar to him. But now she looked at him clear-eyed, almost defiantly.

"I don't know, Wyatt," she said. "Why *did* you take me out of Nadine's?" A note of perverse satisfaction was in her voice.

Was she actually enjoying this? Wyatt couldn't conceive of finding any pleasure in one of these arguments, but she seemed to be, just the same. For the moment he was flustered.

He took out his watch to check the time and to give himself something to do. "Damn," he said, picking up his hat and heading for the door. "Damn it all."

Out on the boardwalk, a dusty mist lifted off the road and settled on Wyatt's clothes as he stood motionlessly, watching the passing traffic. It was past one o'clock; he knew he should tend to the race, but he stayed where he was. Ike was waiting near the Combination Mine, he thought, probably gloating at the idea of Wyatt not showing. Wyatt concentrated on that thought. Still, he didn't move. Then he saw Morgan step onto Allen Street, a block away, coming from the direction of the O.K. Corral. The sight of his brother jostled him, reminding him about the gray, and made him think that something might be wrong with the horse. That could explain Morgan's taking so long. Perhaps the animal had sickened since Wyatt had last checked on it. Thinking of Ike didn't get him moving, but the idea of his racer being hurt got him off the boardwalk.

"What's wrong with the gray?" he asked when he reached his brother.

"I went to fetch him like you said, Wyatt —" Morgan's words suddenly stopped. He looked uncomfortable with what he had to say.

"What's wrong with him, Morg?"

"The horse isn't there."

"What do you mean?"

"He hasn't been there for two days," Morgan said.

"Why the hell didn't Gonzalez tell me?"

"He said he thought you had taken the horse yourself, early in the morning sometime when he wasn't around."

"You mean when he wasn't sober," said Wyatt. "Someone took it right from under his nose." He turned agitatedly. "God damn!"

Riding past him was Johnny Sturm, a gambler from Charleston, headed for Toughnut Street. That was where the Combination Mine was. Considering that Charleston was a hangout of Ike's, Wyatt had no doubt that Sturm had heard about the race and was on his way to see it now. Another sporting man from Galeyville also rode by. Wyatt figured a crowd was already waiting for the race to begin. "Damn," he said.

"You've got to call it off, eh Wyatt?" said Morg.

Wyatt said nothing at first as he pulled in the reins on his anger. "Come on, Morg," he finally said. "Let's tell Ike."

They turned onto Fourth Street and headed toward Toughnut. Wyatt's irritation was getting hard to sit on as he watched riders go by and imagined they were all headed for the race. One of the riders came up from behind, passing close by, so close that one of the stirrups brushed against Morgan. Out of the corner of his eye, Wyatt then saw the horseman rein toward the left so that the horse's flank bumped against Morg and shoved him aside. Some horses would have kicked at this contact. Glancing at Morg, Wyatt could see that this thought was not lost on his brother. The rider's dangerous handling made his brother flare instantly.

"Son of a bitch!" he shouted.

Wyatt had done his best recently to keep Morg in line, but now he was in no mood to be a nursemaid. "Morgan," he began angrily, then stopped when he saw what had made his kid brother boil.

The rider wasn't a stranger who had made a stupid mistake. It was Billy Clanton, who was looking pretty pleased with himself. Morgan lurched forward after the cowboy. Wyatt put out an arm, but before he could stop his brother, Morgan halted on his own, as if suddenly petrified. Wyatt followed his brother's gaze and stopped in his tracks himself.

Morgan said, "Christ, Wyatt. Look at him."

Wyatt had noticed the color of the horse right away, but not until now did he realize that Billy Clanton was astride his big gray racer. For a moment, Wyatt didn't move. Rustlers in this country were known for their nerviness — Wyatt had heard of cow thieves herding beeves on the land belonging to the stock's original owner — but this topped it all. Wyatt didn't stay inactive for long.

Running hard, he and Morgan caught up to Billy at the end of the block. Wyatt made it a step ahead of his brother and grabbed the bridle to force the horse to a fast halt.

"What the hell —" said Billy. He grabbed the coiled lariat off the pommel and was about to swing it at Wyatt when Morgan pounced on him from the other side and took hold of his arm.

"Get off me," Billy shouted.

Morgan slammed the arm down and held it against Billy's side.

"Where'd you get this horse?" Wyatt demanded.

"None of your damned business!" said Billy.

"The horse's not yours."

"Who the hell you think you are, Earp? You ain't sheriff yet. Get your brother the hell off'n me." He struggled against Morgan's hold. Morg grabbed the back of Billy's shirt and hauled him off the saddle. Billy flopped noisily to the ground on his back. The next second he was up again, but Morgan booted him in the chest to knock him back.

"Morgan. Enough." Wyatt called out.

Billy scrambled to his feet, his face beet red, his eyes flaring. "You son of a bitch. You ain't gonna get away with this. You ain't got no call to take me down."

Wyatt studied the furious young cowboy. This was no bluff, he thought. Billy really doesn't know what this was all about.

"You're riding my horse," Wyatt said calmly.

Billy was still wild-eyed, but was suddenly quiet, his expression locking into place as this information slowly got past the fury and started to sink in. He then glanced from one Earp to the other, realizing that there was more danger behind the Earps' actions than he had first figured.

"I asked you before," said Wyatt, "and now I'm asking again. Where'd you get the horse?"

"One of the McLowerys sold it to me," Billy said quietly. He stared off for a moment, angry with himself for getting caught, and even angrier for being compelled to talk. "I didn't know where they got it from."

"You didn't know?"

"Tell us who they got it from," said Morgan, taking a step toward the cowboy.

"I don't know," Billy said, "I swear I don't know. I didn't ask them."

Deciding not to press it further, Wyatt said nothing. He was ready to believe the cowboy now. For all the wildness in Billy, Wyatt felt that there was a limit to how much he would lie, at least when he wasn't around the likes of Frank McLowery and Curly Bill.

"All right," Wyatt said, "you didn't ask. I guess you Clantons never ask where your horses come from."

Morgan grabbed Billy by the back of the collar, and this time Billy didn't fight. "I'll take him over to Virgil," Morgan said. "He can make the arrest official."

His eyes still on Billy, Wyatt said, "Hold it, Morg."

His kid brother gave him a puzzled look. "What the hell for?"

Wyatt didn't bother to answer him at first. He found himself thinking of the Indian Territory, of a night at Keys Well. Wyatt really didn't think that Billy had much in common with himself at a younger age; just the same, standing close to a young man found riding the wrong horse put him in mind of sitting in a barred wagon from Fort Gibson to Fort Smith.

"We'll just call this a misunderstanding," he said. "Right, Billy?"

"What're you talkin' about, Wyatt?" Morgan said, completely baffled. "We caught him."

"That's right, we did. But we got the horse back."

Billy looked suspiciously at Wyatt, not ready to believe his good fortune just yet.

Wyatt said, "We keep the horse, Billy, and you can walk away. If I was you, I'd watch my step around McLowery horses."

Billy peered at Wyatt, as if trying to divine the reason for this sudden forgiveness.

"I said you can walk away," said Wyatt.

Not about to wait for another change of mind, Billy shrugged out of Morgan's grip and started walking. He glanced back at Wyatt, then jutted out his chin in a last look of cockiness as he headed down the street.

His face set tight, Morgan watched the cowboy leave. Wyatt could easily imagine what his kid brother would like to have done to Clanton. "What'd you let the bastard go for?" Morg finally blurted out.

Wyatt took the reins of the big gray and started leading him down Fourth Street toward Toughnut. Morgan fell into step alongside, waiting for an answer.

"He made a bad move," Wyatt said. "That's not so bad if you make sure not to do it again."

Wyatt saw Morgan shake his head, still worked up and still in the dark. But Wyatt wasn't about to explain any more than that.

The racing strip near the Combination Mine was lined with gambling men, both professionals setting up their latest source of income and miners looking for a way to lose their pay. Ike Clanton, holding the reins of his black mare, was laughing it up with Johnny Sturm when Wyatt and Morgan approached.

"I thought you'd run out on me, Wyatt," said Ike. "Me and Johnny here was just figurin' on a bet about whether you'd show. Good thing you came before we put our money up or I'd have lost some cash."

Ike exchanged a sly look with Sturm, enjoying some joke that wouldn't be shared with Wyatt.

"I don't figure to be racing with you, Ike. That's what I've come to tell you," said Wyatt.

"Why the blue Jesus not, Wyatt? We had us a deal. You don't back out of deals now, do you?"

"I'm thinking a deal with you isn't much good."

Ike cocked his head. "How do you mean?"

"He means," said Morgan, "that he's not havin' truck with a thief."

Ike looked at Morgan as if the younger Earp were simple-minded. "A thief you say? Wyatt, your brother's got an awful way of talkin' to a feller."

"Never mind that," said Wyatt. "I'm just not racing with you because your family and your friends are a little too careless about horseflesh."

Ike's lips pursed as he met Wyatt's look. He then laughed nervously. "You can't just be sayin' such things like that."

"I let Billy go this time, but you fellas keep it up — well, me and my brothers'll go after you."

"What kind of talk is that?" said Ike, mustering up some indignation. "You're talkin' loco."

"Billy's in town. You can ask him for yourself, Ike. He'll tell you."

Wyatt turned the gray and started walking away with Morg.

Ike called after him. "What'd you do to Billy? You tell me just exactly what the hell you did, Earp."

Wyatt stopped to face Ike. He let out a long breath. He didn't hold out much hope that talking to Ike would accomplish anything, but he thought it should be said anyway.

"Billy's your brother," Wyatt said. "You should be looking after him."

29

"You really are out to get John's scalp, ain't you?" said Ray Pullen, propping his feet on his desk in the Golden Eagle Brewery. "He says you're out for blood."

"Not true. I think he's a good man," Wyatt lied. "All I'm saying is I think I can do a better job than him and I can use your vote."

Pullen shrugged. "That ain't what I hear. I hear you're after his job because — well, maybe hate ain't the word, Wyatt, but you two sure ain't friends."

"John telling you that?"

"Near enough. He come by yesterday trying to get my vote for sheriff. He said I shouldn't vote for a man who's just angling for his job out of meanness and spite. I guess that'd be you he was talking about, Wyatt."

"I'll say it again, Ray. I can do a better job than John can."

"Maybe." Pullen didn't sound convinced. To smooth things over he added, "I guess some of these Southern boys just can't forget where you come from."

Since this was not the first time Wyatt had come across this kind of talk in his campaign, he started to get the idea there was little point in fighting it. He told Pullen he would appreciate his vote come election time and then just moved on to try his luck at the saloons along Allen Street. If Pullen had his mind made up, Wyatt wasn't about to waste his time trying to change it.

As far as Wyatt was concerned, his feelings about Sheriff John Behan didn't have much to do with his campaign. That's what he told Virgil and Bat. Even if Behan wasn't in cahoots with the Clantons and the McLowerys — and a lot of people thought he was — Wyatt would still have run against him. Sawtooth Canyon was enough in itself to prod him into trying for the sheriff's job. The fact that he didn't like Behan just added to his desire to beat him.

Wyatt hadn't built up much of an opinion of the sheriff one way or the other until the day he had run into him at the Crystal Palace. Wyatt had been looking for Bat to talk about some gambling business at the Oriental, and Behan had called him over to the bar. Except for passing him on the street, Wyatt hadn't come across the sheriff since the day Morgan had tangled with Frank McLowery. When Behan now asked if he could buy him a drink, Wyatt saw no reason to turn him down.

"How's that kid brother of yours doing?" asked Behan. "You think he'll be able to stay clear of trouble?"

"He's managing all right," Wyatt said.

"I hope so. I surely do. He doesn't seem like a bad feller. Just got to learn to keep from flyin' off the handle I suppose."

Doesn't seem like a bad feller? If Behan was looking for a bad way to start off with Wyatt, he was doing a good job. Wyatt made a point of drinking some of his beer so that he wouldn't have to bother with a response.

Not seeming to care that Wyatt wasn't saying anything, Behan looked into the mirror behind the bar, flattened the sides of his black hair, patted it gently where it was receding on top and then sipped his drink.

"Yep," Behan said, as if continuing a thought, "a peace officer's got to pay a mind to them that might kick up a ruckus. Got nothing to do with your family, mind you. Just a matter of doing the job. But then, you know a thing or two about that, Wyatt, coming from Dodge City and all. You did a sight of law work up there I hear."

"That I did. And there was enough to do up there, for Bat and me both."

Behan seemed to think this over for a few seconds. "I heard you killed a man in Dodge just for shooting his gun off. That ain't true, is it, Wyatt?"

"Mostly true," Wyatt said. "There's more to it than that though."

"You see there, now that's a way we do things different down here. My thinking is, get the feller before he gets too dangerous. That way the shooting never gets started on either side."

Wyatt stared at him. Behan's words were a bit much and Wyatt wasn't going to let them pass. "Is that how the killing happened at the Bird Cage last week?"

Behan shook his head sadly. "That was a real shame, wasn't it though? A lawman can only do so much. Anyways," he added, "that man who got killed, he was no-account. Just a tinhorn I heard. If I kicked up a fuss for every tinhorn getting himself shot, I wouldn't have time for them that counts. You see what I mean?"

Wyatt took a long swallow of his beer. He figured the easiest way to leave was just to finish the drink quickly and say he had business to tend to. He was out the door just a few minutes later.

After this, Wyatt wasn't figuring on inviting the man to dinner, that was for sure, but on the other hand he still didn't give Behan enough thought to work up much bad feeling either. As a matter of fact, for a time, he even started to think Behan was a capable man, for all his damn fool talk.

When the fire wiped out most of the block at Allen and Fourth, the lot jumpers took over. They pitched tents on lots destroyed by the blaze, lots that were temporarily abandoned, and planned on taking possession through squatter's rights. Judge Spicer didn't let them. He ruled that the lots remained the property of those who had possession when the fire struck. That left the job of dislodging the squatters to the police.

All the peace officers were called out: Wyatt and Morgan were enlisted by Marshal White to help him and Virgil, while Behan was there with Stilwell and Breakinridge and his other deputies. Some squatters went easily. Others needed persuasion. Breakinridge saddled his horse, came at one of the jumpers at a gallop and lassoed the man's tent pole. The tent flew off the ground as the horse swept past. The squatter was left crouching on the patch of earth that had been sheltered, a dumb look on his face.

Wyatt himself had to boot one man off a lot, but at least he didn't have anyone throw down on him, which made his job easier than Sheriff Behan's. The sheriff rousted Willie Conrad out of his tent only to find the squatter's rifle suddenly leveled on him. Wyatt saw Behan stand just five feet away from the muzzle, motionless at first. Then, taking a step forward, he started talking. From the other side of the ravaged block Wyatt couldn't hear what was said, but he could see Behan hold out his hand for the rifle and, cool as could be, take another step closer. Two steps later he had the rifle in hand and was showing the jumper the way to the street. Wyatt figured that Behan knew the squatter well enough to know that he wasn't a killer. Even so, it took some nerve.

It was only after he decided to make a run for the sheriff's job that Wyatt saw the bad blood creep in between him and Behan. The way he remembered it, the run-in at Borg's butcher shop was the incident that had made the difference.

Wyatt and Virgil had looked in on Borg to try to make a dent in Cochise County's rustling ring. It was common knowledge that Borg was buying beef from the Clantons and McLowerys, and Borg himself wouldn't bother to deny it.

"Good beef," the Swede said. "Clantons, McLowerys — both sell good beef."

"They get their cows from rustlers," said Virgil, "if they don't steal them on their own. You help them make money on thieving."

"Cows come from their ranch. I know this, Virgil. They own cows. Their beef."

"The beeves come from their ranches," said Wyatt, "but they didn't start there. They're stolen from Mexico and from hereabouts too."

"You prove that?" said Borg. "You prove they stolen?"

Virgil and Wyatt were slow to answer. If they had proof, they wouldn't have bothered with the Swede. The problem was that established ranches like the Clantons' and the McLowerys' provided a secure place to stash stolen cattle until the brands could be altered. And once the beeves were sold to a butcher like Borg, the slaughtering then erased what little evidence there might have been left. Right now, the only trail Virgil and Wyatt could take was to try to cut off the Tombstone buyers for the beeves.

"No proof," Borg concluded from the Earps' silence. "All I know is good beef. You see, good." He brought the cleaver down and whacked off a chunk of the blood-red beef section on the cutting board.

"What're you botherin' this man for?" said a voice at the door.

Wyatt turned to see Behan, standing just inside the shop, staring intensely at Wyatt.

Virgil said, "No one's bothering him, John."

"Don't tell me you ain't botherin' him. I want to know just what the hell is going on here."

Wyatt had never seen Behan so fired up. Most times he seemed completely under control, almost indifferent to what was going on. Wyatt didn't know how to respond at first. Virgil kept up the Earp end of the conversation.

"Now, hold on, John. We can talk to Borg just like anybody else can."

"Talk — hell. I hear you're accusing this man. He's a good business man. Now leave him be."

"I got a better idea," said Wyatt, quickly getting fed up. "You can just back off. Right now."

"The hell with that," said Behan. He took a step forward, but then went no farther. Blood still rushing to his face, he stood, his shoulders straining forward, poised for some action he wasn't quite ready to take.

Borg didn't like the look of things. "They don't bother," he said. "I'm good, John. They don't bother." He smiled as amiably as he could.

Behan took some more time to ease up. When he had himself reined in, an almost sheepish look came to his face, his anger seeming to embarrass him. Turning slowly, he stepped outside without another word but didn't go far. Wyatt could see him through the shop window, standing on the boardwalk, looking out toward the street.

Borg let out a nervous laugh. "John very angry," he said to fill in the uncomfortable silence that descended on the place.

Putting Behan's outburst behind him, Virgil then turned back to the Swede. He tried to explain that Borg could still make money even if he didn't do business with the Clantons and McLowerys. Once the law had gotten the rustlers out of the county, Borg could make money with legitimate ranchers instead of those who dealt in stolen cattle.

"They give good price for good beef," said Borg. "Clantons, McLowerys, both."

Either the Swede's English wasn't good enough for him to catch on to what Virgil was trying to tell him, or he just had no interest in changing a business that was already profitable. There were plenty of men in Tombstone who planned on making their money quickly and then moving on. Borg was probably one of them. Virgil tried to explain once more but got no further.

John Behan was still standing near the store when Wyatt and Virgil stepped out. "Wyatt," Behan called, just barely looking at him. "I want to talk." He was calm now, but still looking ruffled.

Virgil told his brother not to bother. "It'll just be more trouble," he said. "Leave it."

Wyatt looked across the boardwalk at the sheriff waiting for an answer. He had no great desire to talk to Behan, but he was too curious not to. "I want to hear what he's got to say," he told Virgil.

When Wyatt reached the sheriff's side, Behan said, "Let's walk." He led the way off the boardwalk and down Fremont Street, saying nothing for a block, looking from side to side occasionally, then turning down an alley between the Mining Exchange building and the *Tombstone Epitaph* newspaper office. As they reached the other end of the alley, Behan said, "I heard you'll be running against me in the election."

Although Wyatt hadn't started campaigning, he wasn't surprised that Behan had gotten the word. His decision to run was bound to spread quickly to the interested parties. "You heard right," Wyatt said.

They stopped in the lot behind the Mining Exchange. No one else around. Apparently that was the kind of setting that Behan wanted. Wyatt waited for him to get to the point while the sheriff gazed at the ruins left by the fire at the other end of the block.

"Time to time," Behan finally said, "I have call for taking on special officers. Pretty good paying work it is. No sense in us going up against each other. You could work with me as a special officer, then maybe become a deputy after a while.''

"Why should I?"

"Well, that way we'll both be peace officers after the election, instead of one of us getting left out in the cold.''

"If I win the election," said Wyatt, "I won't need the work you're giving me.''

"But you won't win,'' Behan said matter of factly. No doubt entered into his tone or expression.

"Cocky, aren't you?''

Behan said, "This is a town with a Southern way of thinking, Wyatt. A Yankee like you, a Republican — no way in hell you're going to beat me.''

Wyatt considered Behan and tried to look past the smug look on his face. "Why do you want me with the sheriff's office if you can just whup me in the election and be rid of me?''

Behan shook his head and paced off a couple of steps. "Damn it, Wyatt, you can't just push around a feller that's got a business here, a feller like Borg over there.''

Behan's shift from the election to Borg made Wyatt pause before answering. "I got nothing against business,'' he said.

"That kind of business you can't mess with. And I ain't about to let you mess with it — you *or* your brother. Virgil I can't do much about. He's already full-time with Marshal White. But I ain't going to let you stir up any more trouble for me. I gotta keep order here.''

"What kind of order is that?'' said Wyatt. "Order for Ike Clanton and the rest?''

"Don't be a jackass. I didn't get this far by being their enemy. How far you think you'll get? You're acting plain stupid. That's what it is — stupid.''

Blood was rushing back into Behan's face as he stared at Wyatt. Neither man spoke or moved for some time.

Not much more was said after that. Thinking back on that afternoon behind the Mining Exchange once his campaign had gotten underway, Wyatt vaguely remembered there had been more words between him and Behan, but none that he could pin down and none that seemed to matter. All he remembered was the look that had passed between them and how it set the tone from there onward. Not liking Behan doesn't enter into it, Wyatt kept telling himself after that afternoon. Even if Behan is an arrogant son of a bitch, he always added as an afterthought.

On voting day, Virgil went over to the Cosmopolitan Hotel to bring Wyatt along on some claim business; he thought it might take his brother's mind off the election for a few hours. An investor from San Francisco was coming in on the one o'clock stage to talk about buying a couple of the Earp claims along the Mountain Maid Mine. From what Virgil could tell from the man's letters, the purchase could involve thousands of dollars. That ought to distract Wyatt he thought.

Wyatt had kept up a good front through most of the electioneering, but Virgil had known that the disappointment had been growing all along. Right from the start, he thought Wyatt had made a run for office too soon, before he became well enough known in the county. On the other hand, he knew that some good candidate had to go up against Behan, so he hadn't tried to talk Wyatt out of it. The trouble, as far as Virgil could see, was that Wyatt actually thought he had a chance to win. At least for a while.

He found Wyatt sitting on the porch of the hotel, by himself, Virgil was disappointed. He had hoped to go up to the room to fetch Wyatt so that he could see his brother with Verna and find something to report to Allie. Ever since the time a couple of weeks ago when Wyatt had come to dinner with Morgan — and without Verna — Allie had been fussing to find out what had gone on between Wyatt and his common law wife. ''Livin' in common law is no way to live,'' she would say. ''Especially with a woman like that.'' For the time being, it seemed, Allie would have to continue to fuss.

Although it was cool at night, the early autumn days were as hot as any during July and August. Waiting for the Benson stage, already late today, Virgil and Wyatt took to the shade of an overhang and even then had to fan themselves with their hats to create some small breeze. As people walked past them along the boardwalk, Wyatt made a point of smiling and saying hello, and even shaking a hand or two of prospective supporters, but Virgil didn't see any enthusiasm in his brother's last-minute electioneering. The very fact that Wyatt had agreed so readily to tend to other business on voting day told Virgil how little Wyatt thought of his chances.

If there was a reason for the stage being late, it might have been that it was overloaded. The wheels and axles seemed to groan under the extra weight as the team pulled the stage sluggishly through town. Strapped on top was a big base drum, a tuba, several carpetbags and chests, and a rolled-up red curtain. Inside the coach no space was spared as passengers were packed along every inch of the two seats. Stepping closer, Virgil and Wyatt watched the members of a theatrical troupe file out of the stage, first a spry, thin man in a plaid suit, then a middle-aged character actress, then a clean-shaven leading man. A short, dark-haired young woman then followed, stopping at the lip of the coach door. Not moving any farther, she turned to Wyatt, an appraising look in her blue eyes.

''Can't a man help a lady in this town?'' she asked impatiently, and held out a hand for Wyatt to help her down off the coach.

The long ride had flattened and creased her dress and had left her jaw-line streaked with perspiration, but the bedraggled look didn't take much away from her pretty, pert face or her hourglass figure. This was quite obvious to Virgil, and by the look of it, Wyatt hadn't missed it either.

Virgil smiled. Damned if Wyatt didn't look flustered by the girl's demand for help.

Wyatt got around to giving her a hand and eased her down to the ground with a smooth motion. Standing next to Wyatt, she barely came up to his shoulder. The small woman looked him up and down and said, "A tall fellow like you shouldn't mind helping out once in a while."

Even though he opened his mouth, no words came out to answer her chiding remark. Wyatt watched with a lost look in his eyes as she made a coquettish turn and sashayed down the street alongside the man in the plaid suit. Virgil did his best not to burst out laughing.

Cyrus Thornton, the San Francisco investor, was the last off the stage. "An exhausting trip," he said. "But a very colorful one," he added, glancing meaningfully at the troupe members waiting for their luggage and equipment to be lowered from the roof of the coach.

"I'll bet it was," replied Wyatt, saying something at last. He looked down the road at the small woman walking away.

After checking Thornton into the Cosmopolitan, Virgil and Wyatt took their visitor in a buckboard to the First North Extension of the Mountain Maid to show him the claims for sale. Virgil explained that the prices were going up and the time to jump in was now.

"You could do real well with an investment in Tombstone," Virgil said. "You take a look around and see for yourself the next couple of days."

"I will do that, Mr. Earp," said Thornton, turning in his seat to look at the city hall under construction on Fremont. "I have just one concern. The newspapers in San Francisco have published articles on the lawlessness in this area. What with smuggling and raiding back and forth across the border, who is to say that some trouble with Mexico might not crop up."

"We're getting that in hand," replied Virgil. "My brother Wyatt can tell you also. He's been riding shotgun for Wells Fargo for the last month and so has my brother Morgan. Neither one of them has had any trouble. Isn't that right, Wyatt?''

"That's right," said Wyatt. "No trouble." He didn't offer any more than that. He clearly had his mind on something else. Most likely it was the election, Virgil thought, and who could blame him. Virgil preferred to think, though, that his brother's mind was on something more pleasant, like that little, dark-haired girl, who had gotten off the stage. There were some things, he decided, that he didn't have to tell Allie. After all, she had enough on her mind just fussing about Verna.

That night, Morgan joined Virgil and Wyatt as they sat outside the Oriental to wait for the final count of the votes. Doc came by to try to scare up a game of poker, but no one was interested, although Morg wavered for a moment.

"Morgan's staying here with family until we hear," Virgil interjected before the kid brother could get out of his seat. It was enough to remind Morgan of what was expected.

"Suit yourself," said Doc. "I hope you don't mind if I don't stick around."

"We don't mind," Virgil said. When Doc moved on, Virgil added, "You've done enough already." He thought he was saying it under his breath, but the words were loud enough for Wyatt to hear. Wyatt glanced at him, then resumed waiting, saying nothing.

Doc's run-in with saloonkeeper Mike Joyce had been a sore point during the campaign. No one had been hurt in the scuffle, but only because Bat Masterson had been quick enough to take Doc's gun away. Even without gunplay, though, the incident had been juicy enough for Behan to make hay about Wyatt's "desperate friends." The incident was an embarrassment, one that Wyatt preferred not to hear discussed by family and friends. Tonight, though, he didn't bother to object.

Marshal White headed toward them on his way back

from the Mining Exchange, the site of the counting. Fred White's bulk seemed to weigh heavily on his legs, from tiredness or disappointment or both. He placed a foot on the boardwalk and leaned a hand on his bent knee, looking from one Earp to the other, his friendly face blank. When his gaze rested on Wyatt, he shrugged.

"Not much I can tell you," he said. "Bat's over there now and will tell us if anything changes."

Wyatt nodded to acknowledge the news.

White said, "If it makes any difference, Wyatt, I would've liked workin' with the sheriff's office if you were in charge of it." The marshal now stepped onto the boardwalk and leaned against the upright. After a while, he said, "This ain't the last round," addressing no one in particular.

Across the street at the Crystal Palace, a cheer went up, followed by two gunshots and some more cheers.

"Damn," said Morgan.

Virgil turned to Wyatt to see no reaction from his brother, just an empty stare directed across the street.

Ike Clanton and Tom McLowery walked out of the Crystal Palace, Ike's step just a bit more unsteady than his friend's. Clanton stopped long enough to focus on the Earps, then let out a laugh and a rebel yell and told Tom to come with him across the street.

Grinning from ear to ear, Ike said, "You boys hear the election count?"

"Not exactly," said Virgil, doing his best to stifle his annoyance. "But we got an idea."

"We just heard. Johnny Behan's back with the badge," said Ike. "What do you all think of that?"

Ike waited a moment, as if he actually expected a response. He and Tom then had themselves a laugh.

Tom said, "Looks like we're all gonna have us a high old time in Tombstone from now on."

"Get walkin'," snapped Morgan. "We're not listening to that trash."

"Oh, you'll listen all right," answered Ike, turning back

toward the Crystal Palace. "You'll listen and watch, because that'll be all you Yankees'll be able to do. You just watch us boys."

Wyatt got up and started for the Oriental's batwing doors.

"One thing, Wyatt," Ike called out from the middle of the street. "Just because you ain't sheriff, don't worry about a thing. Sheriff Johnny'll take care of it all." He paused to smile. "If I ask him, maybe he'll make sure your woman don't walk around with whoremasters no more. I can ask him for ya."

Out of the corner of his eye, Virgil saw Wyatt stop at the doors, then suddenly spin around and charge across the boardwalk. He was into the street in three long strides before Virgil caught up with him. Wyatt struggled, but his brother got hold of his arms and pinned them back.

"You're not goin' for him," Virgil said into his brother's ear. "You're not goin' to let him goad you. He's trash but you're *not* goin' for him."

Wyatt lurched forward and managed to drag Virgil with him for a couple of feet. Virgil put all of his strength into pulling Wyatt up short.

"You touch him, Wyatt, and I'll arrest you. I swear to God I'll arrest you. Do you hear me?"

He could feel Wyatt straining forward, unable to shake the hold. By now, Ike had made it to the other side of the street, while Tom stayed put, grinning at Wyatt. Virgil only got his brother to slow up after McLowery moved off and joined Ike on the opposite boardwalk; the distance that separated Wyatt from the taunting cowboys seeming to take away some of the sting.

Looking at Ike and Tom, and feeling Wyatt's tensed muscles in his grip, Virgil also began to churn inside, as if Wyatt's rage were passing into him. For a moment or two, Virgil had a notion to let Wyatt go and take after Clanton himself and kick him around the block. Virgil kept his hold on Wyatt until his own violent urge faded away.

30

The gunfire started by 12:30 that night.

Ab Richardson had told Wyatt that the betting men had been putting their money on Ike Clanton as the one to start the ball rolling, and Ike had been giving them good reason to think so. Right after the election count came in he was spreading talk around Allen Street that he was going to tree the town. He said it was his way of celebrating Behan's victory. For his part, Wyatt was ready to believe the odds on Ike because he knew Clanton had plenty of friends around him. Ike was always a good bet to raise hell when he was in the company of genuine hardcases.

But both the betting men and Wyatt were wrong. For all the talk and swagger, Ike ran out of steam by midnight and headed back to his ranch with Ringo, Pony Deal, Indian Charley and brother Billy. That left Curly Bill and the two McLowery boys to shoot up the town.

Listening to the first crack of gunfire while standing in the Oriental doorway, Wyatt judged that the shots came from the western end of Allen Street. Another round of

... with it two screams from the same direction.

Wyatt was out in the middle of Allen when Virgil jogged over from Sixth Street. Together they came upon Marshal White a block farther west. Before any words were said, they started walking side by side.

"It's Curly Bill and the other two," said the marshal. "Ab told me they're over by Third, headed toward Fremont."

Another cluster of shots rang out in the night. The three men walked quickly now, pulling their guns and letting them dangle by their sides.

"Anybody hurt?" asked Wyatt.

"Don't think so," the marshal answered. "But Ab said they've run off some folks."

By the time they reached Fourth Street, the gunfire stopped, leaving the town in an unnatural silence that put Wyatt on edge. With no sound to lead them on, he, his brother and Marshal White came to a halt. They listened for something that could point them in the right direction: footfalls, hoofbeats, the sound of a scuffle. A faint commotion reached them from the west end of Allen, in the direction of the Mountain Maid, but Wyatt figured that was probably only some confusion that the cowboys had left behind them. They could be blocks away by now. For all Wyatt knew, the cowboys could have reached the residential area.

Wyatt said, "Best to split up. If one of us finds them, the other two can move in to help."

Marshal White didn't take long to consider this idea. "I'll go down Fourth," he said. "Wyatt, you take Third. Virgil, move over to Second. We'll all work toward Fremont, then move west."

They each moved off at a jog.

Reaching Third Street, Wyatt walked into the night shadows untouched by the street lamps on Allen. He stopped for several moments to allow his eyes to adjust to the deeper darkness before advancing. Two more shots roared, one right after the other, but not coming from the same place. One was to the left, over near Second, and the other was straight ahead, at least another block farther on. Wyatt started running for Fremont.

Tom McLowery was weaving as he stepped over to the alley behind the *Epitaph* office. Leaning against the back of the building, he reloaded his Colt .44, taking extra time with the job to let himself catch his breath. He heard two shots to his left, followed by the shattering of glass. Tom laughed. That would be brother Frank, he thought, finally hitting one of them street lamps. He had sworn he'd hit the mark sooner or later.

Just now realizing exactly where he was, Tom peered through the back window of the *Epitaph* office. Wouldn't it be such a bad idea to shoot up the place, he mused, considering all the bad-mouthing the newspaper gave the McLowerys and their friends. With the butt of his Colt, Tom smashed a hole in the window and then stuck the barrel through it to take aim. In the dark, he couldn't make out anything in particular inside the office, just a jumble of dimly outlined shapes. It then occurred to him that he had no idea what to shoot at. What was the point of shooting a printing press? Dragging it out with ropes and a strong team, maybe, but that took a bunch of fellers. Hell, I got better things to do, he told himself, and triggered just one shot inside and started diagonally across the lot toward Safford Street.

Along a row of adobe homes and jacales, Tom stopped to take a look around. "Gettin' too far away from town," he said out loud. "Where the hell'd Curly Bill go?" He took a step back toward the center of Tombstone, then stopped again between two houses, a big grin on his face as an idea registered with him.

"This town is our'n!" he bellowed and fired his gun three times into the air.

It was Tom's cry that got Virgil's attention as he moved

past Fremont. He was after the cowboy who had shot out the street lamp just a few minutes before, but now Tom's firing turned him around in a completely different direction. Knowing he was close, he cut across the near lot at a run, and then stopped in a back yard shared by two houses to listen for the next sign. Footsteps were coming along Second, just to the other side of the houses. Virgil crept down the strip of ground separating the homes, and as he reached the front corner of the house on the right, Tom McLowery came into view. In the shadow of the house, Virgil remained unseen while Tom cocked the hammer for another cluster of shots. Bolting forward, Virgil reached him before Tom could pull the trigger.

Virgil grabbed Tom's gun arm and slammed it against his raised knee, getting a yelp out of him as the Colt flew out of his hand. Virgil spun the cowboy around and, with his other knee, pounded McLowery once in the lower back. The cowboy buckled and dropped to the ground.

"Get up when you can," said Virgil. "I'm not carrying you to the calaboose."

Wyatt was pleased to see Curly Bill at the other end of the alley. Brocius was the one he wanted.

Wyatt was walking along the back lots of the buildings along Fremont when he saw Curly Bill draining a whiskey bottle and tossing it down the street. The cowboy took a shot at it and missed. After a bottle of whiskey, Wyatt thought, it was no surprise that he'd miss a small target with a pistol, or for that matter, with any weapon. But that wouldn't keep him from hitting something or someone he wasn't aiming at.

Taking a step down the alley toward his man, Wyatt stopped when he heard a voice from Fremont Street.

"Hold it, Brocius." It was Fred White's voice.

Without hesitation, Curly Bill turned and started running down Fremont, away from the marshal. Wyatt doubled back to run across the back lots. He moved as fast as he could across the garbage strewn ground to get ahead of Brocius along a parallel route so that he could cut him off. He was already past the next building when he heard running footfalls, just behind, probably at the opposite end of the alley he had just passed. He moved back, staying close to the adobe building, and peered down the alley to see Curly Bill headed toward him.

Knowing White would be closing off the Fremont Street entrance, he didn't bother to wait for Brocius to reach him. As long as the alley would be bottled up, he wouldn't need to rely on surprise. He swung out into Curly Bill's path, his thumb pressed against his gun hammer.

Wyatt braced himself for the possibility that Curly Bill might throw down on him, but the cowboy spun around at the first sight of Wyatt and ran back the way he had come. As Brocius turned away, Wyatt caught a brief glimpse of the cowboy's face in the light of a window; Curly Bill had an almost mischievous look about him, a glint in his eye, as though this was nothing but a game. Wyatt was certain that the cowboy hadn't recognized him in the darkness. If he had, the game would probably have come to a sudden halt.

When Fred White appeared at the other end of the alley, Curly Bill pounded to a stop, his gaze going from one end of the passage to the other as the marshal and Wyatt approached slowly from both sides.

"Put the gun up, Curly Bill," said Marshal White.

Wyatt could see the cowboy's block of a face take on a smile as he kept an eye on the two men drawing nearer. Wyatt still saw no sign of recognition from Brocius. Probably too drunk even to care who was trapping him, Wyatt thought. He casually considered how easy it would be now to even the score for the treeing in Dodge. One bullet might erase the memory forever.

"Aw, Marshal," Curly Bill said, "you know we was just funnin'. Just havin' a good time celebratin', is all."

White was the first to reach Curly Bill. The marshal still

had his gun at his side. "Just give me the gun and we'll talk about it." White held out his empty hand.

Beginning to slouch in resignation, Curly Bill let his gun hand drop. He sighed and said, "All right, Marshal. All right."

Curling his finger around the trigger guard, the cowboy turned the gun butt-first toward White. From where he stood behind the cowboy, Wyatt saw the marshal extend his hand farther to take the gun. He then heard Curly Bill say in an almost wistful tone, "Wait till Ringo hears about this." That's when the cowboy executed the border roll.

In one sudden motion, he spun the gun around the pivot point of his curled trigger finger and reversed the butt so that it slapped into his palm. As it smacked into position the gun roared.

For a moment it looked like nothing had happened to Marshal White. Then the expression on his face shifted from impassiveness to pained surprise and froze that way. With a blood stain spreading across his white shirt, he crumpled slowly and collapsed to the ground.

Curly Bill's move happened so quickly that Wyatt didn't react at first, the action in front of him seeming to last much longer than the few seconds it required to begin and finish. When the marshal hit the ground, Wyatt's reflexes snapped alive and he hurtled forward. Swinging from the heels, he clubbed Curly Bill across the top of the skull with the barrel of his Colt. The cowboy dropped like he was shot through a trapdoor and lay in a curled heap at Wyatt's feet. Wyatt stood over him for several moments trying to think of what else he could do to him, before long settling on a swift kick to the stomach that rolled the cowboy farther down the alley.

Virgil held the new badge in his palm and gazed at it a long time. The way he studied it in the square of light thrown from the front window of Fred White's house, he might have been judging the value of a chunk of stone chipped from a prospecting site. If he was pleased with the promotion Mayor Clum had just handed him, he showed no sign of it.

Wyatt had no trouble understanding his brother's reluctance. Like Virgil, he wasn't one to be leery of taking a top peace officer's job, but taking a man's job not an hour after his death was something else. Not knowing what to say, he simply stood by as Virgil came to grips with his new position.

Virgil slipped the badge into his vest pocket, still not quite ready to pin it on, and turned to look at Dr. Goodfellow comforting Fred White's widow in the small, struggling garden at the side of the house. Wyatt thought the time had come for his brother's first act as city marshal.

"We best be checking on Curly Bill and McLowery at the jail," he said. "Breakinridge was on duty when I left them there."

Virgil turned to his brother, concern taking the place of the uncertainty that had clouded his face before. "Breakinridge you say? Was Behan there too?"

"Not when I left."

The two brothers stood in silence for a moment, each knowing the thoughts building in the other's mind. "You're right," said Virge. "Let's take a look."

They left the house behind, moving in long purposeful strides.

Once Virgil had reached the alley, only seconds after White had been shot, the Earp brothers hadn't given much thought to the handling of the prisoners other than stashing them somewhere until White had been seen by a doctor. If Morgan hadn't been on a Fargo run, they might have sent him to the jail to keep an eye on things, but other than that, no alternatives had occurred to them.

When he had brought Curly Bill and Tom McLowery to the calaboose, Wyatt had taken some comfort in seeing that Breakinridge, a deputy that he thought he could trust, was on duty. But Breakinridge was still Behan's man, and that thought nagged at the back of Wyatt's mind. Once Fred White was pronounced dead and there was nothing more that could be done for him, the idea of Behan's man guarding the outlaw cowboys had begun to loom large.

Approaching the adobe calaboose now in the early hours of the morning, they saw Behan walk into the jail just a half a block ahead of them. Wyatt judged that something was on the sheriff's mind because the man seemed too preoccupied to notice the Earp brothers drawing near. If Behan's our worry, Wyatt thought, we might have come just in time to stop him.

The front door of the calaboose was open when they arrived. Billy Breakinridge was nowhere to be seen. Floyd Stilwell sat on a corner of the desk while Behan paced before him, agitated, rubbing his jaw. Stepping inside, Wyatt could see the lockup in back was open. Open and empty except for a Mexican sleeping it off for the night.

Wyatt wasn't angry. After all the night's troubles, his emotions were too spent to work up a good mad. The only thing he felt was a kind of weariness that left him a little sick at the pit of his stomach. He had figured that Breakinridge would have been square enough to keep the lock-up shut, at least for the night if nothing else. Beyond that, he had counted on Behan as the one to watch. He hadn't figured that Stilwell would start his shift in the middle of the night. Knowing that he had overlooked that possibility made him feel even more weary. He was ready to just turn around and leave right now and not bother with any of it. He stayed only because he could sense that Virgil was digging in his heels beside him.

"There was this ruckus over to Fourth and Allen," Stilwell was saying, his fleshy face not looking terribly concerned. "I had to go look into it, John."

"And you left your lockup keys here?" said Behan.

Stilwell shrugged. "By accident, I suppose."

"Where's Curly Bill?" cut in Virgil.

Behan glanced at the Earps, then stepped away angrily to stare out the window. "Some friends of his took him out. Just a half-hour ago. Curly Bill and McLowery both."

"Some friends of his? Like who?"

"I figure it to be Frank McLowery," Stilwell said. "I hear he was still about when you brought in Curly Bill and Tom. He could've snuck in here when I was out."

Wyatt shook his head. "He wouldn't have to be much of a sneak." He had his eyes on Behan by the window.

"Watch what you say, Wyatt," said Behan. "I wasn't even here. I don't let murderers go. You better know that."

Virgil said, "This stinks to hell, Behan. And don't try to tell me you don't know it."

Behan didn't bother to answer. He turned back to the window and let out a long exasperated breath. After a while he said, "I'm looking into it, Earp. I'll make it right."

"You're too damn late," said Wyatt, his pulse starting to pick up again. "You should've looked into it before you hired this thief here as a deputy."

Deputy Sheriff Stilwell got up off the desk. "You don't call me that, Earp."

Behan spun to face his deputy. "Shut the hell up, Stilwell."

Stilwell, checked by his boss's words, continued to bristle as he stared at Wyatt.

"Come on, Virge. There's no more business for us here," said Wyatt. He put a hand to guide his brother to the door, but Virgil wasn't moving.

"Curly Bill's killing Fred changes things," said Virgil. "One thing it changes is it makes me marshal. You and me, John, we're supposed to work together, but I sure as hell won't bother. Being city marshal gives me jurisdiction in Tombstone and being U.S. deputy marshal gives me jurisdiction in the county. That gives me enough badge to do what I have to without your help."

Behan's dark eyes flashed. "Don't you try pushing me out of the picture," he said. "Might be I can make you come up short."

"Don't put your money on it," said Wyatt. "When Virge needs help he'll be coming for me, and he'll be coming for Morgan. If need be he'll bring in Masterson too. That's an awful lot for coming up short, Behan."

Wyatt took hold of his brother's arm again, and this time, with his piece said, Virgil was ready to go. When they stepped outside, they could hear Behan curse Stilwell out for the lowest, stupidest bastard he ever knew.

31

Pete Spence's narrow, pointy face creased around the eyes as he sighted along the road in the glaring sun. A speck, nothing more than a dust devil, appeared on the southern horizon. Spence backed his horse behind the standstone boulder just far enough so that he could be concealed and still keep an eye on the road. When the speck traveled close enough for him to see an outline, he pulled the bandana up over the lower half of his face and drew his gun from its scabbard. He signaled once to his partner on the ledge above, then walked his horse into the middle of the road.

He knew the men in the boot of the stage could see him plainly across the sun-washed flat, but even so the coach showed no sign of slowing down. He was still too far away to make out details about the stage. What he could see, though, was the messenger lean toward the driver, giving him instructions. Then the driver whipped the team to put on some speed. Spence took comfort in the fact that the stage was still too far off for the Wells Fargo ten gauge to do much good.

The stage kept bearing down on him. Fighting his spooked horse, Spence reined in as best he could and let the animal sidestep off the road, but no farther. With the stage thundering toward him, Spence was starting to get spooked himself. Now was the time to give the signal. He took off his hat and waved it above his head three times.

On the ledge, Floyd Stilwell adjusted the sights of his Winchester .44-.40, leading just a bit ahead of the stage boot, and, after letting out a slow breath, he squeezed the trigger. Flying high, the bullet whined as it ricocheted off a boulder on the far side of the road. Stilwell aimed again, this time lowering the barrel a notch. He fired once more. As the echo of the shot reverberated thinly across the broad valley, the messenger's body jerked, then slumped forward. The rocking of the stage jostled him first toward the driver, then forward and then turned him over the outside edge of the boot. He flopped onto the hard-packed road.

Spence fired twice into the air and shouted, "Hold it up!" With the messenger gone, the driver forgot about running the bandit down. He pulled on the reins and put on the brake. In a blinding swirl of dust, the stage rumbled to a stop just in front of Spence. As the bandit waved the dust away from his eyes, it occurred to him that the driver might take advantage of the clouded air and drive the stage around him. He spurred his horse forward and around to the right side of the coach where the dust was already starting to clear. From there he could plainly see Levi sitting in the boot, his hands on his lap, making no move to prod the team.

Levi worried the inside of his lip with his teeth as he looked from Spence to the spot on the ledge where the rifle shots had originated.

"Throw down that treasure chest," Spence said, cocking his Colt for emphasis. "And put some hurry into it."

Levi reached down, pulled the chest up to the lip of the boot and dropped it over the side.

"You picked a bad run to hit," said Levi. "Ain't hardly enough for killing a man."

Spence laughed. "Is that right?"

Turning his slit-eyes to the passengers inside the coach, Spence saw them staring fearfully at him and at Stilwell climbing down the ledge. Spence toyed with the idea of marching the passengers out and emptying their pockets, but that temptation was overriden by the desire to take stock of what they had already accomplished.

"Git movin'," he said to the driver. "Ride on."

Levi didn't waste much time. He glanced back at the body left by the road and then put the whip to the team. Stilwell reached Spence's side to watch the coach roll north up the Benson road. When the stage was well on its way, Deputy Sheriff Stilwell pulled the scarf off his face and walked away.

"Floyd," Spence said, "ain't ye gonna look at this here treasure chest?"

"It'll keep. We got something else more important to see," Stilwell said.

Spence looked longingly at the chest lying on the ground beside the horse's hoofs. Unable to restrain himself, despite Stilwell's words, he shot at the lock and missed and then shot again with no better results. Missing three times is bad luck, he thought. He turned his horse and trotted toward Stilwell back south along the road.

His partner was kneeling down beside the tall, thin body sprawled face-down across the ground. He took hold of the dead man's belt and turned the corpse over.

Spence reined in a few feet away. "Which one is it, Floyd?"

Stilwell didn't answer at first. He stood up, put his hands on his hips for a moment, then suddenly kicked the body. "It ain't neither," he growled. He wheeled away toward the ledge. "Damn," he said. "All this damn work for nothing."

Spence walked his horse over to the corpse to take a look

for himself. Sure, he thought after seeing the face, Floyd's got reason to be angry, but sometimes he can be just too hard on himself.

"We still ain't looked inside the chest, Floyd," said Spence to cheer his partner up.

It was no surprise to Wyatt that Bat knew the name of the pretty girl with the theatrical troupe. When they stepped into the Can Can Restaurant, they saw the young woman sitting next to the man in the plaid suit — he hadn't changed his suit since coming off the stage. Her eyes turned toward Wyatt for just a second, just enough for Bat to notice.

"I could introduce you," said Bat.

By not answering, Wyatt didn't say no, which was enough encouragement for Bat.

Wyatt hadn't given much thought to women since coming to Tombstone, and he was sure he didn't want another woman to complicate life with Verna. Trouble with her was trouble enough, he thought. On the other hand, just meeting this actress seemed innocent enough.

"Josie," said Bat, "this here's Wyatt Earp. Wyatt, meet Josie Marcus of Doby's Follies. The fella in the good-looking suit — I don't know who the hell he is."

"He's Vic Doby," said Josie, "owner of Doby's Follies, in case you haven't figured it out. And he's also the one who'll pay for your food if you treat him right."

"Sportin' men always treat me right," said the man in the plaid suit, "because old Vic Doby always gives 'em a heck of a good show."

Josie turned to Wyatt standing at her side. "You can sit down, Wyatt. I don't have any lifting or helping for you today."

She was as impudent as Wyatt figured she would be, but he didn't mind. Not today anyway. Today she fit right in with the easy living he had in mind.

Bat had convinced him this morning to give up his shift

as messenger for the day. Wyatt hadn't been easily budged at first, but his friend had found a way of being persuasive.

Sitting alongside Wyatt outside the Oriental, Bat had been making small talk for a while as Wyatt cleaned his Stevens shotgun. He hadn't fooled Wyatt for a second. For all Bat's casualness and complaints about the heat, Wyatt had known Masterson had something definite on his mind. That something had begun to show itself when Wyatt mentioned he was messengering up to Benson today.

"A damn shame," Bat had said, shaking his head sorrowfully. "There's a heck of a poker game about to shape up over to the Alhambra. I'm sure they wouldn't mind another hand, Wyatt."

"I never knew a game to be short a man around here," Wyatt had responded.

"Not the point. I always thought you were a man to appreciate the company in a game as much as the playing. That's what makes a good friendly game without any business to it. You know that, Wyatt."

Just curious enough, Wyatt had asked if Luke Short would be in on it. "There's him," said Bat, "and also Neal Brown and Cold Chuck Johnny and Ab Richardson. Should be just like Dodge. Except for Ab, of course. He never worked Dodge, as far as I know. But I say he's good enough to have been with the gang back in Kansas."

"You're right about that," Wyatt had said.

Bat had then drifted on about secondhand stories he had heard, about Mysterious Dave Mather leaving Dodge to become a deputy sheriff in Las Vegas, and Prairie Dog Morrow trying out Deadwood but heading back to Dodge, and Charlie Bassett giving Colorado a try. "Bob Wright hasn't left, though," he'd said. "Neither has my brother Jim. He's got a saloon there now."

Bat's voice had trailed off and he watched quietly as Wyatt snapped shut the twin barrels of the ten gauge.

"Things here sure ain't like they were along Front Street, are they?" Bat finally had said.

"I guess they're not," said Wyatt.

"I don't know about you, Wyatt, but when I came here I was figurin' on the good sportin' life. A sweet job dealing faro or poker, buying into one of the saloons. I did my share of law work in Dodge, and I'll probably do it again someplace else, but I can stomach something else for a while, I surely can. For right now, anyway. Thing is, though, I see a lot of sportin' ways around here, but not a lot of what I would call good easy living."

Wyatt had just nodded and said nothing.

"I know you got other ideas, Wyatt. If I had family here too, maybe I'd see it the same way. Maybe I'd get my back up about the Clantons and the rest also." Bat had shrugged his shoulders and looked off down Allen Street. "Hell, Wyatt," he'd said, "that don't mean you can't help out with a friendly game once in a while. I just saw Philpot loafin' around the Occidental with nothing to do. He can messenger up to Benson just as good as you." He checked his watch. "Anyhow, I told Luke and Neal we'd start up around eleven. Not to hurry you, but —"

Wyatt had given it a thought or two, then couldn't help but smile. He couldn't say when it was, but somewhere along the way Bat had succeeded in getting him to think about the times they had had back in Dodge. It was a hot, sunny day, and it seemed to him that it could just as well be a lazy day too.

"Over to the Alhambra, is it?" he'd said.

The game was all that Bat had said it would be, except for Luke Short. He had had to set up the new roulette wheel at the Occidental and couldn't show. But the others — Brown, Richardson and Cold Chuck — had already been at the table in the Alhambra's back room, ready to play, with cigars lit and smoke hovering above the chairs.

They had bet freely and bluffed for all they were worth, but never went for the throat. After two hours of draw poker and five card stud, none of the players had taken much of an advantage, and they decided to call it quits until starting up again later in the afternoon. Wyatt and Bat devoted their playing break to a meal at the Can Can.

Josie kept up her part of the conversation and then some, ribbing Doby and Wyatt about equally and also Bat once in a while. The way she laughed while she spoke made the ribbing easy to take; a loud, throaty laugh that Wyatt liked.

Along the way, Wyatt was interested to hear, she mentioned that she came from San Francisco. "My father wouldn't sit still for me performing in the same city he did business in. He said that was no way for his daughter to behave. 'No vay for you. No vay for you,' " she imitated, using a foreign accent that put Wyatt in mind of Mr. Isaacson back in Dodge. "Actually," she added, "I think he just didn't like my singing."

Doby tried getting in his say, doing his best to compete with his young actress. Mostly, he was trying to pin Wyatt and Bat down to attending one of the troupe's performances at the Bird Cage during the coming week. When that didn't get a response, he tried the tack of singling out Bat.

"Tell me, Mr. Masterson, which kind of entertainment are you partial to — comedy or melodrama?"

"Oh, melodrama, I would think," Josie cut in. "Bat looks like he prefers a good laugh."

Wyatt couldn't remember the last time he had been in the company of a cheerful, bright woman. He found he wasn't sure of what to say to her half the time, but he also found that he wouldn't mind staying close by until he fell into step with her banter. He turned to the waiter and was about to order another beer when Morgan stepped into the restaurant.

The look in his kid brother's eye and the quickness of his stride sprang an alarm inside Wyatt. He pushed back his chair and got to his feet by the time Morgan reached the table.

"Got a wire from Levi in Benson," Morgan began. As soon as he passed on the news of the holdup along the Benson road, his older brother headed for the door.

Josie and Doby looked on with blank expressions as Wyatt made his abrupt exit. Bat got up and took one last sip of beer before stepping away from the table. "Well, Mr. Doby, looks like you're paying after all," he said as he followed the Earps out of the restaurant.

Riding with the Earps in the posse were Bat and Doc, and in addition to the saddle horses, they took a wagon along to carry back the body. At the site of the robbery, they found Bud Philpot lying across the rim of the road, facing the sky, the sun already doing its work on the exposed flesh. Wyatt stood over him, staring at the corpse that might have been his. Glancing at Bat and Virgil standing by the treasure chest, he didn't know whether to thank Masterson for his life or curse him for Philpot's.

The treasure chest was tipped over on its side, its lock blasted off and its lid open. Scattered around it were opened, discarded envelopes and tattered letters.

"For mail," Virgil said softly. "They killed a good man for mail."

Bat said, "There could've been something else in those envelopes. Maybe they knew there was some money coming through."

Stepping over to Bat's side, Wyatt gazed down at the broken strong box but didn't seem to see it. The lowering sun stretched the men's shadows in crisp outline across the chest and the papers lying on the ground. "Maybe the chest didn't matter to them," Wyatt said.

Morgan approached from the flat on the western edge of the road. "Looks like the tracks lead southwest of here. They're plain enough that you can see them a good ways off."

Wyatt left the others in order to take a look for himself. The tracks of the getaway were as plain as the markings by the shoulder where one of the bandits had hidden, and as obvious as the traces along the ledge where the rifleman had made his shot. Sighting along the trail, Wyatt had little doubt in his mind where the bandits had gone.

The slow clop of hoofs and the deep cough behind Wyatt signaled that Doc was approaching on his horse. "Plain enough, Morg says." Doc laughed. "Hell, you could follow that trail at a gallop. Either they're leading us into a trap or they just don't much care if we find them or not."

"They don't care," said Wyatt. He had no concrete reason for believing that. He just felt it.

"Good," said Doc. "Then we can just go and shoot the bastards and be back by nightfall."

As they saddled up, Morgan said they could move faster if he took one of the extra horses instead of driving the wagon. "We could pick up the wagon and the body on the way back," he said.

"Don't count on coming back this way," said Wyatt, tightening the cinch on his saddle. "Besides, we'll find these men soon enough without hurrying."

They followed the trail through a pass in a string of hills, then pushed on across another valley. If there was any glimmer of doubt before, the direction of the tracks across the second valley set them aside. The bandits had headed for Charleston — Wyatt was certain.

At no point did it seem the bandits made any attempt to conceal their trail. On the far side of the hills, they could have crossed a ledge of rock where no tracks would have shown. They also might have dragged a cottonwood branch to cover their markings. But they didn't even bother. Wyatt didn't call this trail plain anymore. Arrogant was the word that came to mind.

Heading straight for Charleston, the posse didn't bother following the markings until they neared the Wiley ranch. There the tracks veered toward the corral, then returned, this time showing different horseshoe prints for both horses. A switch had been made. Virgil called out Jeb Wiley to find out what happened. Jeb made it known right away that the switch had not been a friendly one.

"If'n I got a good look at 'em before they come to the corral I might've got my rifle down in time to do something about it," said Jeb. "Damned if I'll oblige them, but they jerked their guns so fast. They made the swap all to themselves without my help." Jeb gazed bitterly at the bandit horses now lazing in his corral. "Just shows how I'm gettin' slow," he said. "The last time they come here I had 'em covered before they could even call out. Collectin' taxes for the county they said." Jeb laughed.

"You knew who it was?" asked Virgil.

"Hell, it was that damn Stilwell. Had Spence with him. Had Spence with him time he was collectin' taxes too. Him a deputy sheriff — that's what he said." Jeb smiled. "Said it was his right to take taxes for the county because he was a goddamned deputy."

Jeb saw that Virgil and Wyatt weren't smiling at this idea. "You think he really was?" said Jeb.

In Charleston, the posses found Jeb Wiley's two horses standing loose-tied in front of Renfro's saloon. Wyatt walked his horse along the opposite side of the road and reined in to look through the adobe saloon doorway. In the dim twilight, he could only see shapes of men inside and few details to identify them. There were two at the bar, their backs turned to the door, and probably three more sitting at a table to the left.

Virgil led his mount by the reins to his brother's side. "You see who's in there, Wyatt?"

"Only can see how many. Looks like five of them."

"That makes it pretty even with five of us," said Virgil. "But a little better than even for our side. They don't know we're coming in."

"Right enough," Wyatt said, swinging out of the saddle. "Enough of an advantage for us to just go straight in with our rifles. What do you say?"

Virgil pulled his Winchester from the saddle boot. "Sounds fair enough."

When the five-man posse walked through the saloon door, the three at the side table stopped talking and turned to the men holding the rifles. At the table were Pony Deal, Indian Charley and the other half-breed, Hank Swilling. At the bar, the two men still stood with their backs turned, but Wyatt could tell that they knew someone had come in. He saw Renfro, behind the bar, signaling to the men with his eyes.

The taller of the two was Stilwell, standing on the right. He moved his gun hand across the plank counter, starting to angle for the gun on his hip. Wyatt, Virgil and Bat aimed their rifles almost as one, filling the little adobe building with a succession of harsh metallic sounds as the Winchester workings were put into motion. The gun hand on the counter stopped. Indian Charley, Pony Deal and Swilling turned in their seats to face the rifle muzzles of Morgan and Doc.

Stilwell and Spence turned slowly and leaned back against the bar. Wyatt and Virgil moved toward them while Bat stayed behind, positioning himself to be able to swing either toward the bar or the side table.

Stilwell and Spence glared at the Earps, but showed no sign of wanting to make a fight.

"This ain't Tombstone," said Stilwell. "You can't just waltz in here. This town is where our friends be."

"They're not doing you much good now," said Virgil as he took the guns out of the bandits' holsters. He didn't meet with any resistance. "You two are under arrest for robbing the Benson stage and murdering Bud Philpot."

Spence let out an abrupt laugh. "You won't get far with that kind of marshalin', Earp."

"Ain't no problem," Stilwell assured his partner. "A night in the calaboose will be about it and then we're long gone. These fellers just ain't learned the rules yet."

Moving suddenly, Wyatt backhanded Stilwell across the

face. The deputy pounded back into the bar, knocked the plank off the barrels and fell to the dirt floor. Wyatt was on top of him in one step. He hauled him up off the ground.

"You were figuring on killing me on that stage, weren't you?" Wyatt hissed into his face. "Me or maybe Morgan. Weren't you?"

Stilwell shook himself to get his bearings. If he had anything more to say, the cuffing from Wyatt had knocked it out of him for now.

"What do you think our friends're gonna do when they hear tell of this?" Spence said, his slit-eyes cold. "They won't be standin' for this here. That's for sure."

Doc edged toward the bar, keeping his eyes on the three men at the table. "Speaking of friends," he drawled, "how's Curly Bill keeping himself? He hasn't been in Tombstone for a while as far as I know. Seems like getting arrested for murder there has soured him on the place."

"He'll be a big help to you hidin' in a hole," said Morgan.

Wyatt pulled Stilwell toward the door and Virgil took Spence. Morgan brought his rifle muzzle close to Indian Charley. "What about you, Charley?" he said. "What've you been up to? Anything we can take you to Tombstone for?"

"We got what we want," said Wyatt. "They're not fighting so leave them be."

"Nothing wrong with persuading them to fight, is there?" put in Doc. "Pony here is supposed to be a fighting man. And Indian Charley too, when he's found the back of the man he's looking for. Isn't that right, Charley?"

"I work for Spence," said Indian Charley. "At lumber camp. I no fight."

"That so?" said Doc.

Bat stepped between Holliday and the table. "We're movin' on, Doc. Now. Isn't that right, Doc?"

Doc looked quizzically at Masterson, then shrugged his shoulders. "Whatever you say, friend."

The posse left the saloon, Wyatt and Virgil leading the prisoners and the rest walking backward, facing the men at the table and Renfro at the toppled bar until they were all out the door.

It was late at night when they reached Tombstone, leading their prisoners and the captives' murder victim. Doc had been coughing hard and regularly the entire way but he had stayed in the saddle and refused to rest. By the time he unsaddled outside his rooming house on Fremont Street, he was ash white, saying nothing as he went inside, leaving the posse to take the bandits the rest of the way to the jail.

Coming out of the Capital Saloon, Frank McLowery and Ike and Billy Clanton could see the posse farther down the block, crossing the street with Stilwell and Spence in tow. They stopped short, for the moment caught too far off guard to say anything. Ike turned his slack-jawed look toward Frank, then stared at the posse again.

"Well, God damn," he said.

Beside him, Frank gripped his gun belt till his knuckles turned white.

"They got Floyd and Pete with them," said Ike, just to say something.

Frank didn't bother with an answer. Turning slowly, he stepped back onto the boardwalk and faced the opposite direction. He glanced over his shoulder toward Billy. "You go on and get Ringo and Tom. They'll be over to the Bird Cage. You bring 'em back real quick, y'hear?"

32

"I got a mind not to pay the damn bail. We could bust 'em out — that's the right thing. We'd save us some money and teach them Earps a lesson." Frank McLowery paced in front of the Mining Exchange, stopping once to look down Fourth Street to see if Spicer was on his way. Then he started pacing again. "This ain't the way it's supposed to be, John, and you damn well know it."

John Behan watched Frank move back and forth, waiting for the man to cool down before he spoke. He looked at Ike, searching for some sign of support. Ike wouldn't meet his gaze.

"All right, Frank," said Behan, "you had your say now?"

"I tell you one thing, John. I'm finished standin' around and talkin' about the Earps. The time for talkin' is over."

"Frank, you're not bustin' out Stilwell and Spence. You do that and I swear I'm through with you fellers. I don't care if I stay sheriff or not. I'm through. You get that?"

"You tellin' me what to do?" Frank said. "Now ain't that the tail waggin' the dog!" He let out a harsh, short laugh.

"Frank, you know who's down there at the calaboose? Virgil's down there with a twelve gauge, and he's got Masterson to help out. And when they're through, Wyatt and Morgan are takin' over. You want to walk into that? How about you, Ike? You feel like shakin' hands with a twelve gauge?"

Ike looked at John, then checked Frank. "Guess I don't." Seeing he had committed himself, he then turned to Frank to try to make the best of it. "He's talkin' sense, Frank. We can't get 'em out now. Leastways, not tonight."

"I'd expect as much from you, Ike." Frank looked down Fourth Street again, then turned back. "I tell you what — you're so keen on payin' the bail, you wait here for Judge Spicer and you give him the damn money. I'm goin' over to Ringo and the rest." He started down Fourth. "When you're through, you come find us," he added. "You hear me, Ike? We ain't through yet and you're gonna do your share. I ain't tellin' Curly Bill we just rolled over for the Earps."

Frank found Tom, Billy and Ringo in Hafford's. They stayed just long enough for one more round and then started for the door, all except Ringo.

"We got some business to look into," said Frank. "Ain't you comin', Ringo?"

The way the Texas gunman acted, he might not have even heard McLowery. He took another drink and kept staring at the mirror behind the bar. The others waited. They wanted to be on their way, but they didn't think they should leave without giving Ringo the chance to have his say. They waited for a minute, a minute that seemed to stretch on and on, then Ringo finally said, "I'll be along." He took out his makings and started to roll a cigarette and said no more.

Without any discussion about where they would go, the two McLowerys and Billy headed down Allen Street. What exactly would be the business they would look into remained to be seen. For the time being, all three of them were content to play whatever hand they were dealt.

Outside the Oriental they found Morgan and Doc standing on the boardwalk talking. The cowboys veered toward the same side of the street as the Oriental and came to a stop in the middle of the road, some fifteen feet from the boardwalk.

"Scum talking to scum," said Frank just loud enough for Morgan and Doc to hear. When he had their attention he went on. "You Earps think you're ridin' pretty damn high, don't you? Get yourselves a posse behind ya and you think you can take anybody. You think you can take somebody by yourself? How about it, Morgan? You think you could take me in?"

Morgan's face tightened as he put a halter on himself. Any other time he would probably have been out in the street in the blink of an eye, but Wyatt had taken him aside earlier to tell him to be on guard for one of the cowboys trying something just like this. "We'll do our work in the jail, guarding Stilwell and Spence," Wyatt had told his kid brother.

"I'm callin' you out, Earp," said Frank. "You just gonna stand there with your thumb up your ass?"

Morgan was keenly aware of the comforting heft of the Colt on his hip, aware of how easy it might be to go for it now. His mind raging, straining to keep itself in line, he then noticed Ike on the other side of the street, moving up slowly behind Billy and the McLowerys.

"Come on out into the street," Frank said. "Just you and me."

Morgan checked the others. Tom stood smirking to his brother's left, looking just as ready as Frank. The expression on Billy's face, though, was different. Morgan thought he saw a hesitancy in Billy. Not fear, just reluctance perhaps. That was something that could figure to the good if anything happened, Morg thought.

Doc now decided to deal himself in. "You boys don't have to waste your breath anymore. I'm ready right now." In place of the pallid tone of before, a faint whiskey ruddiness now touched his cheeks. He took a step forward to see what would happen.

From the end of the bar inside the Oriental, Wyatt heard some kind of talk going on outside but didn't pay it much attention at first. As he talked to Ab Richardson about the night's take, he then noticed his dealer's eyes pick up something through the window. He turned to look for himself. No one was in sight. Whomever Richardson had seen had now passed out of view.

"I just saw Ike," said Ab. "He was coming off the walk and headed here."

Wyatt took his elbows off the bar. "If Ike's around, chances are he's not alone." He headed for the door.

Stopping just before walking out onto the boardwalk, he saw Doc take a step forward, with Morg to his side and four armed cowboys facing them in the street. Something to the right then got his attention, something he saw out of the corner of his eye. He turned to see Ringo moving toward Morg and Doc, along Fifth Street. The gunman stopped beside a tie rail, just twenty feet away.

"Doc!" Wyatt called before Holliday could step into the street.

Looking over his shoulder, Doc saw Wyatt look in Ringo's direction. Seeing the Texas renegade, Doc smiled thinly.

"Glad to see you could make it, Ringo. We're just about to get started."

"Hold it, Doc!" Wyatt strode over to Morg, who stood hunched slightly forward, his eyes on the cowboys in the street.

Frank said, "You heard him, Doc. You hold on. It's Morgan I'm talking to. You stay clear."

Wyatt could sense Morgan's tension. He seemed ready to bust out any second. "It's their play," he said quietly to his brother, "and it's a fool's play."

"I'm not backing out," said Morg.

"Don't be stupid. Me, you and Doc, we're going inside. Just let 'em stew."

"Aw hell," Doc said in exasperation. "More talk."

Tom spoke up now. "What's it gonna be, Morgan? You runnin' scared? Is that it?"

"Even shit-on-legs there can make a speech," Doc said with a jerk of the thumb toward Tom.

While Tom glowered at Doc, Wyatt took hold of his brother's arm, hoping Doc's distraction could help get Morgan away. "Don't let them goad you," he said to Morg. "We're going back inside."

Glancing back, Wyatt saw Doc lean against an upright and turn toward Ringo, waving the gunman in. "Come on, Ringo. I'll take you too. Everybody gets their chance."

"Lay off, Doc," Wyatt said. This time he didn't snap at Holliday. His voice was low, bristling with urgency. The Georgia gambler seemed to lock up, then turn his head to face Wyatt. "You're not getting my brother killed," Wyatt said.

His eyes shining with the sickness, Doc held Wyatt's gaze. A moment later, he nodded his head in grudging agreement. "All right, Wyatt." Turning to the Clantons and McLowerys, he added, "Looks like you boys'll have to look me up some other time." He checked Ringo once more, then stepped back onto the boardwalk to join the Earps on their way inside. Ike's voice reached them before they passed through the batwing doors.

"What about you, Morgan? Just between you and Frank. You runnin' from Frank here?"

Wyatt glared at Ike as he tightened his grip on Morgan's

arm. He had to yank his brother the rest of the way through the doorway.

But Frank wasn't through yet.

He came toward them and stopped at the edge of the road, the street lamp chasing the shadows from his face. "I tell you Earps one thing," he declared, speaking slowly and deliberately. "Any of you even comes to arrest me like you done Floyd and Pete, I'll kill you. I swear I'll kill you."

Wyatt stopped stock still. His scalp tightened and a cold sensation flooded through him; not an impulse to fight, but a clammy dread. He moved on with his brother to the bar.

The telegram left Bat little choice and precious little time. If he wanted to catch the morning stage, there would be many things to be done and affairs to be straightened away. Most of all there would be talking to Wyatt. After getting Luke Short to take his place at the jail with Virgil, he headed toward the Oriental.

Walking down Fifth, Bat realized with some surprise that he didn't want to come back. He promised himself though that he would come back this way if Wyatt needed him, but he wasn't convinced that he could really do much good.

At the intersection of Fifth and Allen he saw the Clantons and McLowerys in the street up ahead, facing Wyatt, Morgan and Doc. He couldn't hear what was being said, but the look of the men told him enough. He moved on, hoping his presence might help turn back the cowboys, and was drawing close to Ringo's back when he saw Wyatt take Morgan inside.

"You came too late," said Ringo, not bothering to turn toward Bat, his voice a low rumble. Masterson had been facing the gunman's back the entire time he had approached and had never seen Ringo turn his head, but Ringo knew he was there just the same. I'm getting so edgy, Bat thought, I can't even get a drop on a man anymore. Ringo's face was stony as Bat passed, a flick of the eyes the only sign that he was keeping tabs on the man walking by.

Bat found Wyatt at the far end of the Oriental bar talking to Morgan. His back still up, Morgan didn't seem to be listening too well.

"If you're looking for a fight, don't find it with them," Wyatt was saying. "If you see one of them, you can bet one or two more are closing in. That's not the fight you want."

"Damn it all, Wyatt, I didn't just jump out of the cradle," said Morg. "And from talk I heard about you in Dodge, you didn't exactly run and hide whenever trouble came your way."

"No, I didn't. But it was always on my terms if I could help it."

Although he didn't care to cut into family business, Bat didn't think he had the time to wait. He stepped close to Wyatt to get his attention.

"Need to talk to you, Wyatt."

The sight of Bat brought a look of concern to Wyatt's face.

"It's not the jail," Bat quickly reassured him . "Virgil's there with Luke. No trouble there." Bat stopped. Now that it was time to tell Wyatt, he found himself reluctant. He thought it might be easier to tell him alone.

The hesitation got the message across to Wyatt. He turned to his brother. "Go on, Morg, get something to eat. Doc can use some company and so can you." Morgan pushed away from the bar and threaded through the customers to join Holliday at a side table. When he was alone with Wyatt, Bat ordered a beer for each of them.

"I'm leavin' tomorrow, Wyatt. I just got this wire from Dodge and I have to be gettin' back there."

"Is it your brother?"

"Yeah, Jim's got himself some trouble. You remember Updegraff and Peacock? He's in business with them but it looks like splitting the profits isn't something they all agree on. They've already shot at each other once and I don't figure that to be the last of it."

Wyatt nodded in understanding.

"Funny part is," Bat continued, "I'll go all the way back to Kansas and I'll find out it's all Jim's doing. He's got a man-sized temper, enough temper for a couple men I'd say." Bat took a gulp of beer. The easy part of his talk was over. He took another sip in silence, gazing up at the longhorns mounted above the backbar.

"I don't like leavin' you and your brothers here like this," he finally said. "If it wasn't my own brother needin' help, I wouldn't be going now."

"Something you got to do," replied Wyatt.

Mighty cool, thought Bat. He didn't exactly expect Wyatt to bust out crying, but he knew that if he were in Wyatt's shoes he would be troubled. Could Wyatt really not know? He studied his friend. Wyatt looked blankly at the mirror as he drank. Thoughts were clearly brewing behind those hard blue eyes, but Bat could not discern what they were. He had to admit, as long as he had known Wyatt, he could never tell what the man was thinking.

Bat said, "There's something bad comin' here, Wyatt. You know that, don't you?"

Wyatt considered him before answering. "You could be right, Bat."

"You've got to find some way out of it. Do you know that too?"

Wyatt threw back the rest of his beer. "I'm doing all I can. If there's more to do, I'll do it."

Wyatt's mind was set, Bat could recognize that much. He tried to come up with something to say that would make Wyatt be more cautious. Nothing came to him. Wyatt's plans didn't seem to allow for any more advice. Bat ran his hand slowly along the bar's brass rail, then held it out toward Wyatt.

"Best I get things in order before I go."

Wyatt clasped the hand and shook it as he smiled at Bat. Masterson said, "Take care of yourself, Wyatt."

"You too, Bat."

Releasing the hand, Bat turned toward the door, trying to remember the things he had planned to do before morning. He had to sell his buckboard and team and pay off his debt to Neal Brown. He got no further than that as his thoughts jammed into a tangle that refused to be straightened. At the batwing doors, he faced the saloon again.

The place was quiet now with the last shift from the mines almost gone and the next still to come. In the far right corner Bat could see Wyatt going over to the table where Morgan and Doc were eating their dinners. He watched for a moment as Wyatt spoke to his brother and turned to say something to the Georgia gambler. As hard as he tried, Bat couldn't shake the feeling that he would never see Wyatt alive again.

33

The Cosmoplitan was a welcome sight as Wyatt tramped
along Allen Street in the pale light of the first hour of the
day. The street was empty and thoroughly quiet, as though
the town were holding its breath before the outbreak of the
early morning bustle. The hush put Wyatt in mind of the
sleep that was coming to him after so many hours.

After Stilwell and Spence had been bailed out, Wyatt
and Morg had alternated between watching Allen Street
from the porch of the Oriental and patrolling the town to
keep tabs on the cowboys' movements. As it turned out,
the Clantons did not stay long in Tombstone after the run-
in outside the Oriental, but the McLowery boys continued
to make the rounds and, from what Wyatt had heard,
Stilwell and Spence were with them. By five o'clock,
though, even these last cowboys were on their way out of
town before there could be any more trouble.

About to step into the Cosmopolitan lobby, Wyatt
paused to look across the street at the Grand Hotel. Out of

the corner of his eye he thought he saw a curtain move at one of the windows. Looking at the hotel more closely, though, he found the place to be completely still, and he couldn't figure which window he had noticed just a moment before. The thought occurred to him that the Clantons and their friends were known to stay at the Grand. What if some of them hadn't really left? After all, Wyatt only had other people's word that certain members of the bunch had actually ridden out of town. Frank McLowery, for instance. And Stilwell and Tom McLowery. They might have taken a front room at the Grand that would have given them a clear view of — and a clear shot at — the Cosmopolitan entrance. Reflexively, Wyatt sidestepped into the shadows of his hotel's threshold as he searched the Grand's windows again.

The whitewashed hotel facade didn't look very menacing in the early light, and slowly Wyatt came to accept the idea that his tired mind was creating phantoms. He moved inside the Cosmopolitan, but darted an occasional glance across the street just the same.

In the lobby, the clerk slept with his head resting on the hotel register, his mouth slightly open, letting loose a periodic snore. Good thing I'm not depending on him for information about cowboys at the Grand, Wyatt thought. On his way to the second floor, he passed the big, old, yellow dog sleeping at the foot of the stairs — or at least he thought the dog was sleeping. Without raising its head or opening an eye, the animal was somehow alert enough to growl when Wyatt neared.

At the top of the stairs Wyatt could see a crack of light showing at the bottom of the door to his room. That light brought back an uneasy feeling that was strong enough to stir Wyatt despite his exhaustion. It was a feeling that the Clantons and McLowerys had made him forget for the last night and day.

Light in the room meant the curtains hadn't been drawn

the night before, which meant in turn that Verna had been out all night and probably hadn't come back yet. Just out talking to friends, she would say.

Wyatt was surprised that she was at it again. For the last week she had been in bed each night when he had returned. With a sluggish, grim realization he now told himself that she could have been fooling him all along. Just because he had been finding her in bed lately didn't mean that she hadn't been out with Rowdy Joe and his girls earlier.

As tired as he was this morning, he was still ready enough to challenge her as soon as she got back.

Thinking all this through on his way down the hall, he flung his door open. He was sorting out in his mind how he was going to draw the line once and for all when she would finally stroll in, but the preparation was unnecessary because she was already there, right in front of him. She lay in bed, the covers half off her, revealing a good part of her white skin and supple figure. And there beside her was Art MacGregor, sitting on the bed, pulling on his boots so he could make it on time to the next shift at the Mountain Maid mine.

On the table next to the bed was a handful of gold coins alongside an empty bottle of whiskey. Just starting to rouse herself, Verna reached out to the table to make sure the money was still there.

MacGregor blanched when he saw the look on Wyatt's face. Before the miner could spring to his feet on his own steam, Wyatt had him by the collar and was dragging him out the door. A strong push sent MacGregor plunging over the rail and down the stairs, bouncing off the side wood-work, then rolling pell-mell the rest of the way. A long staircase, Wyatt thought — good enough for at least a broken arm. But he didn't wait to see how MacGregor came out. He was back in the room before the miner hit bottom.

Some instinct broke through the fury to tell Wyatt to close the door behind him. Somehow that would make whatever would happen in the room just a little tidier. Verna was sitting up now, holding the sheet across her breasts, as if her modesty applied only to Wyatt. Or maybe it was just fear that made her cover herself. As Wyatt moved toward her she screamed.

A foot short of Verna, Wyatt suddenly stopped. His hands were aching to grab her and punish her, but something told him how foolish it would be. After putting up with her for so long, why start hitting her now, now when it was all over? The thought put him in control of himself again, still furious but in control. Turning away from her, he went to the bureau that held her things, pulled out a drawer and dumped its contents on the bed.

"You can take one of my carpetbags if you want," he said, "but just make sure you pack it all up."

She flinched each time he made a move in her direction. Disregarding her, he went to the bureau again and pulled out her other drawer, but when he turned back to the bed to dump it, her scared look was suddenly gone. In the time it had taken to turn his back on her and cross the room, her expression had been transformed from fear to a pouty sort of anger.

"Throwin' me out will make you feel good, won't it, Wyatt," she said.

Put off balance by this switch, he studied her, trying to figure where she was headed.

"You throwin' me out makes you seem like a fine, up-standin' man," she said. "And you flirtin' around with that Jew tramp."

"What the hell you talking about?"

"In the Can Can with Bat yesterday. You think I don't hear things, Wyatt?"

"What does she got to do with you being a goddamned slut? Tell me that, Verna."

"You think she can be your woman, that actress? That's funny, Wyatt. I knew some of them Jews back in St. Louis. All they know is how to get a man's dollar away from him. She'll sharpster you out of everything you got. You'll see.''

Wyatt stood perfectly still. At first Verna's talking about Josie Marcus infuriated him, but now it meant nothing, because something else she had said put it completely out of mind.

"St. Louis?" he said. "What the hell do you know about St. Louis?"

"I was on the line there, that's what the hell I know about it. About goddamned time you knew."

"You said you grew up on a farm in Iowa. That good family and upbringing you're always talking about."

"Yeah, that's right. Till I was twelve and I run away. In St. Louis I learned the trade young enough to learn real good. I learned all about you fair-haired bastards and how you were going to do good by me." She forced out a laugh. "Why the hell I thought you could make a difference — damned if I know."

Wyatt suddenly felt disoriented and a little light-headed. For years she had told him about her family and how upstanding they were and how she had let them down — not at age twelve, but years later in Wichita. St. Louis had never entered into it. Did a girl of twelve who left her family to go on the line really come from a decent, God-fearing family? Or had that been a lie also? Any idea that Wyatt had held about who Verna was now started to slip away. All that was left was this snarling drunk whore on his bed.

"You stupid bastards," she said, "how long did you think I'd stay off the line? What the hell did you expect? Was I really good for anything else? You think you were enough to make me forget that? Why couldn't you just leave me where I was? Just leave me be."

She got up now, stark naked, pacing about the room, a whiskey-red tint to her eyes. "I got my bellyful doin' nothing," she went on, "waitin' for folks to point at me, knowin' what I been since twelve years old. Well, they can all know now and all go to hell. You see me, Wyatt? This is what I am. You want any of me anymore, just pay up like the rest. I'm goin' back to what I know and that's that." She stopped, stared off for a moment, then let out a dry laugh. "Maybe Virgil'll be one of my customers. How about that? Won't that be a laugh. Nice old Allie can really get something to poke her nose into."

One swing with the flat of his hand knocked her to the floor. As she thudded to the floorboards, she convulsed in deep, rapid sobs; before long these sobs changed to fitful laughter. Wyatt found himself backing up slowly until he was flush against the bureau. He watched her, sprawled on the floor, her skin now sickeningly pale. He wheeled and stormed out the door as fast as he could.

Halfway down the stairs, he stopped to put a brake on the reeling sensation in his head. Taking several deep breaths, he got a hold of himself and stepped quickly down the rest of the stairs. The only thing going through his mind was that time in Wichita when he had found Verna beaten by the cowboy. He wondered if she had asked for that too.

The dog got out of his way at the foot of the stairs, and the clerk watched, wide awake, as Wyatt crossed the lobby.

34

Wyatt opened the Oriental to get at one of the bottles of whiskey behind the bar. He found an opened one, half empty, but then thought better of it and took a bottle that was still full. Standing behind the counter, he quickly downed three shots. The sting of the alcohol was a welcome sensation as it scalded its way down to his stomach. Then he stopped drinking and waited for some kind of release from the maddened, shuddering feeling. No release came to him, only a sudden weakness in the legs. He took his bottle and glass around the bar to one of the tables.

He drank some more and began to see softer edges around the bottle on the tabletop in front of him and around the frame of the front doorway, which was now filled with bright light. For all that, he still felt no better. Two drinks later he was aware of little else other than the stark fact that he was drinking alone in an empty saloon. Leaving the bottle open on the table, he pushed himself to his feet and, still walking pretty well, he thought, he moved out of the saloon.

His first impulse was to hunt up Virgil, and he even started walking in the direction of his brother's house for a full block before he remembered that Virgil would certainly be asleep by now. Might not be a bad idea to wake him up, he thought. He quickly discarded that notion, though. He then considered finding Morg. No chance of that either, he told himself. He'll be asleep till noon. It's got to be Bat, he decided, he's always good company. He's the man to talk to. In an unsettling rush of thought, Wyatt then realized how drunk he was. He had completely forgotten that Bat wasn't even in Tombstone anymore. His stage must have left an hour ago, which would put him now somewhere along the road north to Benson.

Another realization pressed upon Wyatt: he was standing on the corner of Allen and Fourth, looking stupid, not knowing what he was doing. People were starting to come out on the streets, and the chances were good that news of Wyatt's fight with Verna at the Cosmopolitan was beginning to get around. Rather than let himself be gawked at, Wyatt moved quickly along the street and stepped into the first place that was open.

Sitting by himself in the Can Can Restaurant was Doc Holliday, a bottle half empty in front of him. When he sat next to him, Wyatt could see that the Georgia gambler looked like hell, the worst he had ever seen.

"Any sleep last night, Doc?"

Doc gave him a dim glance. "Maybe some, but I didn't notice." He looked again at Wyatt. "Doesn't look like you got any yourself."

Wyatt took the whiskey and, not seeing any extra glass, took a gulp straight from the bottle.

He wasn't sure he would have actually told Virgil about the fight with Verna; he might not have been able to get himself started, especially if Allie had been around. He might not have even told Morg. With Doc, though, he saw no reason not to talk and, without invitation, told him the whole story, from the time he had found Verna in bed with the miner until he had opened the bottle at the Oriental.

Doc listened quietly and serenely, as though Wyatt's finding Verna back on the line was the most natural thing in the world. When Wyatt was finished, Doc leaned back in his chair and looked off thoughtfully. "Some fellers I know," he said, "don't give a second thought to pimping their women." He sounded like he was making a mild, academic observation.

Wyatt didn't know what to make of the remark, especially coming from Doc, a man who had lived with a whore for several years. Did he pimp for his wife Kate? Wyatt took another long drink from the bottle. When the bite of the alcohol had done its work on his insides, he looked up to see Doc leaning slightly forward, his elbows on the table taking his weight. His eyes glowed intently. Nothing was said for a while as Wyatt took another gulp, then Doc finally let loose his thought.

"It's the demon in her," he said.

Wyatt waited for something more, but Doc left it at that. "What do you mean, a demon?"

"Not *a* demon," Doc said. "*The* demon. Nothing you can do about it. Once it's inside you, there's nothing you can do about it. Yeah," he said, nodding his head, "Verna's got the demon all right."

Wyatt took a stab at pinning him down. "You talking about a ghost? That kind of demon?" Wyatt had known some men who were spooked by ghosts, and he thought Doc might be one.

"No, damn it, not ghosts," Doc growled. "The demon." He turned an unfocused, drunken look toward Wyatt, then waved him off angrily and took the bottle and poured himself another glassful. Shaking his head, he tossed the drink down his throat. Watching Doc stare off, Wyatt knew there would be no more talking. Doc could brood like that for a good hour or two, maybe half a day with another bottle to keep him going. Out of some vague sort of loyalty, Wyatt stayed with him a few minutes longer, then, without a word, he left Doc stewing and walked out the door.

No thinking went into the direction he took. His feet seemed to move on their own, taking him back down Allen to the Cosmopolitan. He tried to sort through all his times with Verna, tried to make some sense out of them. There was no sense that he could see. The one thought that loomed above the others was the realization that somehow everything Verna had done had been leading up to this. Only now did he see it, certain that he had been pathetic and stupid for not seeing it sooner. He just couldn't believe she would go back to that life once he had made it possible for her to leave it.

He started to feel sorry for himself. This was all a terrible burden, he thought, and all I had tried to do was the right thing. The best thing now was to get her moved out, find her someplace else and wash his hands of it.

When he opened the door, he thought at first that she had already gone, even though her clothes were still heaped on the bed. Stepping in farther, he then saw her on the floor, still naked, balled up with her arms twisted, as if they had been writhing before they had stopped. Her jaw was slack, her tongue clearly visible and her chestnut brown eyes stared sightlessly.

Wyatt moved slowly, gingerly, not seeming to feel his feet on the floor. He picked up the small bottle lying next to Verna and looked at it through glazed eyes. For a moment, all the whiskey he had drunk made him lose his balance, and he staggered, then dropped into a sitting position on the bed. This room was always too small, he thought, you can hardly move around in it.

On the table by the bed he saw a slip of paper, next to the money left by the miner. Wyatt reached for it, read it over, then sat quietly, feeling nothing, not one damn thing.

The paper was a receipt from Bauer's store for the purchase of one bottle of arsenic. The first thing Wyatt had noticed about the receipt was that the sale had been made over a month ago. It had taken Verna that long to find the right time.

35

It was all the fault of the Earps. Frank was right about that at least, Ike decided.

Riding away from Lewis Springs toward Tombstone late in the afternoon, Ike thought back to the way things had been before Wyatt and his brothers had come to Cochise County. There had been easy money back then and no griping in the outfit, and there sure as hell hadn't been any days like Ike had today.

All day long Frank and Curly Bill had been stomping around the ranch, telling everybody else what they should have done when Stilwell and Spence had been arrested. Ike wanted to know what Frank was doing at the Clanton ranch in the first place, strutting around like he owned the place. Ike didn't bother to ask him, though. He figured he knew the answer anyway: Frank probably just wanted to be with Curly Bill so they could sound off together. And wouldn't you know it, thought Ike, when the time came to push the blame on somebody it was always me.

Why'd Ike take so long to back up our play at the Oriental last night? Frank and Curly Bill were saying. And how come he took so long to speak up when he got there? Always me, thought Ike. Always me.

Standing by the corral, alongside Frank and Curly Bill, watching Billy break a mustang, Ike had to put up with the worst bad-mouthing of his life. Frank was the loudest of them and the most persistent.

"What goddamn business was it of your'n to tell Morgan to make his fight with me last night?" said Frank.

"You were the one who said you'd take him," Ike tried to point out.

"That's my lookout! If you want to make a play, take on Wyatt himself, or that damned Holliday! If I had to depend on you to throw down a body, I think I'd slit my throat."

Ike leaned against the top corral rail, staring at Billy saddling the mustang, barely seeing his brother as his ears turned red with haltered anger. From behind he heard approaching footsteps, which irritated him even more. Without looking he could tell who was coming. That sneaky step would have to be Floyd Stilwell slipping up to take his shots at Ike.

"And who was it who said we shouldn't bust out Floyd here and Spence?" Frank raged on. "That would'a taken them Earps down a notch, but all you wanted to do was pay the damn bail."

Ike turned to Curly Bill out of desperation. He should have known better, considering how Brocius had been letting him down lately, but he still held out some hope. Maybe his old friend would stand by him after all. Fat chance. All his so-called friend said was, "Frank's right. Can't argue with him, Ike."

Stilwell pitched in now. "I still say the whole problem was the Benson stage job. You told me Earp'd be ridin' messenger on that run, Ike. If you gave me the right information, we wouldn't be worrying about Earp at all now."

A few minutes later, Stilwell said pretty much the same

thing once more. When he started to say it a third time, Ike had taken just about enough and stalked off to find his strawberry roan.

"Yep," he told himself in between sips from his flask on his way into town. "Them Earps really spoilt it all." Sure, the Old Man's dying didn't help. Ike had to live by his wits now that there was no one around to look after his rightful place in the outfit. But everything would still have been all right if the Earps just hadn't pushed it. The harder they pushed, the worse the fellers stuck it to Ike, like it was all his fault. And him a Clanton! Who did they think he was? Wasn't I there at Sawtooth Canyon, he thought, lending a hand when need be? Isn't it my ranch that they keep coming to whenever they need a place to nest? Good thing the Old Man isn't around to see the kind of treatment Clantons have been getting, Ike thought.

He groused some more about Curly Bill, the big man who was telling everybody else what to do. He acts like he's such a bad man, thought Ike, but he's too scared to go back to Tombstone, afraid the Earps will lock him up for good or maybe just shoot him on sight. "A feller's got to be careful," Curly Bill kept saying. That made Ike laugh. Brocius kept on talking about what had to be done to the Earps, but he spent all his time at the Clanton ranch, far away from Wyatt, Morgan or Virgil. Well, just maybe Curly Bill ain't the one to start things rolling, Ike mused. Just maybe that's the job for a Clanton.

In the distance, Ike could now make out the lights flickering along Allen Street in the gathering darkness. A night on the town would set things right — Ike was sure of it. A man could accomplish a lot in one night if he knew how to go about it. "Might even take me a shot at Wyatt," he said to himself. He drained the last of the whiskey from the flask and slipped it back into his jacket pocket.

Stabling his roan at the O.K. Corral, he moved down Allen to make his first stop at Hafford's. That was good for three or four drinks, just enough to loosen up, then he moved on. Along the way, he passed that girl Ginnie from Rowdy Joe's, standing on the corner with another whore.

"You girls want a high old time," he said, "you just look me up. Got money burning a hole in my pocket."

He got a laugh out of them and then turned in at the Occidental. On the third drink there, he judged he was about half-lit and peppery as hell, which made him think of Ginnie and the other girl he had seen outside. A trip to the Bird Cage for a little poontang might be just the thing, he thought. But then again, something about tonight made him think that he had some man's work ahead of him instead, work that would have made Old Man proud. And if Curly Bill and Frank thought he didn't have the sand to do it, then the hell with them, along with the Earps.

When it came to gambling, Neal Brown had no appetite for conversation, which suited Morgan just fine. Sitting in the back of the Alhambra, they played blackjack head-to-head for nearly an hour without anything said except "Hit me" when the time came to ask for another card. It was a relief for Morgan to be doing something that didn't involve some busthead asking him all about the run-in outside the Oriental the night before.

The sporting men along Allen Street all seemed to want to know exactly what had happened when Frank McLowery had called out the Earps, and every time that Morgan had to answer some fool's question, the same thought kept coming back: he had let McLowery get away. Frank had humiliated him in front of his own saloon and Morg had never got his Colt out of its holster.

"Hit me," Morgan said, and Brown dealt him his fourth card. Brooding now about the night before didn't leave Morg much room for thinking through his game, and checking his new card made him realize just how far off his playing was. An eight added to the three and four already showing gave him fifteen without counting the hole card.

All totaled, he was busted, well over twenty-one when he should have been standing pat and bluffing. He shook his head.

That was when he first noticed the voice from the front of the saloon.

It was a loud voice, but the words were unintelligible, and as Morg shuffled the deck for the next play, he paid it little attention. He then began to pick up what was being said before he could identify the speaker.

"The Old Man, he built something in these parts," the voice said, "back when a body *could* build something around here, before these dandies started struttin' around, tellin' folks which way to piss. Enough to make a man sick, I tell ya. But that's gonna change, my friend. I got a bunch of fellers who'll see to it, if I don't do it myself."

The memory of the night before now returned to Morgan with full force as he recognized the voice. He thought of Ike standing next to Frank outside the Oriental, a maddening smirk on his face.

"Things'll be right again," Ike's voice continued, "when we get rid of them. You see if'n I'm wrong, friend. When we take care of them Earps, you'll thank us."

Ike railed on, but Morgan didn't have to hear any more. He was on his feet, shouldering his way through the crowd, headed toward the front, loosening his Colt in its holster. When Morgan reached the bar, Ike was still at it.

"I tell ya," he said, "nothing's gonna stop us from taking what's our'n. Nothing and nobody. No sir."

Morgan clamped a hand on the cowboy's shoulder and whirled him around. Morg's voice was icy. "Here's your chance to get rid of one Earp, you son of a bitch. Go ahead. Stop talkin' and do something."

Ike's mouth seemed stuck for a moment. He then found his voice again, even managing to put some defiance into it. "I ain't armed. You throwin' down on an unarmed man, Earp?"

Morg wasn't about to listen to Ike's talk. He put one

hand on the back of Ike's jacket and the other on top of the right shoulder and dragged him at a fast walk to the door and out onto the boardwalk. His eyes blazing, Morgan heaved the cowboy out into the street and watched him scramble and stagger to stay on his feet.

Morg headed toward him at a quick stride. "Get yourself a gun, Ike, and let's get it over with!"

Wyatt didn't even have his brothers on hand when he buried Verna. He dug the grave himself in the crisp night air at the edge of boot hill and only had Reverend Pryor with him because he couldn't remember what parts of the scripture should be read. It had been too many years since he had buried Willa back in Lamar.

The reverend had finished reading his piece, and Wyatt had shoveled the last spadeful onto the cottonwood coffin, before Wyatt noticed Doc Holliday standing behind him. His pale eyes on the freshly turned mound of dirt, Holliday stood some twenty feet away. The outline of the man was streaked with light from behind him, his sinewy body draped in night shadow. Wyatt had no idea how long Doc had been standing there. He saw no reason to ask when he walked away with the Georgia gambler toward the heart of town.

At Wyatt's side, Doc moved at a shambling, uncertain gait, the consumption leaving him with very little strength tonight. As they neared First Street, Wyatt realized that he still carried the shovel in his left hand. Aiming to plant it cleanly into the ground, he pitched it to the side. The spade clanged against a rock and clattered to the ground.

Without thinking, he turned onto Allen Street and headed toward the Oriental with no object in mind other than to sit in some place that was his. Doc continued to walk silently by his side, his gaze directed straight ahead, shifting neither to the right or left. Crossing Third Street, Wyatt saw Ike hurtling out through the Alhambra's batwing doors, then saw his kid brother stride out of the saloon and into the street to go at Ike some more. Wyatt willed his exhaustion aside to quicken his step and reach Morgan's side before anything further could happen.

Morg had Ike in his hands again and was shoving him down the street when Wyatt neared.

"Get yourself heeled!" shouted Morg.

Wyatt quickly stepped in front of his brother. "What the hell's going on?"

"Ike here's talkin' a fight." Morgan was seething.

Wyatt glanced at Ike, glaring back at Morg with red-rimmed eyes. "Look at him, Morg," Wyatt said. "He's stinking drunk. He's not going to make much of a fight like that."

"He's gotten drunk once too often," said Morg.

"He's right," Doc put in. Walking around Wyatt, he stepped closer to Clanton and gave the man a brief considering look. "You son-of-a-bitch cowboy," he said, as if wishing him a good morning. "We can't put this off any longer and you know it. You can leave these Earp boys alone because I'm ready now."

Moving with a new urgency, Wyatt gripped his brother's lapel and pulled him as he moved to put a straight-arm in front of Doc. "He's dead, stupid drunk," he snapped, jerking his head toward Clanton. "We're leaving him be."

"The hell we are," said Morg. "Last night was the end of it."

"Morg, you walk it off. Take Doc with you. You hear that, Doc? The two of you walk it off now."

Holliday didn't bother to get around Wyatt's restraining arm. He just stayed where he was, his gaze riveted on Clanton, who kept a steady glower on the three men around him. On his other side, Wyatt could feel his brother about to break out. "Move it now, Morg. There's not going to be a fight because I won't have it. Now move it."

Wyatt held his brother in check for several moments more before he saw resignation enter Morgan's expression. A short while later, Morg turned away, glared at Ike, then starting walking, stopping after a few steps to see what Doc would do.

Meeting Wyatt's look, Doc said, "Don't worry, Deacon. I'll go for now." He moved unsteadily to reach Morgan's side and started walking down the street.

"Do yourself a favor, Wyatt," Doc called back. "Kill the little maggot now. Save yourself some trouble later."

"Keep walking, Doc."

Wyatt watched as his brother and Holliday headed down the block.

Ike said, "Your brother's no better than you, Wyatt. Curly Bill said that straight off and he was right."

Wyatt took a long breath. He didn't think Ike was even worth hitting right now. And even if he was, Wyatt didn't have the will to do it. After getting Verna's body out of the room and over to the undertaker, Wyatt had lain in a bed in Virgil's spare room for only a few hours but had hardly managed to sleep at all. Like Doc, there wasn't much left of him today.

He said, "You keep up this sort of talk, Ike, you're going to get yourself into something you won't be able to get out of."

"We've had enough of you Earps," Ike spat. "It started in Wichita and you're still doggin' us here and it's been goin' on too damn long."

Clanton's fighting words didn't concern Wyatt, but the look on his face did. Wyatt had never known Ike to be much good at standing his ground when on his own, but the expression on his face now was unflinching; whiskey-addled, certainly, but unrelenting all the same. Wyatt's stomach began to churn.

"One time," Wyatt said, "I told you to look after your brother Billy. Now I take that back. You can't even look after yourself."

Ike let out a laugh and started moving away, angling to one side so that he could face Wyatt, his feisty resolve still intact. "My friends'll be comin' to town tomorrow Earp. Things'll be different. You can put money on it."

"Don't be stupid, Ike. Sleep it off."

"Go to hell."

His patrol finished at eleven, Wyatt strolled down Fremont toward Virgil's house to tell his brother to take the next shift. By Fly's rooming house, he stopped to look at the second-story window at the back — Doc's room. A light burned there, which gave Wyatt some small comfort. With Doc off the streets there was one less thing to worry about, one less hair-trigger temper that needed to be restrained. Of course, this could be only temporary. No doubt it had been the sickness that had driven Doc to return to his room this early, but that same sickness could keep him from sleeping and make him decide to wander again. Sighing wearily, Wyatt then told himself that Doc would have to be something for Virgil to worry about for the next few hours.

"Is that you, Wyatt?" A woman's voice asked, but its suddenness made Wyatt flinch and cover his Colt with his right hand. He turned to see two figures facing him on the boardwalk. Wyatt eased up when he saw that it was Josie and Doby.

"I couldn't be sure it was you in that dark alley," Josie said. There wasn't enough light to get a good look at her face, but there was enough for Wyatt to see that the usual playfulness was not to be found in her expression.

"Just making my rounds," Wyatt said.

"Didn't see you at the performance tonight," put in Doby, anxious to speak up before Josie shut him out. "A fine show, Mr. Earp. You would have enjoyed it. Perhaps tomorrow night's show?"

"Stop bothering him, Vic," Josie said, taking the troupe owner by the arm and turning him aside. "Why don't you just go on to the hotel without me. I'll be along."

"If you want to," Doby said unsurely, "but I think I should ask Mr. Earp here to escort you on your way back. A young lady at night ought to show care. Am I right, Mr. Earp?"

"Go on, Vic," she said impatiently. "Go on. Go on."

Doby managed to tip his hat to Wyatt before he was shooed away. Wyatt watched Josie curiously, wondering what this was all about. She waited till the troupe master was well on his way before she turned to Wyatt, taking a tentative step in his direction. For a moment she seemed to be groping for words, the last thing Wyatt would have expected of her.

"I heard about your wife," she finally said.

Wyatt tensed. How much had Josie heard? Did she hear about the fight with Verna, or just Verna's dying?

This actress who had been such a flighty chatterbox the day before, now fumbled for words again. "Well, Wyatt, I just wanted to say I heard about it this afternoon, and I thought I should tell you that I'm sorry for your grief."

Wyatt wasn't sure whether it was grief that he was feeling for Verna, but he appreciated the sympathy, just the same. Josie took another step closer, her face catching the light from a rooming house window. Wyatt could see that her sparkling blue eyes were capable of genuine concern as well as sassiness.

Josie said, "She must have been very sad."

"Yes, she was," he replied, not knowing what else to say.

"Another thing, Wyatt, about Vic and him bothering you about coming to the show. Just ignore him. You'll come when you're ready to take your mind off what's happened."

Wyatt smiled wryly. "Vic better not hold his breath for that."

She smiled back at him, then said, "I won't be bothering you any longer. I'll be on my way."

"Josie," Wyatt called to her as she turned away. She

faced him quizzically. "You know, Vic was right about someone escorting you. That would be the thing to do, but the way things are tonight, I think you might be safer walking without me than with me."

She nodded, understanding what he was getting at. "I saw Ike Clanton at the Bird Cage. So did just about everyone else there. He was hard to miss, the way he was talking about you and your brothers." She studied him, anxiety starting to light her eyes. "Does he really mean all that he says about what he's going to do?"

"I don't know anymore. He might."

She considered Wyatt a moment longer, then surprised him by reaching out and gripping his arm. Looking intently up at him, she said. "You be careful, Wyatt. I haven't had the chance to know you yet." Although she stopped talking, she held her grip on his arm, then surprised him again by turning quickly and walking away into the light of Fremont Street on the way to her hotel.

36

Although fitful, Wyatt's sleep lasted till ten o'clock, leaving a web of dream images of Verna that clung to his thoughts and lasted throughout his walk from Virgil's house to the Can Can Restaurant. A venison steak, two fried eggs and a cup of coffee dissolved most of the web and let him gaze out onto Allen Street with a clear head. He was hoping for a second cup, but began to doubt the chances of that when he saw Ab Richardson walk in.

Richardson quickly scanned the nearly empty restaurant until he saw Wyatt sitting alone in the corner. He moved swiftly to reach Wyatt's side.

"What is it, Ab?" Wyatt said.

"It ain't over yet. Ike's been at it all night and he says there's more to come."

Mercifully, Wyatt's memory had allowed him to forget Clanton for at least the first short leg of the morning. Ab's words now brought back the run-in last night outside the Alhambra. The little bastard just won't quit, he thought.

"Is he heeled?" he asked.

"With both hands full," Ab replied. "He's got himself a Winchester and a pistol and he's on the prowl. I got a look at him about an hour ago and he looked like he might still be workin' on the same drunk as last night, but he's ready to go all the same. Clum saw him on Fremont sayin' he was gonna shoot the first Earp he saw. Either an Earp or Holliday, he said."

Staring at Richardson, Wyatt felt an old rage begin to brew inside him, an instinct that would have propelled him out of his seat and out the door with gun in hand at some other time back in Wichita or perhaps even in Dodge. But now he didn't leave his seat. He didn't move at all. There was no mistaking that Ike's actions were backing him into a corner, but he found a calculating calm taking over. There's no rushing this, he thought.

He reached out for his cup and took a last sip.

"Virge told me to come find you," Richardson said.

Wyatt sliced the last strip of venison in two and put one of the pieces into his mouth. "I'll be on my way soon," he told Ab. He finished his steak and the last of his eggs before he got up and headed toward the door.

The day was cool, the northerly breeze lifting to a gust once in a while to swirl the loose dust on the road. Wyatt found Virgil standing with Morgan outside the Alhambra, their jackets flapping in the wind.

"The last I heard," said Virgil, "he was around Fremont and Third."

"Was he moving toward First?" Wyatt asked.

"Not that I heard."

Wyatt nodded. "He might be still more talk than fight." Virgil's house was at Fremont and First. If Ike really meant to follow through, he probably would've headed that way to set up an ambush.

Morgan said, "If it's not just talk, then it's time to put a stop to it, wouldn't you say?"

"Go slow, Morg," Wyatt told him, "and make sure you get the drop if you see him. Ike might've picked up a trick or two from Curly Bill that could surprise you."

"He won't surprise me," said Morgan.

The search for Ike didn't last long.

As each Earp took a side street, Virgil heard footfalls along Fourth — it seemed Ike hadn't gotten very far — coming from the alley behind the Capital Saloon. At the rear of the saloon, Virgil could see Ike craning his neck around the corner of Blinn's lumber store.

Clanton checked his revolver, jammed it into his waistband and made sure his Winchester was primed. Through it all he kept up a low, disgruntled mumbling, which kept him from hearing the marshal's approach.

"You looking for me, Ike?" Virgil said quietly.

He let Clanton turn his head halfway around, but no more than that. The Colt came down hard on the back of Ike's neck, and, a look of surprise locking onto his face, the cowboy crumpled to the ground.

Ike came to in the courthouse, seated before the judge's empty bench. He stared glassy-eyed at first, then shook his head a couple of times and reached for the back of his neck. His hand retracted suddenly at the painful touch.

Virgil had already gone to find Judge Spicer so that they could arraign Ike for carrying firearms within city limits. The paying of a fine would be all that would be needed to release him, but it would still give him a message. Morgan stood to one side, Ike's guns in hand, keeping a close eye on Clanton slumped in his chair. Leaning against the side wall, Wyatt watched as Morgan strolled across the room and stopped in front of the cowboy, only a row of seats separating them.

"You livin' again?" Morg barked.

Ike grumbled in reply, something too faint for Wyatt to hear. It was loud enough, though, to tell Morgan he could get a rise out of the cowboy.

"We don't gotta wait for Virge," said Morgan. "You

take one of these guns and we'll go outside and settle this now. I'll pay your fine. You just pick a gun."

Ike glowered at Morgan, saying nothing. Wyatt eased himself away from the wall and walked to a seat in front of Ike, where he could face Morg and keep himself between his brother and the cowboy.

"That's enough, Morg," he said. "We already knocked the fight out of him. You put those guns aside."

Morgan looked away from Ike just long enough to glance at his brother, then, shaking his head, he placed the weapons on the bench and headed to the back of the courtroom to take a seat.

Wyatt stayed where he was, in front of Ike, listening to the cowboy's harsh, ragged breath slowly find its regular rhythm as the effect of the buffaloing wore off. Still facing forward, Wyatt said, "You've pushed it far enough, Ike. Your threats are going to stop."

"The hell with that."

Wyatt turned slowly, fixing a penetrating stare on the cowboy's face, anger prickling the back of his neck. Ike glared back with a cockeyed, almost rabid look; dazed, hung-over and hateful all at once.

"You stupid son of a bitch," said Wyatt, "you keep on talking a fight, that's what you'll get. That's my last word."

Ike sneered. "Wait'll my friends get here, Earp. Just wait."

Wyatt gave him an icy glance. Disgusted, he then got up and strode through the spectator section and headed for the door. A minute ago, he would not have wanted to leave Morgan alone with Ike, convinced that his brother might spark a fight. But now he saw no reason to stay. At this point, Wyatt wasn't in the mood for holding back any more than his brother was. Besides, he told himself, Virgil would be back soon enough with the judge.

Don't let the anger run away with you, he thought as he stepped out of the courthouse. That was when he bumped into Frank McLowery. One look at Frank's murderous glower made the venom boil inside of him.

"Bail out your friend," Wyatt snapped. "Bail him out and leave. You hear me?"

Frank seethed, but didn't answer. Wyatt saw a look of calculation in the cowboy's eyes, a hint that he might try his play here and now.

"I said, bail out Clanton and get going," demanded Wyatt.

Frank's voice was low and menacing. "You've buffaloed your last man, Earp. I swear it."

"More fight talk." Wyatt grimaced. "If you got a gun under that jacket, use it."

Frank stood before Wyatt, and turned ever so slightly to the right, in that moment exposing the pistol butt peeking out from under the jacket. He reached for the gun, but Wyatt was already swinging his left arm. He jolted Frank across the face with his open left hand, then pulled his Colt with his right and whipped it toward the cowboy's head. The smack across Frank's face had knocked him off balance which put him out of the gun's direct path. The Colt only grazed the back of his head; it was enough, though, to stagger him to the side of the courthouse, where he slumped against the wall, stunned. Wyatt stormed off to the street.

He didn't bother to glance back at Frank, keeping a swift pace as he walked down Fremont. Angling to the other side of the road, he happened to glance down an alley, by Fly's rooming house, and saw something that made him slow down. At the other end of the alley, at the O.K. Corral, he saw three men with four horses. They appeared to be putting up their animals. As Wyatt came to a stop, the three men turned his way.

The bare blond head highlighted in the midday sun identified one of them as Billy Clanton. Wyatt was able to recognize one of the others as Tom McLowery, but the third man turned back to his friends, apparently to say something, making him impossible to identify. Wyatt figured the fourth horse belonged to Frank McLowery.

If they turned their horses around when Frank returned with Ike and went back to their ranches, Wyatt thought, then the fight might not happen. But he didn't count on it. Even if they left today they would be back some other time. Wyatt moved on, turning at the next corner and shifting over to Allen to work his way back along the other side of the corral.

Reaching a good vantage point on Allen, he stopped to light a cigar, giving himself an excuse for taking a long look. He heard some men on the other side of the corral's bleached adobe wall, and he waited till they revealed themselves in the open gateway. He saw two men, neither of them Billy nor Tom nor, by the look of it, the third cowboy he had just seen with them. Wyatt flicked the spent wooden match away and continued down Allen.

Seeing how well Frank was bearing up after *his* buffaloing, Ike did his best to look cocky as they crossed Fremont on their way from the courthouse. He had taken enough guff from Frank lately without having to listen to him say how much better McLowerys could stand up to some manhandling. And Frank would say that, Ike was sure of it. He was that mean-spirited.

As much as he resented him, though, Ike had to admit something about Frank: he was sure going strong, buffaloing and all. There was determination in his step, a swagger to the roll of his shoulders and fire in his eye. Wyatt must've gone easy on him, Ike told himself.

As he and Frank reached the other side of the road, Tom, Floyd Stilwell and brother Billy were walking along the lot behind the O.K. Corral, approaching Fremont. Tom had his horse by the reins, while the other two had left their animals behind.

Frank faced his friends, then looked down Fremont, checking the street in both directions. "This here's goin' to be the last day for the Earps."

For a moment, nothing was said. Ike noticed Billy glancing apprehensively at the two McLowerys. This irritated Ike deeply. What's wrong with that fool kid? he thought. Every time there was talk about taking on the damn Earps he had that same undecided look. Comes a time, Ike decided, that a feller's got to take his kid brother in hand. He was about to say something when Stilwell spoke up to break the silence.

"You think we can get 'em all, Frank?"

"Could be," Frank answered. "We play this right, we can settle up all at once."

Billy said, "I didn't come for no fight. I just come to fetch Ike back to the ranch."

Ike barked at him: "God damn it, Billy. What the hell's with you? Don't you know what they done to me this morning? They buffaloed me. Just like they done to Frank here. Jesus Christ, Wyatt lets you off the hook once and you think he's your best friend in the world."

"I don't neither. I just figure you been on a bender and need to ease up."

"The only reason Earp didn't arrest you that time was because he didn't have the guts. You hear me, Billy? He caught you with the damn horse. Why the hell else wouldn't he take you in? No guts, is all."

"I don't think so," muttered Billy, looking like he wasn't sure he wanted the others to hear.

Frank said, "None of that matters. You got your gun on, Billy, and it's time to use it. You other fellers're throwin' in, ain't ye?"

Tom said that he was and so did Stilwell.

"There you are," said Frank. "This here's a long time comin'."

"Damn right it is," Ike chipped in.

"What's it gonna be, Billy? You gonna stand with your brother and your friends?"

Billy dropped his gaze to the ground, then looked up, red in the face and angry. He looked at Stilwell checking his revolver chambers.

"All right," Billy said. "I'm in."

Ike was about to clap his brother on the back, but a sharp look from Frank told him no more time was to be wasted. McLowery stepped farther into the lot, away from the street, and waited for the others to gather around. He jerked a thumb at the frame building behind him. "This here is Holliday's rooming house. We can start here, leave a couple boys waitin' for him."

"What about the Earps?" Ike asked.

Frank pulled a .36 Navy Colt from his jacket pocket. "First we gotta get you heeled, Ike. Take this. That'll keep you in the game."

Past Frank, on the near side of Fremont, Ike could see Dr. Goodfellow walking by just as he was taking Frank's extra revolver. Ike didn't give the doctor much thought as he rotated the Colt's cylinder to check that it held five loads.

37

Dr. Goodfellow found the Earps on the boardwalk outside Hafford's at Allen and Fourth.

"I saw them in the lot in the back of the O.K. Corral," Goodfellow told them as he gave his derby a nervous tug over his white-haired head. He glanced over his shoulder. "Tom McLowery and Bill Clanton are with them, along with Stilwell."

The figure Wyatt hadn't been able to identify at the corral now registered with him. Stilwell throwing in with the Clantons and McLowerys only meant more trouble. The stage-robbing deputy had already killed one man that Wyatt knew of.

"They're armed and they're talking a fight," Goodfellow continued. "I thought you boys should know."

"Thanks, doctor," said Virgil. "Better make yourself scarce."

Goodfellow nodded and, not waiting for another warning, headed down Allen. Wyatt turned to Virgil, about to say something, but was distracted by the racking coughs coming from the doorway to Hafford's. Doc Holliday, wearing a gray greatcoat on this cool day, stepped out of the saloon and stopped to lean on the cane in his left hand, his handkerchief clamped to his mouth, his body bent to one side as the coughs deepened. None of the Earps went to his side; they knew better than to try to help. Instead, they watched in silence and didn't continue their conversation until the coughs became less frequent and Doc had himself under control.

Wyatt took a step closer to his older brother. "What do you say, Virge? There are five of them in the lot. Do we go down there, or wait for them?"

Virgil gazed down Fourth toward Fremont, as if there were some way for him to see around the corner and take stock of the cowboys. He shifted the weight of the Stevens shotgun in the crook of his arm.

"Ambushing is their style," said Wyatt. "We wait, and we may be dead."

Virgil let out a long breath. For a stretch of time there was no sound other than the wind whistling down the block, rising then ebbing to a mild breeze. "Let's go," Virgil said.

They started down the boardwalk toward Fremont, Wyatt positioning himself in the middle so that he could talk easily to either brother. They had been walking for only a few moments when Wyatt's ears pricked at a new sound to their rear, a steady scraping sound. He looked over his shoulder to see Doc a few feet behind, his face ghastly white, his eyes feverish. He had to rely on the cane to keep up. The three Earps stepped off the boardwalk and began to veer toward the Capital Saloon on the left corner where Fremont intersected Fourth. Doc continued to keep pace with them.

"This is Earp business," Wyatt said over his shoulder. "You best steer clear." Looking back, he saw Doc staring at him, his cheeks turning pink with emotion. It might have been anger.

Doc said, "I go where I damn please."

The tone of Doc's voice made it clear to Wyatt: the man was offended. Not angry or disappointed, but indignant that Wyatt would leave him out of whatever would happen. Wyatt wasn't about to lose time in discussing it. He slowed his gait. Virgil and Morgan slowed with him, then watched Doc come alongside Morg.

The Earp party rounded the corner and walked four abreast down the middle of Fremont.

"You best take the shotgun," Virgil told Doc, handing the weapon to Wyatt who then passed it along to Holliday. "I got a better chance of getting them to put up their guns if I talk to them without it."

They moved on, mindful of the back lot of the corral. For the moment, they could see no one, not at the entrance anyway. Keeping his gaze directed straight ahead, Wyatt spoke quietly to Morgan. "If it comes to it, I'll take Frank McLowery. He's supposed to be the best shot. You take Billy."

With his eyes closed, John Behan could savor the cool sensation of the shaving-soap foam freshly applied to his face. He settled himself in the reclining barber's chair, listening to the rhythmic rasp of Tyrone sharpening the blade along the strop. He toyed with the notion of dozing for the next little while. Behan considered Tyrone to be a master with the razor, able to glide it across a stubbled chin without a hitch or nick. Behan thought it just might be possible to sleep through one of the barber's shaves.

Something, though, made Behan open his eyes. It might have been a slight delay in one of Tyrone's honing strokes, a second's hesitation that disrupted the rhythm. When Behan opened his eyes and gazed through the shop window onto Fremont, he had a vague idea that it might have been some instinct that had told him to check the street. If it was an instinct, it was rewarded by the sight of the four men, three in black suits, one in a gray greatcoat, moving deliberately from the intersection at Fourth Street. Wind-swept and etched severely in the bright sunlight, the four men triggered a flutter of alarm in the pit of Behan's stomach.

"Good God, what're the Earps up to?" he asked.

"Whatever it is," said Tyrone, "it's in this direction. And they got Holliday with them."

Behan took hold of the barber's bib around his neck, about to rip it off, but he told himself to hold up. Take it steady, he thought.

"Tyrone, go to the window. Take a look outside."

Without a word, the barber did as he was told.

Behan said, "Look over to the lot, next to Fly's house. The one behind the O.K. Corral. Are the boys still there?"

"Sure are, John. All five of 'em."

"Damn it to hell," said Behan. He got out of the chair, struggled with the bib, got it off, wiped his face quickly and hurried out the door. With foam still spotting his face, he jogged over to the approaching Earps.

"Damn it, Wyatt. What the hell is this?"

The Earp party continued walking. A breeze shifted one side of Doc's greatcoat to expose the Wells Fargo shotgun underneath.

Wyatt said, "Ike and his friends want a fight. We'll disarm them if we can."

"Don't go down there. Let me try talking to them. I'll get them to hand over their guns. Let me talk to them."

Virgil came to a stop, and the others followed suit. "Go ahead," he told Behan. "See what you can do. We won't fight if we don't have to."

"Better make it fast," Wyatt added as Behan moved quickly away.

Behan turned into the lot to find the five cowboys wheeling toward him, ready to go at it.

"Hold it, boys," the sheriff said, "the Earps're comin'."

Crouched with his hand poised above his gun, Frank

now straightened and considered Behan. He scratched the whiskers at the edge of his goatee as he narrowed his eyes. "Bringin' it here, are they?"

"Give up your guns and there won't be trouble," said Behan.

"We ain't givin' up nothing," said Tom.

Behan looked desperately from one face to the other. He saw Ike's mouth twitch nervously as he took a half-step behind Tom McLowery. Other than that, Behan saw no weakening. "Listen to me," he said. "They got Holliday with 'em. They're ready for you."

Frank said, "You best get movin', John."

Behan turned to the street to see the Earp party coming into view. They weren't waiting anymore. He wavered for a moment, a moment that stretched and then stretched some more. Finally, Behan glanced back at the cowboys and then ran to the side door of Fly's house and hurried inside.

Nearing the lot, Wyatt scanned the line of cowboys quickly, searching for the first sign of a hand reaching for a gun. For the moment, there was no such movement. But there was motion of another kind. The five cowboys started to fan out, making themselves as much of a spread target as possible in the fifteen-foot width of the lot. Stilwell was posting himself to the far left. Next to him was Ike, then Tom McLowery, shifting slightly back of the others, still holding the reins to his horse. To his side was his brother Frank, his arms hanging loosely at his sides, his body taut and coiled. Billy Clanton sidestepped to the wall of the Harwood house on the right. He planted a foot at the base of the building, bracing himself against its side.

Wyatt glanced at Virgil. Did his brother still think they could disarm these men? To do so they would have to draw close, but Wyatt was already finding himself coming to a stop at the mouth of the lot, and Virgil was doing the same. To Wyatt's other side, Morgan and Doc also halted, all of them now nearly twenty feet away from the cowboys. It seemed the most natural thing to do, as though the patch of earth before them was something forbidden.

If there was something to be said, Wyatt was going to let Virgil say it. For now, though, Virgil was silent. Wyatt noticed the stock of the rifle sticking up above the back of Tom's horse, booted on the far side. Tom was reining the animal around to stand in front of him, to act as a shield and to bring the rifle within reach. He would be the last to bring his weapon into play, Wyatt judged. The other four all had revolvers close to hand. While keeping the entire line of cowboys in his sights, Wyatt focused most of his attention on Frank.

All of this passed through Wyatt's mind in two or three seconds, his mind racing while the time crawled. Then Virgil spoke.

"Put up your guns, boys," Virgil said.

He didn't have the chance to say anything more.

Almost as one, Frank and Billy went for their revolvers. His senses ablaze, Wyatt flashed his right hand to his hip and jacked the hammer back as he pulled the Colt from its scabbard. On the fringes of his mind, he was aware that both Billy and Frank were firing at him. Billy's shot stabbed a hole in the skirt of Wyatt's jacket — he could feel the bullet whizzing past his thigh — and Frank's shot was high, just above his hat. A split-second later, Wyatt dropped the hammer.

The Colt bucked and the .45 slug crashed through Frank's midsection. McLowery wrenched, doubled up, but somehow stayed on his feet. Almost keeling to his side, he then corrected himself and staggered blindly forward.

By then, gunfire exploded all around Wyatt in one continuous roar, punctuated by the whinnies and shrieks of Tom's terrified horse. Wyatt swiveled to his right to check Billy. The young Clanton brought his gun up to shoulder level, sighting along the barrel, cool as could be. His sights were trained on Wyatt. Before Wyatt could snap off a shot, he heard the crack of gunfire to his left, coming from Morgan.

Morg's first shot had buzzed wide of Frank McLowery as the cowboy caved in with the impact of the bullet from Wyatt's Colt, but Morg then swung his gun sharply to the right, toward Billy, and lined up fast. Morg triggered twice in rapid succession. With the first round, Billy's gun hand whipped back, blood spurting from the forearm. The second shot punched a hole in Billy's chest and drove him backward. The young Clanton slammed into the side of the Harwood house. A look of consternation frozen on his face, he slid down along the wall, his arms and legs splayed until he sat, stunned, on the ground.

In the pounding chorus of gunfire, Morgan's ears now singled out the squeals of Tom's horse. Reflexively, he turned toward McLowery.

The first thunderclap of fire shook Ike to his bones. He was conscious of nothing but riotous noise and swirling shapes, all of which encircled him with tornado force. He didn't see Frank McLowery get hit, but he was certain that they would all die.

His initial wave of panic then suddenly withdrew, allowing him to see and hear with some clarity, while also leaving his nerves exposed to every sensation. In that instant, he had enough presence of mind to turn and look at his brother Billy, just in time to see him pounded to the wall by .45s. Without absorbing what he had just seen, Ike then swung to his other side. Tom McLowery fought with his horse, pulling on the reins to keep him in front while at the same time lunging for the rifle in the saddle boot.

The horse bucked so hard that it nearly yanked Tom off his feet. Spewing curses, Tom tugged the bridle down and took hold of the rifle stock and pulled the weapon clear. Still holding onto the reins, he aimed his rifle and fired across the horse's back. The close gunfire brought the animal to a sudden standstill, fear stopping it in its tracks.

As shots boomed back and forth, Ike could think of only one thing. He ran toward Wyatt. Grabbing Wyatt's left arm, Ike shouted to be heard over the volleys of fire.

"Don't shoot! Don't shoot me, Wyatt! Don't shoot!"

A shrug of Wyatt's arm tossed Ike away. For a moment, the tall man in black looked straight at Ike with an icy rage that made Clanton think his pleading was wasted: Earp would kill him anyway. Wyatt then barked, "Get to it or get away!"

Ike hesitated, just long enough to realize he wasn't going to be shot. He then ran as fast as he could, his pistol still in his waistband where it had been since the fighting had started.

Stilwell was firing a wild shot at the Earps when Ike bolted past him. The stage-robbing deputy snapped off one more shot, then, getting an idea from Ike's getaway, turned and ran behind Clanton down the alley toward the corral.

Doc never liked Frank McLowery and was disappointed when Wyatt's first shot plugged the cowboy before he could let him have a barrel of the shotgun. Unwilling to give up just yet, Doc kept the ten gauge trained on McLowery as he staggered between Virgil and Wyatt and stumbled on into the street. When Frank went down, Doc swung the shotgun back toward the lot.

He saw Ike run off, followed by Stilwell. Not about to let Ike get away scot-free, he triggered one of the barrels. Most of the twenty-one pieces of buckshot scattered without hitting a thing, but a few caught the side of Ike's leg. They didn't make much of an impression. Clanton yelled, faltered only a couple of steps, then ran on down the alley. Doc considered trying another barrel, but he decided the range was too long.

For the first time since the firing started, Doc now realized that the cane was no longer in his left hand. Without thinking, he had discarded it when Frank and Billy had gone for their guns. In the thick of it, Doc's feebleness was forgotten.

Just then, Tom's horse finally bolted, snapping the reins out of the cowboy's hands as it charged toward Fremont. Out in the open, Tom aimed the rifle and turned it on Morg who swung his revolver around at the same time. Before either of them could shoot, though, Doc had the shotgun lined up and fired the second barrel. No buckshot was wasted this time. Tom screamed as he was laced across his chest and stomach and legs. His rifle flying from his hands, he reeled to the side, colliding with the side of Fly's house, staying upright and moving out of control, one shambling step at a time, along the side of the building toward the street.

Seeing that McLowery refused to drop, Virgil kept him covered with his revolver, on the chance that Tom might still be able to pull a hideaway gun.

Virgil was being careful about the wrong cowboy.

If he had been looking to his right, he would have seen Billy Clanton, sprawled in a sitting position against the Harwood house, trying to shift his gun from his incapacitated right hand to his left. The pain of the effort forced streams of tears from his eyes, but his left hand managed to grip the revolver, and the index finger slipped inside the trigger guard to complete the process.

Sobbing, he brought the gun up, steadied himself as best he could and let loose a shot. The bullet lanced through Virgil's right thigh. Earp buckled, lost his balance and fell.

Billy cocked the gun to aim once more.

Frank McLowery collapsed face-down in the street. Mustering everything he had left, he placed his hands beneath his chest and slowly powered himself up to his knees to find himself behind the Earp party, with Doc Holliday standing straight ahead.

He commanded his gun hand to lift itself and take aim, but the arm gave up after he'd gained only a few inches. Taking hold of his right wrist with his left hand, he moved the pistol up to chest level with agonizing slowness and tried to aim at Holliday with his wobbling gun, only to see Doc turn toward him before he could fire.

Doc tossed the spent shotgun aside. While Frank aimed, Doc drew his nickel-plated gun from its shoulder rig and turned so that he presented McLowery his narrow side as a target. He squared off in a dueler's stance.

Morgan turned just in time to see Frank fire. The shot grazed Doc along the leg, scratching a thin red line across the side of Holliday's gray pants. Doc never flinched. He took an extra second to aim, fired a single shot and blew a hole in Frank's handsome face.

After seeing Frank sag to the ground, Morgan turned back to the lot. That was when the shot rang out from the side of the Harwood house. Billy was still firing with his left hand. The slug tore through Morgan's shoulder, punched its way out the other side and knocked Morg down.

Wyatt had also been worried about Frank, but Billy's shot now made him wheel about. Billy, his face in a tight grimace, was cocking the hammer and aiming again at Morg. Wyatt swung his Colt around. In that instant, Morgan, swiveling on the ground toward Billy, also leveled his gun. The brothers fired almost as one.

Morgan's shot plowed through Billy's left shoulder. In the next split second, Wyatt's bullet smashed through the left side of Billy's rib cage, shattering bone from sternum to spine. In criss-crossing red streaks, blood splattered from both wounds across the young cowboy's torso. Flattened against the side of the house, as if he were pinned there, Billy finally let his gun hand drop.

Wyatt swept his gaze from one side of the lot to the other, his Colt still leveled. The gunsmoke hung suspended in the air, mixed with dust, stinging Wyatt's eyes, its acrid smell filling his nostrils. He drew his second gun from his left hip and switched it with his other Colt to give himself a full chamber in his right hand. He waited for the next move. The sudden hush in the lot made his ears ring.

To either side of him, Morgan and Virgil pushed themselves to their feet. Over to the far left, Tom McLowery dropped to his knees, clutching his buckshot-ravaged stomach, then struggled back up to tramp into the street where he collapsed and died just ten feet away from his brother.

Turning back toward the Harwood house, Wyatt then looked at Billy, watching transfixed as the young Clanton turned his head, breath somehow still coming from him in faint rasps. When he found the strength to talk, Billy's voice was cracked, little more than a murmur, but loud enough to be lifted by the breeze across the silent lot.

"Give me more cartridges," he pleaded. "Give me more cartridges."

38

Ike saw his plan for revenge slip through his fingers in just a few minutes of speechifying as Judge Spicer delivered his opinion to the court.

It had been a damn good idea too, Ike was certain of that. If the Earps wanted to use the law, then the law could be used against them just as easily, he had figured. "I'm a witness, ain't I?" he'd told Curly Bill at the ranch house. "And so is Stilwell here. And Johnny Behan, too. If we all say it right, we can really nail those bastards."

There it was — Ike's big chance to avenge Billy and at the same time put himself back in the picture with Curly Bill and the rest. He had to congratulate himself on coming up with such a simple idea that would pay off in spades. Maybe it wasn't the way Old Man would have handled it, but it sure made sense. There had to be an inquest after the gunfight and Ike would be there with his friends and with a story that would give those Earps a good licking. All they had to do was say that they had been on their way out of town when the Earps and Holliday showed up at the O.K.

Corral lot. They had put up their hands, had said they wanted to give up, and damn it all, the Earps had just started shooting. "At point-blank range it was," as Ike said on the witness stand. That was something that just came to him on the spot, a bit of inspiration.

But then that just goes to show how pointless it all is when everyone's set against you, Ike decided.

Sitting there in the back row of the courtroom with Stilwell, Spence and Behan — Curly Bill still didn't like the idea of coming back to Tombstone — Ike had to bite his tongue and listen to that fancy-talking Judge Spicer talk about the Earps doing their duty.

"Marshal Virgil Earp was carrying out his duty as a peace officer," said Spicer. "When Wyatt and Morgan Earp and John Holliday were deputized by the marshal, they shared this duty. They acted properly in confronting men who had repeatedly threatened their lives." As for Billy and the McLowerys getting shot with their hands in the air, Spicer wouldn't budge. He just fiddled with his moustache and droned on about the coroner's report, something about the angle of the bullet wounds. Spicer had said the wounds would have been different if the deceased had had their hands up. A sorry thing, Ike told himself, when the word of a Clanton doesn't carry any weight anymore in Cochise County.

As soon as the decision was delivered, Ike got to his feet and walked out of the courtroom with Stilwell, Spence and Behan. He didn't want to see the Earps looking high and mighty and gloating over his failure. Virgil with his limp and Morgan with his arm in a sling, the two of them parading their wounds around, looking for sympathy — it made Ike sick.

"Sorry it didn't work out better, boys," Behan said outside the courthouse. "I don't know what else I can do. We tried anyway."

Stilwell said, "This thing ain't over yet. Not hardly."

He turned on his heels and started walking away. Ike and Spence left Behan behind to catch up to him.

"What're you talkin' about, Floyd?" Ike asked, quickening his step to keep pace with Stilwell. "You can't change that damn Spicer. You just can't talk to that man."

"We still ain't through."

"Floyd's got some other ideas," Pete Spence said, his weasel face looking sly as he read his partner's grim expression.

Stilwell came to a stop in front of the *Daily Nugget* office and turned to Ike. "Pete's right," he said. "And I'll tell you something else, Ike. You got us into it this far, you're gonna see it through." Stilwell started walking again. "Let's talk to Curly Bill." He led the way to their horses stabled at Dunbar's Corral.

The walk to the *Epitaph* office would do him some good, Virgil figured. The leg was starting to mend and a walk could help to strengthen it some more. At the same time, he could tend to some business with Mayor Clum.

Clum had been on the Benson stage that had been attacked four days ago, and the mayor believed that attack might have been an assassination attempt. The cowboys might have wanted to gun him down for his support of the Earps, Clum said. Virgil thought that in the quiet of the *Epitaph* newspaper office at night, he could talk with Clum and see how much he really knew, how much he had seen of the attackers. All told, there might have been five or six of them. Anything Clum might have noticed about any one of them could lead to an identification.

Virgil left the Oriental just before midnight. The warm autumn night was unusually quiet. Miners had passed through the Allen Street saloons and dance halls in the afternoon and had stayed on through the evening, but the next shift had not come aboard yet. Perhaps they would let this night pass them by, as hard as that might be to believe.

Even miners desperate for a good time have to lie low once in a while, Virgil thought.

He still walked with a slight limp, but the leg didn't trouble him nearly as much as it had. Crossing the intersection of Allen and Fifth, he felt no strain as he kept up a brisk pace and decided that he would be back to normal within the week. To test the leg, he put his weight on it as he stepped up to the boardwalk in front of the Golden Eagle Brewery. Before he could take the next step, gunfire erupted from the half-constructed building across the street.

The Golden Eagle Brewery window crashed behind Virgil, broken by a load of buckshot. Another load shattered Virgil's left arm, searing him with a sudden cutting pain and splintering the bone just above the elbow. He toppled forward, managed to right himself before he fell and lunged for the upright in front of him. If I can brace myself, he thought desperately, maybe I can reach my revolver and fire back. At least get one of them.

The wall of buckshot roared again. Virgil grunted in uncomprehending shock as his left side was ripped open. He lurched back toward the Golden Eagle, completely insensible to his jarring fall to the boardwalk. The next thing he was aware of was the sound of running booted footfalls, somewhere to his side, and then the drumming of hoofs, growing fainter and then vanishing into the night.

Other footsteps approached, moving quickly, but by now Virgil couldn't hear them. He was only able to focus dimly on his surroundings again when Wyatt and Morgan grabbed him by the armpits and hauled him up to his feet.

Dr. Goodfellow visited the house once a day for a week. The first day after the shooting he said he wasn't sure that Virgil would last through the night, and when Virgil made him a liar, the doctor stopped making predictions. He simply tended to the wounded marshal, gave Allie instructions for his care and then just shrugged at Wyatt and Morgan on his way out.

The policy of no predictions, though, ran out after the first week. Goodfellow finished his examination, put away his instruments and then faced Allie, a hint of a smile on his face. Getting up from his bedside chair, he patted his patient's arm said, "See you tomorrow, Virgil," and crossed the room to Allie's side. Virgil watched through half-closed lids, content for now to remain perfectly still.

"He has most definitely improved over the last few days," the doctor said. "He still has a ways to go, but I take back that talk about dying."

Allie's worn, drawn face didn't return the doctor's smile. She was able to manage only a thankful nod. Not one to waste time with talk when doing something was possible, she walked past the doctor and took the seat by Virgil's bed and applied a wet cloth to her husband's forehead.

Goodfellow glanced at Wyatt and Morgan and motioned with his eyes to the next room. When they were out of the bedroom, Wyatt closed the door behind them and asked, "What else, doctor?"

Goodfellow ran his fingers through his thin white hair, as if trying to overcome some reluctance before speaking. "I didn't want to tell Allie just yet, but I have serious doubts."

"You had doubts before."

"True enough, but his improvement so far has been due only to the fact that he's strong as an ox, not because the injuries are minor. There's only so much his constitution can account for, as remarkable as it is. After taking about twenty buckshot from his side and four inches of bone fragment from his arm, I can't say I'm very hopeful. There's a good chance his left side will be paralyzed, and as for his arm . . . ." The doctor shrugged, then looked from brother to brother, his eyes tired and guardedly sympathetic.

Wyatt nodded. Although not surprised, he had still counted on his older brother's recovering completely, or nearly so, through sheer sturdiness and willfulness. As much as he now wanted to argue that the doctor was being pessimistic, Wyatt could see no point in even trying. Morgan left his side and stopped at the front window to gaze out at the street.

"I wouldn't worry about telling Allie," Wyatt said to Goodfellow. "She's probably stronger than all of us put together." He tried an encouraging smile but quickly grew impatient with it.

The doctor secured the clasp on his black bag. "Maybe tomorrow I'll tell her," he said wearily. He didn't bother saying goodbye on his way out the door.

Wyatt sat at the big table in the front room, an area that was a combination kitchen, parlor and, now that Wyatt and Morg were staying here, guest room. Still looking out the window, Morgan was the first one to speak.

"We should've taken care of them all while Virgil was still marshal," he said, his voice hoarse with pent-up emotion. "We could've killed them legally then." When Morg turned toward him, Wyatt could see his kid brother's eyes were red-rimmed. "Don't look at me like that, Wyatt," Morg snapped at him. "You heard what the doctor said. Virge is going to be a cripple for life. Those bastards need killing. Now more than ever."

Wyatt had no answer to that. He looked away from his brother and tried not to think of how their father was going to react to the news.

A knock on the open door turned Wyatt around. Standing on the threshold was a broad-shouldered man in a brown frock coat. His features were sharp, accented by a trim moustache and goatee. The visitor considered Wyatt for a moment before speaking.

"Would you be Wyatt?"

"Yes, I would. What can I do for you?" Irritation quickly set in. Reporters from newspapers in Tucson and Prescott had already come around the last couple of days to collect all the grisly details of the attempted assassination. Wyatt thought this man might be another newspaper vulture.

The man in the brown frock coat came forward to shake hands. "Wyatt, my name's Crawley Dake. You might have heard I'm the federal marshal for the Arizona Territory and I was the one appointed your brother Virgil deputy U.S. marshal for Cochise County a while back."

"I remember Virgil mentioning you," Wyatt said. He then introduced Dake to Morgan and asked the federal marshal to have a seat.

"Wyatt, the territorial authorities in Prescott have been looking into the troubles in and around Tombstone," Dake said. "There's always been concern about things here in Cochise County, but now matters have become much more alarming."

Wyatt waited for him to continue. The silence made Dake self-conscious; he apparently realized the foolishness of explaining Tombstone troubles to the Earps. "I don't have to tell you any of this," the federal marshal said to try to correct himself, "certainly not now. But what I do want to tell you is that Prescott's biggest concern is Sheriff John Behan and his cooperation with the rustler element in these parts. I've been in Tombstone the last few days to snoop around for myself, and I've found that still no arrest has been made in the shooting of your brother. If I needed any more persuading, that would do it."

"Persuading yourself about what?" Wyatt asked.

"I understand Virgil was relieved of his city marshal responsibilities since the attempt on his life."

"They put a new man in," responded Wyatt.

"The council thought us Earps'd just make more trouble if we stayed on as peace officers," Morgan said bitterly.

Dake glanced at Morg then turned back to Wyatt. "Well, Wyatt, I think I may be able to do something to put Sheriff Behan and his friends on notice. Since Virgil is incapacitated for the time being, I would like to appoint you to take his place as U.S. deputy marshal for this county.''

Wyatt leaned back in his chair and exchanged a look with his brother. ''I would like that, Mr. Dake,'' he said. ''But I have to know if I would have full authority to handle things the way I see fit.''

''You'll probably have problems with John Behan, Wyatt, but the territory would be behind you.''

''You better be right,'' said Morgan.

Dake studied Morg, but didn't seem to take offense at his challenge. ''My one concern, Wyatt,'' he said, ''is your getting the men to back you up here in Cochise County. Will you be able to round up enough men for a posse that you can trust to do the job?''

''Well, there's Morgan here,'' said Wyatt. ''And Doc Holliday will stand by me.'' Wyatt paused, pursing his lips as he mulled it over. He didn't have to think very long.

''For the rest,'' he said, ''it may take a few days, but I can round up a couple more.''

39

Gray hairs were more plentiful in his hair and beard, but otherwise Turkey Creek Johnson looked much the same. Even his broadcloth suit looked like it was the same one Wyatt had seen him wear back in Newton.

Turkey Creek rode down Allen Street flanked by three other hardcases. One of them was Johnny Green, his face showing more creases, his eyes just as rock-hard. Wyatt didn't recognize the two other men. One was a short, burly man wearing a duster, the other a lean, dark-skinned plainsman who looked like he might be part Indian.

Wyatt was standing on the boardwalk outside the Oriental when Turkey Creek and the others dismounted.

"Well, God damn it, Wyatt," said Turkey Creek, clapping him on the back. "How the hell are you?"

"I've been better."

Turkey Creek nodded. "I guess you have." He gave Wyatt's shoulder a slight squeeze. "I'm sorry as hell about your brother Virgil."

"Hello, Johnny," said Wyatt to change the subject.

Johnny Green gave him a curt wave of the hand and nothing more as he appeared to look right through Wyatt to the saloon facade behind him. Wyatt turned back to Turkey Creek.

"Your wire said you were living the sporting life up in Gunnison."

"Sporting life," Turkey Creek laughed. "Hell, that just meant I wasn't workin'. But I'm ready to go at it now."

Wyatt's first wire to Deadwood had gotten no answer, and the next one to San Antonio hadn't produced anything either. The rumors Wyatt had heard about Turkey Creek passing through those places may have been true, but apparently the man had passed through some time ago. Wyatt then had sent a telegram to Shotgun Collins in Leadville who had answered that Turkey Creek was definitely in Colorado. Two more wires had brought Wyatt's message to Gunnison where he had finally found his old friend.

Wyatt turned his smile away from Turkey Creek to look pointedly at the two men he didn't know.

"Those fellas," Turkey Creek said, "they're good friends of mine. Your wire said you wanted good men and they're the best I know outside prison. That fella over there in the duster, that's Sherman McMasters, and next to him is Texas Jack Vermillion. If you need a posse, Wyatt, they'll ride like hell for you. And you can count me in for that also."

"If you're speaking up for them, that's good enough for me. But I don't think there'll be any riding right now. I'd guess you'll be wanting to shake the dust off before doing anything else. Am I right?"

"Well, to tell you the truth, Wyatt, we wouldn't mind that, but then again, the way your wire sounded, I think the best thing would be to sit ourselves down and figure how we can help. Johnny there can take his beauty bath later on."

Inside the back room at the Oriental, Wyatt and Morgan

talked with Turkey Creek and his outfit about the best way to move ahead, helped as they went along by a bottle of whiskey. Wyatt considered bringing Doc into the talk also, but then thought better of it. Even if Holliday agreed to sit down with these strangers — and there was no telling if he would — he wouldn't be interested enough to make himself useful. He would be ready to ride or fight when the time came. That was all Wyatt was counting on and all he really wanted from the man.

Between the two of them, Wyatt and Morgan had not been able to find any witnesses who could identify the men who had ambushed Virgil. A miner had seen four riders leaving Tombstone after the attack, but he hadn't been able to get a clear look at their faces. With the help of Turkey Creek and his friends, the Earps would begin to cover the rest of the county.

"It was either Curly Bill's bunch or it was gunmen that Curly Bill hired," Wyatt told his U.S. deputy marshal posse. "That much we're ready to put money on. That means the men we want probably passed through Charleston or the Clanton ranch. Tomorrow we can start to hunt up somebody around those two places who might know something."

Wyatt figured on trying Charleston first. The plan was to split the posse, one half to ride into the town of Charleston itself, the other half to scour the outlying area.

Sitting next to Turkey Creek, sharing a bottle with his old friend, Wyatt couldn't help but think of the years that had passed since he and Johnson had prowled the streets of Newton. He pictured himself in those days — green and ignorant. More than that, though, he kept picturing Morg and Virge in those days, days when both of them were in one piece.

Wyatt and his posse loosened up some that night, in preparation for the hard riding they would be facing the next morning. For his part, Wyatt was ready to saddle up tonight and not even bother with any sleep before setting out. He knew Morg felt the same way, but Turkey Creek and the others were fresh from the trail and just getting them to start up again tomorrow was as much as a man had a right to expect.

Wyatt showed Turkey Creek some of the sights along Allen Street, careful to keep an eye on all the windows and alleys on either side as they walked down the road. This wasn't lost on Turkey Creek. "It'll make it easier," he said, "if you just watch on the left and me take the right."

After the Occidental and the Alhambra, they doubled back to rejoin the others at Hatch's billiards hall. Morgan was playing a round with Johnny Green, while to the side of the narrow room, McMasters and Texas Jack were giving the players advice even though none was needed.

Turkey Creek said, "You play a wicked game, Morgan. You're up against Johnny Green and you still have your shirt."

"He can have my shirt," said Morg, "I'll take everything else." He lined up the cue for his next shot. His wounded shoulder no longer hampering him, he could extend well across the table to strike the ball.

Wyatt and Turkey Creek leaned against the wall to watch the game. After a few minutes, Wyatt had no trouble seeing that his old friend didn't have his mind on watching Morgan's billiards shooting.

"I almost passed through Dodge a couple of years ago," Turkey Creek said after a while. "I was haulin' freight through Kansas, figured maybe you could stand to see me." Although his thought wasn't finished, he stopped there for some reason. Wyatt gave him some time to go on, then decided his friend might need some encouraging.

"I might've been able to stand it," he said. "Any reason you didn't reach town?"

"Well, it really wasn't along my route, mind you. I figured I just might make a swing your way is all. I'd been hearing enough about you, thought maybe I'd see for myself." Through all this Turkey Creek looked straight ahead, never glancing at Wyatt.

"But hell," he continued, "I ain't one to hunt up folks just to pass the time. All the same, I regretted it — not looking you up that time. I guess, going back the way we do, I think of you as a kid brother or the like. I figured I had a stake in seeing what kind of a big noise you turned out to be." Darting a glance at Wyatt from beneath his full, graying eyebrows, Turkey Creek became quiet again. Wyatt knew that nothing more needed to be said. He let the silence return. Through the sheet of glass fitted into the back door, he thought he saw some movement, and then the quiet was interrupted by a burst of gunfire.

The back door window exploded. Shards of glass were driven halfway across the room by shotgun blasts from the rear alley. In the path of that fire stood Morgan, his back to the door as he lined up his next cue shot. With terrible, pulverizing impact, the buckshot, stormed through his lower back, crashing through his spinal column and shredding all vitals on the way out the front of the body. As glass shards flew past him, Wyatt watched his brother contort in a brief, cruel jig, then flop onto the corner of the billiards table and bounce off to the floor with a hollow thud.

Wyatt was vaguely aware that there were running footfalls outside in the dark, charging away from the rear of the billiards hall, the footfalls of the men who had just gunned down his kid brother. He made no attempt to go after those men. For a span of time that he had no way of measuring he felt like he was keeling to one side, an impression that was so strong that he was surprised to find himself still on his feet when he finally got a hold of himself again.

He heard the others running past him on their way out the back door as he knelt beside Morg. His brother had landed on his back, his eyes staring straight up, unblinking and glazed. Wyatt knew that behind those eyes was over-whelming, paralyzing pain. Morg's body twitched and he let out a thin, tortured moan.

Wyatt took his brother's hand while, beside him, Turkey Creek lowered himself quietly to one knee. On the edge of Wyatt's mind it occurred to him that Turkey Creek was one of the men who had run out the back door. His return could only mean one thing: the ambushers had gotten away. But the ambushers were meaningless. Everything fell away beside the sight of his brother's ruined body and horrible gaze.

His grip feeble, Morgan let out a rasp, an attempt to say something. As Morg continued to try to squeeze his hand, Wyatt leaned forward to bring his face next to his brother's.

"What is it, Morg?" His own voice sounded peculiar to him.

Morgan's lips moved, tried to form the words, then slowly retracted at the corners to bare his teeth. Arching his head back, a bone-dry wheeze escaped through his mouth and everything about him suddenly stopped. Wyatt held tightly to his brother's hand and watched for several minutes before he allowed himself to realize that Morgan was dead. The agony is over, he told himself, over before I had to do anything about it. If Morg had held on much longer, Wyatt was certain he would have had to shoot his brother to stop the pain.

40

Wyatt got the names from a woman named Inez Rojas, and later that same day he got the warrants to go with those names.

With Turkey Creek to help him, he found Inez after talking to the people who lived and worked along the alley behind the north side of Allen, starting at the Fifth Street end and working his way building by building toward Third. When he asked her what she had seen the night before, she made it plain right from the start that she was the witness he needed.

She had been taking down laundry from the clothes line behind her house when she had heard the shots from Hatch's billiards hall and, a few moments later, had seen the five men running down the alley in her direction. "I know Spence," the thin little Mexican woman said, speaking slowly to give herself time to translate her thoughts into English. "His wife is Mexican woman and I know her. And I know he is bad man. I see him first. His wife, she comes here much and I go to her house too. I see the others at her house a few days ago.''

"You knew who all of them were?" Wyatt asked.

"I know the five. The men in the alley."

Wyatt scrutinized her carefully, his eyes narrowing quizzically. "You say that like there were others, maybe somewhere else."

"Please, Señor Earp. Let me say it my way or I get it confused. My English is slow."

Wyatt felt Turkey Creek's hand on his shoulder, taking a firm hold, which made him realize that he was starting to lean across the table, about to badger this woman. He couldn't get her to tell the story fast enough. Letting his friend guide him, he moved back slightly. "Please, Señora Rojas, tell me what you can," he said.

"I see Spence in the alley, running to me. Also I see the Indian one, they call him Indian Charley I think. I know him from Spence's house, too. And there was also Bill. He was there."

"Curly Bill?"

"Yes. Him. And the big, quiet one. I think he is Johnny."

"That would be Johnny Ringo."

Inez nodded in agreement, her face solemn, pensive, as she sorted through the foreign words. "The deputy, Stilwell, he was there, running with the others."

A small, serene smile came to her face to say she was done. All five men were named.

"Señora Rojas," Wyatt said, as patiently as possible, "you said before you knew the five men from visits to Spence's house. You also made it sound like there were other men. Is there any more you can tell me?"

"Yes, there was one more. I see him down the alley. The five men, they run down the alley and they go to this other man. He had horses for them."

"Did you see him? Who was he?"

"He was away from me. Too far away. It was too

dark.'' She shrugged forlornly. "I am sorry, Señor Earp. I know Spence is a bad man. I know how he treats his woman and I want to help you get these men, but that is all I see. I am sure of Spence, Señor Earp. Him and the others in the alley.''

Five names were more than enough to get Wyatt started, and he was grateful to Inez for that much, but the grim realization came to him that he would have to wait before hitting the trail. Family business had to be tended to first.

Although Virgil wouldn't agree to Wyatt's suggestion at first, Wyatt kept at him most of that night, and with Allie's help he was finally able to persuade him. "Please the Lord, Virgil," Allie said, "you think you can ride with a posse the way you are? Or maybe you think you can just stay here in town and get out of the way of shotguns on one good leg? You don't have to tell me you're getting around some now when you got help, and thank the Lord you can do that much, but you can't have Wyatt fretting about you when he's got business to take care of.''

When the members of the posse met outside Virgil's house the next morning, they brought two wagons around to the back door where they wouldn't be easily seen from the street. One wagon carried Virgil and Allie and those possessions that they cared to take with them to California. The other, driven by Turkey Creek, carried Morgan's coffin. The posse flanked the two vehicles, shotguns and rifles in hand: Wyatt and Doc to one side, Johnny Green, Sherman McMasters and Texas Jack to the other. They headed north out of town, moving slowly to check every possible hiding place along their route, ready to spring into a gallop if need be.

Driving up the Benson road, Wyatt sent Johnny Green ahead as an advance rider to scout the blind turns in the road and check potential sniper nests along high ground, all the places Wyatt had committed to memory on his Wells Fargo runs. They took the road as far as Contention, where they waited at the depot for the train to Tucson.

From Tucson, the train would start the journey westward to Nicholas Earp's home in San Bernadino. Virgil had finally, reluctantly agreed that their father's ranch was not only the right place to bury Morg, but the proper place for him and Allie to stay until the trouble cleared.

The train at Contention wasn't due for another two hours. Wyatt considered putting Virgil up in a hotel for that time, but preferred staying close to the tracks, out in the open, where no one could sneak up on them. They made Virgil as comfortable as possible on a bed of blankets in the back of the wagon, their guns out and ready at all times.

As he put a cushion behind his brother's head, Wyatt noticed a man down the street, a block away, looking toward the wagons. Wyatt kept an eye on him and watched as the man turned about and walked quickly into a nearby store. For no more than a few seconds at a time did Wyatt take his eyes off that store, waiting for the man to walk out. But he never saw him reappear. If the man was one of the five, he had been too far away for Wyatt to identify.

Once the train was in and all possessions and people were aboard, Wyatt settled into a seat by a window, the shotgun across his lap. He felt the urge to go to that store down the block and find out who it was that had been watching the wagons, but he shunted the impulse aside. He didn't want to leave his brother and his friends a man short unless he had a very good reason. The thought of the unidentifiable man then made him think about the sixth man and wonder who he might be. He had some favorites to fill the one hole in Inez's story — for all that was worth, which was nothing. He would have to wait, to get the whole story as he went along.

They arrived in Tucson that night. Knowing that the stopover would be an hour, Wyatt looked at his brother's drained face, made even more haggard than usual by the full day's traveling, and decided a walk through the streets would be worth the risk in order to get Virgil some rest at

Porter's Hotel. Hiring a buckboard to carry his brother, he told Allie to take the reins and drive slowly, slowly enough for the posse to keep pace on foot on either side of the wagon.

Wyatt saw no sign of trouble on the way to the hotel, and the path was clear when they returned to the train an hour later. He posted Doc and Turkey Creek on one side of the train and the rest of the posse on the other as he helped Virgil aboard. He then saw to the luggage and was putting his brother into a seat when he looked out the window to see Turkey Creek jogging over to the train. By the look of it, Johnson was returning from a scout, coming from the sidings farther into the depot yard. Turkey Creek looked back at him and motioned with his eyes to the freight cars standing on the siding to his rear. Wyatt's body tensed with anticipation.

"Allie," he said, "you look after things. Something I've got to tend to."

He felt Virgil's grip on his arm as he picked up his shotgun and turned to leave.

"Hold on, Wyatt," his brother said. "I'm not dead yet. You can tell me what's going on. And you can tell Allie, too, while you're at it."

Wyatt took a long breath. "Turkey Creek's seen something out there. I've got to move now."

"Not yet, Wyatt." Virgil maintained his grip, still strong after all that had happened to him. "There's just one thing I want to tell you."

"Not now, Virge."

"I said, wait."

Wyatt forced himself to hold still, straining inside to be on his way.

"Plenty of times," Virge said, "I've told you to hold back. There was a reason for that once, but I just want to tell you there's no reason for that now. Do whatever you have to do, Wyatt. I'd do the same."

Virgil's pallid face showed the reserve of determination

that had lived through all the buckshot that had crippled his body. Beside him, Allie looked closely at Wyatt, a quiet fierceness lighting her eyes. "Go on, Wyatt," she said. "You go on now."

Turkey Creek was waiting for him outside the train, his eyes sweeping the dim, dark shapes along the yard's sidings. Wyatt followed his friend's gaze.

"I saw something move back there when you went aboard," said Turkey Creek. "That's when I went for a closer look. Somebody's slippin' around there all right, but I couldn't see who it was without showing myself. Figured I'd tell you before doing anything."

The suspicious-looking man in Contention, thought Wyatt, had probably been a lookout. He could have wired ahead to someone waiting here to tell him the Earps were coming.

"You just cover my back," said Wyatt. He opened his ten gauge, checked the shells and then set off across the inky, moonlit yard.

At the first standing freight car, he stopped to listen, waiting for the sound of a boot step to lead him in the right direction. The engine for the train carrying Virgil was being primed and was now snorting bursts of smoke high into the night air, a noisy mechanical pulse that made it impossible for Wyatt to pick up any other sound. If he was to find his man he would have to do it by sight.

Stepping over a coupling, Wyatt flattened himself against the end of the car and, turning slowly, peered around the corner. One car down, the shadowy figure of a prowler crept toward a coupling, something looking very much like a rifle in his hands.

The pulsing engine now worked in Wyatt's favor, drowning out his footsteps as he crept toward his man. As he neared, he watched the prowler reach the gap between the two cars and line up his rifle, aiming for Virgil's car across the yard. Wyatt quickened his step and lunged across the last few feet. Slamming the barrels of his shotgun across the rifle, he knocked the man's weapon to the ground. He then grabbed the back of the man's jacket, spun him around and held the shotgun muzzles up to the prowler's face.

Floyd Stilwell stared at the twin muzzles, his mouth open, his face drained white.

Wyatt lowered the Stevens shotgun and pushed it into Stilwell's chest, shoving him back a foot. He moved up to stay close. "Tell me, Stilwell," he said, his voice cold and even. "Was it a ten gauge or a twelve gauge that you used to kill Morgan? Which was it?"

"It wasn't me, Wyatt. I didn't use either of them shotguns. I was just one of the lookouts. I swear to you, Wyatt." Reflexively Stilwell stepped back away from the shotgun. Wyatt stepped with him.

"I'm not someone you should be lying to, Stilwell," Wyatt said. "Not now." He pushed the deputy back again with the gun. Stilwell almost lost his balance. His eyes were wild with desperation.

"All right, I had one of the shotguns," Stilwell blurted out. "But it wasn't my idea. It was Curly Bill. He thought of it. He made me do it."

Wyatt closed in and pressed the shotgun against Stilwell's stomach, feeling the rise and fall of the killer's breathing against the weapon. He paused for a moment, scrutinized the fleshy face before him, then slowly cocked both barrels.

"Wyatt don't do it! Just bring me in! I'll help you get the others! I'll help you get Curly Bill! I swear, I'll help!"

"You will?"

"I'll take you to him. I'll be a witness. That's it — I'll be a witness."

"I don't think so," Wyatt said mildly. "I took you in once before, for robbing the stage and killing Bud Philpot. But that didn't stop you, did it? I can't let that happen again, Stilwell." Wyatt said no more, letting the words sink in.

As he stared at Wyatt, unbridled, sweat-streaked panic swept across Stilwell's face. An expression that wasn't half as bad as the look on Morgan's face when he died, Wyatt decided. Suddenly, the outlaw deputy grabbed the barrels of the shotgun and tried wrenching the weapon aside. Wyatt strengthened his hold, forced the muzzles by inches back against the cowboy's sternum and, staring into the man's eyes, he triggered both barrels. The force of the twin blasts threw Stilwell back some five feet and drove him to the ground, a hole the size of a melon in the middle of his body.

Breaking open the gun, Wyatt took out the spent shell casings and inserted fresh ammunition as Stilwell's shirt ignited from the close-range powder burns. He left the burning body behind, its flame spreading from head to toe, and started back toward Virgil's train. Two days since Morgan was killed, he thought, and one of the bastards gone.

41

Wyatt and his federal marshal's posse returned to Tombstone the next morning. Grouped in a loose double-file, they rode down Allen Street, each line responsible for keeping an eye on the near string of buildings and, more important, the windows along the second stories. At the Oriental, Wyatt and Doc dismounted, leaving the others saddled and ready while they went inside the saloon.

With Doc stationed at a side window, Wyatt finalized the sale of his and his brothers' share of the Oriental to Ab Richardson. Still too early for the Tombstone trade, the saloon was closed, leaving the bar unoccupied except for Ab and Wyatt.

"I surely wouldn't mind owning the place," said Ab, "but're you sure you want to sell out?"

"I've got a feeling I might not have a choice," said Wyatt. "I might not get back here, and even if I do, I don't think some people will let me do business."

Ab shrugged. "I guess you know best, Wyatt."

A commotion at the front of the saloon made Wyatt swing around. He grabbed the shotgun off the bar and brought it about, his thumb on the hammer. He then froze when he saw Josie Marcus trying to push her way past Doc at the door.

"Doc, leave off," said Wyatt.

Holliday glanced back at him, a thin smile on his face as he held the girl's arm a moment longer, then let go. "Thought maybe Johnny Behan was sending a woman to do his work for him," he said. Stepping back to his position by the window, he added, "Would've been a shame to have to shoot her." He coughed and continued his watch.

Josie settled her ruffled white dress as she walked over to Wyatt. "Behan's not sending over women," she said. "He plans on sending himself. That's what I came here to tell you, Wyatt."

Wyatt gazed out the window, looking for some sign of the sheriff. "He plans to arrest me?" he asked.

"I hear he's got a warrant for you, for the murder of his deputy. That man Stilwell."

"A very loyal employer," Doc drawled from the other side of the room.

Wyatt said, "Do you see him, yet, Doc?"

"Not yet, but I'm looking."

Wyatt crossed to the window opposite Doc's position. With some satisfaction, he saw that Josie followed him, no more than two feet away. "Better move back," he told her. "This window could give a rifleman a clear shot." He put out an arm to guide her away, then, after a look down the street, stepped back with her.

Although the hem of her dress was already dusted with bits of Allen Street, the rest of her outfit was still pure white, its brightness sharply setting off her dark hair and blue eyes. She was striking enough to make Wyatt take his mind off other things, but only for an instant, as his thoughts returned to backshooters and the trail northeast out of Tombstone.

"I appreciated you coming by to tell me," he said quietly.

"I've heard enough about Behan and his friends since coming here to know what's what," she said. Turning away, she looked idly out the window. "I also thought I might as well say goodbye." She glanced at him. "You won't be coming this way again, will you?"

"No, I won't."

"I think I know what you have in mind to do when you leave here, Wyatt," she said. Her lips pressed tightly together for a moment as she seemed to search Wyatt's face. "I just hope it takes away some of your grief by the time it's over."

Wyatt dropped his gaze to the floor, saying nothing.

"I also wouldn't mind hearing that you came out of it alive," she went on.

"I don't intend to die before it's through."

"I'm glad to hear it," she replied dryly.

Outside, Turkey Creek rode down Fifth Street, leading four fresh saddle horses to the Oriental.

"If Behan wants me," said Wyatt, "he better come now or he'll miss the show."

He started for the door, but then Josie put out a hand to rest on his arm. "I meant that about hearing what happens to you, Wyatt. Doby's taking us out of here next week to go to Tucson. Then after that we go to Denver. I just wanted to tell you."

Wyatt studied her, and she held his gaze. For a moment, he wished he could imagine settling in with a woman sometime when this was all over. It was a notion that seemed too far off, too painful, so he set it aside for now.

"I'll keep that in mind," he said as kindly as he could. Walking off, he pushed his way out through the batwing doors.

Wyatt and Doc were saddled and the posse ready to pull out with its extra mounts when John Behan and his deputy Billy Breakinridge headed toward them from the Crystal Palace.

"You came back," Behan said. "I didn't think you'd have the nerve."

"Don't worry," Wyatt replied, "I won't be long. My business is already settled."

Holding up a sheet of paper, Behan took a step forward. "You'll stay longer than that, Wyatt. This here's a warrant for your arrest, for the murder of Floyd Stilwell."

Wyatt didn't bother to answer. He reined his gray stallion around and started up Allen at a walk, followed by Turkey Creek, Doc, Texas Jack and McMasters.

Behan hurried to keep up. "I said you're under arrest, Earp!"

Continuing to ride, Wyatt took a folded piece of paper from his jacket pocket, flicked it open and tossed it at the sheriff. Behan watched it flutter down to his feet.

Wyatt stopped his horse. "That was my warrant for Stilwell," he said. "You'll have to do better if you want to serve yours."

Behan faced the five heavily armed horsemen, then turned to see that he was alone; Breakinridge hadn't bothered to follow him. A moment later, Behan watched the U.S. deputy marshal's posse ride out of Tombstone at a lope.

Four days after Morgan had been killed, Wyatt and his men threaded their way down the western slope of the Dragoons to a high tableland bordered by lodgepole pines. Ahead of them lay Pete Spence's lumber camp.

In the distance, along the base of the right-hand slope, was the mill, showing no sign of activity, and straight ahead was a field of tree stumps marking the work that had already been done. Riding farther on, the posse drew abreast of a lumber crew splitting a pair of lodgepole trunks, the only crew in sight. To the left, sitting by a hummock, was a beefy worker. He was rolling a smoke, his battered hat tilted forward on his head in what might have been an attempt at jauntiness. Wyatt turned his stallion in the worker's direction.

"Pete Spence around?" Wyatt asked.

"Nope," said the beefy man, "can't say that he is. Hasn't been for a while."

Turkey Creek said, "Kind of peculiar for a man not to show up at his own lumber camp, isn't it?"

The worker shrugged. "Him being peculiar ain't none of my business. If he don't want to show that's up to him. Old Jim Boyle here don't care."

"That right?" said Turkey Creek. "Does old Jim Boyle see this Spence fella workin' here at all?"

"Not a whole lot, now that you ask. Sometimes it seems like Pete got this place just so's his friends can pass through time to time, but then, like I say, that's up to him."

"Who are the friends?" asked Wyatt.

"They didn't tell me who they were. Didn't see no reason to ask them, neither."

Wyatt shifted his weight in the saddle, taking a casual look around the camp. "I hear Indian Charley picks up wages here. He's a half-breed. Maybe you know him."

"Well, I can help you out on that one." Boyle paused to light up his smoke and took several languid pulls before bothering to go on. "I saw the 'breed over the next hill just a while ago. Probably still there. Damn Indian — probably lazin' off, as usual."

No one in the posse took the time to ask Boyle how that was any different from what he was doing. Wyatt turned his horse, said "Obliged," and headed for the next hill. The others filed behind.

Rounding the hill's shoulder, Wyatt could see a man dressed like a Mexican, nooning under a cottonwood, his back to the posse's approach, some fifty feet ahead. Wyatt glanced at Texas Jack and then at Johnny Green. Texas Jack nodded and ranged off slowly to the left while Green angled toward the right.

The posse came within thirty feet before the man under he tree turned to take a look. After his eyes focused on Wyatt, Indian Charley jumped up and ran away from the tree. Texas Jack lifted his horse to a lope and so did Johnny Green. In a pincer movement, the two riders moved ahead of Indian Charley, curled toward the center and cut off the half-breed's escape. Charley pounded to a dusty stop. Turning on his heels, he started to bolt back the way he had come, but then saw Wyatt, Doc, Turkey Creek and McMasters coming on at a walk, four abreast, bottling him up. Suddenly helpless, the half-breed looked desperately from one end of the posse to the other. He then averted his gaze. Slowly, he lowered to a crouch, his head down, assuming the peon's position of submission. He'll try anything, Wyatt thought.

Wyatt reined in a few yards short of the half-breed. "You out of the water business, Charley?"

Indian Charley didn't raise his eyes. "I like wood," he said. "Is good work."

"You know where your boss Spence is?"

"He went away. I do not know where. I promise it is true."

"That means I'm going to have to talk to you instead of Spence, doesn't it?"

Indian Charley began making circles with his fingers in the dust. He didn't answer.

Wyatt leaned forward in the saddle. "I know you were in on my brother's murder, Charley. You're going to tell me what you did."

Now the half-breed looked up. His black eyes roamed nervously from Wyatt to the other members of the posse. "I was only lookout man," he said, his voice already thin with desperation. "This is all I do. Curly Bill, he shoot your brother. Him and Stilwell. You want them. Go find them and kill them, Wyatt. I was only lookout."

"Who else were the lookouts?" asked Wyatt, keeping his voice as level as possible. "Was it Ringo and Spence?"

"Yes, that is all. We just look. Spence look at the door with a pistol. At Hatch's. Ringo and me, we look down the alley with rifles. That is all. Curly Bill and Stilwell, they shoot.''

"There was a sixth man," said Wyatt. "He held the horses. Who was it?"

Indian Charley was eager to please. "Is Ike. Ike Clanton. Him and Curly Bill, they make plan. Not me. I just look. I had nothing against your brother, Wyatt," he added. "I don't even know him." He looked at the rest of the posse as he groped for something that might help his case. "I just do it for money. That is all. Just money. I don't hate your brother."

Wyatt felt like he must be trembling, although a glance at his hands told him he was still in control. "Just money?" he said. His throat was God-awful dry. "That was your only reason?"

"Sí. That is all."

Wyatt held himself perfectly still, his hands resting on the pommel, giving himself the time to steel himself for the change in course. The time for questions was over. "You're in a bad business," he finally said. He stepped down from his horse and took a couple of steps toward Indian Charley.

"Get up," he said.

"You want Curly Bill! I tell you already!"

Wyatt took a moment to settle himself. When he spoke, his voice sounded matter of fact. "I want to take care of this thing right away. We have others to look for."

Wyatt lifted the Colt from his left holster and tossed it to the half-breed. Indian Charley watched it land a foot in front of him.

"Heel yourself," Wyatt said.

Still crouching, Indian Charley eyed the pistol, then glanced fearfully at the other posse men. Wyatt glanced at them also, and without anyone saying a word, Turkey Creek, Doc and McMasters drifted to the sides. Behind Charley, Texas Jack and Johnny Green also moved off.

"Don't worry about the others," Wyatt said. "This is between you and me. If I die, there's no more reason for this posse. These men will have no business with you."

"I do not believe you," said Indian Charley.

"It doesn't matter what you believe, you son of a bitch! You took money for my brother's life. You don't have any choice now."

Wyatt shifted back the right side of his jacket to expose his holstered Colt. He let his right hand hang, a prickling sensation running up and down his arm, his muscles aching to spring into action. Indian Charley stared at him, then at the gun on the ground in front of him. He took a long breath, then another, then a crafty look came to his face, as if he had just discovered his way out. He grabbed for the gun.

As Indian Charley brought the pistol up, Wyatt swept his Colt out of its holster. He fired and the half-breed's shoulder jerked back with the force of the bullet. While Charley's gun discharged into the ground, Wyatt fired again and blasted the man through the chest. The half-breed shambled back, dropped clumsily to the ground and groped blindly with his left hand for a brief moment before flattening against the parched dirt.

Charley lay there motionlessly, but Wyatt strode over to him and, aiming precisely, fired three more times into the torso. The body flinched senselessly with each shot. Reaching into his pocket, Wyatt took out his warrant for Indian Charley, tossed it onto the corpse, then yanked the gun out of the dead man's hand and turned away.

Wyatt was reloading the chambers of his Colt by the time he got back to his horse's side. He holstered the gun, reached up for the pommel, then noticed Turkey Creek staring at him. Turkey Creek's eyes were boring into him, looking like he was taking Wyatt apart.

Wyatt stopped for a moment under the force of his gaze, then, with an abruptness inspired by irritation, swung into the saddle and neck-reined the gray back toward the slope.

If he doesn't like it, Wyatt thought of Turkey Creek, then he's riding with the wrong damn posse. Wyatt spurred the stallion to a lope as he led the way to the trail through the Dragoons.

Soon after, Jim Boyle found the time to leave his hummock and made his way to Indian Charley's side of the hill to take a look at the corpse. When the next bunch of riders came through, he forgot about minding his own business and told them all about the shooting of the half-breed.

42

Just short of the Babocamari Valley, Wyatt led his men across a dry wash. Moving his gray stallion at a slow walk, he let the animal pace himself to conserve strength for the last leg of the journey to Fairbanks. If Jeb Wiley's information was right, Ringo had holed up there just after Morgan's murder. With luck he might still be there.

Riding in a ragged line, the posse started down a long, grade, a sun-dried shelf that grew nothing but cacti and in the distance a stand of yucca plants. Past the hoofs of Wyatt's gray, a chuckwalla lizard skittered, the first sign of animal life Wyatt had seen for a couple of miles. Turkey Creek brought his horse up alongside Wyatt's and turned in the saddle to look at their back-trail. It was the second time Wyatt had seen him do that in the last half-hour.

"Someone's behind us," Turkey Creek said.

Wyatt hadn't noticed anything that day, other than Turkey Creek's turning, but he knew enough not to question the man's judgment. Turkey Creek's instincts had gotten him through too many years on the plains for Wyatt to doubt him.

"Any idea how far behind?" Wyatt asked.

"Can't really say. Couple of miles, maybe more."

"You think you can do something about it?"

"I can get a good look at 'em, for one thing. If I take Texas Jack with me, maybe I can lead 'em down the wrong trail."

Wyatt thought this over, remaining silent as he reached his decision. "What if you take Doc with you?" he said. "Could you still throw them off?"

Turkey Creek gave him a questioning look. "Probably could, if you think he'll do what I say."

"He'll do it if I ask him."

"Any reason he should go and not Texas Jack?" Turkey asked, still sounding uneasy about making Holliday his trail partner. "You plannin' on there being some fighting out there?"

"No, I just got a feeling that it's Behan on our trail with a posse to hunt me down. I also figure he might have some of the men we're looking for in that posse. If he does, Doc'll know who they are. You and Texas Jack wouldn't."

"Sounds fair enough." Turkey Creek said. He started to turn his horse. "But that Holliday better do as he's told."

A series of racking coughs making him slump forward in the saddle, Doc rode off with Turkey Creek, the two of them angling east, back across the wash, and disappearing over a bald hill. The rest of the posse rode on with Wyatt toward the Babocomari.

Although back in Tombstone they had been more talkative than Johnny Green, McMasters and Texas Jack turned out to be just as silent when on the trail. That suited Wyatt just fine. He had enough thoughts about Fairbanks and what they might find there to occupy him.

That night they were camped along a stream running

through a narrow cut, sheltered by cottonwoods, when Turkey Creek and Doc returned. The two men unsaddled their exhausted horses and left them ground-hitched before sitting with the others. Wyatt poked at the embers of the fire to give himself something to do while waiting for their report.

"I think we got 'em confused enough," said Turkey Creek. He let out a groan of relief as he leaned back on his elbows to allow his muscles to stretch.

"With Behan leading them," Doc drawled, "that didn't take an awful lot of confusing."

Ignoring the comment, Turkey Creek went on. "We had 'em leaving the trail, but then the sheriff took a few riders to double back. I think he might be back on your trail but there's less of 'em coming this way and he's lost some time."

"What about the other part of the posse?" Wyatt asked. "The part you led away."

"As far as we could tell, they kept on riding to the northwest. Maybe to circle about, try to cut us off."

"Most likely," Texas Jack put in, "that'd take them through the Whetstones."

Wyatt figured their way to Fairbanks was still clear. The Whetstone Mountains would take that section of the sheriff's posse out of the play for a good while.

"We saw who was in that bunch," said Doc. "The one headed for the Whetstones. We didn't see all of them, but Pony Deal was there and so was Hank Swilling." He brought his knees up and hooked his arms around them, exposing sheet-white wrists. Offhandedly, he added, "You also might want to know that Ringo and Curly Bill were in the bunch too. Looked like Curly Bill was leading. I guess that'd make him a deputy, just like Stilwell, right, Wyatt?"

Wyatt stretched out on the ground and rested his head against his saddle. He wanted to get back on his horse and move on now, defying the weariness that he knew must be obeyed. "If we forget about Fairbanks, we just might find them in the Whetstones tomorrow."

Thinking of setting out at first light, he closed his eyes to try for the sleep that he would need. A foolish notion, what with his heart pumping so, he soon realized. He got up a few minutes later and walked off to the cut, where he sat down along the rim.

His legs dangling above the stream, he listened to the water and stared off at the bleak skyline. Images of Curly Bill and Ringo raced each other in his mind, competing for his attention. His mind brimmed with anticipation of tomorrow's hunt and he felt it would burst at the seams. His head pounded. Perspiration beaded his face and his back on this cool, autumn night. He sat on the rim of the cut for an hour before he tried sleep again.

Sunrise brought in the sixth day since the killing of Morgan. Wyatt's posse was already mounted and well on its way, striking northwest across the plain, pointed toward the first line of Whetstone ridges. The early daylight hours were cool, the riding easy to take across the open stretches and even more brisk in the long shadows at the foot of mesas and mountain saddles. By late morning, though, the sun got its teeth back again and lanced across the posse's trail with a punishing heat.

When they reached the foothills of the Whetstones, Wyatt sent Turkey Creek and Texas Jack up ahead to scout for sign of riders. The rest of the posse plugged away without stop to keep themselves as close as possible to their advance horsemen. They moved up the slope past a patch of talus and sweeps of piñones to the sharp outcroppings and limestone cliffs that signaled the next level up the range.

They were well into the mountains by the time Turkey Creek and Texas Jack rejoined them. The look on their faces made it plain that they didn't have good news.

"Damned if we couldn't find a sign of 'em," said Turkey Creek. "I'm sure they came this way, but we couldn't cut their trail once."

Wyatt sat his horse for several moments without speaking, oblivious to the stares of the men who waited for his next decision.

"We could try another swing to the east," suggested Turkey Creek. "Maybe they turned south before getting this far."

Still not answering, Wyatt swung his horse around and walked him over to the game trail winding downslope. His thoughts locked. He wanted nothing but to just ride on and let his mind clear. He heard his men follow his lead.

Turkey Creek might be right, he thought. Another scout to the east might be all that was needed, although Wyatt couldn't quite settle on it. His disappointment was too keen to let him be decisive. He kept riding, waiting for the next idea to come to him. Maybe they should just give up on the Whetstones and head back toward Charleston, or perhaps Galeyville, someplace where the cowboys would congregate after a long ride. Wyatt thought his posse might even reach one of those hangouts before their prey did and give themselves the chance to wait and surprise them. A lot of possibilities, but none that Wyatt was ready to latch onto.

He kept riding, steering his gray toward the far stand of willows and the faint scent of water. For the time being, a rest at a waterhole seemed like a good enough idea.

Months later Wyatt would wonder if he had had a premonition as he turned his horse into the clearing.

The way everybody was lazing about, Ike figured he could get to one of the horses and slip away without anyone noticing. Hell, Spence had managed to leave the posse yesterday, he thought, no reason why I got to stick my neck out any longer. I've done my share.

Spence had said he was going to Tucson to round up

some more men. Ike didn't believe it for a second. He couldn't help but notice that Spence started talking about getting reinforcements only when he had seen Indian Charley filled with lead at his lumber camp. Spence just might find some more men, but only to stand around him while he stayed in Tucson and waited for Earp to come for him.

Sitting under one of the willows, Ike took stock of the rest of the posse. Ringo was stretched out on his back by the springs, his hat over his face as a shield against the sun. Pony Deal and Hank Swilling were asleep at the other end of the stand of trees, and Curly Bill seemed only half-awake just a few feet away. To the other side were the two new men Curly Bill had brought along, Barnes and Fuller, two toughs Brocius had known in the Panhandle. If he thought those two were such handy fellers, Ike told himself, then they could take up my slack when I'm long gone. The trouble was, Barnes and Fuller were still awake, playing cards under a tree, and they might stop Ike from making a getaway.

Ike was beginning to think that even Curly Bill was starting to get jumpy. If he wasn't, then why was he traipsing around these mountains instead of trailing the Earp bunch for real? Perhaps Curly Bill was just trying to steer clear. And as for Ringo, Ike had seen him look over his shoulder more than once the last couple of days, and he wasn't one to get jittery for no reason. All in all, they couldn't blame Ike for slipping out and heading for the border, just to play it safe.

With Barnes and Fuller turned away, Ike got up and took a couple of casual steps toward the horses. Take it slow and maybe nobody'll notice until it's too late, he thought. Barnes and Fuller kept on playing cards, seeming unconcerned about everything else, and Ike was just about halfway to the mounts when suddenly Ringo got to his feet. The Texas bad man stopped to listen for a moment, while Curly Bill stirred and did the same. Brocius shook the sleep off and crept low to the ground on his way toward the eroded bank on the other side of Mescal Springs. He stopped long enough to whisper a command at Ike. "Wake up the other two," he said, motioning toward Pony Deal and Hank Swilling.

Resigned that there was no getting away for now, Ike did as he was told and, after waking the two men, crawled over to Curly Bill and Ringo's side as they reached the top of the bank. His mouth went dry in a flash as he sneaked a look over the crest.

It was only a glimpse, as the riders on the other side of the clearing passed beyond the gap between two outcroppings, but Ike had no doubt: Wyatt Earp was leading his posse right toward them.

"We'll, I'll be damned," said Curly Bill.

Wyatt dismounted as he entered the sandy hollow that led to Mescal Springs. The rest of the posse rode their animals at a listless pace, both horses and men near the end of their string, but thankful to be nearing a wet camp.

Halfway across the hollow, they saw the heads and shoulders and weapons of the cowboys appear above the bank around ten yards ahead.

The first volley boomed. Bullets from rifles and pistols kicked up sand on all sides of Wyatt's posse, slugs seared past them and ricocheted with a whine off boulders to the rear. Turkey Creek, Doc, McMasters and Texas Jack wheeled their horses, sand flying all around them, and dug their heels into the sides of their mounts to pound back across the hollow to the cover of the rock shoulder.

With the first crack of gunfire, Wyatt swung his gray stallion to his front, grabbed the pommel and braced himself for the jump into the saddle. But as his men drummed away, snapping off pistol shots toward the outlaws' embankment, Wyatt suddenly stopped, frozen in place for a roaring, suspended moment, exposed and alone in the middle of the hollow. Over his horse's saddle, his eyes trained on one end of the eroded bank. Leaning across the bank at that spot was the blocky face of Curly Bill Brocius.

All thought of riding for cover suddenly vanished from Wyatt's mind.

Curly Bill fired his revolver, a shot that buzzed past the stallion's ears. While his friends continued to cut loose, he then stopped, meeting Wyatt's stare for an instant, as he put the pistol down. In its place, he picked up a double-barreled shotgun.

He swerved the weapon from side to side as he tried to line up on Wyatt, now shifting back and forth with the bucking of his stallion. Wyatt steadied his horse long enough to grab his Stevens ten gauge looped around the pommel. With his left hand still holding the reins, he snapped the stock of the weapon to his shoulder. He took aim. The stallion reared, pulling him off balance.

He yanked the animal back down and lined up again. Just a foot from his face, the pommel exploded, shot off by one of the other outlaws. Standing his ground, he sighted over the barrels to see Curly Bill finding his aim. Morgan's killer triggered one of the barrels.

Wyatt felt something sting across his side, but nothing more. The rest of the load went wide. In that moment, he locked into place and let loose.

The two barrels of the Stevens thundered as one, and buckshot ripped through Curly Bill's midsection, exploding muscle and bone, and scattering blood wildly across the bank. For a fleeting instant, Wyatt thought he saw the top half of the outlaw's body break off just above the belt. In the next instant Curly Bill dropped from view.

The outlaws' gunfire stopped for a brief, stunned pause. Seizing the opportunity, Wyatt threw the shotgun aside and pulled his colt before the barrage began again. Backing off slowly, using his horse as a shield, Wyatt shot back at the cowboys. He saw Ringo's face above the bank. He snapped off a shot, but his bullet thwacked into the ground in front of the outlaw, doing nothing but raising a gout of earth. He then heard, above the roar from the bank, a volley of fire from his rear, from his posse behind the shoulder. Their shots sprayed the outlaw posse's cover and slowed their fire. But not enough to prevent a cowboy bullet from smashing through the gray stallion's neck.

The horse keeled over and thudded to the ground, nearly pinning Wyatt underneath. Trying to use his downed animal as cover, Wyatt drew his second Colt and returned fire as best he could. Out of the corner, he saw a slight figure moving quickly through the rock field on the left, headed toward the outlaw posse's flank. Another glance told him that the figure was Doc Holliday. He then heard the drumming of hoofs behind him. Turkey Creek galloped across the hollow and reared his horse into a tight, sudden, sand-spewing turn by Wyatt's side.

As Wyatt turned toward Turkey Creek, he saw Doc open up with his nickel-plated Colt just twenty feet to the left of the cowboys. His first shot bored through Pony Deal's throat. His continued fire turned the other cowboys' attention away from the hollow. Wyatt took a running step toward the rear of Turkey Creek's horse and vaulted onto its back. Turkey Creek spurred the animal as gunfire pelted the sand around them again. They rode furiously for the cover of the shoulder of rock.

Once safe, Wyatt put his second Colt to work as he and his posse kept up the pressure on the bank. Wyatt had to duck beneath a spray of stone chipped by a .45 slug, but he and his men didn't have to keep up the fire much longer. Unnerved by Doc's flanking maneuver, the cowboys soon dropped below the top of the embankment; their firing became sporadic and then stopped altogether.

Wyatt told his men to hold up. The sudden silence that followed was quickly interrupted by the sound of hoof-beats on the other side of the bank, headed away from the springs. Wyatt held still for several moments, not even thinking of pursuit.

He later crossed the sandy hollow alone to take a look at

what the cowboys had left behind. Climbing over the embankment to the far side, he saw three bodies: Pony Deal, his neck blown away; a man he didn't recognize who was just as dead; and Curly Bill. Brocius was sprawled across the downslope, his body almost completely cut in half, only a strip of skin and muscle connecting the upper and lower sections.

All at once, while he stared at the mangled corpse, Wyatt's strength evaporated from every part of his body. He took a couple of faltering steps, then sat heavily on the slope, just a few feet above the remains of Curly Bill. He pulled out his warrant for the outlaw and, for lack of anything else to do, read it over several times, the words not registering no matter how many times his eyes ran over them. He then crumpled the paper in his palm and gazed ahead at the willows and at the switchback trail beyond. His thoughts abandoned the manhunt of the last few days and drifted back to a more innocent hunt, a deer hunt in the Missouri hills. Morgan had been with him then. Wyatt could picture Morg crouched in the brush, just ahead of him, waiting for the game. The sunlight sliced through a gap in the tree tops to brighten Morgan's profile in sharp detail and shine on his blond hair. There had been many hunts with Morg, but Wyatt remembered that this one in particular had taken place while he had been courting Willa. His throat tightened convulsively, the urge to cry almost overcoming him.

"It's almost over, Morg," he said softly. "It's almost over."

A breeze lifted across the hollow, rippling the water and rustling the branches of the trees with a faint whisper. Farther back, a quail moved quickly from one of the willows to the thicket that bordered the field of rock to the right. Under the lowering sun, Mescal Springs became a cool, sheltered place that somehow had nothing to do with the three bodies bleeding along its edges.

43

Ringo got the jitters from the killing of Indian Charley.
That's how Henry Corcoran put it to Wyatt.

"I've known John nearly two years," said Henry, "and
I couldn't tell you one thing he was thinking all that time.
You know how he was. But last night — maybe it was all
that tequila he drank — you should've seen how he talked.
The first time I ever seen him talk that much."

Corcoran ran a saloon in Antelope Springs, nine miles
outside of Tombstone. He told Wyatt and the others in the
posse that Ringo had come to his place last night, already
about half-lit.

"As soon as he started his first bottle, he began talking
about Spence. 'That damn Spence,' he said. It turns out,
Wyatt, that Spence gave himself up in Tucson, for robbing
the Benson stage. You hear about that?"

"I heard," said Wyatt.

"Well, Ringo says Spence gave himself up because he
was scared. Scared and tired of looking over his shoulder
and expecting to see Earp coming at him with a shotgun, is
how he put it."

By the time Ringo finished with the first bottle, Henry said, he was talking about finding Indian Charley all shot up at the lumber camp.

"Charley had hardly anything to do with Morgan's murder," Ringo said. "No more than I did. We were just lookouts. How can you shoot a man for that?"

He fell silent for a while after that as he got started with bottle number two. Then he told Henry about Curly Bill, about how he got cut in half two days before. "First that stupid Stilwell," said Ringo, "then Indian Charley, then Curly Bill. Stilwell and Bill had it coming, I can't kick about that. That's what they dealt themselves in for when they shot Morgan. But Charley — that makes no sense."

Henry said Ringo kept talking about Indian Charley and kept hitting the bottle. "He was just about blind with the tequila," said Henry, "and then, damned if it ain't so, he started looking over his shoulder. At first I thought I was seeing wrong, getting the wrong idea, but then he did it a couple of times more. That's when he stopped talking. After a while he just paid me for another bottle and left. I guess you know the rest, eh Wyatt?"

Two miles before reaching Corcoran's saloon that night, Wyatt's posse had stopped along the road when Texas Jack saw something partially illuminated by the moonlight under the big oak to the side. Seeing that it wasn't moving, whatever it was, Wyatt had dismounted and gone over to take a look.

The big old roots of the tree were wrapped around a rock that served as a resting place for people looking to take a break from traveling along the road. On that rock, Wyatt found Ringo, leaning against the tree, his head hanging forward on his chest. In his left hand was a half-empty bottle of tequila, and in the other, his revolver. A blue bullet hole, surrounded by a powder burn, was in Ringo's right temple.

"Guess there ain't much you can do to Ringo now," said Henry.

Wyatt didn't bother to answer.

The saloonkeeper then said, "I also heard about Ike Clanton, from down in Sonora," He paused to make sure he had everyone's attention. "Some cowboys passed through here today and told me."

"He didn't die horribly, I hope," said Doc, leaning against the near adobe wall. Henry looked at him curiously as he tried to figure the man's sarcastic tone.

Wyatt finished his beer and placed the mug on the plank bar before getting the saloonkeeper back on track. "What happened to Ike in Mexico?" he asked.

"Well," said Henry, "it seems Ike got himself killed." He waited for a reaction from Wyatt, but got none. "They said it was over a card game down to Mex Nogales. Some beaners said Ike was fooling with the deck and then shot him in the back when he tried to walk away with the winnings." Henry was disappointed. He wasn't getting any response from Wyatt. In fact, Earp didn't even seem to be looking at him anymore. He appeared to be gazing at something just to the side of the saloonkeeper's ear.

Something about the story struck Wyatt as funny. After hating Ike for so many years, ever since Wichita and then Dodge, he now knew Clanton was dead, and Wyatt had had nothing to do with it. The funny part was that Wyatt didn't much care. The way things looked to him now, he figured that getting shot in the back over a card game seemed just about right for his old enemy, perhaps more appropriate than a straight-up showdown over Morgan's murder. What else would have been right for a horse-holder and loudmouth?

Wyatt reached in his pocket to pay for his posse's round of drinks, gave Henry Corcoran a nod and walked out the door.

In the breezeless night, the crunch of the posse's boots against the ground sounded loud and harsh as the reins of horses were gathered from the saloon's tie rail. Wyatt gazed down the road at the four other buildings that comprised the town and then faced his men.

"I figure Spence to be on his way to Yuma Prison before long, which'll take care of him. With Ringo and Ike gone, that finishes. We might as well split up and see if we can get out of Arizona ahead of Johnny Behan's posse." He paused to study the hard-looking faces before him. "Thanks to all of you," he said.

Wyatt led his horse into the road and mounted up. As he settled into the saddle, he saw Turkey Creek, still holding his reins by the tie rail, staring at him, the plainsman squinted with the effort of scrutiny. Wyatt remembered the look Turkey Creek had given him after he had killed Indian Charley, a memory that was interrupted by Doc bringing his horse alongside.

"They tell me they're striking silver up in Colorado," said Doc. "Seems like the next place to go, wouldn't you say?" He touched the brim of his hat. "Be seeing you up there, Deacon."

Wyatt was going to answer him, but before he could manage any words, Doc gigged his horse onward, headed north up the road. Watching Doc go, Wyatt smiled and shook his head.

"Think you're gonna be hitching up with him again?" It was Turkey Creek, mounted and reined in beside Wyatt.

Wyatt didn't have to give the question much thought. "I don't think so," he said.

Turkey Creek grunted in acknowledgement, then smiled and motioned with his head toward Green, Texas Jack and McMasters. "Well, Wyatt, we're going to be on our way. Me and the fellas thought we'd give New Mexico a try for a while. How about you?"

Wyatt nodded pensively, still looking at Doc receding into the darkness. "Something I want to ask you, Turkey Creek."

"Go ahead."

"After I took care of Indian Charley," said Wyatt, "you didn't much like what I was doing, did you?"

Turkey Creek studied Wyatt for a moment. "I didn't blame you for one second for what you were doing, Wyatt. A brother crippled and another killed — there's no arguing with that. It's just that, after Indian Charley, I saw a look in your eye. Something spooky, it was. It just got me to wondering if your killing was going to ever stop, even after this business."

For a moment there was no sound except the creak of leather as Wyatt shifted slightly in the saddle to face his old friend directly. "You think that now?" he asked.

"No, I don't. I been watching you close, especially since Curly Bill and Mescal Springs. I think you're different. It's behind you now, most like."

"I hope you're right," said Wyatt.

"Don't bet on me being right," Turkey Creek laughed, "but this time, I probably am."

The clip-clop of the hoofs of Doc's horse was faint now, but it still carried down the road. Wyatt could see that Turkey Creek was also listening to it. They sat their horses side by side, without speaking, watching Holliday's night-blurred outline rolling onward. Wyatt then fought a final reluctance and reined his horse around.

"Be seeing you, Turkey Creek," he said. "We best be moving on — all of us — if we want to get clear."

"Know what the hell you're gonna do now, Wyatt?"

Wyatt took a long breath as he thought. Nothing came to mind right away. He shrugged his shoulders. "I'll make my way as I go along I suppose," he said. "You taught me that much." Wyatt gave Turkey Creek a wave, returned the man's smile and rode off. He trotted up the road for a while, then let his new horse pick its own pace.

HOLLYWOOD, CALIFORNIA

44

He moved freely across the back lot, a familiar figure known as a friend of Tom Mix. Always dressed in a black suit, his thin white hair and full white moustache always carefully trimmed and groomed, he looked more like a banker than the old desperado he was rumored to be. But then a banker wouldn't spend so much of his time with wranglers and cowboy stuntmen, both on the Fox sets and, when it could be managed, at some speakeasy along Gower Gulch. To those film crew members who bothered to notice, there was also something else that betrayed the distinguished, polite appearance.

Once on the set of a William S. Hart picture a few years ago, the tall old man had been standing by a corral built the day before to be used in a scene that Hart wanted to add at the last minute. A young cameraman by the name of Parker was moving the camera for his next shot and found the old man was in his way.

"Let's go, Pops," Parker said, "make yourself useful and get off the set." Not content merely to tell him what to do, Parker then took hold of the old man's sleeve and started leading him to the side. The way Parker told the story later, the look the old man gave him stopped him in his tracks. "Something spooky about the way he looked at me," Parker would say. It didn't make sense to him that he would be scared of a white-haired old fellow, but he decided to leave Wyatt Earp alone. The old man moved off soon enough on his own, when he was ready.

The hard lines on Wyatt's face had drooped some and softened over the years, but he still moved with a long-legged spryness that most men his age couldn't have lain claim to. Just a month ago, in March of 1923, he had turned 71, an age that most of his contemporaries had not reached, not Bat Masterson, not Luke Short, not Ab Richardson, and certainly not Doc Holliday who was now long gone and who had somehow managed to die in bed with his boots off. Wyatt told himself he couldn't complain.

Walking across the sun-filled Fox lot today, Wyatt contented himself with telling stories. That was not something he ordinarily cared to do, but Tom Mix was late as usual, and Wyatt's companions seemed especially interested.

He came to a pause in his story as he looked at the set on his right, a courtyard for a medieval castle where a historical romance was in production. Next to that was a Southern plantation similar to the ones that had existed when Wyatt had been a boy. He still couldn't get used to these make-believe worlds erected overnight, side by side, one having nothing to do with the other. He shook his head and walked on.

"Young Billy Clanton turned out to be the gamest fighter in the bunch," he continued. "After he wounded Virgil, he put another bullet through Morgan's shoulder."

Rafer Jackson, the cowboy stuntman walking to Wyatt's left, passed him the flask of bootleg whiskey. Wyatt took his sip and then handed it to Jack Ford on his right.

Wyatt kept hearing that this young, round-faced Irishman was a rising young director on the Fox lot, a rumor that pleased Wyatt. He knew Ford from the director's days at Universal when Jack would complain about Wyatt getting his cowboy-actors drunk during lunch. Ford liked to think of himself as a tough piece of work, and Wyatt knew he could be tough with other movie people, but he was respectful with Wyatt, more respectful as they got to know each other, a feeling that was mutual.

Wyatt went on with his story. "When I saw Morgan hit the ground, I turned on Billy and threw down. Morgan got off a shot at the same time and poor Billy took both bullets. Years later I heard that he was the only one in the bunch who wanted no fight that day."

"Where did Ike Clanton end up?" asked Ford. His tone was casual, but Wyatt could see he was soaking up every detail.

"He ended up in a Mexican dance hall on the other side of town. And he was the one who started it all. He killed his brother as sure as if he pulled the trigger."

They came to a stop just before the western street set. Wyatt looked around in the faint hope that Tom might actually show up, only forty minutes after he had said he would arrive. No such luck.

From behind came Kyle Fisk, one of Mix's wranglers. With him was an old-timer, dressed in a threadbare brown suit and a new stetson; by the look of him, Wyatt judged that he was a Gower Gulch hanger-on. Wyatt thought Fisk might have word from Tom, perhaps a new meeting place or a new time for the appointment. He better have word, Wyatt told himself. It had been Tom's idea to meet in the first place.

"Wyatt, there you are," said Fisk. He indicated the old-timer next to him. "I just met this here old buzzard over to Frannie's speak. He was talking up the old days in Kansas and such, so I figured you two should get acquainted and chew the fat."

376

No news from Tom, then. Getting irritated, Wyatt gave the old-timer nothing more than a quick glance. Not that he had anything against meeting someone from the old days — there were only a few of them left, that was certain — he just wasn't in the mood now that it seemed that he had been given the grand runaround by Mix.

But then there was something in the old timer's look that made Wyatt move his eyes back to the man.

Fisk started the introductions. "Joe Duncan, this here's Wyatt Earp. Maybe you two crossed trails in one of them cow towns. Wyatt, this is Joe Duncan, the best cowboy in all of Texas, if you can believe half of what he says." Fisk stood there grinning from ear to ear as he waited for the old coots to walk hand-in-hand down memory lane.

Ford said, "I've got to be back in the office, Wyatt. I'll see you around when my cowboys need to get drunk."

Wyatt said, "Goodbye, Jack," as he kept his eyes on the old cowboy Joe Duncan. Rafer Jackson said he also had to be on his way and walked off, joined by Fisk, to leave the two old-timers alone.

Wyatt wondered idly how much his own face had changed over the years, how recognizable it would be to men he had known a long time ago. In Joe Duncan's case, Wyatt could see that old age, with the help of liquor, had made the eyelids sag heavily, while puffy cheeks had replaced skin that had once fit closely to the bone. The change had been drastic enough to keep Wyatt from recognizing the man for a few moments, but no longer.

Wyatt looked into the apprehensive eyes before him. "Ike," he said simply.

Old Ike Clanton said nothing, his gaze becoming resentful as he chewed his lower lip.

"They told me you were dead in Mexico," said Wyatt. "More than one man told me that."

Ike took a shuffling step to the side to put some distance between himself and Earp. He stood with shoulders hunched forward, his body taut. "I started them rumors

myself," he said almost proudly. "What the hell was I supposed to do? How else was I gonna get you off my trail?
God knows my so-called friends weren't about to back me
up." He looked like he wanted to say more about those
friends who had let him down, but another, more important consideration took hold instead. He turned to get
away from Wyatt.

Reaching out quickly, Wyatt gripped Ike's arm which
felt spindly now, and kept him from going any farther. Ike
looked up, his eyes wide with an old fear. He worked his
mouth nervously, not sure what he should say. Suddenly,
he blurted out, "You're not gonna do anything, are ya,
Wyatt?"

Wyatt narrowed his eyes. "I'm not so old I've forgotten
you held the horse that night. I ought to do something."

Ike was perfectly still for a moment, held in Wyatt's
stare. He then pulled furiously on his enemy's grip. "Jesus
Christ! Leave me be!" He struggled a while longer, but
Wyatt's long hands had lost little of their strength. He
soon tightened his hold enough to quiet Ike and make him
still again.

"I wouldn't worry too much," Wyatt said. "It's too late
to be doing something about it now, I figure."

Ike studied him, as though trying to decide if this was
some kind of trick. He then darted a glance at a group of
propmen passing by with some western saloon orna-
ments — a spittoon, a faro bank, a trophy made of longhorns. Finding reassurance in the sight of harmless people
nearby, Ike took a step to the side. Wyatt let him slip out
of his grip. As more people passed on their way to the set,
Ike even managed some defiance.

"You know, Wyatt," he said, "I got this writer friend
now, and he says he's gonna write him a book about the
old days in Arizona. He's gonna tell the Clanton side of
the story. When folks read that book I'm gonna be able to
tell 'em I'm a Clanton again. You'll see."

Wyatt scrutinized the old but still cocky Ike. "Good

enough," said Wyatt, "get your book written. Then all you'll have to do is explain why you were Joe Duncan for forty years."

As this sank in, a flicker of doubt passed through Ike's eyes, but in a moment his feisty front returned.

A voice from behind Wyatt said, "Earp, good to see you. You're just in time. I've got a few minutes before our first shot." Wyatt turned to see Tom Mix, in that funny cowboy costume of his, an entourage of five tagging along with him. His hand was out and Wyatt shook it.

"Hello, Tom." As Wyatt suspected, Tom made no mention of his being late.

Tom put an arm around Wyatt's shoulder and began guiding him toward the set. "Now, I had a reason for asking you to come by, Earp."

Wyatt glanced back to see Ike watching him bitterly.

"I wanted to ask you about one of your fights," continued Mix. "That one at Mescal Springs I think you called it, where you killed Texas Bill."

"Curly Bill," Wyatt said.

"That's the one. I think there may be a scene there."

Wyatt started to tell the story, and, as he knew Tom would, the cowboy star got distracted before Wyatt was halfway through. In another moment, Mix was off, entourage and all, solving some production snag, and Wyatt was left alone.

He turned back to take another look at Ike, but Clanton was no longer there. Probably on his way back to Gower Gulch to hunt up some free drinks, Wyatt decided. He had wanted one more look to prove to himself that the old rustler had really passed through after all.

There had been nights when Wyatt had felt a sharp twinge of regret for not taking care of Ike himself. Those were the nights he thought of Morgan and how much longer his brother's life should have been. Just believing Ike was dead wasn't enough at those times.

But now, seeing Ike alive, old and wasted, calling himself Joe Duncan and threatening Wyatt with a book of lies, Wyatt wondered why anyone had bothered with Ike in the old days.

Wyatt walked through the clutch of production people and strolled to the other end of the set where the mock-up buildings were still empty and quiet. He stopped at the end of the street to get the full view of the reconstructed boom town.

The facades weren't too badly done really, though Wyatt never remembered these towns being so clean. Squinting, he found he could almost see a real street, and if he tried hard enough he could almost see Dodge City's Plaza. But then, that wasn't how the set would look on the movie screen after Tom Mix started jumping around with all his busthead riding tricks. At least Bill Hart used to make an attempt to put something real in front of the camera. Not so with Tom. Wyatt had to admit, though, that Mix had a way about him. Full of piss and vinegar, as Virge would have said.

Wyatt checked his pocket watch and decided it was time to get back to the car and drive home. He certainly had said his piece for one day, and, besides, Josie expected him to spend some time with her relatives from San Francisco. As it was, he had already managed to slip out of the better part of a day's visiting and was pushing his luck by stretching it any further. As he turned away from the set, a chorus of pistol shots suddenly crashed to his rear. Knowing full well that it was only blanks fired for Mix's picture, Wyatt broke stride for only the briefest of moments, the small hairs tingling on the back of his neck, before he moved on to reach his car by the lot entrance.

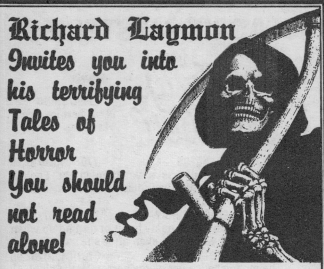

FREE!!
BOOKS BY MAIL
CATALOGUE

BOOKS BY MAIL will share with you our current bestselling books as well as hard to find specialty titles in areas that will match your interests. You will be updated on what's new in books at no cost to you. Just fill in the coupon below and discover the convenience of having books delivered to your home.

PLEASE ADD $1.00 TO COVER THE COST OF POSTAGE & HANDLING.

- -

BOOKS BY MAIL
320 Steelcase Road E.,
Markham, Ontario L3R 2M1

IN THE U.S. -
210 5th Ave., 7th Floor
New York, N.Y., 10010

Please send Books By Mail catalogue to:

Name _____
(please print)

Address _____

City _____

Prov./State _____ P.C./Zip _____

(BBM1)